RAÐIANT
BROW

The Epic of Taliesin

H. Catherine Watling has written two factual books 'The Sacred Word' and 'Wood Wisdom', and designed a pack of tree oracle cards. She has also written articles on various subjects, including the Celtic bardic tradition. She is a bard of Gorsedd Ynys Witrin and a druid with the Order of Bards, Ovates and Druids.

H Catherine Watling

RADIANT BROW

The Epic of Taliesin

WildCat Arts

Publishing

RADIANT BROW
The Epic of Taliesin
Second Edition
©2014 H. Catherine Watling

ISBN 978-0-9928530-1-3

ALL RIGHTS RESERVED

Cover illustration by H. Catherine Watling

Published by:
WildCat Arts Publishing
wildcatarts.glasto@gmail.com

A catalogue record for this book is available from the British
Library.

Printed and bound by
Short Run Press Ltd, Exeter, EX2 7LW

Dedicated to Master Taliesin,
source of inspiration,
and to all bards, past and present.

CONTENTS

Part One

Flesh or Fish

I have borne a banner before Alexander;
I know the names of the stars from north to south;
I was in the court of Don before the birth of Gwydion.......
I shall be until the day of doom on the face of the earth;
And it is not known whether my body is flesh or fish........' 1

CHAPTER ONE

The woman clutched a sleeping infant to her breast as she stared out across the waves. Their rhythm pounded in her ears: a hollow voice, goading, testing.

She was numb to the chill water that swirled around her ankles, dragging at the hem of the cloak which made her no more than a shadow in the failing light, and though she had draped a fold over her head, for concealment rather than warmth, the wind caught at wisps of silver-fair hair that had blown free. Spray stung her eyes so the world became a blur, the salt of the sea mingling with the salt of tears.

It was only a faint movement from the infant in her arms that broke her trance, and the woman retreated up the beach to where a coarse-woven sack lay beside a coracle of bowed willow spars. The tide was at full flood, but soon it would begin to ebb. She knew she must act now. Before her resolve broke.

She crouched on the wet sand, scarcely looking at her child as she reached for the sack. Yet she had to gaze at his face just one more time, the face that was more precious than any other. Pale lashes rested on rounded cheeks as he breathed softly from between slightly parted lips. He did not wake when she placed him inside the sack, nor when she tied the top with a cord. If he lived, he would be a good child, and clever, she felt sure. His brow was unusually high and his eyes seemed to hold the wisdom of ages. But torturing herself was pointless.

She got to her feet, the sack cradled in one arm, and dragging the coracle with her free hand, waded out thigh deep, the force of the waves making her stagger, struggling for balance. When she could go no further, she steadied the craft and placed the sack on the willow spars at the bottom.

Believing that she heard her child's cry, she hesitated, clinging to the coracle, fighting the current and buffeted by the storm.

Finally, she let it slip from between icy fingers.

'May the gods watch over you.'

Her whisper merged with the wind and was carried away with the coracle as it rose and fell on the tide, one moment visible on the crest of a wave, the next plunging down, then rising to view again, each time further from the shore.

The woman watched the receding shape until it was no more than a speck in the distance. She began to shiver and wrapped her cloak more tightly about her, but it made no difference.

So bitter for the time of year, she thought. In two days it would be Calan Mai, the start of summer. Light days lay ahead. And she pictured the bright face of her child surrounded by the darkness of the sea at night.

The weather was fitful the day before May Eve as Elffin sat beside the central hearth in the feast hall, a cup of mead in his hand. Lulled by the fire's warmth, he listened to the wind blowing in from the Hibernian Sea which washed the coast of Gwynedd - a blast that whined through every crack in the walls and around the barred shutters.

Opposite Elffin sat his father Gwyddno, brother to King Mealgwn of Gwynedd. As his only son, one day Elffin would be master of the fortress of Braich y Dinas and its surrounding lands, but though Gwyddno was greying and growing stout he was still in good health and shrewd as ever.

'The salmon weir always yields well at summer's start.' His gritty voice competed with the cry of the wind. Elffin nodded vaguely, thinking of the coming festivities. 'Son, I've decided to let you raise the nets this May Eve, to call the catch your own. God knows, you need some good fortune. What

6

honour have you won lately, eh? Ill luck, and blunders, foolish blunders......'

At last he had Elffin's attention, his face burning red as his beard. 'I meant no insult to our guest, he misunderstood my meaning, and it was no fault of mine that the horse I paid a good price for turned lame, or.......'

Gwyddno sighed. 'Do you intend to accept my offer or not?'

Stifling his words of defence, Elffin replied respectfully. 'Your offer is generous. I am glad to accept.'

He knew this was his father's gruff way of showing love, and wondered how it would be with his own children when they were grown. Would they bring shame to him as he did to Gwyddno? Across the hall, the two eldest scampered after a hound pup, while his wife Eilonwy suckled their six-month-old son, a sturdy infant with a thick crop of red hair and a strong resemblance to his grandsire.

Turning back to the men gathered about the hearth, Elffin put aside thoughts of how he displeased his father, and joined their talk of the Saeson who were pushing ever westward under the leadership of the warlord Cynric. Since Arthur Pendragon's death at the battle of Camlann, the Britons had become disorganized and been defeated in a series of bloody battles, their land and goods stolen. The long years of peace that followed Arthur's victory at Mount Badon thirty six years ago, a peace which had lasted since before Elffin's birth, had been broken.

Fear over-shadowed his easy-going nature - a fear that the Britons might fail ever to expel the Saeson from their sacred land, the island that was their mother, their life-blood. But surely the enemy would never reach Gwynedd. He could not, or would not, imagine that his children's future could be endangered.

* * *

The following morning when Elffin dragged himself from bed Eilonwy was long since up, and frowned at him for rising late. He replied with a grin, seeing that the shutters had been opened wide and that sunlight flooded across the two long tables to either side of the hearth.

The change in the weather from the storms of the previous night, combined with his father's offer, lifted Elffin's spirits. After breaking his fast with ale, freshly baked barley bread and cheese, he got to his feet and turned to Gwyddno.

'The nets should be heavy with salmon by now, I'll go with the men to oversee the drawing.'

Whistling a tune, he sauntered across the courtyard to the stables where two attendants were polishing harness. He ordered his horse to be saddled, and the three men set off with the sun full in their faces. A rutted track led down from the fortress, joining another which took them east over high ground before descending again to the pass, slopes towering above them to either side. They continued through woodland, following Afon Conwy downstream, its waters glittering between the trees.

As the tree cover thinned, Elffin looked towards the twin summits of Deganwy on the far side of the estuary, the larger hill crowned by fortifications. His uncle Maelgwn Gwynedd feasted his warband at Deganwy when he was not at his main stronghold of Aberffraw on Ynys Mon, and as a boy Elffin had dreaded visiting the place, afraid of the arrogant, viper-tongued king. Now he was a man he enjoyed baiting Maelgwn with jests, though it was a dangerous game, one of skill in judging the limits of provocation.

Riding ahead of his men, Elffin kept up a brisk pace until he reached a round-hut built where the river widened into the estuary. He reined in and, raising his voice above the rushing waters, called out,

'We come to draw the nets.'

'Summer greetings to you, Lord Elffin.' An ageing man, stooped and grizzle-haired, stepped from the shadows of the doorway. 'Should be a good haul today - May Eve.'

'It's a fine day for catching salmon.'

The men dismounted and went with Elffin to the strand, where they set about helping the weir-ward haul in the nets that were suspended between alder poles. Closing his eyes, Elffin turned his face to the sun and stretched. He was looking forward to the sight of the silvery salmon, symbol of wisdom. Surely they would herald an improvement in his life, respite from being ridiculed for his folly.

When he opened his eyes again, he frowned.

'What delays you? Where is the catch?'

Drych, the elder of the attendants, spoke in an undertone. 'The nets are empty, my lord.'

Elffin examined them as they were brought to shore, though he could see no breaches in the knotted cord. He found it impossible to believe. Such a thing had never happened before. They were always so heavily laden that it took two strong men to pull them in. He felt a nagging sense of uneasiness. Nor was he looking forward to Gwyddno's forebodings or Eilonwy's derision.

Concealing his anxiety, he waved a hand in the direction of the weir.

'Re-set the trap, perhaps there will be success tomorrow.'

The men dragged the nets back into the water, the weir-ward still hunched beside Elffin, grim-faced. They watched the attendants work until Drych's yell broke the silence and, throwing the nets to his companion, he waded out to the remains of an abandoned trap further from shore, its rotting timbers half-fallen and cluttered with driftwood. Once more Elffin frowned, but said nothing. He had grown weary and felt little interest. Let the man swim the estuary if he pleased! The fact remained - they had no catch. Instead of returning to the hall triumphant, again he faced humiliation.

'There…..' Drych called, 'caught between the poles…..'

The younger attendant waded out after him, while Elffin moved to the water's edge, followed by the weir-ward. His curiosity roused at last, he waited for Drych to work the object loose. After growing anticipation, he gave a bitter laugh. It was merely a fisherman's coracle, which must have been blown from its tether during the storm.

Drych reached the shore first, holding one side of the coracle in a tight grip. The second man clambered up after him and lowered the other side onto solid ground at Elffin's feet. Questioning why they had troubled to bring it to land, he glanced down, and felt a stab of excitement. Within the vessel lay a full sack tied with a cord.

'It will be quickest to cut it open,' he said, his voice tense. 'But have a care, lest we have won a valuable prize.'

With a nod, Drych unsheathed his knife, though before he had time to use it the sack moved. The weir-ward caught his breath, and the younger attendant gave a start, instinctively stepping back. Drych laughed at him, but Elffin noticed that he discretely made the ancient sign against enchantment. His own optimism reawakened, he half expected the bag to contain one single magnificent salmon, one that would be the envy of all and silence his father's criticisms for ever.

Carefully, Drych sliced the sack open from end to end, and in his expectation Elffin thought that he did see a salmon inside, then he blinked, dazzled by the sun's reflection on the water, and cursed. It was no salmon, but an infant wrapped in a woollen shawl, almost newborn by the size of him. The weir-ward was already on his knees, muttering prayers. Elffin stared in disbelief and bitter disappointment, then crouched down and lifted the child from the sack.

The boy winced in the sudden brightness after his dark prison, gave a cry, and stretched out tiny fists. Even in his disappointment Elffin felt a growing wonder. Such a striking child: his skin clear and fair, almost translucent, his hair silvery blond. Elffin's own children had never looked this way when they were newborn. The boy in his arms gazed up at him with green-blue eyes, like the sea from which he had been rescued, their expression strangely knowing. A fading memory of the Otherworld? Elffin shook the thought away. Above anything, he was relieved that the child appeared healthy and seemed not to have suffered any harm.

The weir-ward stood at his shoulder, open-mouthed.

'Behold a radiant brow!' he whispered.

Elffin was brought back with a start. 'It seems you have just named our catch,' he said. 'He shall be called Taliesin - Radiant Brow........We must get him to the fortress immediately so my lady Eilonwy can make sure he is properly fed and tended.'

Still angry and embarrassed at having no salmon to bring back, Elffin offered up a silent prayer of thanks that the child was saved; in that at least he had not failed. Though what mother would leave an infant to the mercy of the seas? Perhaps he had been born to an unwed girl on Gwyddno's lands who could be traced and persuaded to accept her son. But he did not look like the offspring of a bondman. It seemed more likely he was a bastard of noble blood.

He turned to the weir-ward. 'Guard the weir with care. I'll return in a few days to see what the nets hold then.'

Elffin handed Taliesin to Drych, then mounted his horse and had the boy passed up to him. Throughout the return journey he often looked down at his small pale face, anger slowly fading in the knowledge that he was far more important than the expected salmon. Even if Taliesin's mother could not be found, Elffin had no doubt that any childless couple would

11

be glad to foster him. He could help them work the land and be a comfort to them in their old age.

When Elffin entered the hall he found Eilonwy embroidering with her companions, their infant son Glinneu asleep in a cradle at her side and two year old Dyfnarth playing on the rug.

'Was there.......?' Eilonwy got to her feet, her gaze followed by the two women seated beneath the window. Dyfnarth, who tried to run after her to see his father, was held back by one of them. 'Elffin, why are you carrying a child?'

She crossed to where he stood, looking first at Taliesin, then up at her husband, ignoring Dyfnarth's angry screams. 'Elffin?'

'My throat is parched. I need some ale.'

Eilonwy sent a servant boy to answer his master's request before resuming her questions.

'Did Drych take the salmon to the fish house?'

'There is no salmon. Come, sit down, it is a long tale that I have to tell.'

The outer door creaked shut behind Gwyddno.

'No salmon?' His voice filled the hall, echoing the words he heard. 'Who is that infant?'

Elffin sat by the hearth and took a draught of ale, then recounted what had happened, all who were within earshot putting aside their tasks to listen.

When he had finished, and life in the hall resumed, Gwyddno mumbled into his beard. 'This does not bode well, Elffin. For generations the weir has yielded a valuable catch on May Eve. You are dogged by misfortune. I must speak to Brother Docmael, perhaps he can offer advice, and I'll ask the brothers at Bangor-Fawr to offer up prayers for you.'

'Is it such ill luck to rescue a child from almost certain death?' Elffin replied defiantly.

Eilonwy reached out and took the infant from his arms, her

expression softening. 'A child's life has no price.'

'He is named Taliesin.'

'So you even have a name for the brat.' Gwyddno scowled. 'Curse it, that weir may never yield again as a result of my stupidity in letting you draw it at such a time. What use to us is some unwanted bastard? And what do you intend to do with him, eh?'

Taliesin pressed his face against Eilonwy's breast, whimpering.

'I think he's hungry,' she whispered. 'Hush, little bright one, I'll feed you. You're safe now.'

Cradling him, she went to join the women, throwing Elffin a glance as she left.

He looked back at his father. 'We must make certain that he is in good health before we try to find foster-parents.'

'Do what you wish with him. He is no concern of mine. But you are, as is the ill fortune that attends you.'

With a certainty he had never felt in his life before, Elffin met Gwyddno's eye.

'There will be no more ill fortune, father, I know it. And no need to get the monks to pray for me. Taliesin is a better omen than any amount of salmon.' He finished his ale and wiped a hand across his mouth. 'Let us hunt this afternoon, and I will bring down something larger than salmon for tomorrow's feast.'

The fires which were kindled that night to celebrate the start of summer blazed throughout the dark hours, and the servants and young people from the fortress had been out in the woods since before dawn, gathering the white-flowered hawthorn.

All around the hall, walls and rafters were being decked with boughs. As Elffin sat at one of the tables, the youths and girls worked around him, laughing and singing, stealing a glance or a touch. Not so many years ago he and Eilonwy had gone with them to the woods, holding hands as they crept away from the others. This was a time for celebration; in nature the sap was flowing, and in men too. Though Gwynedd was Christian, and the monks at Bishop Deniol's monastery decried the May celebrations as Pagan, they had never been banned, nor could Elffin see any reason why rejoicing in fertility should be unchristian when everyone needed children to till the soil or fight for the clan, and life depended on having grain to harvest, cattle to slaughter.

The weather remained glorious. The hall was filled with the rich scent of may blossom, and sprigs of celandine brightened the shadows where no daylight could reach. Elffin's oldest child, four year old Tanwen, skipped at her mother's feet, wearing a chaplet of the golden flowers and carrying a bunch in her hand. Eilonwy smiled at her as she cradled an infant in each arm, and it seemed to Elffin as if his son Glinneu radiated the fire of the sun, with his ruddy complexion and shock of copper hair, while Taliesin was kin to the silvery moon. Since the moment Eilonwy fed him with her own milk, Elffin knew deep down that they would not now be looking for foster-parents in the surrounding farmsteads.

The day passed in contests and dancing, the air alive with laughter as young people jumped the May fires, praying for luck and fertility. At dusk, the clan gathered in the hall to feast on the boar Elffin had speared the previous afternoon. While the company ate, Gwyddno's Chief Bard Cadfarch led the lesser bards in poetry, music and song, celebrating the season and the noble household.

Dazed from the mead he had downed throughout the evening, Elffin stared at the scene before him. He took another draught, then cut a chunk of boar's flesh and savoured the fine flavour, filled with pride at his success in the hunt. But mixed with pride was wonder - in the past all too often he had failed to bring down his quarry. And earlier that day, at the games and horse races in the valley, he had won over men of great skill.

Summer had arrived after the harsh winter, and with it Taliesin. Elffin's life had been blessed in the short time since Drych fished the coracle out of the weir. Through the muzziness, he questioned if perhaps the boy was a faerie child sent to him by the old gods, though he had a powerful pair of lungs and as healthy an appetite as any ordinary infant. Again, Elffin emptied his cup, his thoughts drifting on the mead, filled with memories of the hunt, of riding with his comrades and hounds, of cornering the boar, fearless in the face of its ferocity, the other men shouting behind him.........then Cadfarch's voice rose above it all, stilling the clamour in Elffin's head. Agile fingers rippled across harp strings, his words mingling with the music.

'I have a new tale, made this day in honour of Lord Elffin's triumph.'

Elffin straightened his back as he sensed heads turn in his direction, but he kept his gaze on Cadfarch.

As he related how Taliesin was rescued from the weir, and how the boar they now feasted on was brought to bay and speared, Elffin felt Eilonwy's hand slip into his. He turned to her, noticing that her expression was unusually pensive, and when the bard paused in his recital, she spoke softly, her grip on his hand tightening.

'How can we send Taliesin away after this?' she said. 'He belongs here with us. Why else was the coracle trapped in our weir? I know you feel as I do, Elffin, I have seen it in your eyes. He is so close in age to our Glinneu, when they grow a little they'll be good companions.' She smiled, but he heard the tremor in her voice. 'And he is......beautiful.'

Elffin inclined his head, then kissed her. 'I do feel the same, cariad. From today we have not three children, but four.'

They raised their cups, glancing at the partition which divided the hall from the chamber where the children slept. Elffin knew that Gwyddno would not be pleased. When there had been talk of fostering, it had been centred on a chieftain's son from Elmet, an alliance of noble clans. He would never accept them taking on some foundling of unknown parentage, but both Elffin and Eilonwy already loved the child; and, as shouts and applause filled the hall, it seemed to him that their decision was celebrated by all who heard Cadfarch's tale.

Chapter Two

Taliesin sat on a flat stone beside the waterfall, elbows resting on bare knees, his chin in his hands as he watched the rushing water. He had slipped away from Braich y Dinas on the first really warm day of the year, a week after his ninth birthday, which was celebrated on May Eve, the day of his finding. He knew he was forbidden to go beyond the walls unaccompanied - his mother and tutor, Brother Docmael, warned of accidents and outlaws, and the punishment for disobedience was to be beaten with a birch rod, but he had never seen an outlaw nor met with any harm. And it was worth the risk of discovery to be alone, away from the drunken bragging of the warriors, from the arguments of his brothers and sisters, to be enveloped by the lush greenery of the glen.

A breeze rippled through the leaves overhead. To his ears it sounded like harp music, mingling with the sound of the water until it resolved into a perfect tune. Dappled sunlight danced and flickered to the music. As he stared unblinking, Taliesin noticed that the ferns by the water's edge had taken on a radiance that seemed to come from deep within, shining with all the colours of the rainbow. When he looked around, the stones at his feet and the trees above also had their own colours, their own voices. Each one was whispering words of poetry, chanting, singing. The glen was no longer green and gold, but a tapestry of many hues, and Taliesin felt as if he was a thread being woven into that tapestry, or that he was the tapestry, feeling all the threads being drawn through him.

He was everywhere and nowhere, in every time since the day of creation and beyond time itself. His head filled with music and verse that came from a source beyond his knowing,

'I have borne a banner before Alexander;
I know the names of the stars from north to south;
I was in the court of Don before the birth of Gwydion.....
I shall be until the day of doom on the face of the earth;
And it is not known whether my body is flesh or fish...' [1]

The glen had vanished, replaced by a cascade of images, of strange places, bright stars, vibrant colours. Suddenly Taliesin felt overwhelmed and frightened. He shook his head to try and banish the visions and voices, but they only became more vivid. And encompassing all that he saw and heard, he sensed a presence that filled him with still greater terror.

He jumped to his feet and knelt in the pool at the base of the waterfall, splashing his face with the cold water until the clamour in his head was silenced. When he eventually looked up everything had returned to normal, and all he could hear was the song of a blackbird on a branch nearby and the bubbling of the stream. He pushed wet strands of hair from his eyes and took a deep breath, then stood up, his legs weak and shaky.

Taliesin had had glimpses of other worlds before, but no more than glimpses, he had never been entangled in the web. He wished there was someone he could speak to, to calm his fear, but he knew that he would either be ridiculed or punished for lying. He had heard that hermits and holy men had visions, but he could not imagine that they were in any way like what he had just experienced. Bishop Deniol had had visions of Christ, and the scriptures said that angels were sent as messengers to those favoured by God. But he was not holy and, according to Brother Docmael, was not even good. He thought then of the tales of the bards. Great heroes and druids, too, had visionary experiences, but no sooner had the thought occurred to him than he dismissed it, knowing that he was no more a

18

druid than a hermit.

He sat back down on the stone and unwrapped the hunk of bread he had brought with him. As he ate, the last traces of shimmering light vanished and he began to think of everyday matters. The shadows had deepened while he had been in the glen and, though it was a quick descent from the fortress, he had a long climb ahead.

Leaving the bread, which had become stale after hours in the sun, he put his shoes on and bound the straps around his ankles. With a final look at waterfall and sun-dappled ferns, he began to walk.

The sun was low over the sea as Taliesin slipped through the gates of the stronghold in the wake of a group of men returning from Penmaenmawr with sacks of fish. He was breathless after his climb, and the smell of cooking that wafted across the courtyard from the hall reminded him of how hungry he was. There were few people about and they were occupied with their own business, so unless he had been missed...... As he took in the familiar sights and smells, he was pleased to be back home amidst the bustle of life.

He had just begun to cross the courtyard, keeping to the shadows, when his brother Glinneu appeared from behind the stables. Taliesin pretended not to have seen him, and continued walking until the stocky red-haired boy planted himself in his path, feet apart, eyes challenging.

'Where have you been?' he demanded.

'Watching the smith at work.'

'Then why is your hair wet, and why do you have mud on your tunic? Lying is a sin, Brother Docmael says so, and you'll go to Hell.'

'Then you will too.'

Taliesin took a step forward, but Glinneu put out a

freckled hand and grabbed his shoulder.

'I'm not a liar......I know you've been out of the fortress, and you'll be beaten for it.'

Taliesin pushed the other boy's hand away. 'Let me alone.'

The words were barely out of his mouth when Glinneu grabbed him and wrestled him to the ground, each boy trying to pin the other down, Taliesin forgetting his hunger and tiredness, determined to make Glinneu surrender. Though his brother was half a hand shorter, he made up for it in breadth, and they were equally matched. They rolled over and over, cursing and grunting, unaware that they were being watched until strong hands took them by their belts and hauled them apart. While he was still close enough to be heard, Taliesin hissed in Glinneu's ear,

'The buckle is yours if you keep silence.'

Elffin looked down at his sons, both covered in mud and scratches.

'Why must you boys always fight?' he asked. 'What was it about this time?'

Taliesin straightened his tunic, glancing at his older brother whose hazel eyes gleamed defiantly. He knew that Glinneu was longing to tell, to gloat over his punishment, but greed stood in the way. He had coveted a bronze buckle of Taliesin's ever since he was given it by Maelgwn's son Rhun the previous Christmas. Taliesin was unsure what the other boy was going to say. He was simply glad that it was his beloved and easy-going father who had found them, not the grim Brother Docmeal, who enjoyed inflicting a severe beating.

'I'm sorry, father,' Glinneu murmured. 'I accused him of lying.'

'I should send both of you to bed without supper, but if you are truly sorry for your behaviour.......Taliesin?'

Feeling a secret sense of victory, he nodded.

'Very well, we will speak no more of this, but I do not

expect to have to separate you again.'

Elffin placed his hands on his sons' shoulders and, walking between them, herded them towards the hall.

Dyfnarth and Glinneu were out in the courtyard with a group of boys playing at mock battles. Their shouts carried on the sleepy air, at odds with the harp music which filled the hall. Taliesin's fingers glided across the strings as he sang in a high boyish voice which hit each note effortlessly, while Cadfarch sat on a bench above him, nodding approval.

The tune rippled to an end and Taliesin looked up questioningly, silvery hair framing his high forehead and falling in waves to his shoulders.

'You are progressing well,' Cadfarch reassured him. 'Play 'The Song of the Swans' to finish, then I have other work I must attend to.'

But instead of returning to his music, Taliesin continued looking up at the calm figure clad in fine robes. He was deeply in awe of the Chief Bard, but he also liked and trusted him.

'Master, may I ask you a question?'

'Of course. I'm here so you can learn.'

Taliesin tried to summon his courage. 'It is not a question about music......not exactly. In the ballad of 'Gwinwydden and the Forest' she saw the spirit of the oak tree, and in the song about the swans, the warrior sees the ancient god of the sea.......Um......do you know anyone who has really seen such things?'

Cadfarch raised a brow, meeting the boy's intent green-blue eyes.

'Do you?' His voice was gentle, coaxing.

There was a pause, filled with yells from the courtyard and the buzzing of a fly which traced lazy circles above the table.

'I think......perhaps.......I have.'

'There are many ways of seeing, Taliesin. Tell me about it.'

'Sometimes the trees and plants seem to have new colours, to shine, and when this happens I hear music but don't know where it is coming from. It's not like the music we play here, it's.........it's lovely but frightening. I see other things too, fortresses of polished stone, towers, and moving stars. And I feel that there is someone watching me, someone beautiful and powerful. I think I can just see her and then she is gone. In the songs and tales it seems exciting, but when it happens to me I don't like it. I....I wish it would stop.'

Taliesin waited, every muscle tense, feeling hot and anxious, but Cadfarch only smiled.

'There is no need to fear these things, though I can understand why you are afraid. What you have is rare gift, and you should not wish it away but treasure it. I myself have had similar experiences, but not when I was as young as you, and I had to work hard for a long time in order to achieve them.'

Taliesin's eyes widened. He wanted to ask a hundred questions but felt he had asked too much already. It was Lord Gwyddno's Chief Bard he was speaking to, a man respected throughout Gwynedd, not another child in the courtyard. But why had Cadfarch had to work to see what he had seen without effort? What kind of work did he have to do, and why do it at all?

'When this happens again, sit still and breathe slowly,' the bard said. 'Remember all that you see and tell me afterwards as if it is a lesson. Will you do that?'

'Yes, Master.' Taliesin chewed one of his finger nails. 'But you'll not tell anyone else, will you?'

'I'll not tell anyone else. And remember, thank God for the gift you have been given. It is nothing to be ashamed of. Perhaps when you are older you will be able to make good use of it.'

Taliesin ran his fingers across the harp strings, feeling as if he was listening to the voice of a beloved friend. He stopped puzzling over Cadfarch's words, and his tense muscles relaxed as he began to sing of how two sisters were transformed into swans, the cruel sister into a black swan from May Eve until All Hallows and the good sister into a white swan from All Hallows until May Eve, when she again became a maiden. It was a song Taliesin loved because it seemed to reflect his own life, rescued from the weir on May Eve with no knowledge of who he truly was. Sometimes when his brothers mocked him he found himself thinking that he too would like to return to the river as a swan or salmon.

The time of harvest approached, and the bards told tales of ancestral kings who sacrificed their lives for the land so that their people would not go hungry, and of the corn god who also went to his death as a sacrifice. According to the tales, his spirit lived again each year in the grain that was cut down to feed the people. Taliesin listened, not understanding everything but sensing the power of the ancient mysteries.

Sunlight glanced off the head of the spear which Glinneu let fly through the air towards a rough wooden target that the boys had constructed. The weapon struck the edge of the target, but did not hold fast and fell to the ground.

Dyfnarth looked at his younger brother with disdain in his black eyes, then positioned himself opposite the target. He stood to his full height and took careful aim, radiating confidence. He was the eldest son and proud of it, and at eleven regarded himself as almost a man.

He cast the spear, hitting the target midway between the centre and the rim.

'If any of those filthy Saeson come here, that's what they'll get,' he declared. 'Soon I'll not be aiming at wooden targets but at the enemy. We will drive them back to the eastern sea so they drown.'

'I'll be at your side. I'll kill more Saeson than any man.'

'Not if you throw like that.' Dyfnarth waved a hand at Glinneu's spear lying in the dust.

'It was bad luck......I had a fly in my eye. Watch.'

Glinneu ran to retrieve the two spears, glanced at the dark-haired boy beside him, and took aim. His second throw hit the target and remained where it struck, but Glinneu's look of triumph was met with disinterest.

'You'll improve with practice,' was the only reply he received.

He knew better than to protest, and instead turned to Taliesin who was sitting on the ground, carving a piece of wood and eating an oat cake by turns, apparently paying no attention. Yet he had heard every word and knew how desperately Glinneu wanted to prove himself to his elder brother, whom he worshipped like a hero. But hoping for praise from Dyfnarth was like expecting the piece of wood he was carving in the shape of a dog to jump up and bark.

'Why are you not practising, Taliesin? Do you not want to drive the Saeson out? Or will you grovel to them like a slave.......or a girl.' Glinneu hissed out the words, swaggering in front of him.

'You waste your breath.' Dyfnarth was taking aim again. 'He'll never be a warrior. All he wants to do is tell stories and play the harp.' The spear flew through the air, and as it hit its mark Dyfnarth laughed derisively. 'He probably thinks that he'll frighten the Saeson away with poetry.'

Taliesin gave a start, his brother's words stirring a latent memory, a knowledge long buried, but he did not stop to question it. Instead, he got to his feet and turned towards the hall.

'See, he's running away,' Glinneu taunted.

Taliesin stopped in his tracks and faced him. 'I've better

24

things to do than watch you trying to throw a spear.'

Dyfnarth looked at them with a cold gleam in his eye, then offered his own spear to Taliesin.

'Perhaps you can teach him your skill,' he sneered.

In silence, Taliesin took the weapon, his palms clammy with sweat. He had never had much interest in battle games and dreaded humiliating himself in front of the two people who would gain the most satisfaction from it.

Dyfnarth scratched a new line on the ground, close to where Glinneu had stood. As he watched, praying fervently for success, Taliesin felt a sense of unreality creeping over him, and when he came to stand behind the line and take aim he was scarcely aware of what he was doing. As he balanced the spear it felt as if another hand was guiding his.

Only the sound of it humming through the air, and the thud as it hit the wood, brought him back to reality, and he blinked in the glare of the lowering sun. He thought for a moment that his eyes were tricked by the light, tricked into seeing the spear-point at the centre of the target.

'You cheated.' Glinneu's voice was shrill.

Taliesin looked at him, then glanced back at the target. He had the uneasy feeling that perhaps Glinneu was right, but he could not explain why.

'How could I?' he said firmly. 'I stood behind the line that Dyfnarth marked.'

'You stepped over it, I saw. You are nothing but a cowardly cheat.'

'Forget it, Glinneu, what can you expect from a foundling?' Dyfnarth narrowed his eyes at Taliesin. 'He does not even know who his blood parents are. They were probably liars and cheats too. Slaves.......Saeson.....who knows.'

Taliesin turned, retrieving his knife and carving before walking away. He was determined not to cry, even when he was alone, because then they would have won. He wanted to humiliate his brothers as they did him but knew he was powerless. There was no point in keeping on fighting Glinneu or having word battles with Dyfnarth because it changed nothing. He was still different. Deep down he felt he would have sacrificed all his musical talent just to be Elffin's and Eilonwy's true blood son, to see their reflection in himself. He hated his fairness that made him stand out from the others, though it had often been praised by visitors to the stronghold. He wished he was dark like his foster-mother, like Tanwen and Dyfnarth. Dyfnarth's swarthy complexion gave him a look of maturity and strength. He wished.......and wished.

As he neared the hall his sister Alarch ran up to him, turning a freckled face towards him with a look of concern. She was the youngest of Elffin's children, born a year after he was rescued from the weir, and as they grew had become his ally.

'Taliesin, you are unhappy. Has Glinneu been trying to pick a fight again?'

He shook his head. 'It is nothing.' He stopped, and placed the dog he had just carved in her hand. 'Here, it's a present for you.'

Alarch's face lit up. 'You are so clever. I wish I could carve and sing and play harp like you.'

Taliesin forced a smile. Did she really wish it? As much as he wished he was her real brother, Elffin's son.

'You do sing well.'

She grinned. 'But you are Master Cadfarch's pupil.'

They went into the hall and sat in a corner playing, as the aroma from the great cauldron that simmered above the hearth filled the air. Warriors were gathering at one of the long tables, drinking and laughing, while Eilonwy presided over the cauldron, measuring out herbs. Tanwen, the image of her mother, brought the herb containers from the storage chest with a look of self-importance, and held them as Eilonwy took a pinch of thyme or a sprig of mint.

When Taliesin looked up to see if the food was ready, he saw Dyfnarth and Glinneu march through the door like heroes returning from battle. Dyfnarth cast a contemptuous glance in his direction, and walked ahead of his younger brother. But before they reached their places at table, Glinneu stopped, scanning the hall with a predatory look until he found his quarry. Dyfnarth ignored him and took a seat, leaving Glinneu to approach Taliesin and Alarch alone.

The girl looked at him defiantly.

'Go away, you cannot join our game........unless you carve me a wooden horse.' She indicated the toy animals scattered on the floor around them. 'What are you staring at?'

'I would not play such silly games anyway. I'm going to be a warrior. And I'm surprised you want to play with him.'

'He does not argue all the time. And you never stay at the same game for half a moment.'

Glinneu snorted.

'I don't play with cheats.'

Taliesin got to his feet and glanced at his sister. 'Come on Alarch, I'm hungry.'

Glinneu's hazel eyes were blazing. 'At least I know who my real father is,' he spat. 'You're just a peasant's son......or perhaps you're a........'

Taliesin's body stiffened, and Glinneu fell silent. He had never seen such an expression on Taliesin's face before. Alarch pulled urgently at his arm.

'Come on, come on, he doesn't mean it.'

But Taliesin seemed not to hear and shook himself free from her grasp. He stood motionless, then took a step forward, raising his hand as if to push Glinneu, though in all the brothers' fights he had never been the one to move first.

In that instant Glinneu gave an agonized scream and fell to the ground, clutching his head with both hands. Everyone in the hall turned, then hurried to where he lay. Taliesin was the first at his brother's side, kneeling close to him. The blinding anger was gone, as if an arrow had been loosed from a taught bow and, despite his fear for Glinneu, he felt dazed and empty.

Eilonwy crouched beside them and took Glinneu into her arms. He was no longer screaming but sobbing weakly like a small child, his bravado forgotten.

'Mother, what is the matter with him?' Taliesin asked desperately. 'I didn't touch him.'

'He didn't, I was watching,' Alarch said. 'Will Glinneu be all right?'

'Yes, my sweetness, he will be all right. Don't worry.' Eilonwy stroked Glinneu's brow, then spoke to him softly. 'Are you still hurting?'

He shook his head, though the usual fiery spark in his eyes had been replaced by fear.

'Then I'll take you to your bed. You can have some supper there.'

She helped him to his feet, and with her arm around his shoulders led him to the family's sleeping quarters. Those gathered about them watched, then slowly returned to the tables, talking under their breath, and Tanwen took over her mother's role of supervising the cauldron and serving its contents.

Taliesin had lost his appetite, but followed the others and sat down with Alarch beside him. He could hear a couple of women murmuring nearby.

'Our kin has never been afflicted by fits. I've not known one uncle, aunt or cousin to suffer a fit.'

An elderly crone replied in a croaky voice, unaware than anyone but her companion was listening. 'I once knew a youth who was taken by a fit - a clever boy, favoured for kingship. Afterwards he could neither move nor speak, and he died two weeks later. They said he'd been cursed by an evil satire, that the father of another lad wanted his son to be favourite........'

Taliesin could bear it no longer. He leapt up and ran from the hall to look for Glinneu, terrified that he might find him a motionless corpse. Sometimes when his brother mocked him he thought he hated Glinneu, but the shock of seeing him collapse made him realize that was not truly what he felt.

He pushed a hide curtain aside and entered the area where the boys slept, his heart throbbing. But when he looked around the dimly lit room he found Glinneu sitting up in bed, sipping from a cup while Eilonwy was trying to get him to explain what had happened.

'Ah, Taliesin.....' Her face was pale with worry.

'I.....I had to see how Glinneu was. I couldn't eat until I knew.'

The brothers looked at each other warily but the earlier hostility was gone.

'I had a pain, but I'm better now,' Glinneu said with some of his usual spirit.

'Taliesin, perhaps you can tell me more.' Eilonwy's voice was gentle but firm.

He shook his head. 'We weren't fighting. I didn't hit him, I swear.'

'No one is accusing you, do not upset yourself. And now you've seen that your brother is all right you can go and have some supper. He needs to rest.'

Shuffling his feet, Taliesin made his way back to the table. He sat with his head lowered and said little as he ate, replying to Alarch's questions with one word answers. He knew he had not touched Glinneu. He had done nothing except feel angry, but over and over he questioned himself. Had the incident been his fault? Then he thought of the crone's words, again not fully understanding. Cadfarch's stories told how a bardic satire could harm, but Brother Docmael dismissed any talk of magic. Feeling confused and frightened he played with the food in his dish, wishing the world was less complicated, that it was safe and simple as it had seemed when he was small, when he and Glinneu trotted round after Eilonwy, pulling at her skirts, and fell asleep together with their heads on her lap.

chapter three

The summit of the mountain where Taliesin stood was higher than any he had climbed before, higher even than Eryri Gwyn, so he seemed not to be on the earth at all but balanced in the sky. Yet there were no clouds to obscure his view. He could see the entire land, from the northernmost isles of Pictland to the tip of the Dumnonian peninsula jutting out into the Great Sea; he could see the marshes and dunes of the east and the chalk downs of the south, kingdoms now in the grasp of the Angles and Saeson. As he watched, a great white dragon appeared from the east, advancing across the land, trampling the crops in the fields, its fiery breath burning forts and settlements. People scattered before the dragon, screaming as they fled, the venom it breathed on those who tried to escape making their flesh erupt in black boils, and they ranted in delirium. Still, the dragon advanced, facing a red dragon that stood in its path, fighting valiantly. But the courage of the red dragon was not enough to stop the white from pressing westward, its body enveloping the land, becoming the land, as far as Mor Hafren.

The white dragon's eyes stared into Taliesin's, locked in a deadly battle of wills, as the red dragon stood behind him, weary from its wounds. A stream of strange words poured from his throat, words that made the white dragon falter, but he felt his strength beginning to ebb. His heart pounded and he struggled for breath..........

Filled with growing panic, he found the world had turned dark; the dragons had vanished, so had the wide vistas of Ynys Prydein. He opened his eyes, and realized that he was lying on his bed, with the faint light of a wintry dawn creeping through the cracks in the shutters and no sound but the sleepy breathing

31

of his brothers. He sat up, then got to his feet, and wrapping his blanket around him left the sleeping quarters and made his way barefoot across the feast hall, where the previous night's fire was banked down in the central hearth and the beams were decked with greenery for the festive season.

Holly berries, red as the dragon of his dream, nestled between leaves sharp like its claws - the weapons of the Britons. Brother Docmael said that the berries represented the blood of Christ, the saviour born in this season, who died to bring eternal salvation for mankind, as the evergreens lived on through the dead of winter. Cadfarch, too, said the holly represented life at the time of Alban Arthan, the shortest day of the year.

Taliesin had to stand on a stool to raise the top bar of the door, then he pushed it open and peered out onto a scene of all enveloping peace, the courtyard and huddle of buildings within the ramparts covered by snow. All the mountains of Eryri were white, their peaks veiled in cloud. The scene was so tranquil, so beautiful, that it calmed Taliesin's throbbing heart, and he breathed deeply of the chill air.

He knew that Cadfarch must be told of the dream, it felt important - too important. He shuddered at the thought of what it might mean. Or perhaps it was only his grandfather's foreboding talk of the Saeson that had disturbed his sleep. Cadfarch would know and understand. Taliesin was coming to realize that the bard knew a great deal more than he allowed most people to see, more even than the learned Brother Docmael. Not only could he transport the noble company in the hall to another world when he performed, but he could read the trees, the stars, dreams, and even men, like the monk read a manuscript.

But it was Brother Docmael whom Taliesin saw first that day. He and his brothers sat at one end of the hall, scratching letters onto wax tablets which could be melted and reused, while their tutor's voice droned monotonously.

Taliesin remembered the white dragon's eyes, filled with greed to devour the land, and in his head he heard Dyfnarth jeering at him, 'He probably thinks that he'll frighten the Saeson away with poetry.' In the dream that was what he had tried to do, to repel the beast with words.........

'Taliesin!'

He jumped and looked up into the monk's pale severe face. Stony grey-brown eyes, that matched his hair and the coarse cloth of his robe, replaced the flashing yellow eyes of the dragon.

'You are not attending. Look, you have omitted a word. Write the last sentence again, three times, with no errors.'

Pursing his lips in concentration Taliesin obeyed, laboriously forming the letters, his hand unsteady as he felt his tutor's eyes boring into him, afraid that he would make yet another mistake.

He had been told how important it was for a chieftain's son to be well-educated, though he wondered how such a tortuous process could ever bear healthy fruit. Reducing the beauty and melody of words to straight lines, hammering them into him until their magic was lost. His stylus slipped and Brother Docmael grunted disapprovingly. Taliesin hesitated, then continued painfully slowly until the exercise was done.

'Dedication, application and obedience are as important as knowledge.' The monk frowned at Dyfnarth's sneering smile. 'So is humility. It is one of the heavenly virtues.' He began to gather up the writing tablets. 'Lessons are over for today. You may go.'

The brothers stood, but waited for their tutor to leave first, then grabbed fur-lined jerkins against the cold and ran out into the courtyard, across snow already dirty and trampled from the passage of many feet. They ran without stopping until they reached an area beyond the last roundhouse where it lay undisturbed, three sets of footprints marking a jagged path.

Dyfnarth scooped up a handful, rolled it into a ball and flung it at Glinneu, who gave a yelp of shocked delight. He fired back at his elder brother, aiming a second ball of snow at Taliesin. Shouts and laughter filled the air as they jumped and skidded, throwing and dodging, forgetting the rivalry which so often got in the way of comradeship.

Though they were soon wet through, excitement kept them warm. White missiles flew through the air, the snow underfoot now churned and scuffed. And, hearing their shouts, other children came to join them, forming two battle lines, then breaking up into small laughing groups.

They stopped only when Tanwen's voice called above the noise.

'Mother says you're to come in.'

Dyfnarth nodded obediently, waiting for her to leave. Taliesin and Glinneu, standing behind her, grinned.

'Come in. Now! I am no fool,' Tanwen scolded, resting her hands on her hips. 'You must practice your lessons and, Taliesin, Cadfarch wants to see you.'

Suddenly he remembered his dream, and all the thrill of the game drained out of him. He realized that he was cold and wet, and with pretend reluctance began to shuffle in the direction of the hall. Glinneu looked towards Dyfnarth's dark lanky figure, not prepared to do anything without his approval.

'When I am a man, I shall not take commands from any woman,' Dyfnarth said as he sauntered past Tanwen, who laughed.

'Some day you might change your mind about that, little brother.'

Taliesin was grateful to sit in front of the fire in dry clothes, his hands cupped around an earthenware beaker of hot milk. His brothers sat beside him, telling jokes they had heard amongst the warriors and which they pretended to understand, trying to impress each other.

When Cadfarch entered the hall, the boys got to their feet as a mark of respect, but only Taliesin went with him through the snow to the bard's roundhouse. He glanced at the familiar symbols carved on the door-posts as he stepped between them into the fire-lit interior, the berries, leaves and feathers there speaking a wordless welcome, and on a chest stood Cadfarch's harp, the smaller one that Taliesin played waiting beside it.

The house was filled with a bittersweet aroma from a bronze dish which rested in the embers at the edge of the fire. As Taliesin watched curls of smoke rise into the air, he recalled the fiery breath of the dragon wasting the land.

Cadfarch took a seat beside him, and looked at him with concern.

'What is troubling you?' he asked.

Without looking up, Taliesin described his dream, only raising his eyes when he had finished.

'Does the white dragon mean the Saeson?' he asked in a trembling voice.

Cadfarch nodded thoughtfully, making Taliesin question again.

'Did I really see truth?'

'I think you saw truth, but you must not be afraid. You said the red dragon fought back valiantly.'

'Yes.' Taliesin's voice brightened.

'And you did not see it vanquished, only retreating, gathering its strength to continue the fight.'

'But what of the villages it burnt, the people it killed?'

Cadfarch sighed. 'Sadly the foreigners have already done these things. You have seen into the past as well as the future.'

Taliesin met his master's deep brown eyes, which reminded him of the warm forest earth, and searched for any shadow of uncertainty. He had the feeling that Cadfarch was trying to soothe him with false encouragement, though he saw nothing to either confirm or banish the thought.

'There is no need for such melancholy,' the bard said. 'In two days time the Mabon will be reborn.'

Taliesin frowned.

'The child of light, who incarnates after the longest night.'

'Oh, the baby Jesus.' Taliesin's frown became a smile. 'Mab Mair.'

'Yes, the Mabon is, and has been, known by many names in many lands. He lets us know that there is always hope, that after darkness there is light, after winter's hardship, summer. You, and your brothers and sisters, are the hope for our future.'

Cadfarch waved a hand in the direction of the harps, and Taliesin ran to fetch them. 'You can make that future bright with your music.'

A group of figures clustered around a stone beehive hut which was partly sheltered in the lee of a rocky outcrop. Snow still lay on the ground, and scattered from the thorn bushes nearby each time the wind blew, though there had been no fresh fall for two days.

The villagers of Penmaenmawr stood respectfully apart from the chieftain's family, with their silver brooches and fur-lined cloaks. Taliesin pulled his more tightly around his shoulders as he huddled between Tanwen and Glinneu, who stamped restlessly, rubbing his hands. But the hermit Beulan, thin to the point of emaciation and wearing only a sparse undyed tunic, seemed oblivious to the cold.

'Have no fear for your children.' The sea moaned in the background as his voice rose through the brittle air. 'As the master Pelagius says, they enter this world free of sin. Even those who die un-baptised may enter the Kingdom of Heaven. We are all born innocent in the eyes of God, and all have a choice whether to follow in the ways of good or evil.'

Glinneu had begun to blow on his icy hands, and Tanwen gave him a nudge.

'Be still. Listen, and you may learn something. To be sure you need to.'

Taliesin and Alarch exchanged glances. Then he turned back to the gaunt figure of the hermit, whose eyes shone in his wan face. Yet, despite his passion, he possessed great gentleness. And Taliesin wished that it was Beulan, not Brother Docmael, who tutored him. He seemed to feel his faith in his heart, rather than to think about it with his mind as Brother Docmael did. Cadfarch, too, felt his faith in his heart, though Taliesin was becoming aware that the bard's beliefs were not entirely Christian.

'I repeat, we have the choice, brothers and sisters, whether or not to condemn ourselves, as Adam did. If we follow our conscience and do only good, we remain as untainted as on the day of our birth, though some say that the first sin committed by the first man is visited upon all his descendants..... I say that the path we walk is our own. It is our own choice whether or not we walk with God.'

Snow from the bushes whirled about the listeners, driven by the biting wind.

'God has infinite compassion, as does his son Jesus, who came to earth to show us the way.' Beulan paused, looking directly at the children from the fortress gathered around Tanwen, and smiled kindly. 'Choose the right path now, at the commencement of your life's journey, though it is only natural that sometimes you will stray and stumble. Because if you travel but a short distance along the way of sin and selfishness, you will have to retrace your steps over harsh and rocky ground to start again on God's path of righteousness.'

Glinneu fidgeted under the hermit's gaze and looked down, but Taliesin held Beulan's eye, his expression wistful as he thought of Eryri Gwyn and the slopes leading to its peak.

On the journey towards God's kingdom, or the Otherworld of the bardic tales, there were the dangerous routes followed by those who were evil, like the Saeson, which led the climber to fall, but also good paths. He was sure that even if Cadfarch still followed some of the Old Ways, his path was as holy as Beulan's, and perhaps all good paths became one near the summit.

He shivered, his awareness returning to the cold shore and the mournful music of the sea. Longing for the warmth of the fire at Braich y Dinas, he wondered how a frail man like Beulan could endure the winter alone in a windowless stone hut. But he seemed to possess strength greater than Gwyddno - a hardened warrior and veteran of many battles.

Once the snows cleared, Elffin took his sons hunting in the wooded glens below the fortress: galloping over the frost-hard ground, brittle twigs crunching beneath hooves, leaping streams swollen with melt-water that gushed down from the mountains of Eryri. The hounds bayed as they chased deer, though Dyfnarth bragged that he would spear a boar and the bards would sing of his courage.

Taliesin had no such ambition, all he thought of was the thrill of riding with the wind in his face, as he had enjoyed sitting by the waterfall in the summer. The mountains towered over them, icy and treacherous, but he saw as much beauty in the stark brutality of winter as in the soft green of summer.

When they paused to retrieve their kill and he had time to reflect, he remembered Cadfarch's words, reminding him of how light followed darkness, and the many other things the bard had begun to tell him during the long winter evenings. He never thought of this as tutoring, not like the lessons he endured with Brother Docmael, and for the first time he found learning exciting. There were no dull writing exercises, everything he learnt was spoken or sung. And though Cadfarch asked him to repeat what he had been told, memorizing came easily and naturally.

Early twilight was falling when they returned to the fortress. Tired but exhilarated, they sat by the hearth, and Tanwen removed her father's riding boots, her cheeks rosy in the fire-glow.

Alarch looked at Taliesin.

'Did you enjoy the hunt?' she asked. 'What did you bring down?'

'Dyfnarth killed a deer,' he replied flatly.

'I wish I could come. I hate cooking, the bread I bake is always hard. And the thread I spin is uneven. But I can shoot an arrow.'

'Perhaps you could come next time.'

She shook her head. 'Mother would never allow it. She is always comparing me to Tanwen and saying I should have been born a boy.'

Taliesin gave one of her auburn braids an affectionate tug. 'I wish you were, but wishing doesn't ever change things.'

Alarch tugged at a handful of her brother's hair in return and giggled, then led Taliesin across the hall to persuade Tanwen to give them the jar of hazelnuts.

'Tell me about the hunt,' she begged as they sat cross legged on a sheepskin rug by the fire, the earthenware jar on the floor between them.

Taliesin straightened his back and began. 'Three princes galloped through the golden gates of the caer which stood on the highest mountain in all the world. The eldest prince was tall and dark, the second strong and red-haired, the youngest fair......'

Alarch listened intently, the hazelnuts forgotten.

'On and on they rode, over mountains, through glens, their hounds following the scent of a wild beast......

'All day and all night they followed it, and by the light of the full moon at last they saw their quarry - a pure white hind with a silver torc about its neck.'

Taliesin paused, seeing the wonder in Alarch's eyes, then, more slowly, he continued, taking her as a companion through the world of his imagination.

'When the hind leapt a stream and vanished into the mist, the princes brought their horses to a halt. The two eldest turned back, but the youngest rode deeper into the forest, until he came to a clearing where he heard sorrowful music. As he looked about him the mist parted, and the white hind stood in the clearing, less than a spear's throw away........ The prince did not throw his spear. He stayed very still, feeling pity for the hind.

'Then a cloud passed across the moon and all became dark. When the prince was again able to see, it was no longer a hind that stood before him, but a maiden clothed in a white gown, with a silver torc about her neck.

'She walked towards the fair-haired prince and spoke, 'You have broken the spell cast by my jealous sister. Instead of chasing me and trying to kill me, you let me come to you, and so the curse is lifted.'

For a moment Alarch sat entranced, then she raised her head and saw that Elffin was listening with her.

'That was a wonderful tale, Taliesin,' he said softly. 'But now you must leave fantasy for another time and attend your lessons with Brother Docmael.'

He turned, and the children walked beside him, Taliesin glancing up at his father, whom he loved more than anyone else, who was strong and protective but who often seemed like a boy himself. To his surprise, he thought he saw Elffin look back at him with an expression normally reserved for Cadfarch.

After lessons were finished, Taliesin sat by the fire playing his harp, idly wondering where Tanwen had put the jar of hazelnuts. Or had Alarch taken it into the sleeping quarters, so she could eat in secret under the covers?

From the corner of his eye he noticed Glinneu prowling about looking distracted. But Glinneu was always restless and he paid no attention. He played another tune before putting his harp aside, and went to see if Alarch was awake.

As he entered the sleeping compartment, he noticed a flicker of light from the far end where the boys slept. Then the dividing curtain was tugged open, and Glinneu stood in front of him, scowling.

He marched to Taliesin's bed, and pointed beneath it. Curious, Taliesin crouched down, seeing Glinneu's bow on the ground.

'I have been looking for this,' his brother hissed.

'Why? When you must have put it there yourself.'

'Liar. Thief.'

Taliesin thought that perhaps Dyfnarth or one of the other boys had hidden it as a prank. He spoke in a whisper.

'Well, you have it now. Let us leave before we disturb Alarch.'

'Did you tell her to steal it?'

'I'm leaving.......'

'I think you moved it by magic.....because you're the son of a demon.' Glinneu's eyes shone in the lamplight. 'Who else has white hair like yours? All white, all washed out. Strange. Stranger.'

'Stop it.' Taliesin's voice was no more than a whisper but he felt as if a mountain torrent roared in his head, as if lightning flashed across his vision.

Glinneu screamed, staggered, and fell across Taliesin's bed. His fingers clasped his temples, but as he lay face down all Taliesin could see was a halo of red hair. From behind him he heard Alarch's cry, though he did not turn. Instead, he stood frozen, staring at his brother.

'I must never become angry again,' was his only thought, beating at his brain like a drum. 'Never. Ever. I never want to hurt anyone this way again, and if I get angry I cannot help it.'

He shook with fear, fear at a part of himself that he did not understand and could not control. A demon, Glinneu had said. He thought of Brother Docmael's warnings, filled with terror that perhaps he was born evil. But the holy Beulan had said that the choice of good or evil was his own to make.

chapter four

The feast of Gwyl Fair was past and the first lambs had been born on the lowland pastures, but winter still held the peaks of Eryri in its grip and the ground inside the fortress complex was hard as iron.

Taliesin had been helping tend the horses and had run back to the sleeping quarters to fetch a warmer tunic. As he pulled it over his head, he heard his father speaking in the hall, followed by Cadfarch's voice. When he heard his own name, he stopped to listen, then edged closer to the partition that separated the chamber from the hall.

'But the boys are receiving tuition from Brother Docmael, a very learned man. He is well versed in both Greek and Latin.'

'Lord Elffin, I am not speaking of literacy or calculations.......nor of the scriptures. I speak of the ancient arts of this land.'

'I know what you speak of,' Elffin replied in an undertone, 'and that is why it troubles me. I am uncertain what to do for the best. I was raised a Christian, and so are my sons; the time for druidic magic is past.'

'I understand your position, my lord, but I feel bound to offer my advice, which is not given lightly. With respect, magic will never be a thing of the past. It exists in the world, and you cannot deny that Taliesin has natural powers. You may see these as a gift of God, along with his musical talent but, if not, you cannot overlook them simply because they do not fit in with Christian theology, nor will they diminish by being ignored. When someone with such power is untrained, when it is not under the conscious control of the mind, it can be dangerous as a sword in the hand of a child. Surely you do not wish to witness a repetition of the episode with Glinneu.'

Taliesin pressed a clenched fist to his mouth, scarcely daring to breathe, as Cadfarch's words lightened the shadow that had hung over him all winter.

He heard his father grunt, though he gave no reply, and Cadfarch continued in a firm voice.

'The boy is distressed because he does not understand the nature of his powers. Would you deny him the chance to use them for the benefit of others? The clan, our countrymen, our land. Instead of accidentally and innocently causing harm, he could be trained to help and heal. I would not be encouraging him to forsake his religion, only to find harmony within himself and in the world, and of course to improve his bardic technique. Though he is agile, and reasonably skilled at arms for a boy his age, I believe it is his destiny to be a bard, not a warrior.'

Taliesin stood motionless, silently pleading with Elffin to agree. He would be like Cadfarch - hold a place of honour in a chieftain's hall. He would travel across the land, play the harp, sing of ancient gods and great heroes; he would be wise........powerful. He had never thought of the future in this way before, it had always been vague, somehow frightening, like half-seen images in the mist.

To his dismay Taliesin heard the men's footsteps receding across the hall, their voices becoming indistinct as they moved away, mingling with other voices and sounds. He struggled to make out what they were saying, but when it proved impossible he backed away from the partition and sat down on the clothes chest. He had lost interest in helping with the horses, unable to think of anything but Cadfarch's suggestion, which seemed to answer his every prayer.

He waited, in his mind seeing a hall filled with warriors listening to his song, entranced as little Alarch had been by the tale of the transformed maiden. He stayed where he was for a long time, not wanting his father and Cadfarch to know that he had overheard their conversation. Then, realizing that Drych

44

would wonder what had become of him, he finally emerged and headed back towards the stables.

In the courtyard he passed Glinneu and one of the warrior's sons returning from sword practice, talking excitedly. In the past Glinneu would have shouted out some insult, now he fell silent, cast a wary glance in Taliesin's direction and increased his pace. It had been this way since their last argument when Glinneu collapsed, and it pained Taliesin more than the cruellest taunts. Though he had avoided his brother as much as Glinneu avoided him, afraid of getting angry again, the sense of isolation created a hollowness deep inside. If only he was a bard like Cadfarch, then surely he would no longer feel so weak and alone. If only Elffin would agree to let him begin training.

'There is plague in Deganwy now.' Eilonwy twisted the wool deftly as her spindle whorl twirled towards the floor. Her rounded, usually serene face was lined with worry. 'No one from Braich y Dinas must cross the river. It may even be dangerous in the village.'

'The epidemic spreads like fire through thatch.' Gwyddno banged his fist down on the table. 'Saeson. Disease. Our land is being devoured..........'

Taliesin looked up from polishing a belt buckle. An image sprang to his mind, one he had not thought of for months, that he had chosen to forget - a white dragon wasting the crops, the people's faces erupting in black boils. When he had the dream he had not known about the plague, now talk of it filled the hall, and talk of what happened to those who fell sick. He shuddered, and continued polishing, as if he could polish away all that was wrong in the land.

'They say it started in Gaul and came over The Narrow Sea on the trading ships. Now it has infested all the British kingdoms.'

'That Saeson cur, Cynric, makes the most of our weakness.' The man who spoke had once fought under Gwyddno. Now he, too, was ageing, his skin like leather and his hands gnarled. 'A traveller from the east brought news that Cynric has taken Sorbiodunum. The young warriors here should take up their swords and ride out to meet the foreigners. They should stand beside our comrades from Powys and Dumnonia.'

There was a pause. Cups were raised slowly and thoughtfully. A gust of wind rattled the shutters.

'What sin have we committed?' It was Gwyddno's gruff voice. 'Is this divine vengeance for our folly?'

Cadfarch sighed. 'We have forgotten much, my lord. We have forgotten what is truly sacred, the sanctity of the land itself.'

'Nor have we ceased to fight amongst ourselves.' Elffin took a draught of mead. 'Even now Uncle Maelgwn argues with King Elgan of Dyfed, and there is talk of war.'

'There was a time when we found unity. I remember our great victory at Mount Badon. And once, when I was a boy, I accompanied my father to Caerleon when Arthur visited the fort of the legions. I've never forgotten the charisma of the man. Where is such a leader now? Where?'

Taliesin listened to his grandfather's voice, picturing the heroic warlord - the finest of Roman and British blood. All the fire and courage of his own people, but in battle he wore the Roman breastplate and helmet, and used the tactics of the Empire. Taliesin thought that if ever such a leader emerged again he would serve him, in whatever way he was able.

'Taliesin, we must not go too far. Tanwen will kill me when I get back.'

He grabbed Alarch's arm and pulled her onwards.

'Perhaps she'll use the skinning knife, or the serving ladle, or even.........a meat hook.'

'Don't tease. And is it not dangerous away from the fortress? With the plague......'

Taliesin gave an indulgent laugh. 'You get that from people, not from trees and rocks.'

His sister tramped after him, clothed in one of his tunics and a pair of breeches that were too long for her and had been rolled up at the ankles. Both wore sturdy boots, and over his shoulder Taliesin had slung a cloth bag containing bread and cheese.

They reached the glen, where the sound of water broke the stillness and branches were just breaking into leaf. Taliesin paused beside an alder tree, pressing his hands against its grey trunk.

'Feel the energy, Alarch.' He placed her hand on the trunk beside his own. 'Cadfarch has been telling me this tree's secrets, but I think it can tell me some more.'

She stood unusually still, looking confused. It never occurred to Taliesin that the pulsing life he felt within the tree could not be sensed by everyone, especially someone he felt as close to as Alarch.

Suddenly she pulled her hand away, and with a laugh leapt the stream and began running through the trees and tangled undergrowth on the far bank. Taliesin chased after her, soon racing past and leaving her to follow.

He finally stopped in a chasm where cliffs rose to either side, stealing the sunlight. Breathless, Alarch skipped up to him, her freckled cheeks rosy from the run and the mountain air. Taliesin's face, too, was flushed, his sea-green eyes sparkling. They walked a little further, Taliesin whistling a tune. Then he paused and looked around thoughtfully. He whistled louder, and Alarch raised her head in surprise as the cliffs whistled back.

Taliesin took a deep breath and sang a long clear note. While the echo still sounded he sang another, and another, bringing the chasm to life with a chorus that seemed to come from the Otherworld. Alarch's spine tingled. She had experienced nothing when she touched the tree, now she felt light-headed, and the distant sky appeared over-bright.

When Taliesin stopped singing, and the echo faded, she was left with a numbing sense of loss. He folded his arms, then turned to her and grinned.

'You try.'

Alarch hesitated. She looked up at the cliffs, almost expecting to see faerie singers there.

'Go on.'

Nervously, she drew in a lung-full of air and sang as loudly as she was able. Her own voice returned to her, clear and tuneful, but disappointing. Something was lacking. Perhaps there had been faerie beings singing with Taliesin after all, and they would not sing with her because she was not Master Cadfarch's pupil.

They took turns to sing again before sitting down and tracing patterns in the dust with a stick. Gradually their talk of friends and games dwindled into silence, broken by occasional birdsong.

Taliesin stared down at one of the patterns he had drawn, his gaze travelling round and round until the lines melted from view and he saw a woman standing on the shore of a lake overshadowed by mountains. A wind swept across its surface, catching at her barley-coloured hair and the folds of her dark cloak. She was stirring a pearl-rimmed cauldron, its contents swirling and spiralling, revealing glimpses of living creatures: a hare, a hound, a salmon, an otter.........then a circle of stars, a ring of stones.........

'Taliesin.'

He felt that he had fallen into the depths of the cauldron,

that he was dissolving.

'Taliesin!' A high-pitched, terrified cry penetrated the darkness. He was not dissolving after all. He had a head, a body, arms, and someone was clasping his arms so tightly that it hurt. Someone was shaking him.

'What's the matter? Taliesin. Please.......'

Slowly the ground swam back into focus and, still feeling disorientated, he looked up at the white, wide-eyed face in front of him.

Alarch released her hold and sighed loudly.

'Oh......You went really peculiar. Your eyes were staring and you were saying strange things, they were all nonsense.'

'It's all right.' Taliesin tried to speak calmly. 'I was daydreaming.'

'You're lying. Don't treat me like a baby. I thought you were going to stay like that and I would be here alone, and not know what to do.'

'I......I cannot talk about it.' Taliesin gave an apologetic smile, grateful that she was there, even though she would not understand. He rubbed his eyes, then got unsteadily to his feet, eager to be away from the place of the haunting echoes. 'I think we should go home.'

Alarch nodded enthusiastically, fear of her elder sister nothing compared to the fear she had felt when she looked into Taliesin's eyes.

Afternoon sunlight shone across the entrance to Cadfarch's round-house as Taliesin tapped once on the door.

'Master.'

'You may enter.'

He stepped inside, finding it pleasantly cool and dark after the heat of the courtyard. But Cadfarch stood up, reaching for his hazel-wood staff.

'Come, let us walk.'

'Shall I bring the harp?'

'No, not today.'

He did not say why that day should be different from any other, and Taliesin had learnt not to ask for explanations. He sensed there was something on Cadfarch's mind that he would discuss when he felt the time was right. Since the festival of Calan Mai, Taliesin's birthday, the bard had begun to take him out into the woodlands to give instruction, and as the weeks passed the lessons came to mean more to him than anything else: his hope and his refuge.

Cadfarch picked up a leather water skin, then led the way across the courtyard. The children who were playing there stared and, knowing that they looked at him with envy, Taliesin felt a growing confidence in his new status. Their games held no interest for him as he headed towards the fortress gates, where a guard was posted, standing in the shadow of the wall.

'Greetings, Master Cadfarch......Taliesin.' The man wiped a hand across his dripping brow and took a swig from a flask. 'Tis hot for walking.'

Cadfarch smiled. 'Not if you understand the subtle elements, my friend. And not if you drink only water.'

The guard frowned, then laughed, loud and hearty.

When they were clear of the gates Cadfarch stopped, and Taliesin stood silently beside him. Together they looked at the unbroken vistas which extended in all directions, melting in a haze towards the horizon. Gulls' wings glinted silver above them, and to the south the peaks of Eryri yearned towards the blue arc of the sky.

'See, Taliesin.' Cadfarch raised his staff and pointed. 'You have looked at this view many times, but have you really *seen* it? This land is the mother of our people, to be loved and honoured. She bestows generous gifts on us, gives us nourishment and strength. We depend on her, and you must serve her as I do.'

He pointed to the north-east. 'There lies the kingdom of Rheged, where the young warrior Urien fights beside his father Cynfarch against the barbarian Angles. Like your foster-father's clan, the house of Rheged is descended from the great chief Coel Hen. Some day you will travel, and meet our comrades who dwell in the north.' He turned in a sunwise direction, still pointing. 'And there lies Deva, Roman military headquarters of western Ynys Prydein, where many roads meet like the spokes of a wheel. Its stone buildings, erected in pride, are falling into ruin, as the Empire has crumbled. Nothing is constant except change, all things are forever dying........and renewing.'

Taliesin put up a hand to shield his eyes, peering into the distance, seeing far-off ages and places pass in procession before him. Cadfarch continued turning, past the ramparts of the stronghold, until he faced west.

'On the strand of Ynys Mon, the Britons' death blow was struck; druids and wise-women massacred by the Romans under the command of General Paulinus, because he feared their power.'

Completing his circle, Cadfarch pointed north-west.

'In this direction, Hibernia, whose men were once the dread of Gwynedd - wild and ruthless, raiding our land and settlements. Now they are tamed by Christianity. There are many who are very wise amongst them, some who even journey to the Saeson kingdoms and to Gaul to spread the Christian word. And between the two coasts lies Ellan Vannin, sacred to the ancient sea god, Manawyddan.

'You are born of this land, Taliesin, rooted in it. Always remember that, when you share your gifts with your people.'

The bard lowered his staff and began to walk briskly down the track from the fortress, Taliesin struggling to keep up, the sun burning his fair skin. He had never heard Cadfarch speak to him this way before, and felt overwhelmed and puzzled by it. But for the moment all he could do was concentrate on matching his master's pace and trying not to slip on the loose stones of the track.

They were heading in the direction of the village, and Taliesin wondered if they would go past Beulan's beehive hut to the shore. The heat made him long for the cool sea breeze, but Cadfarch veered from the track, and they began to climb an increasingly steep slope until they came to an ancient circle of eighteen stones. Whenever Taliesin visited it with Elffin, he felt disorientated by its primeval energy, and always avoided crossing the threshold.

He was thankful that Cadfarch did not enter the circle, but lowered himself onto the grass outside, in the shade cast by one of the megaliths. The bard took a drink of spring water, then handed the flask to Taliesin as they sat in quiet companionship, looking out over the sea.

'I have brought you here because it is a place held sacred by our ancestors,' Cadfarch said softly, 'and by the race of people who dwelt here before them, who built the circle in a time beyond memory. And it is here that I had my first visionary experience.'

Taliesin continued looking into the distance, feeling the strength of the earth beneath him.

'You've progressed well with your music and natural studies.' Cadfarch spoke again. 'But more importantly, you have shown that you possess certain powers that only the few are born with.......These gifts are unique and should not be wasted, which is why I've spoken to your father concerning your future.'

Taliesin turned, his muscles tensing, though he dared not hope. He had waited so long since he overheard Elffin's and Cadfarch's conversation that he thought it had been forgotten.

'I suggested to him that you should begin full bardic

training. At ten you are old enough........and your parents have agreed. You will start under my tuition, though perhaps in time you may come under the guidance of another master. I have to warn you that it is not an easy path.' Cadfarch met Taliesin's eyes. 'Is it your wish to begin bardic training?'

Taliesin's spirit soared. He felt like jumping to his feet with a shout, like leaping and running. But he forced himself to show maturity.

'It's my greatest wish, Master. I'll work as hard as I can, every day.'

Cadfarch nodded. 'I'm sure you will. Though, before we start, there is something I must make clear. It has not escaped my notice that you often leave the fortress alone, or accompanied by your sister. You do as you please without a thought for the consequences, and she follows you like a hound pup. If you are to train seriously you must learn to curb your wilfulness. Rules are not simply for the amusement of those who make them, they exist for a reason. There may come a time when you will be grateful for having been taught self-control and discipline.'

His joy dampened, Taliesin hesitated. He had never suspected that Cadfarch knew about his adventures, he thought he had been too clever. But, unlike Brother Docmael, Cadfarch did not threaten any punishment. Being denied bardic training would have been worse than the severest beating.

He spoke under his breath. 'I understand.'

Cadfarch's expression lightened, and he got to his feet. 'Then let us enter the circle together.'

They followed the outer perimeter until the bard turned, leaning on his staff. 'We stand in the east, the quarter of new beginnings. As we trace the path of life and light, think of what you will work to achieve. Not for yourself, but for your people, your land.'

Taliesin walked beside him between the stones, feeling the

surge of power. And, side by side, they spiralled sunwise towards the centre.

Part Two

Oak, Broom
and Meadowsweet

A maid from the flowers
of oak, broom and meadowsweet.....
skin, milk white,
speech of honey.

CHAPTER ONE

Icy rain was lancing across the courtyard as Elffin rode out through the gates of Braich y Dinas. Eilonwy stood at the door to the hall, arms folded, and watched him go.

That year he would be away from his home and family over Christmas, staying at the fortress of Deganwy where his uncle was holding a feast set to last seven days. Their own hall would be empty without his kindness, the fireside dull without his boyish humour, but Maelgwn Gwynedd was not a man to be refused, and he had favoured Elffin over recent years.

Eilonwy stared at the falling rain, then turned and closed the door against the weather.

Though her husband was away, at least she had the rest of her family around her. But for how long? The boys were fast approaching manhood, her two youngest sons already thirteen. Even Alarch was scarcely a child any more.

Angry at herself for indulging in self-pity, she bustled across to the fire and stoked it, warming her hands before leaving for the storage hut. The dark interior was filled with the aroma of the herbs which hung from the rafters to dry, and Eilonwy's mood lifted as she kindled a light and looked round at the sacks of flour and jars of preserves that lined the walls, at salted meat and smoked fish suspended from iron hooks. At least no one would question the generosity of her table, nor would there be hardship before summer brought a renewal of fresh food.

The following day broke clear and bright, and Cadfarch left at dawn to visit his ailing sister. Throughout the morning Taliesin worked alone, practising the tale of Llew, ancient god of light, but by noon he was growing restless and made preparation to ride in the glens with his comrade Henwyn.

Once he would have taken Alarch. But now she sat with a group of other girls, spinning as they spoke in undertones beside the fire, their talk broken by a giggle or peel of laughter. As he passed them she looked up, her freckled face framed by braids entwined with gold ribbon, and instead of borrowed breeches she wore a fine embroidered gown.

'Enjoy your ride, Taliesin,' she called out.

A couple of her friends smiled in his direction, and he hurried on, trying to mask his awkwardness.

Over his shoulders he slung a worn plaid cloak, and fastened it with his favourite brooch - a gift his father had given him on his tenth birthday. Glimpsing the stylized beasts that encircled its central boss, he recalled the wooden animals he and Alarch used to play with, realizing that he had not thought of them for months, and wondered what had become of them.

The youths returned to the stronghold under a brittle winter sun, disappointed at having to abandon their ride after Taliesin's horse turned lame. Slouching against a doorpost, windblown hair falling across his eyes, he watched Drych check the hoof.

'.........we suffered heavy losses at Dinas Brea, which the enemy call Beran Byrg in their barbarous tongue.' Drych spat on the straw of the stable floor. 'They massacred dozens, including women and children, the rest were forced to flee. Now Cynric is ill his son Ceawlin leads in his place, drooling over the West Saeson chieftainship.'

Reflecting on the talk he had heard in the hall, Taliesin replied thoughtfully. 'The warriors speak of going to help our kin on the borders of Dumnonia.'

Drych grunted, and reached for the hoof pick.

'Glinneu would go if he was old enough. He longs to fight.'

'That time will come soon enough.' Drych shook his head. 'Dinas Brea stands in a strategic position on uplands that cross the country to the south-east of Gwynedd. The Saeson are grasping territory nearer home with each passing year.'

'What is this? Talk of defeat?'

Fifteen-year-old Dyfnarth swaggered into the stable, a new cloak draped across his broadening shoulders, secured by a large, flashy brooch. 'We are only biding our time before we slaughter the Saeson and drive any that survive into the sea that spawned them. I intend to be amongst the victors.' He stopped, as if realizing that his listeners were unworthy of such heroic speech, and assumed a tone of command. 'Drych, saddle my horse. I have important business in Bangor Fawr.'

There was a pause. Taliesin's easy posture stiffened and he stood to his full height. He was tall for his years, as tall as Dyfnarth, but still narrow-shouldered and boyishly lean.

He looked into eyes that were dark and arrogant. 'Can't you see that Drych is occupied?' he said. 'Gwyn has a stone embedded in his hoof.'

'Then remove the stone yourself. Or do you fear dirtying your 'fine' clothes.'

'Are you unable to saddle a horse? Would you like Drych to help you mount it too?' Taliesin gave a dry laugh.

'How dare you, fatherless peasant.....'

Drych put Gwyn's hoof on the ground and straightened. 'Now, lads! There's no need for such talk.'

'Keep out of this. He forgets his place.' Dyfnarth turned to Taliesin. 'One day I'll be master of this fortress, Glinneu and I will possess these lands. And what will you be? For all your pride, you are no one.'

Drych stood ready to separate them if the argument turned to violence. But Taliesin did not move, his expression set, concealing a hurt so bitter it was a part of his very self. Like an old battle wound, whenever he thought it healed it would reopen, though after three years training under Cadfarch he no longer feared his own anger. He could allow himself to feel it, knowing he would not accidentally unleash its dangerous power.

'I'd rather be no one,' he said softly, 'than driven to brag to convince others of my worth.'

Dyfnarth had turned white, his pupils dilated, and Drych took a step forward. But before he could intervene, the door opened and a youth entered the stable.

He looked at the brothers. 'The Lady Eilonwy summons you. There is trouble at Deganwy.'

Dyfnarth tried to compose himself. 'Trouble? What manner of trouble?'

'I believe......I believe that Lord Elffin has displeased King Maelgwn.'

'Oh God.' Dyfnarth turned on his heel, and with a dramatic sweep of his cloak strode out into the courtyard, closely followed by Taliesin.

They found Tanwen at her mother's side, seated on a couch by the fire. Eilonwy's hands were clasped together, her face distraught.

Dyfnarth crouched on the ground in front of them.

'What has happened?' he asked.

'Your father has........has been imprisoned by Maelgwn.'

'Imprisoned? His own clan and kin!'

'I never wanted him to leave for this feast, he should have been at home with us. I always had a sense of foreboding.........He was ever too open and honest. But he meant no harm. He is a good man, your father, a good man.' Eilonwy looked close to tears. 'I fear for him so, the king can be merciless.'

'But father is one of Maelgwn's favourites. How did he anger him?'

Tanwen answered for her mother. 'They say that in the hall last night, after Maelgwn had retired, there was a discussion. The company all agreed that Queen Perwyr is the most beautiful and virtuous lady in Gwynedd, that Maelgwn possesses the bravest warriors, the finest horses and hounds, the most gifted bards. Then father spoke out in praise of mother's virtue.'

Dyfnarth's eyes flashed. 'It would have been dishonourable not to. A curse on Maelgwn! He had his own uncle murdered to gain the throne and........'

'Be silent.' Eilonwy's voice had taken on its old authority. 'I'll not have such slander in this hall.'

'I'll ride to Deganwy and teach him a lesson for his insults.'

'You will do no such thing,' Tanwen said. 'One day your arrogance will get you killed.'

Taliesin sat quietly, thinking. He was making his own plans but did not share them. Instead, he laid his hand over Eilonwy's as Tanwen continued,

'I think it was Chief Bard Heinin who told Maelgwn. He took offence because father claimed that his own bard possessed greater skill than any of the king's bards.'

'That is no lie. Cadfarch's skill is......'

Tanwen shook her head. 'Not Cadfarch.........Taliesin.'

Taliesin felt his heart begin to pound, and Dyfnarth turned sharply, remembering the unresolved argument in the stables. He grimaced to see the fair-haired foundling sitting beside his own blood mother, her hand held lovingly in his.

'Father must have been taunting Heinin to test his credulity. Taliesin! The man's a fool.'

Eilonwy looked at her foster-son, thinking of the praise he received whenever he performed in the hall. 'I fear Elffin drank too much and forgot himself. When we were first wed he used to bait his uncle in jest. I thought he had long since given up such games.' She clasped Taliesin's hand. 'What shall we do?

As Gwyddno is away on the border, perhaps I should go to Deganwy myself and speak to Maelgwn.'

'You are too distressed.' Tanwen spoke calmly. 'Let Cadfarch go.'

After a moment's thought, Eilonwy inclined her head. 'I'll send for him when he returns. He can leave at first light tomorrow. That will give Maelgwn's temper time to cool.' She sighed, and turned to her sons. 'Dyfnarth, Bishop Deniol expects you at Bangor Fawr.......Taliesin, do you not have studies?'

As Dyfnarth stode away she called after him. 'You are not to go to Deganwy. Do you hear me? You would do your father more harm than good, and I do not want to insult Bishop Deniol as well.'

Taliesin did not wait for Cadfarch's return, and at sunset he crossed the courtyard to the stables.

After checking Gwyn's hoof that had given trouble earlier in the day, he saddled and bridled the horse, talking to him like a confidant, then went in search of Drych's seven-year-old son who was feeding the other horses. He held out the best of the carved wooden animals, which he had retrieved from a dusty corner, and watched the boy's eyes widen.

'Will you do something for me, Collen?' he asked.

'Depends.' The boy looked nervous but defiant.

'Can you give a message to Tanwen at supper time?' Taliesin placed the carved horse in Collen's outstretched hand. 'Tell her that I've gone to Deganwy. But say nothing 'til supper time. You will remember that, won't you?'

Collen nodded, admiring the toy. 'I'll remember.'

Taliesin returned to Gwyn and guided him to the stable door. He glanced round the courtyard, then led the horse to the gates, passing the guard with a polite nod and a brief word about needing to make certain the lameness was cured.

Outside the palisade he mounted, descending the track as the last sunrays gilded the peaks of Eryri. In the wooded valley east of Penmaenmawr bare branches formed a tracery against the deepening blue of evening, and in the shadow of the mountains it was already growing dark. Taliesin told himself that if he kept up a steady pace he should be in Deganwy by the time it was fully dark; and by the time Tanwen received his message - too late for anyone from Braich y Dinas to stop him entering Maelgwn's fortress.

The air became chill as night drew on, and his breath rose in clouds of vapour as he rode, pressing his heels against Gwyn's sides where the going was smooth. He had no illusions about what he was doing, defying Cadfarch as he had never defied him before. And tomorrow he would have to face his master. But he prayed that Cadfarch would understand and forgive him if he succeeded with his plan.

The trees appeared increasingly sombre in the twilight, reminding Taliesin of elders with stooped forms and thin limbs, rebuking him for his disobedience. Trees lived long. Those that survived the generations possessed wisdom that could be passed down to men who were willing to learn, as Cadfarch shared his wisdom. Was he, by his action, putting his apprenticeship at risk, sacrificing all the knowledge that the master he honoured still had to impart? But he loved and honoured his foster-father. Was it so wrong to try and help in the way only he was able?

In near darkness Taliesin reached the salt marsh at the mouth of Afon Conwy, and made his way to the landing stage where the ferry was moored beside the ferryman's hut, relieved that he would not be delayed while it crossed from the far shore. He called out, and as he waited, staring at the waves, he sensed the presence that was often with him, that took form in his dreams and visions.

The tales named her Ceridwen, ancestral goddess of the bardic mysteries, though he dared not speak of such things in front of his Christian foster-parents. He knew he should not acknowledge any deity other than the one God, but the more he tried to deny her existence, the more she impressed herself upon his consciousness.

'Yes, lad?' A gruff voice made him start. 'It's late for someone of your years to be abroad.' The dark, squat ferryman eyed him suspiciously.

'I need passage to Deganwy. I can pay.' Taliesin opened his hand to show a bronze ring.

'You seem familiar.' The man frowned, taking in his rich attire.

Taliesin gave no reply as he led Gwyn onto a craft made of logs bound together with hide. Nor did he speak as it moved out across the waters, swaying gently as the paddle broke the surface with a steady rhythm.

Across the estuary he could see the silhouette of the fortress where the king's guests were assembled. Back at Braich y Dinas, Cadfarch would have returned, and Collen would be delivering his message to Tanwen. Taliesin tried not to think of his master's disappointment when he found out what he had done, to think only of what lay ahead. The Deganwy shore was drawing ever closer, a widening expanse of water separating him from those who might come in pursuit.

Feeling both relief and anxiety, he watched the ferryman bring his craft in, looping a rope over the mooring post to secure it for the night. And, under the man's suspicious gaze, Taliesin placed the ring in his palm and stepped onto dry land. Now that he stood at the foot of the flat-topped castle rock, like a great beast crouching against the sky, his fear intensified. He clutched the reins and rested a hand on Gwyn's neck, breathing deeply of air which carried the salt tang of the sea. Eventually, he managed to recapture some of his earlier confidence, and without taking his eyes from the stronghold, rode up the track towards it. At first the ascent was easy, but the way became steeper as he neared the top. Then, above the echo of the sea, the hum of voices reached his ears, coming from within the ramparts. The feasting had begun, and soon he would be amongst King Maelgwn's guests.

At the fortress gates, set in an outer wall of dry stonework, Taliesin dismounted. He shook out the creases in his cloak, and, with all the boldness he could muster, raised his voice.

'Taliesin, foster-son of Elffin ap Gwyddno, seeks admittance.'

The gates opened with the creak of timber, and a giant of a man appeared, holding a flaming torch aloft. He paused as the light shone on Taliesin's silver brooch and pale serious face, then stood aside.

'You are welcome to Deganwy, with the blessings of the season.'

A groom took charge of Gwyn, and the gatekeeper led the way towards the stone and timber hall at the centre of the stronghold. The sound of festivities was clearly audible now, and a warm glow shone from within as the door opened.

While the gatekeeper spoke in undertones to an attendant, Taliesin looked round the hall. He had been there many times, secure in the company of his family, but that night the place seemed larger, crammed with more people, than ever before, and he felt very alone. He knew that if he could not achieve some composure he would make a fool of himself and, far worse, disgrace or even endanger his father.

He turned at the boom of a full-bodied voice.

'My lord, the foster-son of Elffin ap Gwyddno is here to pay his respects.' The words were followed by a chuckle.

Taliesin held his head high as he made his way towards the royal table where Maelgwn sat with Queen Perwyr, the king's rotund figure clothed in a scarlet and purple tunic trimmed with gold. Though his sparse hair had long since turned grey, Maelgwn's beard still showed streaks of red, and his complexion was ruddy like Elffin's and Glinneu's. The kinship was obvious. Taliesin seemed to see Glinneu looking out at him through the king's eyes, and the familiar pain of hurt and rejection gnawed at his guts, aggravated by indignation at Maelgwn's treatment of Elffin.

He bowed before the king, then before Perwyr, whose array of jewels swamped her small frame.

'My lord, my lady.'

'Young Taliesin.' Maelgwn looked him up and down, holding his goblet in a plump hand, each finger adorned with a ring. 'By God, how you've grown.' His tone hardened. 'We have been awed by tales of your skill, have we not?'

He looked past Taliesin at his guests as he laughed, a sound which echoed from every throat in the hall. Mocking, like Glinneu. But Taliesin was used to mockery; he had learnt to hide his feelings and remained impassive.

'So you are a great bard now, the greatest in Gwynedd.' Maelgwn laughed again. 'I should be proud to have such magnificent talent in this clan.'

'I make no claim to greatness, my lord. I am but an apprentice.'

'Ah ha, that is not what your father would have us believe.'

Taliesin remained silent. He would not argue, nor try to prove himself with boasts.

'Well, you must join the feast now you are here. Drink, eat and make merry. And you can listen to a true master - Heinin, Chief Bard of Gwynedd. You can learn the nature of the highest inspiration.'

'My lord.'

'Find him a place.' Maelgwn waved his hand dismissively. 'Let the entertainment commence.'

Taliesin was shown to a table where noble youths were

seated, and a goblet was set in front of him, together with a platter of food. He made no attempt to befriend the other youths, nor did he eat or drink. His every sense must be finely tuned, not dulled by a full belly or made hazy by wine. Though he did allow himself to steal a glance at Heinin: hair and face white as lime, gold glinting at his throat and on his bony fingers, his robe of the richest cloth embroidered in many colours. He was the personification of dignity, but also of arrogance. He had none of Cadfarch's gentleness and humour, which blended with his gifts in a sweet mixture that made others truly respect him.

Taliesin had never spoken to Heinin, but observed his humourless pride. Intimidated, even at a distance, he was seized by a panic that turned his stomach, making him wonder how he had ever been foolish enough to conceive the idea that had brought him to Deganwy. He felt ready to give up, to accept his error, and with a trembling hand reached for his wine goblet to seek consolation there. Then, he was no longer alone - once more he felt Ceridwen's presence, pouring her sacred elixir into his heart. He experienced a rush of power, and the youth next to him shifted uneasily as if he felt it too.

Taliesin looked at Heinin with new eyes. The Chief Bard was so jealous of his dignity, wooden as the boards of the table, incapable of moving with the spirit of the moment. Such self-conscious dignity seemed ludicrous now, wildly funny. Laughter bubbled in the depths of Taliesin's being and he longed to give expression to it, but held the energy, tingling with it, the anxiety gone. He knew that Heinin was afraid, afraid of losing his reputation, afraid of being dragged out from behind the mask he had carefully moulded over the years.

The bards of Maelgwn's noble guests gathered around the Chief Bard in a swirl of bright robes, ready to present their verses in praise of the king. Taliesin's green-blue gaze focused unerringly on the first man to make his way to the centre of the hall. He set his goblet down, the wine untouched, his hand now shaking from mirth rather than fear. And as the bard from Pengwern passed, he began to hum, an undulating vibration, just audible.

Though he was aware of the youths at his table looking askance at him and whispering, he paid no heed.

Taliesin smiled secretly as the bard faced Mealgwn and bowed, proud as Heinin. But instead of reciting noble verse, he staggered and began to mumble incoherently, a stream of nonsense mingled with obscenities pouring from his mouth.

There was silence amongst the company, before the second bard stepped out to take the place of his colleague, thinking he had been taken ill. When he, too, rambled and cursed there were rumblings of laughter in the hall. Taliesin's smile widened, though he continued to focus his energy.

Maelgwn was torn between mirth and rage. His face had become the same shade of scarlet as his tunic.

'What is the meaning of this?' he bellowed. 'It is an insult to my hospitality. Are you drunk? Insane?'

Heinin swept to the front of the gathering with long strides, his brow furrowed. He drew in his breath, ready to pronounce upon the other bards, when a bemused expression took the place of anger and he began to recite a child's rhyme. The tension and suppressed hilarity in the hall burst free as the company laughed, banging cups on tables, holding their aching sides. Taliesin finally released his own mirth, unable to hold it any longer, and joined them, the spell broken.

He watched Maelgwn's ruddy face mould into an unpleasant grin, thinking the king must resemble one of the demons that Brother Docmael used to threaten him with in the days when he was under the monk's tutelage.

'My lord.' Heinin's lips formed the words cautiously, like an unpractised pupil reciting before his master. 'Be it known to you, my lord, that it is not from the effects of excess alcohol that myself and my noble colleagues lost the power of correct speech and seemed like men drunk with wine. No, there is evil magic at work in your hall tonight.'

The laughter died as Heinin turned and surveyed the company with a frosty stare. The guests fidgeted beneath his gaze, then he flung out an arm, his fore-finger pointing at Taliesin as if to strike him down.

'There is the one responsible.'

Maelgwn frowned. 'Nonsense, man. You truly have lost your wits.' Nevertheless, he turned to an attendant and spoke in an undertone. 'Bring Elffin's foster-son to me.'

Taliesin walked beside the man who had come to fetch him, maintaining the poise that Cadfarch had worked hard to instil, but which usually slipped away when he was not performing.

He bowed to Maelgwn, feeling Heinin's eyes on him like dagger points.

'Taliesin, I am advised that you are responsible for what has just taken place.' Maelgwn took a noisy gulp of wine and wiped his moustache on an embroidered sleeve. 'If you have come here to disrupt my festivities, believe me I will have no hesitation in sending you to join your father. Explain your behaviour.'

Taliesin met the king's gaze, but his thoughts were of the jovial, easy-going Elffin, and of Eilonwy, steady as the solid ground on which Braich y Dinas was founded.

In a clear, melodious voice he began to speak, letting the words flow from a source beyond himself.

'Bard am I to Elffin,
And my original country
Is the region of the summer stars........' [2]

He became enveloped in a vision he had had once before,

many years ago, sitting by the waterfall in the glen, but this time he felt no fear. As he recited, though he looked at Maelgwn he saw instead the turning patterns of the galaxy, his mind the infinity of space pin-pointed by stars that told of past and future. He saw the world through the eyes of many men, singing with their joy, struggling with their pain. He was flung into the waters of the flood, he was the waters of the flood, he was a leaping salmon in the weir, then......he was Taliesin.

Fighting his dizziness, he breathed slowly and evenly, as he had been taught, and at first was unaware of the thunderous applause that filled the hall.

'So.....' Maelgwn's eyes glinted. He enjoyed a good fight and saw the chance to give his guests an evening they would not easily forget. 'You do indeed have some skill. But can you match Heinin in a contest? Eh?'

Taliesin bowed his head. 'My lord, if I can prove that my father spoke true about my ability, will you free him?'

Maelgwn laughed. 'Not so fast. First you must win the contest.'

Taliesin turned to face Heinin and smiled his most innocently boyish smile. The bard gripped his staff, his knuckles white, his face set in immobile lines.

'I defer to you as my elder to begin, Master Heinin.'

The hall fell silent, and only the thud of a cup being replaced on a table broke that silence. Heinin gave a barely perceptible nod. Taliesin continued smiling.

Standing tall and dignified, the Chief Bard moved to the centre of the hall and prepared to recite, but a mess of senseless words tumbled from between his tight lips.

Maelgwn chuckled, taking another drink, eagerly awaiting the next development. Heinin looked as if he would suffer a seizure, or assault the boy in front of him. Again, laughter erupted amongst the listeners.

Taliesin waited for it to subside, then turned towards the

company, seeing beyond the bright tunics and golden brooches, beyond the stunned faces. His gaze focussed on a world visible only to him as he spoke.

'I am trying
To secure the prize, if I can;
By a gentle prophetic strain.......' 3

He cleared his mind of all thoughts except his need to free Elffin, invoking the essence of freedom. He could see the wild windswept mountains of Eryri, the gale whipping up over the sea, he could feel its energy, its chill blast, its gathering strength. And he gave voice to that elemental power, breathing it, weaving it, directing its currents. Each breath was inspiration rushing through him.

'Strengthened by my muse I am powerful;
Mighty on my part is what I seek
For three hundred songs and more
Are combined in the spell I sing.......' 3

The gale seemed to lift him clear of the earth, to rid him of his body, so he became the wind itself. His breath, his words, had the rage of the tempest, the tornado, circling around the walls of Maelgwn's hall.

The strong creature from before the flood....
How the sea whitens
When first it come!
Great are its gusts
When it comes from the south;
Great are its evaporations
When it strikes on coasts.
It is in the field, it is in the wood,

Without hand and without foot.......' ₃

The power was so great he fought to stay in control, not to be lost forever in the vortex.

'It is mild,
It is strong, it is bold,
When it glances over the land.
It is silent, it is vocal,
It is clamorous.....
It is concealed......
It is noxious, it is beneficial;
It is yonder, it is here.....' ₃

The guests were no longer laughing. As Taliesin's voice rose to a soaring pitch, the gale howled across the ramparts, straining at the timbers of the hall until the heavy oak doors flew open. The guests looked at each other, searching for someone to stop the enchantment before the fortress was smashed into the sea, carrying them with it.

Taliesin did not hear Maelgwn's bellowed command, nor did he see the two men who ran out into the teeth of the wind, forcing the doors shut behind them. He was beginning to concentrate the power, to direct it.

'One being has prepared it,
Out of all creatures,
By a tremendous blast...........' ₃

'Taliesin. Son.'
Elffin's voice reached out across the void and Taliesin felt himself sinking, solidifying, contracting into human form, no longer at one with the storm he had generated. He continued to recite as his vision focussed, and he saw his father standing

74

in front of him, flanked by two guards and with chains binding his ankles.

Gradually, Taliesin's incantation grew fainter, and the gale subsided. But the tension held, oppressing the company who waited. Then, with a supreme effort, he drew the power into himself on a long breath and sang one lingering note that made the hall and everything within it tremble. The guests leapt to their feet, ready for flight, then froze as they watched the chains that bound Elffin crack and fall away.

In the silence that followed, Taliesin collapsed at his father's feet, and Elffin's triumph turned to dread. He knelt on the ground and, raising him, looked with horror at his glazed stare.

chapter two

As Taliesin opened his eyes, his gaze fell on the brightly-coloured landscape of the tapestry at the foot of the bed where he lay, and it seemed to him that he had died and journeyed to Heaven or the Otherworld. Confused and disorientated, he turned to see Elffin at his side, his face drawn.

'Father.' Taliesin's voice was so hoarse he could barely speak.

'Thank God.'

Elffin took his hand, while an aged man raised Taliesin's head and held a cup to his lips.

Though the room span, and he thought he would lose consciousness again, he managed a sip of the bitter liquid. Its taste was nauseating, but he took a second mouthful, and a third, until he was allowed to lie back once more.

'Where are we?' he whispered.

Elffin's worried expression returned. 'Do you not remember? We are at Maelgwn's stronghold of Deganwy.'

Taliesin closed his eyes, dazzled even by the soft glow from an oil lamp. Had he been lost in a storm and rescued? There was no storm now, no sound at all in the vast fortress. Then slowly the memories began to surface, the concentration making his head throb so he wanted not to think at all, to retreat into a world of darkness and oblivion.

'Let him sleep,' he heard a voice whisper.

'Will he be all right? He seems so........vacant.'

'Yes. Just let him rest.'

The voices faded, carried away on a summer breeze, and Taliesin found himself sitting on a mossy bank beneath the shade of an apple tree. A silver-haired woman was beside him, her green robes flowing across the ground.

'You have your mother's gifts and your father's strength.'
Her aquamarine eyes glinted. 'You have demonstrated them
well.'

Taliesin knew she did not speak of Elffin and Eilonwy, but
before he could form the question he longed to ask, but feared
to, his attention was drawn away from the spirit woman. He
sensed another presence encompassing them both, her hair the
golden barley, her mantle, billowing storm-clouds. All
creatures were born and died through her magic, their spirits
issuing from her cauldron and returning to it at death. On her
brow, in the starry indigo of the heavens, shone the waning
moon, curved like a sickle; and with a sickle that reflected light
as it slashed the corn, she reaped, the poppies that grew
amongst the stalks falling like drops of blood on the earth. So
she took back the life she gave. Taliesin saw land that was hard
and barren, forest leaves wrinkled and leathery as the face of a
crone - her face. Her knotted fingers were the bare branches of
winter trees. And Taliesin knew that she was Ceridwen, giver
and taker, forever changing……..initiator and inspirer.

He felt her arms around him, holding him as a mother
holds an infant. Her breath filled his nostrils, the breath of life
and health, reviving him, flooding his exhausted body with
strength. As her name sounded in his head, a ray of winter
sunlight touched his lids, and he opened his eyes. Elffin was
still beside him, with Maelgwn's physician, and Cadfarch.

Elffin looked at Taliesin with a particular tenderness he
had not seen since he and the other children were very young.

'Do you feel any better?' his father asked gently.

'A little. How long have I slept?' Taliesin struggled to sit
up, his body aching.

'It is close to sunset.'

'I'm hungry.'

Elffin laughed, relief in his eyes.

Taliesin now remembered everything that had happened

the previous night, though not the words he had spoken during trance. At first he felt pride, as he re-lived his performance before the awe-struck company. Maegwn's guests had seen a bard of skill, of power, not a foundling whose true lineage was unknown. He had been someone, admired and respected by noble warriors from across Gwynedd. Then pride was replaced by shame. Though he had liberated his father, and shown the arrogant Heinin for what he was, he had failed. Unable to handle the energy he had raised, he had made himself ill. It had been a humiliation, not a triumph. And he dared not look at Cadfarch because he knew the moment he dreaded had come, the moment when he would have to answer for his defiance.

He was brought a little diluted wine, and some broth and bread, which he ate distractedly. After he had finished, Elffin and the physician left him alone with his master.

The bard's nut brown gaze rested on Taliesin as he waited for him to speak, but when he said nothing, it was Cadfarch who broke the silence.

'I knew something like this would happen,' he said. 'Sooner or later.'

Taliesin tried to conceal his apprehension.

'Bards have to learn through experience, but most apprentices do not possess your power......or your recklessness.' Cadfarch lowered his voice. 'You see now why I counselled you against following every impulse.'

Taliesin stared at the embroidered bedcover and at his hands resting on it, strong, long-fingered harpist's hands.

'I'm sorry,' he murmured. 'I will never do anything like it again.'

He raised his eyes and met Cadfarch's, reading affectionate concern rather than anger.

'I trust not. You're fortunate to be alive, and sane...... Thank the gods your mother was not here to witness your collapse and suffer the anxiety your father has suffered.'

'I.......I meant to help him, to show King Maelgwn that he did not lie. I never wanted to make father suffer.'

'Then in future you must think more deeply before acting.'

Taliesin got up from the bed and wandered unsteadily over to the window. He unbarred the shutters and stared at the red winter sun setting over the Conwy Estuary, its waters reflecting the crimson sky. Eventually, he forced himself to face Cadfarch, his eyes asking the question his tongue dared not frame.

Cadfarch spoke firmly. 'You will work twice as hard at routine exercises: meditating, controlling mind and body. And you are not to perform in the hall until after Calan Mai.'

Taliesin exhaled.

That was all? He had not been told that he was unfit to be a bard, the one true identity he had, the only path he could see into the future. He would have accepted anything as long as he could continue training. He returned to his master and sat at his feet, head bowed so he would not see the tears of relief.

Cadfarch rested a hand on his shoulder. 'I know what you were thinking,' he said. 'But you have been punished enough through the pain you brought on yourself. And you have the potential to be a bard, a great bard. You just have some growing up to do first.........'

Over the feast of Christmas Taliesin and Elffin remained at Maelgwn's stronghold as the king's guests, and a fortnight passed before they rode for home beneath a watery blue sky, the day still and tranquil, with no breath of wind in the valleys.

Taliesin had never been away so long, and felt an overwhelming sense of joy when he entered the gates of Braich y Dinas - the security of knowing that nothing had changed, except perhaps himself.

He found Eilonwy waiting in the courtyard with Tanwen

and Alarch at her side, after a lookout spotted the riders approaching on the road from Deganwy. As he jumped from the saddle, Taliesin forgot his fear over what his mother would say and the punishment he knew awaited him. Instinctively, he ran to her, calling out a greeting. For a moment she looked at him, then reached out and held him close. Though he now stood a head taller than Eilonwy, suddenly he felt like a child. All the show and posturing of the noble company at Deganwy, the praise and attention that had been lavished on him, forgotten in the comfort of her warmth.

Tanwen's affection was guarded, but Alarch gave him a lively embrace.

'I hear you stirred up the king's feast!' she laughed. 'They're all talking about it. You must tell me everything.'

Taliesin shrugged. 'I'm sure there's nothing you have not heard already.'

She stepped back, puzzled. She had expected him to enjoy telling a tale with himself as hero, one she could repeat to impress her friends. Instead, he was sullen and withdrawn as they stood side by side, watching their father dismount in the courtyard.

With a sparkle in his eye, Elffin pulled Eilonwy to him, his kiss lingering on her lips.

'It's good to be home,' he said. 'We'd have left earlier, but Uncle Maelgwn insisted we accept his hospitality. I did not think it wise to refuse!'

Elffin speared a piece of mutton with his knife, and ate with more appetite than he had any of the fancy dishes at Deganwy. He washed it down with a draught of mead, then looked at his family seated around the feast table. When he spoke, it was on a note of triumph.

'The king is holding a race at the new moon,' he

announced. 'We're invited to compete.'

'I'll wager our champion can beat the other horses.' Glinneu leant across the table, his voice bold.

'There'll be young warriors there,' Taliesin heard Alarch whisper to her sister. 'I can wear my new saffron gown and red enamelled bracelet.......No one interesting ever comes here.'

'I thought we would be settled at home over the cold days until Candlemas.' Eilonwy sighed, looking at the enthusiastic faces of her children, all except Taliesin who stared down at the table.

'Mother, it will be wonderful.' Alarch grinned. 'And Tanwen needs to find a husband before she gets too old.'

'Hush, girl.'

'You need to have your lips sewn together,' Tanwen muttered with a dark look. 'No man could put up with your brainless chatter.'

Elffin smiled at his daughters. 'Any man would count himself lucky to be favoured by either of you. And our champion is indeed the fastest in Gwynedd. We'll bring home the prize and the glory.'

Over the following week preparations for the race began amidst an excitement Taliesin could not share. The day before they were due to leave, he sat with Henwyn on a bale of straw, watching the cascade of rainwater that poured from the stable roof into the courtyard.

'Do you want to play dice?' Henwyn asked.

Taliesin shook his head.

'What ails you? Since you returned from Deganwy your mood has been as vile as the weather. D'you dislike glory? Now you're going back, the king will honour you before his guests.'

Taliesin continued to stare at the rain. 'Cadfarch sees no

glory in what I did.'

'My God! You freed Lord Elffin, your adventure is news from Deganwy to Caer Seint........and you fret about upsetting Cadfarch. You remain his pupil and, whatever he says, he must be proud.'

Taliesin plucked a loose straw and broke it between his fingers, wishing he shared Henwyn's uncomplicated view of life. 'Don't ask me to explain,' he murmured, half to himself.

'Well, I am looking forward to riding in the race tomorrow. And to winning.'

Taliesin's tone brightened. 'Make sure you do.   I'll be laying a wager on you.' He gave his comrade an affectionate punch on the shoulder. 'And I'll compose a poem about your victory, though of course I cannot perform before the company because Cadfarch has forbidden it.'

A change in the weather accompanied the party's departure for Deganwy.   When the time came, Taliesin had reconciled himself to the idea of going, and the festive atmosphere was beginning to lift his spirits as Elffin's entourage made their way into the valley.

The weather held until the hour of the race, when a colourful gathering assembled on Morfa Rhiannedd, across the river from the rock of Deganwy. Pale gold in the hazy sunlight, Maelgwn's fortress balanced above them as if floating between worlds, and the air rang with the voices of the crowd, vapour pouring from their lips in the chill afternoon. Standing with the royal company, Glinneu surveyed the horses in the enclosure. Though he reached no higher than Taliesin's eyes, his brother was stocky and muscular, proudly wearing an amber cloak that emphasized his fieriness.

'They're lining up,' he declared.

Taliesin frowned into the sun, picking out Henwyn

amongst the riders, sitting astride the young grey that Glinneu had helped train.

Tension mounted, and with it the uproar. It reached a peak, then trailed away into silence. All eyes turned to Maelgwn, who got to his feet, raising a jewel-hilted sword. He paused, the blade held high, then brought it down with a sharp stroke.

To a cheer from the crowd, the horses surged forward. Soon Taliesin was cheering with the rest, loud as Glinneu and Alarch, their new-found maturity forgotten.

As the horses passed once, twice, three times, Henwyn held his position at the heart of the race, and each time they bellowed out his name, their voices lost amidst the tumult.

On the sixth circuit he was beginning to advance - fifth from the lead.

Bridles and brooches flashed in the sunlight, and the riders approached again, Henwyn now third.

'Faster!' Glinneu yelled, striking the air with his fist.

But as they sped by in a whirl of steam, the horse in front stumbled and fell in Henwyn's path, throwing its rider. The crowd gasped, and Glinneu swore. Taliesin's breath caught in his throat as he prayed for his comrade, with all his strength willing him to safety.

He felt Alarch clasp his arm, uttering a stifled scream, but Henwyn swerved clear of the fallen horse. Swiftly, he regained his balance, digging in his heels.

Glinneu glanced at Taliesin, wild-eyed.

There were two circuits to go. His heart pounding, Taliesin watched Henwyn gain ground as the crowd chanted his name.

He kept his gaze on his comrade, unaware that Alarch still clung to him in her excitement. Glinneu leant forward, beating the air to the rhythm of the chant.

Again he horses flew past, Henwyn's level with the

leader's rump. The shouts grew frantic. Glinneu and Taliesin stood together, yelling for victory, Dyfnarth's voice loud behind them.

As the final lap began the pace was relentless, the leaders neck and neck, the crowd insane. With a final spurt, Henwyn overtook, storming ahead, past Maelgwn's raised sword, to triumph.

Sighing, Alarch released her hold on Taliesin's sleeve, and he and Glinneu turned to each other, breathless and laughing. As he faced his brother, united in comradeship, Taliesin's victory poem poured into his mind, born from the roar of the crowd and the thunder of hooves.

As darkness fell, the gathering retired to the warmth of Maelgwn's hall, to mead and heroic tale.

Though there were warriors from the length and breadth of Gwynedd amongst the company, many only a few years older than Alarch, Taliesin noticed that she ignored them as she sat beside Henwyn, looking into his eyes and smiling. And he saw how Henwyn returned her gaze. At first it seemed funny. Henwyn of all people! After Alarch's talk of boredom at home. Then his amusement was replaced by a vague disquiet. With the knowledge of what they felt for each other, he sensed the wheel of change creaking into motion, ready to carry away all that was certain and secure.

He forgot where he was, the people around him, as he thought back over the past weeks, the past year. The wheel was already turning, faster than he had realized. It was only the sound of Cadfarch's voice that brought him back, the rich notes rising to the rafters as he sang of Coel Hen, ancestor to Maelgwn and the clan at Braich y Dinas. Too tired to question the future, Taliesin let his dreams drift into the past with his master's words.

When Cadfarch plucked the last note, and the guests called out in appreciation, Maelgwn beckoned to Taliesin. He glanced at the fair-haired man who was about to perform, recognizing him as Tegai, the master who ran the bardic college attached to the royal household at Deganwy. Then his gaze fell on Heinin, who stood stiffly behind Maelgwn. He had avoided Taliesin during his previous stay, and now stared through him as if he was beneath the Chief Bard's notice, but Taliesin sensed there was fear mingled with the contempt.

As he turned to the king, Maelgwn spoke in a tone that was the closest he ever came to affection.

'We have not yet heard your fine voice this evening. You will follow Master Tegai.'

Taliesin's stomach tightened and his inner-self screamed, yet he managed a steady reply.

'You do me honour, my lord.'

In despair he looked across at Cadfarch, and realized that he knew what Maelgwn had asked of him. There was disapproval in Cadfarch's eyes, but he gave a curt nod, granting his permission because he had no choice.

With head lowered, Taliesin returned to his place and waited for Tegai to finish. To perform was the thing he wanted most in the world, the time when he felt most truly alive, forgetting his insecurity, yet now he was torn. Why could Maelgwn not let him remain in the shadows, numbing his senses with mead? But as the tale with its poetic refrain continued, Taliesin was unable to ignore it, drawn in by familiar names and places: the battles of Sorbiodunum and Dinas Brea, the feats of British heroes from Dumnonia before they were overcome by Cynric and Ceawlin's barbaric invaders. Taliesin saw the furrows of grief on the faces of hardened warriors who had joined the fight on the border. They listened, mourning those they had known, comrades who were briefly restored to life through the words of the bard, revived at the moment of their greatest glory.

'And the land weeps,
the Great Queen weeps......'

came the refrain. Taliesin felt the pain of a loss so intense it was
one with his own deepest suffering. But in this he was not
alone. He saw suffering, but also pride, in the eyes of those
around him, and knew that as long as they felt the inspiration,
the connection to the sacred land, there was hope; as long as the
voices of the bards were never silenced - the voices that kept
their world alive: breathing, laughing, crying, loving. To win
battles with sword and spear was not enough, the chains of
tradition must remain unbroken.

'King Cynan Garwyn, the open-handed, from whose door
no visitor is turned away, whose hall is bright with jewels and
mead, shouts in defiance against Cynric, the cowardly. The
shields of Powys are strong......'

Warriors reached for their cups and drank deeply. Others
sighed, easing taut muscles.

Tegai's voice never lost its power to inspire, even when he
told of defeat. Now it rose, filled with hope.

'Arthur's spirit fights
in Prince Urien of Rheged,
Bull of the North.
The land lives,
the Great Queen lives.....'

When Tegai's performance drew to its end, Taliesin
remembered that he was next to recite before the company, and
the realization struck him with cold fear. How could he follow
Tegai? How could his verse seem anything but dull after the
skills of a master bard? He wished that he had never returned

to Deganwy.

As he began to walk towards the centre of the hall, he saw Tegai standing beside Maelgwn's chair, watching him. Not with Heinin's hostility, but with a question in his eyes. When he drew nearer the expression vanished, replaced by a look of encouragement.

Taliesin bowed to Maelgwn, then spoke with a confidence he did not feel.

'My king, lords and ladies. I would like, with your blessing, to celebrate the events of this day with a poem I have composed.'

He paused, stilling his mind as Cadfarch had taught, opening up the channel of inspiration. And when he began to recite, suddenly he was freed from doubt. Through his verse he took his listeners back to Morfa Rhiannedd in the winter sunlight. With him, they saw the swift horses, the riders, bold and courageous, felt the grip of fear and the thrill of victory.

As he finished, the roar of the crowd on the Morfa became the roar of the company in the feast hall. It did not fade but grew louder, more insistent, resounding in Taliesin's ears, and, as Henwyn was hauled to his feet by his comrades, the boys caught each other's eye across the hearth and grinned in triumph.

The following morning Taliesin and Henwyn were sharing a dish of honey cakes when Elffin came to the door, his face flushed.

'Son, Maelgwn has called for you.'

Taliesin frowned. 'Is anything amiss?'

'No, no, but do not keep him waiting. He is not a patient man.'

Wiping his hands on his tunic, Taliesin glanced at Henwyn and got to his feet.

He went with his father to the hall, where Mealgwn lounged on a couch by the hearth, drinking wine from the jewelled goblet that never left his side. Taliesin was surprised to see Cadfarch there, and Eilonwy. If nothing was wrong, why did they seem preoccupied? All but Maelgwn, who appeared in good humour.

'Sit down, boy,' he waved a hand in the direction of another couch. 'And you Elffin. No need to hover like a fly.'

Taliesin sat opposite the king, straight-backed and tense.

'You did well last night, pleased my guests. Less spectacle than last time,' Maelgwn chucked, 'but pleased them nonetheless........I have been speaking to Cadfarch and your father.'

'My lord?'

'I have suggested that you come to Deganwy and continue your training under Master Tegai at the bardic college.'

Taliesin's gaze clouded, though he continued looking at Maelgwn. He could think of nothing to say. The wheel of change.........revolving faster and faster, dragging him away from home, from the refuge of childhood.

Cadfarch turned to him, his brown eyes wise and gentle.

'It is time for you to move on,' he said softly, 'or your growth will be stifled. You need to work with other young people, not just with an old man like me.' He smiled at Taliesin's stricken expression. 'At Braich y Dinas they are training warriors, not bards, though we, too, play our part in the struggle.'

Taliesin found it hard to conceive of any master other than Cadfarch, but he knew he could not remain at home for ever. In a few years Glinneu and Dyfnarth would be away fighting, and by that time he had always planned to be following his own path. Only now that he was faced with it, the reality felt very different from the dream. Then the thought struck him that at the bardic college no one would know the circumstances of his birth. And after all his brothers' taunts he, the youngest, would be the first to seek his destiny.

Feeling a new strength, he addressed the king.

'Thank you, my lord.'

'You are to come to Deganwy after Calan Mai, when you are fourteen,' Maelgwn said jovially. 'Not long to wait, heh.'

chapter three

In the shade of an oak grove, a circle of eight apprentices were assembled with Tegai.

'Your mind is a store-house of great treasure, and when the Awen flows through you, you become a channel for the living spirit of inspiration.' He paused, looking at the youths with his ice blue eyes. 'Here, there are no dead words scratched on parchment, like a child stillborn. Our tradition grows and evolves, as each one of you has grown from an infant into a young man, and will continue to grow in wisdom until you draw your last breath. And, as the spirit never dies, so the sacred tradition is reborn into a new cycle with each generation.'

The apprentices sat still and attentive, drawn in by the master's words.

'Listen always to the message of the trees, of the animals, the rocks,' he continued. 'They are your teachers, more than I shall ever be. Your ordinary consciousness is limited. When you think you see most clearly, you are blind; when you think you hear most sharply, you are deaf. As bards we observe in new ways, communicate in new ways. The time has come to open to other realms, for then the path to full awareness is revealed.'

Tegai threw a handful of wooden staves onto the ground in the centre of the circle.

'Show me you have understood.' He nodded towards a large, open-faced boy with sandy-hair. 'Meriadoc.'

With an air of confidence, the boy did as he was told and took up one of the staves.

'How does it speak?' Tegai asked.

'It speaks of protection and vision.' Meriadoc studied the

stave in his hand. 'Cerdinen forms a shield against malediction and stands at the portal where the veil is thin, bearing the bright berries of inspiration.'

'Who follows it? Taliesin.'

He reached forward and picked up another of the staves. 'Gwern, nephew of the raven-king Bran, follows it. His sacred tree is strong by water, but the element of fire consumed Bran's nephew.'

'How so? Rhys.'

The boy looked down, fidgeting nervously. 'It.......um.......'

As he hesitated, a starling swooped across the clearing, and Tegai watched its flight.

'An ally comes to help me teach the lesson. Though you forget the reason for Gwern's fate, do you recall the role of this bird?'

There was a long silence.

'Was he a messenger?'

'Do you ask me or tell me?'

'The starling was........a messenger, to Bran from his sister Branwen.'

'I would like you to recount the whole tale on the evening of the full moon. One of your comrades will help refresh your memory before that time.' The bardic master turned to a fourth boy. 'Ewyn, I give the task to you.'

The instruction continued as the sun passed its zenith. When its slanting rays shone into the grove, finally Tegai dismissed his pupils. Two of the youths sauntered further into the woodland, the rest gathered around Meriadoc.

Ewyn gave a crooked-toothed grin and shouted excitedly,

'Let us hunt. Divide into two bands and see who can catch the most rabbits. The losers must.........'

He was interrupted by Iddig, the oldest of the group. 'Childish games. I shall see if any of Queen Perwyr's

maidens are walking on the strand. The fiery-haired one is.......'
he made a gesture and the others laughed, 'worthy of a bardic
song, at the least.'

Meridoc picked up the staves that Tegai had left behind
and placed them in their leather pouch. When one fell to the
ground, Taliesin retrieved it, finding that it was hawthorn, the
tree of his birth month. Looking down at the stave, he said
absently,

'I think I'll ride to the far side of the headland.'

'Excellent idea.' Meriadoc's voice made him start.

The rest called out in agreement, and Taliesin shrugged.
He had lost his chance for solitary contemplation, for letting the
music of the waves give him a new song. More than anything,
he wondered why the other boys bothered with him. The
youngest, and the latest newcomer.

As they headed back towards their quarters in Deganwy,
Meriadoc walked at Taliesin's side, sharing the bread and
cheese that he had wrapped in a piece of cloth.

'You have brothers who are warriors?' he asked.

'Dyfnarth is. Glinneu will leave for Dumnonia when he's
sixteen.'

'I have three already fighting. I began to train with them
in the use of arms, before I realized that was not my path.'

Taliesin looked at him questioningly.

'I felt I must study here. Someone......something,
demanded it. I thought that by learning how to inspire, I could
best fight the Saeson.'

Taliesin nodded. 'I have felt the same. Perhaps all of us
have.'

'Even Iddig? He's already been responsible for one of
Perwyr's maidens,' Meriadoc raised a brow, 'though she's no
longer that, being sent home in disgrace.'

Taliesin gave a wry smile. 'Iddig misunderstands Master
Tegai's instruction to work with our animal nature.'

Meriadoc's laugh was loud, making the others glance over their shoulders as they ran on ahead. He and Taliesin lagged further and further behind, talking, joking, sharing the bread and cheese, and in the brief intervals of silence they listened to their comrades' voices fading into the distance until all they could hear were shouts and snatches of a song that Tegai had forbidden.

When they were out of earshot, Meriadoc became serious. 'Now Cynric is dead and Ceawlin not acknowledged as his successor, d'you think internal conflict will make the West Saeson fall back?'

'I doubt it.' Taliesin was reflective. 'Like a worm cut in two, both halves will continue to thrive.'

'Worms, yes!' Meriadoc turned, roused by his words. 'And worms must be crushed underfoot.'

Taliesin spoke with equal vehemence. 'When my training is completed I shall travel to be where the battles are fought.'

'I'll go to Dumnonia. I have been twice already with my father. I hope to be there when the......worms......are driven back, to watch the smoke rise from Ceawlin's funeral pyre.'

Taliesin looked into the distance, through dappled sunlight between the trees, seeing instead a bleak country, dark beneath low cloud, spanned by the great wall built by the Emperor Hadrian, which marked the land like a scar. When he spoke again his voice was remote as the vision. 'Some day I will visit Rheged. Perhaps I can become bard to one of the noble warriors fighting under Cynfarch and Urien.'

'Many compare Urien to Arthur, they say he will be a mighty leader after his father. In Rheged you would see action, and glory. It's certain they expect great feats of their bards, as they do of their warriors.'

Taliesin glanced at Meriadoc, suspicious of a veiled insult, but his comrade's expression was easily read and he knew he had been mistaken. He turned towards Maelgwn's fortress, a gaunt silhouette now visible above the trees.

'Race you,' he said, starting to run. 'First to the stables wins.'

Taliesin soon found that he had little time to himself, and over the following weeks the hours spent taking instruction from Tegai increased as the work became more intense. It was close to Alban Hefin, the longest day of the year, and the woodland no longer hummed with the vibrancy of spring but summer brought a drowsy stillness.

Lulled by the heat, Taliesin was sitting on a fallen tree, fingers rippling across the harp strings, when he heard the rustle of someone approaching along the overgrown path. He stopped playing and looked up, expecting one of the bardic apprentices. Instead, he saw a girl of his own age, alone, carrying a basket overflowing with medicinal plants.

He got to his feet, unsure what to do or say.

'Sorry if I disturbed your playing.' The girl was the first to speak and, despite the slight wariness in her voice, there was a quiet self-assurance about her. 'You are Taliesin, are you not?'

'Yes........'

He stared at the ground, not daring to look at her, though one glance had been enough for her to be imprinted on his memory. She was the living image of a maiden in one of the tales the apprentices had learnt, 'hair black as a raven's wing, complexion like snow, lips blood-red.' The more he thought of it, the more self-conscious he became, convinced she saw him as the freak his brothers told him he was.

'I've only recently come to Deganwy,' she said. 'King Maelgwn is a distant kinsman of mine and I'm here as companion to Queen Perwyr........I heard you sing in the hall the night I arrived.'

Rather than raise his eyes, Taliesin fixed them on the

contents of her basket, noticing feverfew, periwinkle of the women's mysteries, mint to give prophetic dreams, fern for divination. He and Cadfarch had used both as offerings on the fire at Alban Hefin the previous year. The girl was clearly herb-wise as well as beautiful. He tried to gather his thoughts, knowing he had to say something.

'I've come to train under Master Tegai,' he replied quietly. 'I'm staying in Deganwy, though I live only a short ride away, across the other side of the river.'

'My home is in Dyfed, near Caerfyrddin, the old Roman fortress of Moridunum.' The girl stepped into the clearing, and Taliesin finally looked up.

'You know my name, but I do not know yours.' He was surprised at his boldness in the face of painful confusion. He had scarcely noticed the girls he had grown up with at Braich y Dinas, even when they started wearing fine gowns and glancing sidelong at him. He had certainly never been so eager to impress, yet so incapable of doing so.

'My name is Gwenddydd.' The girl smiled, and Taliesin turned away again. Now he was afraid that if he looked at her he would stare. He bent down and retrieved his harp.

'I should return to the fortress. Master Tegai gives us so much work that I practice from supper time until deep into the night.'

'I know.......He drives his apprentices hard. My companion Rhian has a brother who is studying with you.'

'Oh? Who?' Without thinking Taliesin plucked the harp strings as he spoke, a trickle of confidence flowing into him with the music.

'His name's Ewyn. He has.......he seems to have more teeth than most.' Gwenddydd gave a soft laugh, then stopped herself. 'No, I should not be cruel.'

'He also shouts more than most. But he's a good comrade.......'

They had begun to walk side by side down the woodland path, Taliesin finding his tongue now they talked about others rather than himself.

As they started up the steep ascent to the fortress, he indicated the herbs in Gwenddydd's basket.

'You practice the healing arts?'

'I learnt from my grandmother, but there is still much to learn. And not only herbs for healing, but for seeing. But I suppose you know more about that than I.'

'I'm sure Master Tegai wishes I did.' Taliesin managed a smile, and Gwenddydd immediately smiled back.

'When will you next be singing in the feast hall?'

'I cannot say. Only when my great uncle Maelgwn requests it.'

'Great uncle Maelgwn? Then we must be related.'

Taliesin shook his head, regretting the words that had escaped when he was off-guard. 'King Maelgwn is my foster-father's uncle, not blood kin of mine.'

'Who is your blood kin?'

Taliesin bit his lip and walked on in silence. He had invented heroic genealogies whenever the subject arose with his new comrades, but for some reason he was not prepared to lie to Gwenddydd. 'I will tell you another time,' he said. 'We are almost at the gates.'

She looked at him quizzically, but asked no more questions before they parted. He was already wondering when they would meet again as he watched her walk away across the courtyard, her gown swaying with the movement of her narrow hips, her head held high.

Then a familiar laugh at his shoulder made him turn.

'So that's why you went to the woods alone! Don't make the same mistake as Iddig.'

Taliesin felt his anger kindle, fuelled by the thought that Iddig might lust after Gwenddydd as he did after the other maidens.

He hurried towards the hall without replying, Meridoc hastening after him.

'Taliesin! It was only a jest. Slow down.'

The hut was windowless. Its stone walls excluded all sound, and the heavy oak door had been barred from the outside and covered by a hide curtain.

Taliesin lay on his back on a pallet bed, in a darkness so intense it seemed that he could reach out and touch it. He knew Rhys had panicked when he had been shut off from the world to seek inspiration. Meriadoc had received some powerful verse, but had told him of thoughts and images that he could not reveal to Tegai.

At first Taliesin felt sleepy. They had worked harder than he had ever thought possible, until he felt his brain would be torn apart with the tales, poetic theory and correspondences of word, beast, bird and colour that he had memorized. Many nights he had deprived himself of sleep to go over and over the material that he would have to repeat for Tegai the following day. For weeks he had scarcely seen anyone but his master and the other apprentices, and though he often thought about Gwenddydd, their meeting seemed far distant amidst the accumulation of myth and verse in his mind.

His eyelids grew heavier, his limbs relaxing against the wooden planks of the bed. The darkness cocooned him - soft, rich and warm.

Then he saw the figure of the spirit woman standing over him, her face framed by silver-fair hair.

'Tell me who you are,' he whispered. Finally, he had managed to voice the question.

'I am your guide, your companion. The gods chose me to walk with you, and I will show you mysteries far beyond all you have dreamt of or feared.'

'But what is your name? Where are you from?'

'My name I cannot reveal, though one day you may learn it.' She smiled at his dismay. 'As to your second question........a part us both resides in the Otherworld, and together we walk between worlds.'

She raised her hand, indicating for him to get to his feet. As he did so and faced her, the woman took the form of Ceridwen.

'Do you know me?' For the first time she spoke to him - in a voice of eerie beauty.

Taliesin inclined his head, and from the depths of his being reached out to her, with a longing, a yearning, a love beyond any human love.

'Most do not recognize me any longer,' she said. 'But without my nourishment - the elixir of inspiration that awakens the people to the living spirit of the land - Ynys Prydein becomes nothing but a barren waste. Without me there is no true motivation to valour; the souls of the Britons are dry without my mead, the sacrament from my vessel, my mother's milk.'

Taliesin listened, shaking as if wracked by fever........as if he stood in danger of his life. And he knew then that he did. They all did: his foster-kin at Braich y Dinas, his companions here, the heroes, the distant figure of Urien of Rheged, the farmers and herders - each one.

'It does not have to be this way.' The goddess spoke again. 'There are a few who can make the life flow again through the Awen. A few who can give the Britons back their inner strength so the land will not be devoured by the wolves from across the sea. You are one of those few, Taliesin. But I will test you, test you to your limit.'

'My Lady Ceridwen.'

The words seemed to strangle him, as he watched her face

turn black, with a single eye of fire. The locks of her hair transformed into writhing serpents, and vaporous breath poured from between broken teeth. He saw a barren wilderness, earth scoured by scorching winds and icy blasts, his own body burning and shivering by turns.

The hag was screaming at him, words he could not understand. Taliesin knew only that he had to escape, and began to run. He ran until his lungs ached. He could hear her breathing closer and closer behind him. He was not fast enough. His legs felt like stone. His heart hammered like hail on a roof........Faster.........faster. Which animal could run faster than he? A hare. A hare.

In terror, he was racing between clumps of withered vegetation, past rocks that towered above him. The landscape flashed by to either side. His four legs moved with ease, lithe and strong. But it was not enough. She was on his heel, as a hound with swift stride and slavering jaw. He must go faster......

The wilderness had become a plain. Across it flowed a river. The rushing water, his refuge. Instinctively, he dived, down to the cool green depths, gliding smoothly, salmon tail propelling him onward. But, shifting shape from hound to otter bitch, Ceridwen was pursuing. Drawing nearer. He could feel the pull of the water as she closed in.

With a mighty sweep of his tail, he leapt.......

Then all was dark. He looked from side to side, seeing nothing. Clumsily, he sat up, the panic rising. He stared into a void, not knowing who or what he was. With trembling fingers he felt his own face and hair and limbs.

In the silence he could hear rapid breathing, and at first thought it was a predator, that still he was pursued. The sound seemed to be coming from outside himself. He was about to flee again when he realized where he was, and lay back with a sigh.

He tried to think, to understand whether he had been dreaming or journeying out of his body. He remembered when he was a very small child, sitting on Eilonwy's knee as she told him how he had been found by his foster-father. It had always seemed like a bardic tale, not real, not a part of his own life.

Elffin had been hoping for a haul of salmon, instead he had found Taliesin. The old question returned, pressing itself on his mind. Who was he? He had no blood parents. Elffin had been expecting salmon. Salmon. That was what he had been in his vision. If it was a vision. He sat up once more. He was going insane. He had thought Rhys cowardly for hammering on the hut door and crying out until Tegai went to him and gave him a sedative draught.

Taliesin sat in the darkness and solitude, desperately searching for some lost memory that would answer all his questions. That would make him whole.

chapter four

'You seemed to be in favour with the Master today,' Meriadoc said, casting Taliesin a curious glance as they stood looking out over the estuary.

He knew that was his comrade's way of asking him to tell of his experiences, to be as open and honest as the other boy had been. But just as Taliesin had not told Tegai everything, nor could he tell Meriadoc. The only person he could have spoken to without reservation was Cadfarch.

He watched the ferry move across glassy waters that reflected the bronze light in the sky, heading for the far shore - the direction of Braich y Dinas. And, though he was happy at Deganwy, he felt an unexpected homesickness.

'So the results were worth the ordeal.......'

Taliesin brought his attention back to the present. 'I think so.'

'Your time wasn't wasted with the kind of things that came to my mind?' Meriadoc laughed, a little nervously, remembering the way Taliesin had reacted when he joked about Gwenddydd.

'Nothing like that.......My spirit clothed itself in animal form to travel in the realms of vision. Master Tegai believes that animal will be important to me in future.'

'What animal was it?'

'A salmon.'

Meriadoc looked impressed. 'I had nothing so meaningful. Perhaps next time......But do you think Rhys has the courage to last the apprenticeship? What of the more demanding ordeals to come?'

'He had a bad experience,' Taliesin said evenly. 'It could have happened to any of us.'

'Ha! You don't really believe that. You'd be ashamed to show such cowardice.'

Taliesin bit back his instinctive reply, not wanting to seem weak, to risk the status he had in the group. He had seen how Meriadoc treated Rhys in front of the others. In his brash, careless way he could be as cruel as Glinneu, not knowing the harm he did.

'The bardic path isn't supposed to be easy,' he said with a note of finality.

Meriadoc frowned. Then, with a shrug, he picked up a stone and skimmed it across the water, cheering when it made five leaps before sinking.

When they returned to Deganwy, Taliesin sat on the ground beneath the low eaves of the apprentices' quarters. The evening was still and oppressive, and inside it was too hot to work.

'You said you'd help me with the chorus of "The Boar Hunt".'

He looked up at the sound of Rhys' voice.

'Sorry. I had forgotten.'

Rhys sat next to him. 'No.......I'm sorry. You undertook the trial in the house of vision only yesterday.'

Taliesin turned, thinking carefully before he replied.

'I understand what you went through,' he said gently.

He saw surprise in Rhys' eyes, followed by a look of shame. 'But you did not fail.'

'No. But I felt......felt a great fear. I'm sure the others did too, even if they say different........And you did not fail.'

Taliesin watched Rhys' expression lighten.

He struck the harp strings, and smiled. 'Let us keep everyone from their rest!'

Effortlessly, he sang the chorus that Rhys had been struggling with.

'I am a boar of seven battles.
Kill me but I never die......'

He sang until Rhys took up the tune, then let his voice fade, allowing the other boy to continue alone, accompanying him only when he faltered. Repeating the song over and over as darkness deepened.

After two months' seclusion, Tegai's apprentices were amongst the company gathered to celebrate the festival of Gwyl Awst, the first harvest. They feasted also in honour of the king's guest, a chieftain from Dumnonia, who had brought news of an enemy raid near Mor Hafren.

In the feast hall, Taliesin sat between Meriadoc and Ewyn, remembering the words Ceridwen had spoken.

'Without my nourishment - the elixir of inspiration that awakens the Britons to the living spirit of the land -Ynys Prydein becomes nothing but a barren waste.'

Each year more territory was lost, more people slaughtered or driven from their settlements. As an apprentice of but five years' training he felt helpless. Another seven still lay ahead before he would hold the silver branch of a master bard and wear the feathered cloak of power; before he could ride with the warriors to battle.

Recounting tales of Maelgwn's ancestors, Heinin and Tegai entertained the company as they dined, the warriors becoming drunk and noisy, following the king's example. Numbing their minds to the Saeson threat. Escaping from it in a wine cup. Taliesin watched, thinking how they should be drinking instead from Ceridwen's cup of wisdom. Yet she was acknowledged only in secret, by initiates and their pupils.

The night wore on, and he was growing tired when

Maelgwn called out in a slurred voice.

'My nephew's foster-son, a youth with much talent. Taliesin, what will you sing for us?'

When he hesitated, Meriadoc gave him a push, and he got to his feet, willing himself out of his lethargy. Though the hall was insufferably hot, Taliesin's brow moist under the engraved bronze band he wore, he felt a chill when he looked at the king and saw a shadow behind him - a shadow not cast by any torch. And with spirit sight he saw that a raven perched upon Maelgwn's left shoulder.

Queen Perwyr was laughing drunkenly at his side, her royal circlet crooked, and Taliesin felt contempt rise like a bitter taste in his mouth. A king was bound to his land, which thrived under a man of strength, of honour. But Maelgwn was debauched and weak. Taliesin's first thought was that the shadow meant conquest, death for them all at the hands of the Saeson.

'This weather brings me down, as does our guest's news,' Maelgwn boomed at him. 'I trust your singing will cheer me.'

Taliesin bowed, wondering if he was the only one to have seen the shadow, feeling a weight of knowledge too heavy to bear alone.

Taking up his position between the two great tables he ran his fingers across the harp-strings, shutting out the steamy hall, the company with their red faces and bleary eyes, and began an old familiar song of Arthur's victory at Badon. It was all he could think of to suit the moment, the future he thought he foresaw. If their king possessed the spirit and courage of Arthur there would have been hope. But Gwynedd had no such leader.

There was an appreciative murmur, then silence, as Taliesin was lost to the present, transported to a time before his birth. When the song ended, still he lived in that other time, scarcely aware of the shouts of praise, Maelgwn's louder than any, and before the cheering subsided, his cascade of harp music changed to a new melody.

Taliesin relaxed, letting the tune flow through him, the gift of Ceridwen, radiant and beautiful, no longer the terrifying hag who had pursued him.

'Blodeuwedd -
a maid from the flowers
of oak, broom and meadowsweet,
by Gwydion and Math created.......

He became each word, every emotion that took form and lived through his voice, not knowing why he had chosen this song, one he had not sung since he left home.

'Mistress in the hall,
hostess to Goronwy.
Skin, milk white,
speech of honey.
The wife of another.....'

Perwyr's maidens smoothed their gowns and glanced at the young warriors. Maelgwn put his empty wine cup aside, recollecting his own youth, like a disquieting spirit evoked by the boy in front of him.

The final notes met the company's awed whispers, which rose to a tide of applause, and without looking directly at Maelgwn for fear of what he might see, Taliesin bowed, then walked back towards his master and comrades. Now he was no longer under the spell of song, he felt self-conscious. He wanted to merge with the crowd, into obscurity, when a movement made him glance up.

He noticed that one of Perwyr's maidens had overturned a drinking cup. Then his gaze fell on Gwenddydd beside her, and he wished he had not raised his eyes. At the same time he felt overwhelming joy at seeing her after so long, still and serene, wearing a gown the colour of heather, her hair braided with silver thread and purple flowers.

Their eyes locked for a moment before he turned away and took the last few steps to his table.

'A competent performance,' Tegai said dryly. 'My teaching has not all been in vain.'

The other boys, unsteady with mead, shouted and thumped him on the back.

'Where did you learn that song? The second one?' Iddig's usually pale pinched face was flushed.

'From my first master. Everyone at Braich y Dinas knows it.'

'Impressed the women. You must teach it to me.'

Taliesin ignored him and took a long draught. All trace of tiredness had left him, and he had forgotten the humidity of the hall and the darkness he had seen overshadowing the king. He had forgotten everything except Gwenddydd.

Eventually the temptation was too great, and he ventured to look at her. This time he did not turn away. They gazed at each other: doubtful, tense, compelled. Then, both smiled.

The weather remained oppressive, making tempers short, and each day the people of Deganwy expected a storm but none came.

Taliesin and Rhys sat on a rock by the shore, seeking refuge from the heat, though there was scarcely a breath of wind. Rhys' voice rang out sweet and clear, synchronized with the rhythm of the waves.

'I am a boar of seven battles.
Kill me but I never die.

I......'

Taliesin looked up from the pebble he was engraving, wondering why Rhys had stopped. He felt the tingle of anxiety and anticipation when he saw two figures approaching along the beach - the girl who had overturned the cup at Maelgwn's feast.......and Gwenddydd.

Throwing the pebble onto the sand, he stood, replacing his knife in the sheath at his belt.

'Taliesin!' Gwenddydd came up to them. 'I did not expect to see you here. I thought you would be at your studies.'

'We were given time to practice before this afternoon's instruction.'

'This is my friend Rhian from Elmet. You know her brother Ewyn.'

He nodded towards the other girl, who was plump and pleasant looking but unremarkable. She looked back boldly, sizing him up.

'You have a striking voice. We all said so the other night, did we not, Gwen?' She glanced behind them, a hint of mockery in her smile. 'Good day, Rhys.'

They spoke light-heartedly of the feast and other young people at court, but when the conversation flagged, Gwenddydd became serious. 'Have you heard there is sickness in Deganwy?' she asked.

Taliesin frowned. 'What kind of sickness?'

'The yellow pestilence. A stable-hand and his family have died of it.'

Rhys drew in his breath, and Taliesin felt a chill as he had when he saw the shadow behind Maelgwn. Silence followed, filled only by the murmur of the sea.

'We are attacked from all sides.'

Taliesin felt like laughing as he realized that he sounded like the ageing Gwyddno. He wanted to laugh wildly, madly, to laugh in the face of death.

'It will spread fast in this weather,' Rhian said. 'Drink plenty of strong wine. That helps to ward it off.'

'Even if it doesn't, at least we'd be too drunk to care.'

Taliesin's mirth faded like a doused fire. Now, when at last he had the chance to be with Gwenddydd, the pleasure was tainted. He began walking along the beach, his thoughts in turmoil, trying to escape what he could not escape. She came up alongside him, breathless and struggling to keep pace.

'I did not mean to spoil the day.'

'I'd have found out soon anyway.'

'We must pray the sickness will pass without taking too many lives.' She spoke with maturity, her voice betraying no fear. 'Let us talk of other matters. Dwelling on sorrow only adds to the burden.'

Yet neither could think of anything to say. They walked in silence until finally Taliesin slowed down and turned, for the first time noticing the colour of Gwenddydd's eyes - blue as the enamelled pendant she wore.

She saw him glance at it, and seemed relieved to have found a topic of conversation. 'This belonged to an ancestor of mine,' she said, 'a British princess who was disowned by her family for marrying a Roman soldier stationed at Moridunum.'

Taliesin smiled. 'It would make a good tale.'

'It has already been done. My twin brother Myrddin tells it well.'

'Is he here in Deganwy?'

Behind them Rhian clasped Rhys' arm to hold him back, and Taliesin heard her whisper,

'Are you such a child you cannot see?'

The words hardly registered. Then Gwenddydd's voice made him forget the others.

'No, he's in Rheged with father,' she said. 'We have kin there.'

'Everyone speaks of King Urien. Has your brother met him?'

She nodded. 'Yes, many times. My father has fought at his side.'

That Gwenddydd might have such connections had not occurred to Taliesin, and he was struck with awe.

'They say Urien is the bravest man alive, a second Arthur,' he replied under his breath.

'There is no warrior to equal him. Perhaps some day you will see for yourself. Bards are welcome everywhere.'

'It'll be a long time before my training's done and I can call myself a bard.' Taliesin paused. 'Seven years.'

'No doubt we'll be very different then.'

Both avoided mention of the sickness, the knowledge that neither might see the end of that year. Though it was as if Gwenddydd voiced Taliesin's thoughts when she spoke.

'Myrddin is able to see into the future,' she said, a little shakily. 'I can too, sometimes, but it frightens me so I use the spirit sight only for my healing work.'

As they strolled side by side, talking at intervals, Taliesin no longer felt awkward, and wondered why he ever had. Gwenddydd was unlike anyone he had met before. She seemed to be in his mind, sharing his emotions, her nearness awakening new feelings in his body.

Keeping her eyes lowered, she asked softly, 'You did not tell me of your kin.'

Taliesin could not evade the question a second time, and deep down he wanted her to know the truth. He glanced round to make certain Rhys and Rhian were out of hearing, surprised to find they were now distant silhouettes far along the beach. Then, after a moment's doubt, he began,

'My foster family have been a true family to me, close as blood kin........You ask who my natural parents are........ That......that is something I cannot answer....... When I was newborn my foster-father found me abandoned in a coracle at the mouth of Afon Conwy, and raised me as his own.'

He could not look at Gwenddydd, not wanting to see either pity or contempt.

'I can only imagine how that feels.' He heard neither in her voice. 'You must be always wondering.'

He nodded, and walked on.

'But you have made something of yourself, of your gifts. I suppose you had to, more than most of us. When you sing in the hall the company is uplifted, though you say you cannot yet call yourself a bard.'

She stopped at the water's edge and waited until he faced her.

'Do I prattle? I hope you don't regret telling me. I swear it is in confidence.'

'No,' he answered almost inaudibly. 'I don't regret it.'

It took courage, but he met her eyes, seeing nothing except understanding and affection. Affection was the only word he dared give to it. He stood still, as every emotion he had ever experienced swirled into one with such force that he felt disorientated. He was afraid to stir or speak, to fall back into reality. It was only when a wave broke over their feet that the trance was broken, and they laughed as they leapt onto dry sand.

They continued walking, unaware how far they were from Deganwy, until eventually Taliesin looked back the way they had come. There was no sign of Rhys and Rhian.

Gwenddydd followed his gaze. 'Surely you cannot have forgotten your lessons?' He heard mischief in her voice.

'By the stars! Tegai will.......'

Gwenddydd started laughing, and after the shock of realizing the trouble he was in, Taliesin laughed with her. A part of him did not want to return, daring him to defy his master, but he could not forget how often Cadfarch had warned against disobedience.   And the consequences of defying Cadfarch were nothing compared to the punishment he would suffer if he crossed Tegai.

'We must hurry.' Without thinking, he took Gwenddydd's hand and started to run, but she held back.

'Stop.....stop.....I cannot run in this gown, and your legs are twice as long as mine. You go on.'

He dropped her hand. 'But......'

'I'll come to no harm. Go on.'

'When.......when will I see you next?' A flicker of self-doubt crept into him.

'I often walk in the orchard at sunset. Find me there.'

Taliesin looked at her for a last time, then began to run again, pausing only once before he reached the woods. When he was on solid ground he increased his pace, tearing through undergrowth and ducking under branches like a hunted stag.

As he approached the grove he slowed to a walk, straightening his tunic and wiping the sweat from his forehead.

Tegai's voice resounded in the stillness. '.......below, its roots sink deep, equal to the spread of its branches growing toward the sky.

'The roots of our past reach through the generations, into the soil where our ancestors are buried. Earth houses the dead, and life's new seed. Death and fertility. Tell of this mystery, Rhys.'

So his comrade was already back. Reluctantly, Taliesin entered the grove. He could see that the other apprentices were suppressing laughter. Tegai's expression was unreadable.

'Death and fertility, a sacred mystery.'

The words were now directed at him, on the same note, as if he had been in the circle since the lesson commenced.   He was taken aback, filled with confusion.

'Taliesin, obviously you believe that you do not need my humble efforts at tuition. After all, have you not won great praise in the king's hall? Perhaps there is something you can teach me.'

While Taliesin stood perplexed, Tegai sat down beside the boys. 'Master Taliesin, please proceed.'

Iddig laughed aloud, followed by a snigger from Ewyn. Rhys averted his gaze, twisting his hands together in agitation.

Taliesin took a deep breath, then spoke in a clear voice.

'The sow - mother and devourer.
Great are her origins, many are her gifts......'

After the sixth verse, he fixed Iddig with his gaze, and gave a nod for him to take up the recital. The other youth stopped sneering. He looked uncomfortable, then his close-set eyes narrowed. Taliesin continued to face him as a distant rumble of thunder echoed in the west. There was tension in the air, and he felt the presence of Ceridwen – goddess, shape-shifter - in his mind seeing her take the form of her totem, the sow.

'I will test you. To your limit.' Were those words a blessing or a curse?

Iddig had began to recite, flawlessly but with a tightness around his lips. When lightning flared across the sky, Tegai got to his feet and indicated for him to stop.

'The flash that strikes the tree links Heaven and earth. Divine inspiration comes to the bard, to an earthly frame, to illuminate the minds of his fellows, as Iddig demonstrates.' He gave an ironic smile. 'Let us return to the stronghold. Rain is on the way.'

CHAPTER FIVE

It was dark in the apprentices' house, and the heavy rain which had been falling for days thudded against the roof. Taliesin listened to it as he lay half asleep, though he could find no peace with Meriadoc turning restlessly in the bed alongside his. His comrade turned yet again, then spoke under his breath.

'Taliesin, are you awake?'

He murmured vaguely in reply.

'Remember when we talked of our ambitions? Of travelling to Rheged and Dumnonia to be bards to the great warlords? Do you think that will ever come to pass, or will we die here of the pestilence? A ghastly inglorious death.'

Suddenly, Taliesin was alert. 'I try not to think of what may happen to us. But I believe that one man does not have long to live, and it will mean great change for those who survive.'

'What are you talking about? What have you foreseen?'

'I cannot say more,' Taliesin answered into the blackness. 'I may be wrong.'

Meraidoc sighed. 'Whatever happens, we are trapped in Deganwy, unable to see our kin lest we contaminate them....... like lepers.'

Taliesin pictured his family, strong and in health, as they had been when he left Braich y Dinas, and felt his throat grow tight. He had never missed them so much, needed them so much.

'If only it was an enemy we could fight with sword and spear,' Meriacoc continued, anger masking his fear. 'This is like standing unarmed in front of the Saeson hordes and allowing them to slaughter us without resistance.'

Taliesin's voice was deceptively steady. 'We can fight. We

can use the skills we have learnt to put up a barrier; and do as Master Tegai instructs - gargle with an infusion of sage, rosemary and plantain.......Today Gwenddydd gave me a pouch of rosemary to wear about my neck to ward off the pestilence.'

'At least you have a girl, someone to comfort you.'

Taliesin felt his cheeks burn and was grateful for the dark.

'We are simply friends.'

'Either way, you're fortunate.'

'I know,' Taliesin replied, so softly he spoke only to himself.

The long grass of the orchard was wet, and raindrops clung to the leaves and ripening apples, catching the sun's rays as it set over the Conwy Estuary. Taliesin and Gwenddydd walked between the trees, close but not touching.

'Are your studies going well?' she asked. 'I do not think I would be able to concentrate with.....with the danger that is all about us.'

'I have to, or Tegai would dismiss me and give my place to someone more committed.' Taliesin lowered his voice. 'My studies take my mind off........how things are here. We are learning of Gwydion, magician of the old gods. The tales recount his feats of magic: the illusion of horses and hounds, of an entire army. If I could possess such power!'

'I've heard the tales, how he used trickery and deception. I hope you do not intend to copy that.'

'People are only deceived if they allow themselves to be.' Taliesin smiled. 'But I have no plans to deceive. Not at the moment anyway.'

Gwenddydd raised her eyes skyward, but she was smiling too. 'And who is your living inspiration? Tegai?'

'My first master, Cadfarch. There's no one I respect more;

and he offered me guidance when I was most in need of it.' Taliesin hesitated, remembering the woman he had always regarded as a spirit being, until his experience in the vision hut. But was she of the Otherworld, or in the flesh? Somewhere......in Gwynedd? It was not a question he wanted to dwell on because, though he was unable to reason why, he feared to learn the truth. He hoped Gwenddydd had not noticed his distraction and said hastily, 'There are many who have inspired me.'

She looked at him as they walked. 'Myrddin has heard Talhaearn Tad Awen, Pen Beirdd of all Ynys Prydein, perform in Urien's hall, though he rarely appears before the company now. He gives most of his time to instructing his apprentices, and only takes on the most gifted. I think Myrddin was hoping he might be chosen.'

'He must have so much to tell you. I've seen nothing of other kingdoms. And now Deganwy has become a prison.'

Gwenddydd sounded thoughtful. 'When.....if we come through this, the next time I travel north with my father you may be able to accompany us, to meet Myrddin and see Talhaearn and Urien. You could compose verse about the Lord of Rheged to recite for Master Tegai.'

'Meriadoc would be envious.' Taliesin felt his spirits lift, unlikely as the prospect seemed.

They strolled on until a low-hanging branch barred their way, and he stopped to pick one of the apples that weighed it down, giving it to Gwenddydd.

She took a small bite, then held it to his lips. It was slightly sharp, bitterness blending with the sweetness. All Taliesin's senses were heightened. Then it seemed to him that the two of them stood in an Otherworldly orchard, where fruit and blossom grew upon the branches side by side, where apples were always ripe, and summer never ended.

When the vision faded he noticed that Gwenddydd's eyes

were glazed.

'I saw it too,' she said. 'We were there together.'

The youths who were assembled in the grove were growing impatient. They had never known Tegai to be late, and when he finally arrived his expression was grim. Taliesin tensed as he saw his master's face, knowing the news he was about to deliver, that the time he had foreseen had come.

'I am afraid I bring grievous tidings.' Tegai's ice blue eyes met those of his apprentices. 'King Maelgwn has fallen ill with the pestilence, and the Chief Bard is also ailing. We must pray for their recovery.'

'Soon we shall all fall sick.' Rhys' hands were shaking. 'We shall all die here........we shall all die.'

Taliesin felt a tightness in the pit of his stomach. Hearing the desperation in Rhys' voice made the danger that threatened the community horribly real, more so even than the news of the king's sickness. He could see that the other boy was close to panic, whimpering like a child.

'Control yourself.' Tegai's voice was harsh. 'How do you expect to achieve greatness if you cannot govern your emotions? There are many trials in life and in bardic training, this is but one.'

But Rhys seemed not to hear. He continued mumbling, and the others looked at him contemptuously. Only Taliesin wore an expression of concern.

'Master, shall I go with him to the spring?' he asked.

'Please do, he will gain nothing by remaining here.'

He dragged Rhys to his feet and began leading him away through the woodland, his comrade walking as if in trance. Taliesin kept silent, waiting for Rhys to speak first, as his own thoughts tumbled through his mind. Though he feared the agony that accompanied the final stages of the sickness, he had no fear of dying. Heaven or the Otherworld would be as he had seen in vision - bright and glorious. But if anything should happen to Gwenddydd, that he could not bear. He believed they would never be separated, even in death, but he wanted her with him now in the mortal world, to hear her laughter, to touch her, to feel her warmth.

'Taliesin.......' Rhys stopped. 'I cannot go on.'

'It is not far.'

'I did not mean that.' His voice was barely audible. 'With the training......with anything.'

Taliesin looked at his comrade, who was almost a head shorter and seemed so much of a child, though he was the elder by half a year.

'You will feel differently soon, when there is no more sickness in Deganwy. By Christmas we will be allowed to return home.'

Taliesin knew his words sounded forced and foolish, that he was trying to reassure himself as much as Rhys. They sat down on a fallen tree, face to face, so he could see his pain all too clearly.

'Tegai hates me.'

Taliesin shook his head. 'A master is supposed to challenge us......to make us work harder.'

'He doesn't challenge you.'

'No?' He raised a brow. 'You only notice when it's aimed at you. He wouldn't bother if he thought it a waste of time. You cannot throw away all you've learnt. What else would you do anyway?'

There was a nervous pause.

'Take holy orders.'

Taliesin frowned. 'Holy orders? You have never mentioned this before.......Is it really what you want?'

'I believe it is.'

At a loss for what to say, he listened to the distant babble of water in the green silence of the woods. He struggled to understand how Rhys could think of forsaking the tradition that was rooted in the sacred land they were fighting to save. That he could think of forsaking Ceridwen. Though Taliesin still practised his parents' faith, he had ceased to question whether the Old Ways were wrong, or if it was wrong to honour the goddess. She could be harsh and merciless. But she also gave........so much. Her presence was often with him, lending him strength.

He turned to Rhys, disturbed by the look of fear and loneliness that he saw in his eyes, and tried to sound encouraging.

'Shall we continue to the spring? We can speak of your decision without being overheard, and I'm in no mood for lessons.'

Tegai waited until all his apprentices were present, expecting to receive instruction in poetic metre. The leaves of the grove were yellowing, but the weather was still warm, and a strange heaviness hung over the woodland.

'Sit down.' The bard's usually melodious voice sounded flat and tired. He paused, holding his staff with tense fingers. 'I have just returned from the hall, and am the bearer of sorrowful news........King Maelgwn passed from this world at sunrise.'

The boys stared at each other, saying nothing. Even Rhys was calm, as if he had exorcised his demons three days earlier.

'What is to happen now?' Ewyn asked eventually. 'Will Prince Rhun be crowned?'

'He is in Powys with Cynan's warriors. It would be unwise for him to risk his safety in Deganwy. But, though there can be no coronation with the disease rife all about us, Rhun is lord of Gwynedd, in the eyes of God and of the people. We are not without a leader.'

Taliesin noticed the pouch of protective herbs around the bard's neck, like those he and his companions wore.

'The kingdom is in mourning,' Tegai said. 'There will be no lessons until the new moon. We will reassemble then.........' He looked around the circle of youths, and it struck Taliesin that he was wondering which of his pupils would be alive in two weeks time. Then he waved a hand in dismissal. 'You may leave. God go with you.'

'And you, Master.' It was Rhys who spoke.

The others turned in surprise, then echoed his words.

'God go with you, Master.'

Before the dark of the moon, Heinin too lay in his grave, and there was terror in Deganwy as increasing numbers of the population displayed symptoms of the pestilence. The monks from Abbot Trillo's foundation at Llandrillo, who had come to comfort the sick and give their blessings to the dying, moved about the courtyard and hall, heads bowed, bodies shrouded in rough un-dyed garments. Like spectres, Taliesin thought, and avoided them. As he tried to avoid the disease-ridden fortress whenever he could, roaming the woods or walking along the shore with Rhys and Meriadoc, the three of them speaking verse or telling heroic tales to give themselves courage. And when Gwenddydd could find time from healing and from comforting Perwyr, she and Taliesin met near the now deserted grove.

Throughout the afternoon they had been sitting together beneath the shade of the trees. But as evening approached, reluctantly they made their way back towards Deganwy, walking hand in hand.

'I cannot bear this uncertainty,' Taliesin said, 'not knowing if my family still live.'

'It is the same for all of us. There have been outbreaks of sickness throughout the British kingdoms, though it is worst in the south.'

'And the Saeson thrive.' Taliesin's voice caught in his throat. 'What kind of justice is that? They steal our land, and disease steals our people.'

'Torturing yourself will not help.'

'It seems that nothing will.......As soon as I can, I'll go to Braich y Dinas. It's only the other side of the estuary, yet could as well be beyond the farthest ocean.'

'Perhaps the pestilence will not reach them, if they keep themselves apart,' Gwenddydd replied gently. 'The air is clean in the mountains and there is fresh spring water.'

Taliesin scarcely heard her, as a question arose in his mind. Was Ceridwen testing all her people? Her chosen, and those who no longer honoured her? Those who followed one male god and fought only for physical territory, not for the Great Queen whose spirit manifested in the sacred land, whose lore was held in bardic memory, preserved through the tradition.

'Taliesin. I said that the sickness may not reach Braich y Dinas.'

He turned, struck by Gwenddydd's loveliness, aware of his own youth and strength, of the life within him.

Standing in the shadow of the ramparts, he kissed her lightly on the lips. He had never found the confidence before, but fear and desperation overcame his inhibition. Each day seemed to have no tomorrow. There was only the present.

Gwenddydd smiled and continued holding his hand. He wanted to kiss her again, harder, to draw her close, but was afraid of alarming her. As he hesitated, she reached up and stroked his cheek.

'Let us meet again at noon,' she whispered.

* * *

When Taliesin entered the apprentices' house, he saw Ewyn lying on his bed though it was not yet supper time. His face had a jaundiced pallor and his breathing was laboured.

Taliesin stopped, feeling a weight in his chest, and forced himself not to leave.

'How long have you been like this?' he asked softly.

The other boy opened his eyes. 'Not long……I'm so tired, but I cannot sleep for the pain in my head.'

'I'll fetch some water, and an infusion to drive out the fever.'

'I know what ails me.'

Taliesin paused on his way to the door, and turned as Ewyn spoke in a hoarse voice.

'It is too late for your remedies.'

Taliesin stood in silence, wondering at his comrade's resignation and courage.

'You should keep away.'

He stayed where he was, struggling to accept the truth.

'I'll get the water,' he said after a moment. 'Then, if I play the harp perhaps it will help you rest.'

The next day Taliesin watched Ewyn's condition worsen. Despite the medical skill and prayers of Griffudd, one of the monks from Llandrillo, by evening he was delirious, not recognizing those near him, his lips dry and crusty, his flesh yellow as wax. By the third day he was becoming rapidly weaker, and Rhys and three of the other boys had started to complain of headache and fever. Calmly, Griffudd included them in his prayers and ministrations, showing no sign of despair or of surrendering to defeat.

Iddig had been absent from the apprentices' house since Ewyn sickened, but Taliesin and Meriadoc still slept at the far end of the building where their comrades were being cared for.

As he sat on a timber chest beside Rhys' bed, seeing the fear in his eyes, Taliesin wanted to speak comforting words but knew they were futile. Everything he had dreamed of was futile now. He felt numb and detached, as immune to beauty and joy as he was to terror. Only the thought of Gwenddydd had any power to move him, but letting go of the numbness brought pain. He did not want to feel for her because he believed that soon she too would fall ill.

He rose when Griffudd returned, carrying a wooden cup.

'There is no need for you to leave, Taliesin, is it?'

He nodded, slowly edging away, feeling ill-at-ease with the monk.

'Though I walk through the valley of the shadow of death, I will fear no evil: for thou art with me; thy rod and thy staff they comfort me.'

By chance Taliesin caught Griffudd's eye, and saw such deep compassion that he stopped backing away. He found the monk's expression reminiscent of Cadfarch's, but he could never forget Brother Docmael's severity and threats of hellfire, the years of feeling ignorant and helpless under his uncompromising gaze.

Griffudd was looking at him. 'If you wish to talk, I have time to listen.'

He handed Taliesin the cup. 'Drink this, it is avens root boiled in wine.'

Taliesin did as he was told, watching the monk bathe Rhys' forehead.

'Is there anything I can do to help you here?' he asked.

'You can tell me of your hopes and aspirations.'

Taliesin frowned.

'There is a future, beyond this time of trial, by God's grace. You must look to that future because you are young and still in good health. 'If thou faint in the day of adversity, thy strength is small.' Griffudd's voice held gentle authority. 'But it is my

122

belief that God has granted you strength, not only of body but of spirit.'

That night, though he tried to sleep, Taliesin lay awake listening to Griffudd's muttered prayers by Ewyn's bedside. His comrade had been unconscious since nightfall, his appearance so ghastly that he no longer seemed the same bold youth who would shout in excitement and lead the others in songs he had learnt from the sea-traders of Elmet.

When finally he drifted into sleep, Taliesin felt himself falling, spinning downward through blackness, until he came to a place surrounded by a circle of flame. 'Hell - the pit of fire and brimstone, where the wicked are punished,' Brother Docmael's voice raged at him. Fighting the childhood fear, he shut out the voice, telling himself that fire was protective, purifying. And he saw then that the flames poured from between the open jaws of a dragon, its body curled around the ring it had created, half-concealed by the brilliance.

'Join me, Taliesin.' It was no longer Brother Docmael's voice in his head.

He stared at the blazing circle.

'Do you want to serve?' the furnace roared. 'Then step into the flames, become part of the protection of Ynys Prydein.'

Still he hesitated.

'You have a destiny, if you choose it.'

Suddenly the doubt was gone, and he knew that the fire would not harm him, that he was being asked to choose life, not pain or death. Fearless, he stepped forward, energy coursing through his body as he became one with the flames, consumed in an ecstasy of freedom........

He woke with a start, the radiance lingering like the afterglow of sunset. In the distance, he could hear Griffudd's voice, praying still. Then joy drained from him as he returned to full awareness, realizing the monk's prayers had changed, that he no longer prayed for healing, but for mercy upon Ewyn's soul.

Over the following week Brother Griffudd tended Rhys. He also tended the three other apprentices who were ill, doing all he could to relieve their suffering, though the sickness had progressed too far for him to save them.

Taliesin dedicated himself to helping the monk, as one day merged into the next, the evenings drawing in with the approach of All Hallows - Calan Gaeaf, the ancient feast of the dead, when the veil between the mortal world and the Otherworld was thin, and spirits travelled freely across the threshold.

Taliesin stood beside Griffudd, looking down at Rhys' emaciated face. In his vulnerability he seemed more than ever like a child, much younger than his fifteen years.

'Are.......are you sure he will live?' Taliesin pressed his lips together, his shoulders tense.

'The signs are very hopeful. The fever has broken and he's over the worst, though still very weak. It is almost a fortnight since he showed the first symptoms. Those who die do not fight the sickness this long.' The monk glanced up. 'Have faith........And my fellow brothers tell me there are fewer new cases of sickness in the fortress.'

Taliesin felt so exhausted he could barely think, he could find no energy to hope. Though of one thing he was certain, that he himself would not fall ill. Since his dream on the night of Ewyn's death, he sensed that he had been spared to serve a purpose, one which must over-ride his personal happiness.

As Rhys began to recover, he and Griffudd were often to be found talking in lowered voices and praying together. At other times Taliesin sat with his comrade, but felt more and more that Rhys no longer needed him.

By December the terror was past, replaced by grief, as families all across Gwynedd, all across Ynys Prydein, mourned their dead. It was then, on a bitter morning, that Taliesin left for Braich y Dinas. Over his tunic he wore his threadbare plaid cloak, fastened with the bronze brooch Elffin had given him as a boy, the gifts he had received from Maelgwn put aside. That day he had no wish to wear rich fabrics or shining silver, but clung to the security of what was old and familiar.

He could scarcely believe that Gwenddydd and Meriadoc lived. So many had perished, almost half the population at Deganwy, and he wondered whether he had survived to suffer yet more grief. He tried not to think ahead, to concentrate only on the beat of Gwyn's hooves on the hardened ground, the sting of the icy air on his cheeks.

As he rode up the track leading to the fortress, Braich y Dinas was obscured by low cloud as if it had vanished into the Otherworld during the months he had been away. Throughout the journey he had ridden as fast as he could, but as the outer ramparts emerged from nothingness he reined in, afraid to face what he might find. He sat shivering in the freezing mist for a long time before continuing towards the gates and calling out to the guard to open them. The man greeted him respectfully, but said nothing more, and Taliesin did not question him.

As he approached the hall he noticed logs piled under the eaves in readiness for the cold months ahead, and caught a glimpse of movement in one of the stables. The courtyard was the same as it had been on any mid-winter day for as long as he could remember. Yet..........

He had just dismounted when the door to the hall opened, revealing the ruddy warmth of firelight inside, and a veteran warrior limped out.

He gazed at Taliesin, then grinned. 'Damn it, I'm glad to see you, lad.' Turning, he bellowed into the hall, 'Elffin, Gwyddno........Taliesin is back.'

The warrior clasped him by the forearm with an iron grip, as if he was a man, an equal. Then, seeing the question in his eyes, said in an undertone,

'All is well here. We have been spared.'

But Taliesin found he could not break down the barrier he had taken refuge behind during the epidemic. The words he had been praying for had become empty sounds, and he was unable to feel their truth in his heart.

While he stood in confused silence, Eilonwy emerged from the doorway.

'Thank God. Thank God and all the saints.'

Her voice cracked. She was laughing and crying at once as she hugged him. His family and comrades gathered round, each one holding him, blessing him. Then, with a great wave of relief, finally he felt the tears in his own eyes as he was led into the hall.

'We will hold a feast tonight,' Elffin announced. 'To celebrate the safe return of my son......his miraculous return to us.'

ChAPTER SIX

For three weeks Taliesin stayed at Braich y Dinas, and it was not until the start of Rhun's Christmas celebrations that he set out for Deganwy, warned by Gwyddno that if he delayed any longer the new king would take insult. Miserable at parting from his family, he turned his back on the gates and urged Gwyn onward, only his eagerness to see Gwenddydd making leaving bearable.

At the feast that night he looked round for her, ignoring the full platter in front of him and scarcely listening to Meriadoc's reports of what had happened during his absence. When he set eyes on her, seated with Perwyr, he felt the burden of fear lift, and his pulse quickened with an overpowering urgency to be with her.

She was beautiful as the image he had carried in his mind while he was away. But he found Perwyr greatly altered. She had aged ten years since Maelgwn's death, and sat grim and silent, her goblet always at her lips. Of the maidens who had been her companions, only Gwenddydd and Rhian were in the hall - Rhian's cheerful plumpness gone, her head lowered. A shudder ran through him as Taliesin realized that he would never see the other girls again.

The feast, riotous with forced gaiety, excelled even Maelgwn's in extravagance. And as the mead flowed, the atmosphere became volatile, tempers balanced on a knife edge.

Taliesin had only boyhood memories of Rhun, a wild, fiery-haired youth, who had told him and his brothers jokes Eilonwy would not have wanted them to hear. It was rumoured that he had bedded half the women in Deganwy and that Maelgwn had sent him to fight in Powys to prevent any more bastards at court. There he had remained, marrying

Cynan's niece Olwen, and winning battle glory alongside her father.

'Tegai has been chaired as Chief Bard,' Meriadoc was saying. 'He is to take on Heinin's pupils. Those who were spared will train with us.'

Finally, he had Taliesin's attention. 'I cannot imagine studying without the comrades we have lost, when all has changed.'

'Surely you're not going to give up your training!'

Taliesin stared at him. 'How can you think I'd be so weak? I meant.......' he stopped, unable to finish his sentence.

'I know.' Meriadoc's voice had become hoarse. 'And this hall is full of Rhun's people, strangers.'

'I see Iddig's back.' Taliesin hissed the words, glancing at the dark boy who sat with his hand on a girl's knee. 'They say he fled Deganwy to stay at a farmstead.'

Meriadoc fidgeted. 'There was no cause for him to stay here. Not when he could find a place of safety.'

'He endangered his hosts, and deserted his comrades.'

Taliesin turned away in anger, though it lifted when he saw Rhys at the far side of the hall, edging through the crowd towards them. His bardic robes hung loose on his wasted body, and there were shadows under his eyes, but he had an air of self-assurance that he had never possessed before.

Taliesin got to his feet and embraced him, then made room on the bench between himself and Meriadoc.

'Thank God you're so much better.'

'And you look rested.' Rhys lowered his voice. 'Are your family well?'

'Braich y Dinas escaped the sickness.'

'It cannot have been easy coming back here.'

'I missed my comrades, seeing you again has made it easier.'

'He means he missed Gwenddydd.' Meriadoc's teasing

was like a healing draught; that at least had not changed.

They fell silent as the clamour in the hall faded and Tegai stepped before the company, bearing a branch hung with golden bells that chimed as he walked - the symbol of his office as Chief Bard. Watching his master, Taliesin was thankful Tegai had not brought him to Rhun's notice. He wanted to settle at Deganwy before he performed again; he felt drained, his growing confidence stolen away since the summer.

But as Tegai told an ancient tale of Gwydion, Taliesin's inspiration rekindled, and he gazed beyond the smoky hall, celestial fortresses and phantom steeds alive before his eyes. It heightened his craving to be trained in the skills of an enchanter, to use his powers which were held in abeyance, his early dreams of what he would learn at Deganwy unrealized.

He was still under the spell of the story when Perwyr rose and led her maidens from the table, Gwenddydd walking quietly beside Rhian. She did not look at Taliesin, and he felt angry that they had had no chance to speak. Even one more day apart seemed an eternity. He no longer cared about anything else. And, as the night wore on, his thoughts grew more chaotic, more desperate, until he was overtaken by a kind of madness.

He saw his own turmoil reflected in the chaos around him, in the mirthless laughter and drunken challenges of the warriors which were degenerating into violence. When a fight broke out amongst a group of Rhun's men there was no attempt to separate them. Instead, the others gathered round, cheering the fighters on, downing cups of mead and strong wine. After a man was carried from the hall unconscious, blood streaming from a head wound, the rest continued to drink, until one by one they collapsed into an intoxicated sleep where they sat, Meriadoc and Iddig emulating them, drinking themselves stupid.

It was almost dawn before Rhys and Taliesin left, without

their comrades, and crossed the deserted courtyard to the apprentices' house. Thinking of Gwenddydd, Taliesin watched Rhys coax the embers of the fire into life, the glow illuminating his gaunt cheeks.

Eventually, the other boy looked up from his task. 'There's something I have to tell you,' he began. 'No one except Master Tegai knows.'

Taliesin tried to show an interest. 'Not bad news?'

'Not at all.'

Still huddled in their cloaks they sat on the end of Rhys' bed, while the flames flickered uncertainly and a draught seeped through the cracks around the door and shutters.

'I'll not be joining you when lessons start again after Christmas,' Rhys said, 'but accompanying Brother Griffudd to Llandrillo as a novice.'

Taliesin straightened, frowning in the dim light. 'I suppose I shouldn't be surprised after what you told me before you fell ill. But......'

'Brother Griffudd's counsel gave me hope, made me see things in a way I'd never been able to before. His teachings, his way of life, are what I have always been seeking, though I did not know where to look........You do understand? This is not running away.'

Their eyes met in a look of empathy. 'I never thought it was. We're don't all have to follow the same path.'

Rhys held his hands out to the fire. 'As soon as I had the strength to ride, Griffudd took me to the other side of the headland, where he introduced me to the hermit Tudno, a holy man who lives in a cave, drinking nothing but water and eating no meat. He spends his days in prayer as he listens to the sound of the waves. He also heals the sick. I've heard that he's performed miraculous cures through the power of faith.'

Taliesin saw the gleam in Rhys' eyes, the passion that would have made him a great bard, though he had always been meek and bland when he performed.

'You'd better fatten yourself up on roast pork before you start living on water,' he said with a grin.

'This is no time to mock.' Nevertheless Rhys grinned back. 'Tomorrow Iddig and Meriadoc will wish they drank only water.'

Taliesin stared into the flames, which were at last beginning to emit some heat. 'I'll miss you,' he said. 'Our lives are going to be very different.'

'But we can still be comrades.'

Taliesin nodded, not voicing his thoughts. Whatever Rhys might say now, in the years to come would he want to acknowledge friendship with a bard who honoured the old gods and recalled tales of bloody battles when he performed in the chieftains' halls of the north?

By the light of a blazing torch, Tegai led his apprentices up the slope of the second hill at Deganwy, twin to the rock crowned by the royal fortress. The night was still and bitterly cold, and frost sparkled on the path as they climbed, haloed by smoke and the vapour of their breath.

When he reached the summit, Tegai surveyed the group to be sure that all the boys were present. Then he up-ended the brand with a hiss, plunging them into blackness. For a moment they stood in a void, without bearings. But as Taliesin's eyes adjusted, the sky no longer seemed black but deep indigo, sprinkled with stars as if the frost underfoot had been cast into the heavens.

The silhouetted fortress loomed in the foreground, and to the west the waters of the estuary formed a boundary between earth and sky. Now, instead of being hemmed in by darkness beyond their little circle of light, the whole landscape opened up before them, mountain, hill and wood layered like the folds of a cloak to the far horizon.

Tegai's voice cut through the stillness.

'Raise your eyes to Llys Don.........Iddig, as you are inclined to talk, share your wisdom with us all instead of favouring Meriadoc, and tell us of Gwydion's sacred journeys.'

Iddig cleared his throat, the sound amplified in the clear air, and began speaking with a confidence that verged on arrogance,

'Don, great mother of the gods, gave birth to Gwydion. In the celestial halls of Llys Don he dwelt, and was educated in all the arts, which he excelled in beyond any other youth of his time.' He raised his hand and indicated five stars forming the shape of two valleys in the sky, then pointed at the misty track that crossed the constellation. 'But when he reached manhood, he became lord of Caer Gwydion, the fortress of enchantment, over which he cast a veil of oblivion to render it invisible to us throughout the summer and autumn months. One of his most fateful journeys was to Caer Arianrhod, which we see in spring, shining like a diadem upon the head of the Lady. When he travelled there his own fortress lay in magical concealment. He made three journeys to Caer Arianrhod, the first......'

Iddig's strident voice grew fainter, fading into the distance as Taliesin's attention drifted. The colour of the night sky reminded him of Gwenddydd's eyes, and he recalled how she had looked at him when they were last together. As the understanding between them increased, the need for words diminished, and often they communicated simply by a glance, a touch. He seemed to see her beside him, her lips parted, the warmth of her body close to his.......

'Taliesin, how was her curse overcome?'

He drew in a breath of air so cold it stung his throat, and struggled to concentrate on the question, to decide which of three answers to give. As he hesitated, he noticed the smug look on Iddig's face. Again, he tried to decide on an answer, aware that the other boy was still smirking, waiting for him to betray his ignorance.

Finally, thinking it more foolish to give the wrong answer than none at all, Taliesin turned to Tegai. 'I'm sorry, Master.'

'Iddig?'

'The third time, Gwydion went to Caer Arianrhod as a bard, and by enchantment he created an army which appeared to threaten the fortress. In her fear, Arianrhod gave arms to Llew, so lifting the third curse she had laid on him at birth.'

Taliesin remained expressionless. He knew the tale better than any other, and in the chill of the night his anger burned. Anger at Iddig, who relished the triumph. Anger at himself for giving him that satisfaction. But, vying with the rage, was the vision of Gwenddydd which had distracted him, threatening to steal his attention again.

'Let us now turn to Twr Tewdws.........Meriadoc.'

As his comrade began to speak, Taliesin looked to the skies, to the points of light that held the wisdom of ages, a wisdom that was linked to humanity through the bardic tales. The stars also mapped each year, and guided each man's life journey, as they guided those who sailed the seas. His and Gwenddydd's destiny was written there in the pattern of the constellations, in the turn of heaven's wheel.

'........they are reborn at the time of Calan Mai.'

Meriacoc's voice dragged Taliesin back to the present, and he longed to re-capture the awe he heard in it, the love of knowledge, but only the thought of Gwenddydd now inspired him, dominating his emotions, his mind, his body.

The air was smoky and stuffy, pungent with the odour of sweat and stale meat. Warriors drank, played dice and recounted tales of battle, while two veterans hunched over a gwyddbwyll board.

At the lower end of the hall Taliesin sat with a group of youths, though he took no part in their jests. Their company was simply an excuse to be there in the hope of seeing Gwenddydd, and amidst the uproar the others did not notice his silence. Finally, with a sense of emptiness, he got up from the bench, wondering if Gwenddydd longed to leave Perwyr's bower, if she felt as bleak as he did when they were unable to meet.

Early darkness was gathering as he crossed the courtyard, holding his arms around his chest for warmth. He had no desire to join the other apprentices, to try and perfect his recital of yet more verse. Now Rhys had left for Llandrillo, he found it harder than ever to motivate himself, for the first time understanding how his comrade had felt when he spoke of giving up. The days and weeks and years of training seemed endless. When he began under Cadfarch he had never anticipated the monotony of it.

He continued towards the long building that housed the apprentices, watching the smoke from the central fire seep through the thatch and curl upward. At the entrance he hesitated, wondering if he should go back to the hall. It was still early enough. Perhaps Gwenddydd would arrive later, if he had the patience to wait. But it was too bitter to hover outside, tormented by indecision.

Quietly, he pushed the door open, greeted by faltering harp music and the hum of voices. The boys were gathered around the hearth and, as Taliesin paused, Iddig's voice rose above the rest.

'........compared with Gwenddydd, whose body is so supple, her flesh so soft. I warrant she'd enjoy a man more experienced than.......'

Taliesin stepped out of the shadow. The first thing he saw was the shock on Meriadoc's face.

'He meant nothing. You know Iddig.......' Meriadoc tried

to laugh, but the sound was strangled in his throat.

'Yes, I know Iddig.' Though Taliesin spoke to his comrade, he fixed his gaze on the older boy, meeting close-set eyes, hard and black as jet.

'Grow up, Taliesin. Can't you take competition? Though if the lady desires only you.......'

Taliesin continued to face Iddig. 'Your words dishonour her.'

'Honour! You've learnt too many pretty love tales. This is the real world, where men and women.....'

'Women have no liking for cowards.'

'Taliesin, Iddig never intended........'

'Keep out of this.'

'Who do you call coward?' Iddig's lips were twisted in the semblance of a smile.

Taliesin waited, as the other youths watched in silence. When he spoke, his voice was filled with contempt, driven by hatred of everything that Iddig stood for. 'One who flees danger, who is full of terror and needs a woman to help him forget his fears.'

Iddig stood up and walked calmly towards the door, as if he would pass Taliesin and leave without replying. But when he reached him he stopped and said softly, 'And what of your fears? You may have been the old king's favourite, but he is dead. Does Rhun single you out to play in his hall? Your memory fails. Today you could not recall 'The Tale of Dylan'. Will Gwenddydd want you when she realizes you are a fool and a fraud?'

In his mind Taliesin saw her standing in the orchard, holding an apple out to him, then he seemed to watch from a distance as Iddig stood in his place, fondling her breasts, leaning forward to kiss her, breathing heavily. Contempt turned to rage. He could feel the white fire pulsing in his brain, the power crystallizing, like a knife behind his eyes. He thought he had learnt to master it. He had mastered it, for years. But this was not Glinneu's childish taunts.

Perhaps Gwenddydd herself was destroying him, bleeding him dry, stealing his Awen, his dedication, his gifts. No. She was all that mattered. He could not bear to think that Iddig might lay hands on her. He could scarcely think any more. The pressure, the blazing light, had reached an intensity where he was no longer in control. The power would find release in the direction of his hatred. And he knew that power was deadly.

He stared at the narrow face in front of him, through the glare, the pain. Iddig's smile had faded, but his eyes held it still. Soon Taliesin would be unable to contain the energy. There had to be an outlet for his anger. Insane with agony and confusion, he raised his fist, striking Iddig on the jaw so he fell with a cry. The white fire in Taliesin's head exploded, like glass shattering into a thousand fragments, and he staggered, holding onto a post for support.

'My God! What did you do that for?' Meriadoc's voice sounded remote. 'Iddig, are you all right?'

'Damn lunatic. You'll pay for this.'

Iddig sat up, clutching his jaw, blood trickling from the corner of his mouth, as Taliesin turned and made his way out of the house into the courtyard. Once he was in the open he felt less dazed, and re-lived what had happened with fierce clarity, hating himself, his weakness. He had betrayed Cadfarch's faith. Shudders ran through him - bitter cold and fear. He thought he had mastered his powers. Now he could never trust himself again.

chapter seven

Gwenddydd's hand felt warm in Taliesin's as she walked beside him, clothed in a plain gown, her hair in a braid that reached to her waist. The season lay balanced between winter and spring, the woodland still leafless though the buds had begun to swell. In a month's time Taliesin would have been at Deganwy for a year, a year which seemed the longest of his life.

He could hear Rhian's footsteps behind them, though she always kept her distance. When they stopped, she stopped too, and Taliesin glanced round, seeing that she had turned her back. Gwenddydd followed his gaze and gave a girlish laugh.

'The best keeper of secrets!'

But Taliesin did not share her laughter. 'She must be sorrowful,' he said after a moment, 'missing Ewyn.'

'Soon she'll have yet more sorrow. The man she loves is leaving to fight in Elmet.' Gwenddydd faced him, clasping both his hands. 'Thank God you're not a warrior. I could not bear to think of you in danger.'

'Nothing is certain.'

'No, but to sit in the safety of the hall, not knowing if the one you love has been wounded or slain, what could be worse than that? I'd rather be on the battlefield myself, with no leisure to worry.'

Taliesin looked thoughtful. 'When I ride with the warriors to battle, not fighting but watching, I may feel like a coward.'

'Why? If there were no bards, no one to praise the great victories, if the bards fought and were killed, who would hold the tradition? There are many warriors, few bards. Fewer still with a true gift.'

Taliesin did not reply, shamed by the increasing number of times he had failed in memory or understanding during

Tegai's lessons, the dullness of his recent performances of song and verse.

Mistaking the reason for his reticence, Gwenddydd said, 'You showed courage during the sickness, helping to care for your comrades. God was watching over you, and you were spared so we could be together.'

He wanted to shut out her words when she spoke that way, with such simple conviction, and an uneasiness nudged at the edges of his mind, not allowing him to confront it face to face. Consciously the feeling seemed foolish. Gwenddydd was beautiful and desirable, the most beautiful maiden in Deganwy. She was also bright, and understood his deepest self, his aspirations, his visions.

Taliesin released her hands, intending to walk again and avoid conversation. She looked puzzled, silently asking him not to put up defences. It made him hesitate, then the uneasiness was gone. Her dark eyes, her soft sensitive lips, stopped him from doubting. And, instead of moving away, he reached out, drawing Gwenddydd to him.

Her body felt lithe and eager, and she raised her head, her mouth finding his. Their breathing quickened as Taliesin caressed her, but as they pressed closer he was assailed by confusion. Though Gwenddydd seemed willing, and Rhian would tell no one, he could not go further.

His touch gradually became less urgent until he simply held her, her cheek against his shoulder. After a while she stepped back, looking into his eyes.

'I love you,' she said. 'Many lives can be spent together if the love is deep enough.'

Taliesin felt torn between joy and denial. Then he sensed the presence of his goddess. Felt the helplessness of the hunted animal that could not choose its own destiny. For weeks he had blocked out the truth, pushed it to the recesses of his mind, but that time was over.

'Are you all right?' Gwenddydd's tone had changed. Her voice was very young and shaky. 'Do you not feel the same?'

Taliesin kissed her again, fighting the uncertainty, then answered softly,

'Of course I do, how could you think anything else?'

As the weather became warmer and the trees burst into leaf, Tegai transferred his lessons from the house of bards to the oak grove.

The previous day Taliesin had been back to Braich y Dinas to attend Tanwen's wedding, and recalled the proud face of her husband, a young warrior with lands near Caer Seint. Then he imagined himself with Gwenddydd in the chapel, hearing her vow they would spend the rest of their lives together. She reached for his hand, smiling. But as he looked at her, the woman before him was no longer Gwenddydd in the robes of a bride, but Ceridwen at her most lovely, crowned by a chaplet of blood-red poppies entwined with ivy, a sheaf of corn in her arms.

Tegai's figure swam back into focus, standing at the centre of his circle of apprentices. Briefly, Taliesin met his gaze, certain the master knew that once again his attention had wandered. He felt anxious and on-edge, yet Tegai did not reprimand him, and when the day's instruction was done he prepared to accompany his comrades from the grove as usual.

As he turned, draping his cloak about his shoulders, Tegai's voice made him stop.

'Taliesin, please remain here.'

Meriadoc threw him a glance, before following Iddig down the track towards Deganwy. Though Taliesin guessed he must have persuaded Iddig not to get him into trouble after he lashed out, their friendship had been marred by tension since then.

He watched the others leave, apprehension tightening its hold, and, as the bird chorus greeted evening from the trees above, Tegai sat beside him. He was a detached man, impossible to form a bond with, though he was never unjust and his apprentices respected him for his wisdom.

'I think it is time we talked.' He spoke in an even tone. 'You know why I have kept you behind?'

Taliesin lowered his eyes, at first saying nothing.

'I.........I have been failing in my studies.'

He kept his eyes lowered, trying to find some comfort in the beauty of the birdsong.

'And the explanation?'

Again, there was silence before Taliesin replied. 'It's not laziness, it's just, just.......I cannot say.'

'Cannot?' When Taliesin looked up, Tegai's expression was difficult to read, but his voice was not harsh. 'Very well. We have all suffered greatly over the past year, and have all lost many kin and companions. I'm aware that you are grieving for your comrades who were taken from us. Rhys' change of vocation must have been hard for you too. Perhaps it made you question your own path?'

The bard looked at Taliesin, calm as he wished he himself was, with all the composure of experience.

'I don't question my path, Master. I've never thought to follow any other.'

'I'm pleased to hear that.' Tegai paused. 'Yet you have distractions. In recent months you have befriended Gwenddydd, daughter of Madoc Morfryn.'

Taliesin averted his gaze again, hot with embarrassment, though his palms had become cold and clammy. He could never discuss Gwenddydd with his tutor, analyzing his feelings like Ogham correspondences or star lore.

'You're growing into manhood and no doubt feel a man's desires.' Taliesin stared at the ground, wondering how much more he could take. 'Bards are men, like other men. But we must have a care to act honourably. And must exercise self-discipline in order to fulfil the responsibilities our vocation demands. I have waited to see if things resolved themselves, as you showed such promise last year, but your work is deteriorating with every passing week. I can only give you so much time.'

Taliesin remembered Cadfarch's words of warning, which seemed to belong to a different life. How many chances would he be given? He felt the chill of the evening seep through him with the dread of losing everything.

He took a deep breath. 'Let me prove my commitment. I can concentrate. I'll work harder than before, catch up on all that I've fallen behind with.'

Tegai inclined his head, then spoke firmly. 'I do not expect to have this conversation again. Look within yourself to find your strength and resolve.'

The bard rose. 'The Awen is not a gift to be taken lightly.'

Gwenddydd looked pale and cold when Taliesin arrived at the place where they had agreed to meet - beside a fallen tree which spanned the stream in the woodland below Deganwy. He knew he was late, but gave no apology, and he had been wracked by indecision over whether to go at all.

She called out a greeting, the colour returning to her face as she grabbed her herb basket and ran down the path towards him. Taliesin wished she was angry at having been kept waiting in the cold, he wished she was less beautiful, less radiant. She stood close, expecting him to kiss her, but though he wanted to feel her against him, to smell her soft perfume, to taste her mouth, his lips simply brushed her cheek, barely touching it. Then he took her hand and began walking swiftly. The more he longed for her, the more affectionate she was, the more agitated he became.

He felt her hand grow tense in his.

'Is something amiss?' she asked.

He continued walking, and replied abruptly. 'No......
nothing. I've been studying half the night, my mind is filled
with tree lore and verse.'

'I see.'

'Master Tegai complained about my work, so I must study
harder.' That was the most he was prepared to tell her, the rest,
his utter confusion, he could never reveal. What could he say?
He was not sure what he thought or felt. It would be impossible
to put into words.

Gwenddydd was looking at him. 'You cannot work day
and night. You'll get over-tired and be miserable. D'you still
find the time to go riding or fishing?'

'I've no wish to, now Rhys has left.'

'And Meriadoc and Iddig? You used to ride with them.'

Taliesin stared at the path ahead, at bracken and bramble
hazy in the mist. He felt she was pushing him in a direction he
had no wish to go. Her questions were like dagger thrusts, each
nearer the mark. Though, thankfully, she had never asked the
cause of Iddig's swollen jaw and missing tooth.

He tried to keep his voice steady. 'Things change.......I'll
see if I can visit Rhys soon, see how it is with him.'

Gwenddydd frowned. Then she withdrew her hand from
his and stooped to pick a blue-flowered periwinkle for healing.
She did not take Taliesin's hand again, and he made no attempt
to take hers, nor to put his arm around her waist.

Feeling weary, Gwenddydd stood beneath a gnarled tree,
showers of apple blossom falling around her with each gust of
wind, as clouds scudded across the sky, promising rain. She
wondered if Taliesin had forgotten. He had been distant

recently and was often late, but to forget?

When it began to drizzle, she finally gave up and returned to the fortress, telling herself that Tegai had set his apprentices extra work or taken them further from Deganwy to study. She refused to admit any other possibility. But when he failed to arrive again the following day she asked Rhian to go with her to the grove.

The girls approached as near as they dared, listening to Tegai's unfaltering recital followed by verses repeated less surely by his apprentices. Then the bards' voices were lost on the wind as it veered. Holding her basket under her arm, Gwenddedd looked through a tangle of branches, the air heady with the scent of damp earth and leaves. She could see Taliesin sitting with the others, cross-legged on the ground, his eyes fixed on Tegai, who had his back to her. She breathed a sigh of relief and retreated, leading Rhian away from where they might be discovered.

'Thank God he's not sick,' she whispered. 'I thought that might be why he didn't come to the orchard.'

'Perhaps it would be better if he were.'

'What do you mean?' Gwenddydd's expression darkened. 'Do you have some knowledge that you are keeping from me?'

'Only the knowledge of men. Is that not what drove you to spy on him?"

'I was concerned.' Gwenddydd sounded defensive.

'About his health or his faithfulness?........I'm sorry.' Rhian took her arm. 'No doubt he's as keen on you as you are on him. But bardic training becomes ever more demanding. I'm sure you have no reason to worry.'

Gwenddydd nodded. 'I know the training is hard.....He did try to explain.'

As they began to walk away she glanced over her shoulder, picturing Taliesin seated in the circle with his comrades. She had to force herself not to go back. In her heart she wanted to stay near the grove until the end of the day's instruction so he could not avoid her again. But she realized that if she did Rhian would think her a fool.

Though it was June, the waters of the Hibernian Sea were grey and restless. His vision blurred by salt spray, Taliesin saw Manawyddan's horses rearing out of the deep with their wild white manes and flailing hoofs, otherworldly riders on their backs.

He sensed the elemental spirits alive in the roar of the waves, in the lowering cloud, held in the ground beneath his feet: the energies of the earth, of Gwynedd, of Ynys Prydein. There was power here, and when the Awen flowed through him, taking him temporarily from this world. Like the excitement of being with Gwenddydd, in the feelings which overwhelmed him then. Yet sometimes the intensity became too much, turning it all to pain.

Tegai had not complained about his work again, but whenever Taliesin saw Gwenddydd he became distracted, and so he avoided her, desperately searching for an answer; alone, with no one he could speak to.

He gazed out to the invisible horizon, staring until his eyes slipped out of focus and he felt that he drifted between sea and sky.

chapter eight

Taliesin frowned at the girl standing in front of him, one of Queen Olwen's companions, small and slight as a fey, scarcely more than a child.

'Are you sure those were her words?' he asked.

The girl raised her eyes skyward. 'She said, 'Tell him, if he ever wishes to speak to me again he must come to the orchard at dusk.'

'Nothing else?'

The girl shook her head.

'Do you know what she meant by this? Is she all right?'

'I think so. Why question me? See Gwenddydd yourself.'

With the words barely out of her mouth, the girl turned, and holding her skirts ran in the direction of the hall. Taliesin wanted to call her back, to ask more, but realized it was pointless. She would never tell him enough, even if she knew.

Now, as dusk deepened, he walked restlessly back and forth beneath the trees, biting his lip until it hurt. He had not spoken to Gwenddydd for a full cycle of the moon, and had avoided her in the hall and courtyard, but he could not have stayed away that day. Her message disturbed him: 'If he ever wishes to speak to me again.......'

He sighed, wondering if she would arrive at all, or would make him wait in vain as he had made her wait so often. But eventually he saw a figure approaching, silhouetted against the afterglow in the sky. He stopped pacing and stood still, feeling awkward and guilty.

When Gwenddydd was close enough for him to see her clearly, Taliesin noticed the change in her. At a distance in the hall he had not realized how thin she had become, that her hair had lost its sheen, and that her once fine complexion was sallow, with dark shadows under her eyes.

'I received your message,' he said expressionlessly.

Their eyes met for a moment, and Taliesin longed to offer some explanation for his behaviour, to try and make her understand, but could not summon the courage.

'I shall not keep you long.' Gwenddydd sounded remote, like a stranger. 'I just thought you should know my plans.'

He simply looked at her, distressed by the tone of her voice.

'I have asked Perwyr if I can return to my family. I'll be leaving Deganwy in a week.'

Taliesin continued staring, feeling as if he had been struck in the belly.

'You are not sick are you?'

'No, I'm not sick, though I imagine it would make no difference to you if I were.'

'That isn't true, I care about you.'

Gwenddydd gave a bitter laugh. 'If this is how you treat someone you care about........'

Taliesin did not reply and lowered his gaze, looking at an apple that had fallen to the ground, still unripe.

'You could at least have spoken to me. Did I not deserve that much?' Gwenddydd said. 'I don't even know why you no longer want to see me.'

The silence that followed seemed eternal, broken only by the distant hum of the sea. Taliesin struggled to find the right words, but he knew he had to say something, however foolish and clumsy.

'I was going to explain.' He would not meet Gwenddydd's eyes and continued to look down, wishing he could be absorbed by the dusk, taken through the veil that lay between worlds. 'I've had no time. I needed to concentrate on my studies.'

'A lame excuse.' She began to turn. 'I must go.'

'Gwenddydd!' Finally, Taliesin raised his eyes. He could not let it end with such bitterness. She stopped and looked at him, into him, so he almost lost his resolve. 'I do care, I swear, but.......such closeness.......' He stopped, unable to express the complexity of his feelings. 'I know my life is destined to follow the path where my spiritual mother, my goddess, leads. I lack the strength for both.'

The anger had gone from Gwenddydd's eyes, and when she spoke her voice was tired. 'I only wish you had told me before, before I came to love you. And despite the way you've treated me, and though I've sometimes hated you, I have not stopped loving you......I hope your destined path will bring all the rewards you expect.......Goodbye, Taliesin.'

As he watched her walk away between the trees, he could not believe that she was leaving Deganwy. Her words had sounded more final than the parting of death. He remembered how he had thought they would be together in the Otherworld, beyond time, for ever. Remembered the vision they had shared in the orchard where he now stood, alone.

It had been a tiring journey in the late summer heat, and a fresh breeze blowing down the strait from the Hibernian Sea was like the answer to a prayer. Closing his eyes, Taliesin turned into it, feeling the wind cool on his skin. When he opened them again, he glanced back towards the mainland which they had left, crossing to Ynys Mon in a creaky boat that let in water.

He watched the waves lick the shore, almost touching the hem of Tegai's cloak, the rhythmic swish and scrape stilling his mind, filling it with echoes from the past. On the far side of the strait he saw the Roman soldiers amassing, rank upon rank, like a colony of ants. And he knew that they were like ants, trained not to think but to obey: skilled, disciplined, but inhuman as the cold metal of the short-swords they carried.

Clad in a robe of undyed linen, he stood at the water's edge and raised his arms, directing the lightning power that rushed through him towards the enemy lines, a shadow that foretold the end of the Old Ways. All around him he could hear the voices of the priestesses, their curses mingling with the druid chant that carried across the waves. As they shrieked, they ran into the shallows - raven-women clothed in black, tearing their hair and holding flaming torches aloft. Still the enemy did not advance. Was it possible that the wall of power halted them? Did they feel the curses strike like thrown spears?

'Where we stand, the druids of Ynys Prydein confronted the Romans under General Paulinus, the Governor whose mission it was to extirpate the sacred caste.'

Taliesin heard the anger in Tegai's voice as it drew him back to the present, to a hot summer's evening and the small group gathered on the shore.

'At this place, they were cut down by the first soldiers to reach the island. The few who managed to flee were slain soon after in the sacred precincts of their groves, which were then desecrated and burnt. With the stronghold of the druids destroyed, the Britons' soul and strength was sapped. Though, like a tree felled to the ground, with each generation the tradition puts up new shoots.'

Even now, Taliesin sensed the memory of the massacre held in the earth beneath their feet. And he could feel the presence of restless spirits who had not journeyed on to the Otherworld, though their Roman conquerors had long since left the island. And now a new wave of invasion pressed in from the east. Would there be more death on this shore, he wondered, a clash of arms between Briton and Saeson?

Tegai turned to him, and he thought he would be reprimanded for not attending, though his work had excelled since midsummer and he knew his master was pleased in his guarded way.

'I see you feel the power of this place, Taliesin.'

'It is troubled still.'

'What happened here has affected all our destinies.' Tegai's expression clouded, then he gathered his cloak about him, and, facing the wooded interior of the island, began walking with impatient strides. 'We were promised horses. Where are they? We need time to rest before the king's feast tonight.'

Rhun's fortress at Aberffraw was larger than Deganwy, and the hall filled to capacity. Though the welcome feast lasted until dawn, Taliesin and Meriadoc ate little and left early. For the rest of that day they fasted, following instructions to keep apart from the others and from the drunken court, preparing themselves through meditation.

As twilight gathered, Tegai rode ahead of his two apprentices into the darkly wooded heart of the island, which gave it its other name of Yr Ynys Dywyll. There had been a sudden change in the weather since noon. The wind had risen, bringing rain from the west, and Taliesin sensed the approach of autumn. Last autumn he had been with Gwenddydd, sharing apples in the orchard behind Deganwy, talking in a way he could not talk with anyone else, holding her close........

He blinked the rain from his eyes and looked blankly through the trees.

'Ysgawen, ysgawen,
dark tree, wise tree,
tree of dark dream knowledge.
Ysgawen, ysgawen,
dark tree.......'

Repeating the chant silently, he drove all other thoughts

from his mind. He told himself he must look forward, not back. What lay immediately ahead would take all his resolve, and he embraced that challenge. Neither he nor Meriadoc spoke until Tegai unexpectedly drew his horse up. Meriadoc looked surprised, but Taliesin felt the oppression and grief in the atmosphere as they gazed at an area where the woodland was sparse, the leaves moist and glistening in the half-light.

'The earth remembers.' Tegai spoke under his breath.

There was a look of realization in Meriadoc's eyes. 'This was an ancient grove. How strange that the trees are not re-established after all these years.'

'The seeds of destruction were sown by the desecrators.' Tegai emphasized the final words. 'In time you will understand fully.'

Taliesin said nothing. He longed only to leave the place, and was grateful when they rode on. A growing apprehension tightened his stomach and he felt light-headed. He knew why they had been brought here at this stage in their training. The island was a gateway to other levels of being: the Otherworld, past, future. And at certain times that gate stood ajar. Those who were sensitive could easily slip through.

Once Ynys Mon was the centre - a place of tremendous, dangerous power. But now there was sadness, like the grief of a king separated from his land. Again, Taliesin began to chant silently. He would not let his thoughts follow that path either, because it was the path where past and future threatened to become one.

He was unsure if he felt dazed through lack of food or from the pull of the forces in the earth, a power which seemed to be waxing as night drew closer. Then his thoughts turned unexpectedly to Rhys, praying alone in his hut, or gathering with the other monks to sing the praises of a god remote from mankind and nature. Their paths were already far apart, and at that moment Taliesin felt that his comrade had taken the easier way.

Through the purple light, under the dripping trees, they approached a clearing with a mound at its centre. At the sight of it Taliesin felt a sudden fear, which was at the same time exhilaration, a sense of being painfully alive. This was the place - Bryn Celli Ddu, the Hill of the Dark Grove.

Meriadoc looked at the black entrance to the mound, then glanced at him, and he noticed a flicker of panic in the other boy's eyes. He remembered that it was not so long since Meriadoc had mocked Rhys for being a coward, though this was no mere darkened hut. They would be the first to enter the ancient temple-tomb. Then, each night following, two more of Tegai's apprentices would come to be tested.

The boys gathered wood, and after several attempts Tegai managed to light a fire at the edge of the clearing so they could warm themselves and dry their cloaks. It smoked and hissed in the damp air as Taliesin and Meriadoc stood beside it, knowing that soon they would be deprived of even that small comfort.

Taliesin still felt cold when, without warning, Tegai crouched down and threw soil and leaves over the wavering flames.

Silently, the bard circled the clearing, weaving a protective shield with the movements of his hands. When he had completed the circuit, he faced his apprentices, his expression remote.

'Remember all you have learnt. I will return at dawn.'

Tegai remained by the heap of earth where the fire had been, watching Taliesin lead the way towards the mound, walking with slow even steps. At the entrance, he lowered his head and stepped through the narrow opening, following a passage flanked by vast slabs, though in the darkness he could not see but only feel their stony surface. With each breath he inhaled the scent of earth, not musty but surprisingly dry. In the silence and blackness there was an unexpected sense of security, reminding him of how he had felt as a child in Eilonwy's arms. And he sensed the weight of the stones and earth above them, its solidity below, like the levels of antiquity, deeper and ever deeper, carrying the memory of the ancestors.

As the passage widened, Taliesin moved towards the right, his outstretched hands contacting a stone directly ahead. Then, leaning his back against it, feeling its pulsing energy drawn up from the land, he stared into blackness.

'I wish to remain here,' he said. His voice sounded faint, turned in on itself.

'I think I'll go to the far side.' There was a slight quiver in Meriadoc's reply.

'We will speak again when the master returns........The night is not long.'

Taliesin took his cloak from his shoulders, and threw it onto the ground before lying down with his head towards the stone. For a while he heard Meriadoc moving about, searching for somewhere to face his own ordeal, but finally there was silence.

Taliesin kept his eyes open, watching the swirling patterns of colour that his mind imposed on the darkness. Soon he had forgotten Meriadoc's presence, as the power of stone and the earth grew until he felt dizzy. He felt that he was being pulled back and forth between the two. The earth embraced him, the stone thrust his consciousness towards the stars, spinning amongst them to the constellation of Caer Arianrhod, the goddess' diadem in the heavens. She filled the sky, with the stars on her brow, a delicate silvery being who held the power of all destinies. Earth, suspended in the darkness of eternity, was like a spindle whorl dropped from her hand.......spinning.........spinning.

When he looked into her eyes, Taliesin saw Gwenddydd and Queen Olwen, the ageing Perwyr, and the oldest crone at Braich y Dinas, who said she remembered the days before the battle of Badon. For an instant, all women, all goddesses became one. Then she was the goddess he loved above all others. Ceridwen - his hope, his dread........She smiled at him like a lover, her face beautiful and radiant. But he became afraid, and her smile hardened, showing the bared teeth of an otter bitch ready for the kill. His own body was strong and smooth-scaled, a salmon leaping from the river, as past and present slid together.

He leapt higher and higher, far above the torrent, into the dawn sky. Scales softened to feathers, fins to bird's wings, outstretched, riding the air currents. Free. No, he knew he could never be free, because he had given his life to her. And she would kill him or embrace him. As a hawk she soared, beak dagger-sharp, talons extended. The faster his wings beat the air, the nearer she drew, and his strength began to seep away, like wine leaking from a flask, until he had no energy left to escape. He began to fall, slowly at first, then faster, contracting, becoming ever smaller, oval and golden, life in suspension, a seed........a grain of wheat.

He felt a jolt as he hit the granary floor, dark after the sunlight. Dark as a tomb. His head was spinning and he raised his hands to his temples. For a moment he thought he was back at the house of vision in Deganwy. He would meet Gwenddydd in the orchard, they would walk on the strand.........and they would part.

Suddenly his eyes were burning, tears pushing between his tightly closed lids. The burning was not the pain of grief, but of love, love for his goddess.

Through the darkness, she spoke to him.

'What sorrow there is,
That is better than joy.
I know the blessed gifts
Of the flowing muse.....' 4

153

* * *

Weapons adorned the walls of the hall where Taliesin sat, drinking from a cup of mead as he gazed at the jewel-hilted swords, and shields painted with bright devises. Many of the weapons were ancient, and he found himself wondering who had wielded them in battle. How had they lived? How had they died? Were they remembered in bardic song? Links in the chain of tradition.

He turned when Tegai entered with another man - a stranger. But as he set eyes on him, Taliesin experienced what seemed like a flash of recognition.

He knew that the stranger was of noble rank by the richly embroidered cloak he wore, secured at the shoulder with a gold and enamel brooch. He was short in stature and many years older than Tegai, his lean face deeply lined and weathered, the face of someone who spent much time in the open.

Taliesin rose, and as he inclined his head, he glimpsed the blue spirals tattooed on the man's forearms.

'This is King Rhun's honoured guest.' Tegai gave no name. 'I would like you to tell him of your experiences at Bryn Celli Ddu, and to repeat the verses you received.'

Cautiously, Taliesin met the eyes of the older man. They were dark grey, almost black, and held a power he had never encountered in human eyes before. He was afraid he would recall only fragments of his vision, because he sensed the importance of the moment though nothing had been explained. Clearly, Tegai was testing him. A smile hovered on the bard's lips, but Taliesin could not be sure whether it was a look of pride in his apprentice or of amusement at his curiosity.

The other man did not smile. His face betrayed nothing.

Beginning before fear froze his tongue, Taliesin told all he could remember, gradually relaxing, so the words flowed with an easier rhythm, carrying him as effortlessly as when he performed before the royal company, though that had been rare since Rhun's accession.

When he finished, he saw the stranger nod towards Tegai. It was also he who spoke first.

'The song of the land is alive, Taliesin.'

The man's voice possessed the same quality as his eyes. It was rich and melodious like a bard's, but there was something else, beyond definition. And when Taliesin's own name was spoken in that voice, it was as if he heard it for the first time, realized its true meaning for the first time.

'How long have you been training?' the stranger asked.

'I began with my first master, Cadfarch, when I was ten. At Calan Mai I will be sixteen.'

Again the man nodded.

'I can see you are curious. Before we talk further, let me introduce myself. My name is Talhaearn.'

Taliesin looked back at him, trying to remain calm, to think clearly as his pulse began to race. Chieftains and kings were nothing beside the Pen Beirdd of Ynys Prydein - Talhaearn Tad Awen. Why had Tegai brought him to listen to the dull reports of a youth of six years training?

He felt sure of only one thing. There was a reason for the most painful sacrifice he had ever made in deciding to part from Gwenddydd. And, as he faced Talhaearn, he was liberated by the freedom of certainty. How did it feel to be the man in front of him, he wondered, to possess such depth of wisdom that it radiated though his eyes and voice? One day, he resolved, he would know.

Along with his other lessons, Taliesin spent the time at Aberffraw working on 'Kadeir Teyrnon'. No matter how often he sang it, still he felt he must practice, over and over. There was always some detail he was certain he had not mastered properly. That night, at the feast before they left for Deganwy the following day, he wanted to perform as never before, for the ears of Talhaearn. There would be no other opportunity.

His strong voice carried on the summer air.

'The third deeply wise one,
Is the blessed Arthur.
Arthur the blessed
Renowned in song,
In the front of battle
He was full of activity.' ₅

He stopped, turning towards Meriadoc who sat on the ground beside him in the shelter of the palisade.

'I'll try again,' he said. 'Just once more.'

Meriadoc returned his gaze with an air of frustration. 'I've never heard a better rendition. Why keep repeating it?'

'You know why.' Taliesin ran his fingers across the harp strings, questioning whether Meriadoc could ever really understand, as Rhys would have done.

'We're all nervous,' his comrade replied after a moment's pause. 'But you've less reason to be than the rest of us. I saw how you impressed the Master Talhaearn.'

'If I did, I've got something to live up to.'

'My God, do you never give yourself any peace!'

Taliesin sighed. 'I'm sorry........You practice your song.'

But Meriadoc simply sat in silence, uncharacteristically brooding.

'Tegai won't let me see Iddig,' he said eventually. 'Because he's too ill.'

Taliesin was startled. 'Ill? He seemed well enough when I saw him yesterday.'

'But that......that was before he went to the mound.'

'Yes.....?'

'Don't you see?'

'What? Iddig the brave!' Taliesin laughed, a little harshly. 'Now I suppose I should apologize again.'

'You wouldn't laugh if it were Rhys.' Meriadoc retorted.

Taliesin thought for a moment, then met him eye to eye. 'The worst that can have happened is that he had a shock, an awakening. He'll be better once he's rested........Now, unless you begin your song I shall start mine again.'

Meriadoc forced a grin. 'Anything but that.'

chapter nine

'Ynys Mon has revealed itself in darkness and in light, the lessons of its earth reach deep. Tomorrow we will return to the grove to explore that depth in the shadow of Calan Gaeaf.' Tegai kept his gaze fixed on the path ahead as he and Taliesin walked briskly through the woodland. 'But I did not take time from my duties simply to talk of this.'

Taliesin continued walking in silence, as it struck him that on the rare occasions he had been alone with Tegai it had always been when he was in trouble. They passed close by the oak grove but did not stop. The leaves were beginning to turn, and the undergrowth was dying back, the bracken reddening. Elated and on-edge, Taliesin felt as precariously balanced as the changing season. He had scarcely slept the previous night after the journey back from Aberffraw.

'I have spoken with the Pen Beirdd.'

Taliesin glanced at Tegai, his anticipation increasing. He realized he was holding his breath, though he was unsure exactly what he was hoping for. To learn that Talhaearn had praised his performance? An invitation to perform before him in future?

'It is common knowledge that the Pen Beirdd only accepts pupils who show outstanding potential.' Still Taliesin said nothing, though he was now looking at Tegai as if it were possible to read his thoughts. 'He works individually with those he takes on, never with more than three during the same period. At present he has but one apprentice, and after meeting you at Aberffraw he asked me if I thought you were inwardly prepared to progress to the next phase of training.'

There was no change in Tegai's expression, and he spoke so casually that Taliesin wondered if he had misunderstood.

'Talhaearn Tad Awen is willing to take me as his apprentice?' he asked in an undertone.

'Those were his words.' Tegai's face remained set. 'And I told him that I thought you were prepared, despite some problems earlier in the year.'

Taliesin remembered how, at the time, he had feared that Tegai might dismiss him from training. But that was all in the past, and he had no wish to think about it now. He felt the presence of Talhaearn already with him, as if he stood in the glow of that great fire of renown and inspiration.

'It......it is such an honour.'

Tegai nodded. 'Of course I must discuss it with your foster-parents before I send a messenger to Rheged.'

Taliesin gave a start. In his enthusiasm, he had been thinking only of working under Talhaearn. But that meant he would travel to Rheged, centre of the fight against the barbarian invaders. At last he was to be released from the prison of childhood and of Gwynedd.

'My parents will be honoured too,' he said, trying to keep his voice steady.

'Still, they must be consulted before anything is finalized. I'll send one of my men to Braich y Dinas to tell them you'll be returning for a few days and that I will be accompanying you.'

Taliesin imagined his homecoming, his family's reaction when they learnt his news. 'When will we be leaving?' he asked with forced calm. 'Tomorrow?'

'The bardic path is one of patience. We have only just got back from Ynys Mon and I have an important matter to attend to here. Then we will go.' There was grim amusement in Tegai's voice as he added, 'If you think I am a firm master, you will remember my discipline as soft.'

Alarch smiled sweetly at Tegai as she placed a silver cup of her parents' best wine in front of him, making sure to catch his eye.

'May I get you anything else? Fruit? Cakes baked with honey and nuts? I made them myself.'

'Not at present, thank you.' Tegai's lips curled into a faint smile, and he addressed Eilonwy. 'Your daughter is a fine hostess.'

She inclined her head in acknowledgement of the praise, but when she looked at Alarch her voice held a warning. 'Go and see if your friends want any more to eat. And I'm sure Taliesin has much news you will want to hear.'

Alarch hesitated, then turned and strolled across to the far end of the hall, smiling to herself, her new green gown rustling as she moved. A large group had gathered around Taliesin, mostly youths and maidens, Alarch's own friends, but a few younger children hovered around the edges, wide-eyed and excited. They all seemed to be talking at once. His return was like a breeze stirring up the waters of a stagnant pool.

Alarch bent close to Taliesin's ear.

'Why is the Chief Bard here?' she whispered, glancing over her shoulder to where their elders sat, deep in discussion.

'To perform a song especially for you.'

She slapped him playfully on the arm. 'Do they teach you to keep secrets in Deganwy?'

'That I cannot reveal.'

Alarch laughed. 'You haven't changed.'

'And what has changed here?' Taliesin asked. 'How long since Dyfnarth went to fight for Elmet?'

'Almost three weeks. We've had no news from him, though a traveller from the north said there've been no battles since the new moon.'

Glinneu rested a heavily muscled arm on the table. He was broader and stronger each time Taliesin saw him, his long flame-red hair braided at either temple in the warrior style, framing a face strikingly like Elffin's. 'I shall be going to

Dumnonia before the winter sets in, to train with the men there. By summer I'll be ready to fight, to make sure the filthy Saeson never reach Mor Hafren.'

'Trust you to speak of yourself first.' Alarch narrowed her eyes at her brother. 'Tanwen has wonderful news........but I must let her tell you when she arrives. She will be here soon.'

Taliesin raised a questioning brow, but Alarch only imitated him.

She sat down on the bench beside Henwyn, who put an arm around her waist. As a look of understanding passed between them, Taliesin felt a sudden heaviness. Though he was surrounded by his foster-kin and had a bright future ahead, the future he had always longed for, at that moment he felt very alone.

Disturbed, and angry with himself, he turned back to Glinneu. 'I've heard there's pressure on the Dumnonian border. But if you all leave there'll be no warriors here except the veterans, no one to defend Gwynedd against surprise attack.'

'I've no plans to leave.' Henwyn took a draught of mead and wiped his mouth with the back of his hand. 'I'm training the boys in the use of weapons. Even Drych's son Collen has ambition. I think he'll make a fine spearman, given time.'

'You're an optimist,' Glinneu said. 'The boy's got no backbone.'

'All he needs is encouragement. That is part of my task as trainer.'

'You mean he needs courage.' Glinneu faced Taliesin. 'And what of bardic training? What does that require? Only a couple of years instruction and we risk our lives on the field of battle, but it is twelve before a bard is qualified.'

Taliesin met his brother's eyes, seeing the challenge.

'I can only tell you half of what it requires,' he said dryly. 'You'll have to ask again in six years time.'

There was a moment's silence, then Glinneu laughed.

'Your tongue's sharp as a warrior's sword, damn it. Saeson beware.' He laughed again, and Taliesin found himself laughing too.

Harp music filled the growing darkness in the apprentices' house as Taliesin sat on his bed practising, the strings beneath his fingers like an extension of himself. His thoughts blended and flowed with each note: Alarch and Henwyn together, Dyfnarth and Glinneu now warriors, the news of Tanwen's pregnancy. Her baby was to be born in the spring, around the time of his own birth. Two new lives - one childhood begun, another ended.

The jarring of the outer door and approaching footsteps startled him back to the present. He looked up, his fingers still moving instinctively over the strings.

'Ah, you're back.' Meriadoc's broad figure stood above him. 'Your music seems happy.'

The words sounded like an accusation, and Taliesin peered through the half-light, trying to make out the other boy's expression.

When Meriadoc sat down heavily on his bed, his eyes lowered, Taliesin stopped playing.

'What disturbs you?' he asked. 'Do you wish to talk?'

'Perhaps you're not the person to tell.'

'Are you in some sort of trouble? I'm no stranger to that.'

Meriadoc shook his head. He did not reply for some time, then spoke hoarsely, his voice faltering. 'It's Iddig.......He's given up training.'

The intensity of his reaction surprised Taliesin. He was less surprised that Iddig had been dismissed.

'Because of a girl?'

'Do you not remember? On Ynys Mon. But then you've been away......and now all attention is upon you.' Taliesin forced himself to stay silent, ignoring the bitterness in Meriadoc's voice. 'Something happened to Iddig at Bryn Celli Ddu. He can barely speak to me, as if his reason has gone.' Meriadoc shuddered. 'No doubt you think it is what he deserves.'

'Do not even imagine you know what I think.' Taliesin put his harp aside and got to his feet.

'No........I'm sorry.' Meriadoc's tone had lost its edge. 'I meant no insult to you. All my words are tangled at the moment. Please stay.'

Without replying, Taliesin sat down again, still angry and resentful. His own news would have to wait, or he would be accused of selfishness. Even now, Iddig had succeeded in turning joy to conflict. Again there was silence, Taliesin not trusting himself to speak.

'I never thought it would be like this,' Meriadoc said eventually. 'I had some delusion that bardic instruction would be uplifting. Bloody fool! How many more of us will crack like a stone in a fire? If you saw Iddig you'd hardly know him.'

Meriadoc frowned at Taliesin's lack of response.

'I said I'm sorry. Are you still angry?'

'No,' he replied quietly. 'I was thinking about what you told me.'

'Did you imagine it would have such......effects?'

Taliesin gazed into the shadows. 'All my life I've had.....experiences.....things I could neither explain nor control, at first. For me, training has lessened the fear, not increased it. Through walking the inner worlds under guidance I begin to understand myself.'

'I also begin to understand. That is why Tegai has singled you out. Not because of your royal foster-kin.'

Taliesin could not help laughing, a release of his own tension. 'Did you really imagine it was that?'

'I cannot say for sure, I've not been thinking clearly these

163

past days. I know that the Master Talhaearn spoke to you privately while we were at Aberffraw. I saw him go to meet you and Tegai.' He paused. 'Taliesin, what is happening?'

'I was going to tell you as soon as I saw you, but it did not seem the right time. Believe me, I wish Iddig no harm, whatever our differences.'

'And the answer to my question?'

'I shall be travelling to Rheged in the spring, to study under Talhaearn.'

Meriadoc caught his breath. 'My God, that is news! Not many have such an honour.' Then his expression clouded. 'Do you think you can endure the ordeals? I have heard such things of Talhaearn.'

'I am prepared to face anything.' Taliesin looked at the boy in front of him, aware that of the eight who had come to study under Tegai the previous year, soon only Meriadoc would remain. 'I don't want to stay in Gwynedd all my life,' he said, 'at Deganwy or Aberffraw. At last I have the chance to travel, to see more of the land, to meet men of renown. And Talhaearn can teach things that few men know.'

'If you stand within ten paces of him you can sense his power.' There was awe in Meriadoc's voice, but also fear. 'You are lucky to have been chosen, and I envy your chance to visit the north, but I'm not sure I'd want to be Talhaearn's apprentice.'

Part Three

A Branch of Silver

A branch of the apple tree from the Glass Isle
I bring, like those we know;
Twigs of white silver are upon it
Crystal grows with blossoms. 7

chapter one

As the days lengthened after Calan Mai, Tegai and Taliesin made their way east, accompanied by two attendants, travelling across the wilds of Gwynedd until they came to a gentler land, with fields of young barley, and pasture which stretched between green summer forest. Riding through that unfamiliar country, Gwenddydd was in Taliesin's thoughts again. But he found that the old pain, the conflict, was gone. All winter he had had other preoccupations. Now their time together was locked in the past. He had made his choice, and it was leading him far from her and the scenes of his boyhood.

Places only spoken of before emerged from imagination into reality. Places such as Deva, which Cadfarch had described many years ago, and where the travellers stopped for a night's shelter. A web of straight Roman roads still met there, linking the now deserted forts that once controlled the west of Ynys Prydein.

Everywhere Tegai asked for hospitality they were treated with honour, he and Taliesin repaying their hosts with songs and tales. It was a journey Taliesin had made so often in his mind, he could scarcely believe that at last he was making it in the flesh.

One evening, as a light mist was settling over the land, they reached the border of Rheged, though they still had far to travel. After they had fed and watered their horses, Taliesin stood gazing towards the north where his future lay. Urien was now Lord of Rheged, after the death of his father Cynfarch during the winter, and Taliesin thought how, like himself, the kingdom he had just entered stood on the threshold of a new era.

The weather continued to hold, though the nights were

chill as they passed through an area of mountains reflected in vast lakes. Taliesin sensed the energy of the earth, observed the celestial blues of the waters, the purple hues that rested on the uplands. Yet, amidst such beauty, he mourned for the sea, the salty wind and sound of the waves that had been with him all his life.

Riding became slow and difficult as they continued northward, passing isolated settlements - clusters of buildings surrounded by an oval stone wall or bank and palisade. Or a smaller farmstead would be scoured from the earth of the hillside. There was cultivation in the dales but where the soil was too thin, the slope too steep, sheep grazed, tended by lone shepherds who spent the summer out in the hills.

Gradually, the land began to fall away to lower ground, and around midday the riders paused to eat the bread and cheese given them by their hostess the previous night. The air was heavy, and insects hummed amongst the flowers along the roadside. While the attendants played a game of dice, Tegai sat on his travel-stained cloak, his face bronzed by days spent in the open. He took a drink of ale from a leather flask, then passed it to Taliesin.

'We should make our destination before dusk,' he said. 'Though I feel there's a storm building, and we may have to take shelter.'

Taliesin looked out over the country around them, shielding his eyes against the sun. Though his ambition had been to make his destiny as soon as possible, now the journey seemed too short; a part of him would willingly have continued for ever, travelling Ynys Prydein from one coast to the other, from Dumnonia to Manaw Gododdin, Gwynedd to Elmet. And soon he would have to face the great Talhaearn Tad Awen alone, without Tegai's support. Apprehension intruded on his enthusiasm. He knew the rumours - how the power of Talhaearn's voice could steal a man's mind, that he could physically take the form of a wild beast, that he welcomed any ordeal, however dangerous, and expected his apprentices to do the same.

When he turned, he saw that Tegai was looking at him as if the bard attempted to read his thoughts.

Unable to reveal the truth, Taliesin searched for words to reason away his preoccupation. 'This land is so vast,' he said after a moment, 'and I know little of it even now.'

'Some of it you're unlikely ever to see, as it lies in the hands of the enemy. But the battle is not yet ended. We owe the gods of Ynys Prydein and the spirits of our ancestors, not only courage but our lives.'

Taliesin had never heard Tegai refer to the Old Ways so openly. At Deganwy he had always kept just within the bounds of Christianity. Here, out on the open road, the restraint was gone.

'Is King Urien at Caer Liwelydd?' he asked, trying to keep his voice neutral.

'He may be away, raiding to the east of the mountains. But the Master Talhaearn will be awaiting us. That is all that need concern you. You have not come to be Urien's bard.'

Taliesin stared at the ground, not allowing himself to imagine, and finished off the last mouthful of dry bread.

The storm built throughout the afternoon and broke around sunset. Feeling the tension in the air, each breath tight in his throat, Taliesin watched lightning flicker across the horizon. Closer and closer, the flashes struck earth, approaching over the open landscape which reached as far as he could see, the ferocity of the thunder making the horses restless.

Despite their exposed position, Tegai did not stop to ask for shelter at the walled farmstead they had just passed, and Taliesin was beginning to wonder if his master intended to continue riding into the teeth of the storm, when he inclined his head towards a wooded area, then led the way from the metalled road down a barely visible track.

Recalling the blasted oak that stood alone on a hillside near Deganwy, Taliesin felt relief as he urged Gwyn to follow. He was struggling to calm the frightened horse, and when lightning struck uncomfortably close, Gwyn reared, almost throwing him. Tegai drew to a halt, the attendants watching grimly until Taliesin managed to regain control.

It seemed an age before they entered the woodland, where they made their way in single file down a path worn through dense undergrowth, the first drops of rain drumming on the leaf canopy above. Taliesin had expected Tegai to rest the horses once they were protected from the worst of the storm, but kept silent as they pressed on. The light was poor between the trees, and the air had an acrid smell. Then, through the semi-darkness, a hall appeared ahead of them, timbers and turf roof merging with the woodland.

As Tegai dismounted, a flash of lightning cast the trees and building into relief, illuminating a couple of small roundhouses and an animal shelter close by. Simultaneously, thunder cracked overhead, reverberating in the earth beneath their feet.

Tegai turned to Taliesin, an ironic smile on his lips.

'The gods have arranged a welcome for you.'

Taliesin frowned. 'Here?'

He had thought he was to live in Caer Liwelydd, at Urien's stronghold.

'Here.'

The attendants tied the horses, then followed as Taliesin accompanied Tegai across the clearing, head held high with forced confidence.

Before they reached the hall, the door opened and the Pen Beirdd himself stood at the entrance. He wore none of the fine robes or jewels he had in Aberffraw, but a simple undyed tunic and breeches. His feet were bare and his wiry arms exposed, showing the tattoos that spiralled to the elbow.

'Tegai, greetings.' His voice was deadened by the roar of the storm. 'An ill day for riding.'

The bards clasped each other, then Talhaearn's eyes came to rest on Taliesin.

'You've travelled a long way from Gwynedd. Was the journey rewarding?'

'Yes, Master. The time passed quickly, and I saw and learnt much.'

'Be glad you made the most of it, you'll be staying here for a while.' Talhaearn exchanged a cryptic look with Tegai. 'Though it's as well you have a taste for journeying.'

The Pen Beirdd stepped aside and they entered the dimly lit interior of the hall, where silhouettes lurked half-seen in the gloom: antlers of the red deer, a ram's skull with great curving horns, birds' wings, the head and skin of a mountain cat. Faint embers glowed in the hearth and Taliesin breathed the aroma of drying herbs, not sweet herbs or the kind Eilonwy and Tanwen hung from the roof timbers to use for cooking, but medicinal, and plants of power.

At Talhaearn's invitation the travellers sat on fur-covered benches around the hearth, and a sturdy dark-haired boy came to serve them before retreating into the shadows. As Taliesin took a mouthful of mead, he thought of the companions he had trained with many miles, and worlds, away. The men's conversation buzzed in the background while he became increasingly aware of the energy in Talhaearn's hall, like a forest at night, alert, secret, crouching. Sitting opposite the Pen Beirdd of Ynys Prydein, who seemed to hold the power of that forest within himself, he knew he could only work here if the spirits of place accepted him. After all his training - mastering the lore of nature, of music, the visionary work, the correspondences - he felt like a beginner again. He had

173

travelled beyond the security of Gwynedd, and must continue to travel without fear into realms where all safe boundaries were broken down. Or - he remembered the arrogant but cowardly Iddig - be reduced to a trembling shell.

It was the third night that Taliesin had woken before dawn. He lay on his bed, alone in one of the small roundhouses, a rough blanket covering his naked body. Never in sixteen years had he slept without kin or companions nearby, without the regular breathing that lulled the mind like a chant, without the sound of someone turning, or sighing in a dream. The silence echoed in his ears, all his senses on edge. An occasional crackle from the surrounding woodland, and the hoot of an owl, were the only reminders of life. So this was the great honour he had been chosen for. Meriadoc would have laughed.

In the stillness, Glinneu's voice screamed at him, 'At least I know who my real father is.....' But on Taliesin's last visit to Braich y Dinas there had been a truce between them. Though the tension was still there, now they could talk without arguing, they could even laugh together. There was the chance for understanding. Still the memories arose, like bubbles from the depths of a dark pool. 'You are the son of a demon. Who else has white hair like yours? All white, all washed out.'

Then Alarch's clear childish tones, 'You're so clever. I wish I could carve and sing and play harp like you.'

Faces, voices swirled through his head.

Dyfnarth's disdain, Cadfarch's warmth.

The owl hooted three times, an echo from the Underworld. 'I will test you, to your limit.'

'Look within yourself to find your strength and resolve. The Awen is not a gift to be taken lightly.'

'I am your teacher, your guide.......My name I cannot reveal, though one day you may learn it.'

'Though I've sometimes hated you, I have not stopped loving you.'

Filled with restless energy, Taliesin sat up and pushed his hair from his forehead, finding it clammy with perspiration. It seemed that he was being attacked, his own thoughts and memories waging war on him in the emptiness. He swung his legs to the ground and reached for the blanket, then flung it aside and walked across the beaten earth floor, barefoot and naked.

He had no idea what hour it was, how long he had been awake. He lifted the latch quietly, and pushed the door open. The night smelt of woodland, of earth and leaves. Again, three hoots.

Taliesin stopped on the threshold of the house and raised his eyes. The waning moon was setting, its light sombre, an eerie glow shining through the foliage. He thought how Henwyn or Meriadoc would see the same haunted moon above the mountains of Eryri if they looked into the sky at that moment. In the heavens, amongst the summer stars, time and distance ceased to exist. For a long while he gazed upward, until a movement nearby intruded on his thoughts and made him turn.

Not ten paces in front of him stood a fox, showing no fear. Eyes, innocently wise, met his with a look of.......kinship.   As he looked back, he found peace from his turmoil - conscious only of the vitality of the hunter, of the untroubled spirit that walked lightly on the land.

They stood in silent communication, then the fox scented the air, lowered its head, and loped away through the shadows.

Sitting with Talhaearn outside the hall, Taliesin watched the serving boy, Ieuan, carry a water skin across the clearing. Dew glistened on the ground, and it promised to be another fine day

- a good time for going to Caer Liwelydd, he thought. Tired as he was, he yearned to visit the fortress town which lay so tantalizingly close, to see Urien's stronghold and meet the chieftain famed throughout Ynys Prydein.

Talhaearn laid the pouch of herbs he had been preparing to one side and turned.

'I want you to familiarize yourself with the land at all levels.' Taliesin looked at his master's face, the weathered skin pulled tightly over strong cheekbones, and eyes that reflected light like polished silver. 'To this end we will walk westward towards the coast, journeying by the stream, the lake, the most ancient of trees, seeking contact with the guardians of Rheged, the spirits that will become your allies.......You must also begin to prepare yourself for initiation.'

Inside the building behind them Ieuan dropped something with a clang, followed by a muttered curse.

'Your work until this time has been but a foundation for the true work.'

Taliesin remembered Rhys' panic and shame; and Iddig, who had experienced something so devastating that it sapped his strength and stole his mind.

'You must be ready, free of doubt, when you undergo the ordeal, as Tegai has explained.' Talhaearn paused, his eyes meeting Taliesin's. 'Failure means mental or physical death. Success means you cannot turn back from the path you have chosen. Meditate deeply over the coming week.'

Taliesin inclined his head. 'I understand. But even now I could not turn back. I feel I have not chosen, but been chosen.'

It had become very quiet and Taliesin sensed that Ieuan stood just the other side of the wall, listening. He knew the master must be aware of it too, though he continued to speak as if they were alone.

'Many unexpected doubts arise in the moments before a candidate drinks from the sacred vessel. Do not assume anything. Ceridwen knows the truth.'

'I will meditate.'

Despite his certainty, Taliesin was afraid, but would not show it. He refused to betray any weakness. How many times, he wondered, had Ieuan overheard this same conversation? And how had it ended? Had other apprentices given up? Had any who were unprepared taken the initiation and suffered consequences worse that Iddig's fate? Even silent, sullen Ieuan knew more than he, and he could not ask.

Five men in the robes of master bards formed an inner circle around Taliesin. Beyond, in a second wider ring, stood the younger bards, their apprentices.

Taliesin had fasted since sunset the previous day, and been purified by a ritual bath containing the sacred vervain. Now, clothed in a plain blue tunic with no ornamentation, his fair hair hanging unbound to his shoulders, he appeared young and vulnerable despite his stature.

As the bards began a chant that filled the grove, Talhaearn approached from the west, wearing a robe of seven colours trimmed with gold, and carrying a vessel unlike any Taliesin had seen. Above a silver stem engraved with intertwining plant and animal forms was a bowl of glass so clear, so pure, it refracted a rainbow of light. A silver band inset with pearls shone just below the rim, at the level of the amber liquid it contained, a distillation of herbs that would free the spirit to journey in the Otherworld.

Talhaearn now stood three paces away from Taliesin, the waves of the chant washing over them. Talhaearn's voice harmonized with it, riding its waves.

'Three drops from the sacred cauldron,
the fountain of wisdom.......'

Taliesin reached out his hands and clasped the bowl of the vessel below Talhaearn's, standing motionless as together they sang,

'To taste the waters of knowledge,
to open the eyes that never close,
to die the greater death.'

Slowly, Talhaearn withdrew his hands, and Taliesin raised the vessel, his eyes shining in the reflection of its beauty.

'Without fear,
I loosen the bonds of the physical.
In the realm of spirit,
I am the traveller,
I am the seeker.'

Placing the cool glass to his lips, he took one sip.
'My Lady Ceridwen, all that I am is yours.'
As the chant rose and fell, he drank the remainder of the elixir, light and colour flashing across the vessel's rim, dazzling his eyes. He tasted the sweetness of mead, faint fruit and herb, and a bitterness that lingered on his tongue. In silence, he returned the empty vessel to Talhaearn, who passed it to an apprentice.

A drum-beat had begun to throb, taken up by another and another around the outer circle, which parted for Taliesin and the master to pass through, their steps matched to the rhythm. Bells suspended from silver branches in the elder bards' hands sent out ripples of sound as they followed, the outer circle reforming behind them, chanting and drumming still.

The procession left the shelter of the wood, making its way in a south-easterly sweep across open country barred by long shadows. Before long, Taliesin noticed that the dying light had taken on a strange brightness, burning like the rays from the sacred cup. Even the shadows had begun to glow with luminous colour. The back of his tongue, where the taste of the elixir lingered, felt numb, and the scattered chimes of the bells became amplified, their music creating shimmering waves across the land.

Ahead, Taliesin saw a rise crowned by an oak, its roots and lower trunk twisted into the semblance of steps. Barefoot, he crossed the turf and began to climb, the feel of rough bark against the soles of his feet rasping through his body, filling his head. He climbed higher and higher, gripping gnarled branches, only half aware of the bards who gathered at the base of the tree, intoning the chant of air.

The ground far below him, Taliesin crouched between two boughs. As day died in the west, he turned to the east, and, through leaves that trembled with the sound of bells, watched a speck that appeared on the horizon. It grew larger, gliding nearer, taking on the visible appearance of a hawk. The bird swooped towards the tree, circling before perching on the topmost branch. Its eyes gleamed like red jewels, its wings were of gold and silver.

'Higher, higher,' it called. 'Climb higher and I will teach you.'

Taliesin gripped the branch above and stood to his full height, searching for a foothold in a bewildering maze of boughs criss-crossed by pathways of streaming light. As his hold tightened, he felt the branch give, and reeled dizzily. His heart pounding, he lowered himself back down to safety, trying to stay calm, to re-gain some control.

He could still hear the hawk crying out, 'Higher, higher.'

It seemed to be mocking him.

He paused, listening to the chant of the bards, seeking strength. He knew he must try again. He must not surrender to doubt. And once more he began to climb, testing each branch before trusting his weight to it. When he could go no further, he found himself facing a man in a cloak of birds' feathers and wearing a cap fronted by a hawk's beak, his eyes shining with inner luminosity.

Raising his arms, the man held his head high, emitting the screech of a bird. Great currents of air answered the call, spinning the clouds into a whirling mist, whipping the wind into a gale that tore at the ancient branches. Sick and unsteady, Taliesin heard the creaking of timbers and cried out, fearing he would be flung to the earth. He held fast with aching hands as the boughs thrashed as if trying to be rid of the parasite that clung to them. The wind howled across the land. Still Taliesin held fast, though he felt his hands beginning to slip. The branch shook, again loosening his grip. As he tried in vain to get a firmer hold, the hawk-man lowered his arms, and with a final shrill note dismissed the wind.

It was then that Taliesin realized who stood before him.

'My Lord Gwydion,' he whispered.

The lord of enchantment touched him on the shoulder, and he found himself balanced on the branch with ease, plumage covering his body and wings. Joyfully, he spread those wings, feathers ruffling. He felt the air's caress, then folded them over his back again.

Gwydion laughed. 'Fly. Or do you not trust yourself? ......Fly......fly.'

Once more, Taliesin spread his wings, rising off the branch, touching it with taloned feet, rising again. Then he swooped downward in an instant of ecstatic freedom.

The shock as he hit the ground stunned him, though the turf cushioned his landing. He remained crouched for a moment, regaining his breath, waiting for the pain in his legs to subside, then cautiously got to his feet. Through a blaze of fiercely beautiful colour he looked at Talhaearn. He longed to speak, to tell the master of his experiences, but could find no words. Only a wordless memory instructed him that he must continue towards the south.

He was unsure if he was walking, or gliding above the ground, carried by the sound of bells. His head floated and movement was effortless. It was not until the silver sound fell silent that he stopped and looked back, seeing that he was surrounded by a company with human bodies and the heads of animals. Closest to him, a wolf stared through the gathering darkness, the other animals seeming to answer to its command: the stag, the badger, the boar, the hare and the mountain cat. Breaking down like patterns in a mist, they returned to human form, each crowned with light that emitted rays of colour. The man who had appeared wolf-headed wore the largest crown, dazzling in its brilliance.......and he had the face of Talhaearn Tad Awen.

Branches had already been laid in a cleared area of ground, piled into a cone. Talhaearn crouched beside it, kindling a flame which caught hold of the lower twigs, crackling them into life. He sat down cross-legged to one side of the fire and motioned for Taliesin to sit opposite him, the other bards completing the circle.

Through the smoke haze, Taliesin looked at his master, until he felt compelled to gaze down into the flames. There he saw a battle being waged, swords of fire plunged into the hearts of warriors with golden torcs flashing at their throats, hands and bodies of shimmering heat. He found himself at the centre of the battle, but experienced no pain, only burning inspiration. The power of his verse directed the movement of the warriors, filling them with courage. Their bodies formed the body of a red dragon: flames, scales, warriors, himself - all one. In opposition, a white dragon fought with teeth of iron, slowly retreating into the bleached ashes at the edge of the battle, driven back by the growing size and power of the red dragon that rose like the sun from the Underworld, yet remained eternally as one with the people of Ynys Prydein.

'Do you know me, son?'

Taliesin stood in the midst of the blaze, which had become a beacon lit on the heights at Calan Mai in honour of Beli Mawr, solar lord of life and death. Awed and bewildered, only half-comprehending, he inclined his head, the fiery breath of Beli pouring into him, saturating him. At the point when he could take no more, the brilliance began to diminish and his eyes re-focussed on white hot coals, his ears echoing to the fire chant which spilled from the mouths of the bards. On the far side of the coals, his master rose, gaunt face illuminated by the glow, and beckoned to him. Taliesin rose too. Knowing that he had stood safely amongst the roaring flames, been made one with them, confidently he placed his bare foot on the coals. Unflinching, with steady, even steps he began to walk across them, focussing only on Talhaearn.

As he reached safe ground the chant rose to a crescendo, but Taliesin did not pause to rest. Energized by an inner fire, he headed towards the north-west, seeing more clearly than ever before, having no need of a torch to guide him over the darkened land. Each tree, each leaf, each blade of grass glowed with life. And he knew himself to be part of the pattern, linked to all things like the engraved interlace on a brooch or ring.

The bards walked with Taliesin until they came to the shores of the lake, a place familiar from his expeditions with Talhaearn. They had worked there many times. Yet now it seemed alien, ghost-light shimmering across the surface, though the night was moonless. As the bards shook the silver branches, each bell note struck the wavelets as a spark, and the chant of water began. Standing beside Talhaearn, Taliesin waited, eyes lowered, reading the aeons of the universe in still depths until he was uncertain whether he looked down or up into the skies. Though no word was spoken, he knew what he must do.

The cold water became the music of bells, liquid ringing, welcoming him with each step, gently drawing him in until he stood chest deep. He stopped and inhaled, poised between two worlds, enamel blue and silver-flecked. Then he dived, taking on salmon form, a form worn more easily than his human shape. He felt that had been his first, his true identity, that the body of Taliesin was merely a disguise.

Deeper and deeper he swam, further and further from the shore, through worlds of dark knowledge, scales polished by ethereal light. He reached the bottom of the lake, the oldest time, touching existence from the beginning to the end of creation. It was only when he started to rise that a crippling weakness gripped him. All beauty and wonder were gone. His vision throbbed grey and black, and he barely had the strength to propel himself upward.

Green voices echoed, 'Stay and sleep. Why fight? Why return? This is the place you belong, your home.'

He longed to surrender, to sink back into the depths and find peace. But a faint, insistent chant encouraged him to struggle on, until at last he felt the summer breeze on his cheeks, as fins stretched into arms, tail into human legs.

Taking a gulp of air, he coughed, almost submerging once more. He could see figures on the shore, six figures. For a moment they became twelve, then six again. Far away. With the remainder of his energy he began to swim, fighting the weakness. After a time that seemed eternal he stopped, a tightness in his chest. In desperation he looked up, near enough now to see Talhaearn, his face grim. Taliesin felt the power of his master's will, urging him to continue, and with an effort he managed to swim again, each stroke more painful than the last. His limbs became leaden, too heavy to move. Finally, as his leg muscles cramped, he reached for a clump of reeds and managed to haul himself from the lake. Exhausted, he collapsed at the water's edge, though no one stepped forward to assist him. Only the unbroken chant reminded him that he was not alone.

Lying amongst the reeds, he watched the dance of their life; beneath him he felt the strength of the earth. Eventually, he struggled to his knees, then to his feet, shivering in the mild night. Only by walking again, more slowly than on the previous arc, did he feel his blood begin to circulate, bringing some warmth to his limbs. Each step brought him nearer to the security of the grove, but also nearer to the final ordeal. Through the continuing assault on his senses, he felt a moment's terror. This would be the end. Would it also be the beginning?

When he reached the cairn, he saw a figure standing to either side of the stone-lined hollow leading to its interior. Like the mouth of a predator. Taliesin shuddered and stopped. And at that moment one of the figures moved - a tall heavily built man, robed in black, and masked.

The other man moved too, both lifting the cloak that lay at the threshold. They draped it over Taliesin's shoulders, then stepped aside for him to pass, stooping to enter the low, narrow portal. He thought of neither past nor future, but simply walked, while the chant of earth rose behind him.

Slowly placing one bare foot before the other, he continued deeper into a living darkness peopled with spirit forms that were one with it. Moving forward, time and space uncertain, Taliesin registered the distant sound of stone scraping against stone, and he knew the entrance to the cairn had been sealed, entombing him with the bones of the ancestors, the reassuring chant that had linked him to the world of everyday reality silenced.

Wrapping his body in the cloak, he lay down at the far end of the passage, drawing into himself, flesh holding bones like a husk, the husk of a wheat grain. A small rounded seed containing all potential.

As he waited, a screeching filled the hollow, a flapping of wings in the blackness. Taliesin shook with fear, knowing there was nowhere to hide or flee. He could only lie on the earth, motionless - a grain of wheat that was swallowed, slipping toward the belly of the black hen, of Ceridwen the devourer.

He plummeted downwards, spinning, until the falling ended in a place of warmth and softness, its walls blood red. The wall nearest to him rippled and bulged. He stared, horrified but entranced, then gave a start as a raven burst through. It dived at him, and instinctively he raised an arm to protect his eyes. He felt a hot, sharp pain as the bird's beak pierced his flesh just over the heart, tearing at it. There were other ravens now, beaks slashing deep as daggers, rending skin from bone, ripping muscle, devouring him as they devoured corpses on the field of battle. He screamed and thrashed, mad with agony, helpless to save himself. The arm he held up crumbled away, and one by one the ravens plucked his eyes like ripe berries.

Attracted by the flesh that fell from his body, a sow rooted on the ground, consuming each morsel while the ravens pecked his bones clean, pure white and gleaming. White against red. The ravens tore his heart from his breast, and, as they fought for it, it fell in front of the sow, who swallowed it whole, still beating with the rhythm of an unheard drum.

The pain had subsided as the terror of emptiness grew, worse than all that had gone before. Would he continue in eternity with nothing but despair? Alone in a void? Again Taliesin cried out.

His cry was answered by a whisper.

'I am here.'

Standing beside a cauldron with pearls about its rim, Ceridwen waved a hand towards the scavenging birds.

'Be gone, your work is done.'

As the dry rustling of wings grew fainter, the white sow

began to shift shape, becoming a wraith, merging into the form of the goddess until she and it were one.

Ceridwen reached her hands into the cauldron, then laid them over Taliesin's bleached skeleton, her fingers moving like a craftsman's working the clay of the earth. She sang softly as she moulded flesh and sinew over the bones, flesh that shone like silver and gold. The blood that she chanted into his veins was the sap of the hazel tree, his heart was of oak, his eyes bright jewels. Eyes that saw with new clarity.

She bent over him, cool lips brushing his forehead, her breath the freshness of summer rains.

'Radiant Brow, now you have truly earned your name.'

The sound and scent of her lingered as her image faded. Taliesin rose easily from the ground where he had fallen, renewed and strong. Rejoicing in the power of his new self, at first he did not see how the pulsing walls were contracting, closing in around him. When he noticed, they were but ten paces distant. Five paces. An arm's length.

With a confidence that Ceridwen would not allow him to perish now, he sought the passage, to find that, too, had shrunk. Almost too small to contain him. Yet there was no other way out, no time to think. With a silent prayer, he began to force his way through, scarcely able to breathe, the pressure tightening around his body, moment by moment. Arms pinned helplessly to his sides, he used his legs to propel himself forward, painfully slowly, immersed in darkness.

At last the pressure eased a little, his arms were freed so he could move more rapidly, and a sphere of light appeared ahead, drawing him towards it. Hands clutching the sides of the passage, he crawled out, staring blankly at the light, so brilliant it seemed that he looked at the midday sun.

As he waited, it became less dazzling and he noticed silhouetted figures moving against it. Feeling a longing for human company, Taliesin got to his feet, so unsteady he could barely stand. The ground rocked beneath him and his stomach heaved, but he began to walk, the stony walls that he used to keep himself upright grazing his hands until they bled. The short distance to the entrance of the cairn seemed longer than the journey from Gwynedd to Rheged. One agonized step after another, forcing himself onwards until at last he made his way out into the open air.

He leant against the portal stone, gazing at the wiry man facing him, for a moment not recognizing him.

'Taliesin, we must return to the circle.'

But when he tried to take a step he stumbled, a sickening pain in his head, and he doubled over, retching emptily. For a long while he was unable to straighten his body from where he crouched, eyes tightly closed.

The sound of his name being spoken again with calm authority finally roused him, and Taliesin found that he could stand without falling or losing consciousness. He paused, getting his balance, and looking at Talhaearn and the five bards with him, saw an expression of relief, joy even, in their tired faces.

In the pre-dawn light the land stretched in front of him, fresh and peaceful, the land he knew. He walked to the music of the silver branches carried by the bards, aware of the sound made by his own soft footfalls, bare feet moving over dew wet grass. The light was growing in the eastern sky. One foot in front of the other, over and over. Bells chiming. The distant rhythm of drums, the beat becoming clearer, matching the beat of his own heart, his own steps. Vibrating through the air, pulsing with the earth........The horizon glowed golden.

The drum beat quickened as the seven entered the woodland shade. Conquering his exhaustion, Taliesin's pace increased, exhilaration flowing through him. The circle of bards came into view between the trees, their chant rising on a note of welcome and celebration, blending with a chorus of dawn birdsong.

The circle parted, the chant ecstatic now. And, as Taliesin stepped within it, the first rays of the rising sun flooded the grove with light. He stood at the centre of a double ring, feeling safe and nourished, seeing the bright web that linked each of the bards to each other and to himself.

chapter two

Taliesin remained in the darkness of the roundhouse, though outside the sun shone high and clear. Every muscle in his body ached, and his stomach turned. He sat on the edge of the bed retching, then leant forward with his head in his hands, feeling too ill to move.

At first he ignored the sound of the door being opened, but when he eventually looked up he saw Ieuan standing a few paces away, a wooden cup in his hand and a knowing smirk on his broad face. Fighting the pain and nausea, Taliesin faced him.

'Why do you stare like a fool?' he demanded. 'Have you nothing better to do?'

'I have been instructed to bring you this. You look as if you have need of it.'

Ieuan continued smirking as he handed Taliesin the cup, then walked slowly out into the clearing, whistling a tune.

As the door shut behind him, Taliesin sighed, wanting nothing but solitude and darkness. He could not find the energy to think about what he had been through, to re-live the experiences, and could scarcely believe that he had survived, in body and mind, that he was an initiate.

He looked with disgust at the potion he had been given and took a sip. It was an effort to drink the rest, but he forced himself to drain the cup. Then, putting it aside, he lay back on the bed, soon drifting into a fitful sleep.

Alban Hefin had passed in a solitary rite with Talhaearn, and, though the days were not yet noticeably shorter, the sun's energy was waning, the starry Caer Arianrhod sinking below the horizon. But still Taliesin had not been taken to Caer Liwelydd.

From a hill near Talhaearn's settlement he could see the waters of Merin Rheged to the west and the wall winding threadlike across the country, an epitaph to Roman power, long since dead. Like a rectangular bead on that thread, the great fortress town, centre of the north, was just visible, dark against the green of the land. Each day it seemed less real, less substantial, as if it might fade from sight like the illusions created by Gwydion in the bardic tales. And not only had Taliesin been kept from Caer Liwelydd. Apart from Ieuan, who did menial tasks for Talhaearn and returned to his family each night, and the occasional traveller or cattle-herder, he had seen no one except his master since his initiation.

Talhaearn often left the settlement for long periods, never saying where he was going. Taliesin's intuition told him not to suggest accompanying the bard, though several times he had been tempted to ride to the town when Talhaearn had headed in the opposite direction. But each time, he heard Cadfarch's voice, 'You do as you please without a thought for the consequences.' Then he felt angry with himself, knowing that he should have matured enough, experienced enough, to be patient, not to foolishly defy Talhaearn.

Above them the sky reached unbroken from horizon to horizon, like an upturned cup, overhead the clearest blue, though in the far distance clouds were banked in layers of grey and white. The land hummed with summer, and there was no road, no path, no reminder of human-kind within sight.

Taliesin sat cross-legged beside the Pen Beirdd, relaxed but straight-backed, the blue spiral tattoos that swirled from wrist to elbow like those of his master - the mark of initiation.

Talhaearn held up a lean hand, briefly tracing a sign on his palm, then with rapid gestures touched the ends and joints of the fingers on his left hand with the forefinger of his right.

Conversing in the Secret Language of the Bards, Taliesin soon became oblivious to the lowing of cattle, to the bees in the clover around him. With his inner eye he soared above Merin Rheged, before diving into the waters, swimming through the waters, around the three sacred fountains of Manawyddan's kingdom, the streams of enlightenment from the head of the serpent. His vision flowed with the River Idon into the marsh amongst wading birds seeking food between the reeds; he glimpsed three cranes by the lake: black, white and red; a dark-haired woman walked the ridge to the cairn. Its stones were transparent like Roman glass, revealing the underground passage and chamber where the bones of the ancestors lay. The woman sat above them, silently waiting, her face towards the great wall.

When Talhaearn made the closing sign, Taliesin raised his own hands, barely conscious of the movement of his fingers as he watched foam-haired riders appear from the sea, mounted on white steeds. Over the wall came small dark men and women shouting the war cry, spears flashing; from the south came proud, pale-skinned warriors. And the woman on the cairn smiled. The earth opened and she merged with it, energy flowing out through the land like blood filling its veins, the serpent lines.

Taliesin shuddered despite the heat, and his vision cleared, focussing on a bee that hovered over a clover blossom. He raised his forefinger to his lips in the closing sign, and met his master's eyes.

'Yes, all things are one. There is no separation.' Talhaearn handed him a leather flask of water.

Sitting still and silent, the Pen Beirdd looked out to the horizon, following the flight of a bird with the eye of one who knows its inner meaning.

His voice was low and even when he finally spoke. 'You told me you are concerned about your failure to control the spirit fire.'

Taliesin nodded, suddenly self-conscious.

'My master Cadfarch showed me how to ground it through sacred breath and vision. I thought I had succeeded until......' He stopped, troubled by the memory of his confrontation with Iddig.

'I need no examples. The extent of your power is clear to me, and has been from the time Tegai first brought you to me. Of course you must ensure that you have the skill not to unwittingly unleash dangerous energies. But you must also learn to summon such energies at will, to direct, not dissipate them.'

Taliesin was startled, but said nothing. Cadfarch and Tegai had only ever encouraged inspiration and the pursuit of wisdom. His heart had begun to pound feverishly in fear and exhilaration. Then Talhaearn laughed.

'You did not come to me to learn harp playing!'

Still, Taliesin did not speak.

'I know you want to use your powers. All the sacred arts can heal......or harm. The gifts of Ceridwen must be employed as she intends. You are her instrument, her staff, her sword. And our people are at war.'

Did Talhaearn read his mind? Or simply his face, the language of his body?

'That is why she spared me,' Taliesin replied softly. 'Twice.'

Sunlight shone through the open door to Taliesin's roundhouse, where he sat on the ground, crushing herbs that were recently dry and blending them with measures from the jars scattered in a careless semi-circle around him. He stopped when a shadow fell across the threshold, and looked up.

Talhaearn was clothed in an embroidered linen robe, his

cloak of indigo fastened with a silver brooch. The light that framed his figure reminded Taliesin of the radiance he had often seen surrounding his master when they were meditating together, times when there had been no sun. To him, Talhaearn needed no outer symbols of power. Robes and regalia were the language needed to speak to those without spirit sight.

'That can wait,' the bard said briskly. 'Tidy yourself. We are going to Caer Liwelydd.'

Taliesin inclined his head and laid the wooden pestle down, feeling none of the thrill he had expected to feel at such news. It had been so long, he had locked away all thought of Urien's hall, its feasts and heroic warriors. The anticipation he had first felt had waned as day followed night in isolation. And now, when he was at last to visit Caer Liwelydd, his excitement had lost its edge and he felt cheated.

Talhaearn no longer stood in the doorway when Taliesin got to his feet. He looked at his dusty, grass-stained tunic and breeches, and rubbed a hand across the bristles on his chin. Fine appearances were another thing that had drifted further from his thoughts as the days of summer passed.

After shaving, and washing in a basin of water, he put on the new tunic Eilonwy had sewn for him last winter. Then he had laughed because it was too long, now it barely fitted, and at sixteen he was tall as any man he knew. Finally, he untangled his hair and bound it in the same manner as Talhaearn's, in a single braid, cross-tied with a strip of leather.

With their backs to the sun, master and apprentice rode away from the deepening shadows of the woodland, guiding their horses along narrow tracks until they joined the main road to Caer Liwelydd. After all the times he had gazed at it from a distance, Taliesin was awed by the size of the town as they entered the gates. Houses of wood and stone lined roads laid out in grid formation, the legacy of its birth - a native settlement, founded beside a Roman fort on the wall built to hold back the Pictish tribes to the north. The more recent buildings did not follow the symmetrical plan so neatly, some straddled the road, others were set at crooked angles, and the old paving had become uneven and rutted. The place buzzed with life: craftsmen at work in forecourts, women carrying baskets and jars of water, warriors on horseback, dogs barking, children playing.......

Taliesin found the noise and bustle overwhelming, his senses assaulted. Everything was amplified, exaggerated. He stilled his thoughts, concentrating on his breath, building up a protective shield around himself. And when Talhaearn turned to him, he knew that his master saw the barrier. He knew also that this, like all things, had a purpose - to test and challenge his inner strength.

Within the courtyard of the royal hall, a groom took their horses as Taliesin watched a fine-featured youth in a blue tunic stride towards them.

'Ah, Ysfael.' Talhaearn seemed relieved to see him, and, responding to his look of curiosity, said, 'This is Taliesin ap Elffin.' He indicated the other boy. 'Ysfael has been studying with me for the past year. He will show you round and tell you all you need to know.'

Taliesin nodded greetings to the youth, who appeared stiff and haughty, then accompanied him towards the guest quarters.

'The king has just returned to Caer Liwelydd,' Ysfael said, 'from raiding over the border in Manaw. Brought back some prize cattle. So tonight we feast in triumph.' He paused, a knowing expression in his eyes. 'And the master will be entertaining the company.'

It was late the following morning when Ysfael and Taliesin struggled from their beds, Taliesin's head aching and his mouth parched, though he had drunk only half the amount he used to in Deganwy. Yet his memory of Urien was clear: the bull-like shoulders and heavy brow, dark hair braided at the temples in the warrior style of the golden age before Roman occupation. There had been no lady at his side, but his eldest son Owain sat with the king. Urien's wife, a noblewoman of Gwynedd, had died many years earlier and he had not remarried.

Then, Taliesin recalled the frightening power of Talhaearn's performance. Through his voice, the divine spirit of the land called to her people, inflaming, empowering them to fight and win. He had also spoken the praises of his royal patron, the names and deeds of his ancestors, the root of Rheged's strength.

After a meal of oakcakes, cheese and a little cold beef Taliesin felt less queasy and resolved to make the most of his time in Caer Liwelydd, not knowing how long it would be before he would next visit the town. He and Ysfael were walking towards the road when a group of richly clad youths came from the hall, laughing and bragging. Amongst them Taliesin recognized Owain, swarthy and black-haired like his father.

When the prince saw Ysfael, he stopped and grinned. 'We've been searching for you, the day is half gone. Too much wine?'

The others laughed. But despite Owain's easy confidence, Taliesin noticed the depth of the eyes that glanced in his direction. 'Who is your comrade?'

'Taliesin ap Elffin from Gwynedd. He has come here to train under Master Talhaearn.'

'I heard that the master had taken a new apprentice by the name of Taliesin. Are you enjoying our hospitality?' Owain's voice was strong and proud.

'There's none better.'

'And now you are suffering for it. But I know a cure.

Come swimming with us in the river.'

The group went on foot, Owain at Taliesin's side. As they left the courtyard a full-figured girl carrying a basket crossed their path. She shook her light brown curls over her shoulder and smiled at Owain, who winked back at her. Then they swept on through the crowded streets, Owain exchanging greetings with his father's warriors, while the common people made way.

Once they were beyond the gates, the youths started running, Taliesin glad to escape the pressure of the crowds and Owain's probing questions. He felt free, steadied by the earth beneath his feet, cleansed by the wind blowing in from Merin Rheged. And ahead of them lay the river, its waters dancing in the sunlight. The group raced down a gentle slope, then flung themselves onto the grass, catching their breath.

Owain laughed with his companions as he stretched his legs, then he looked at Taliesin and pointed below them. 'See that flat stone? Excellent for diving.'

He handed Taliesin a decorated flask of the finest wine, but Taliesin had no taste for it that day and drank sparingly before passing it to Ysfael. Turning back to Owain, he forced himself to ask the question that had troubled him since he arrived at Caer Liwelydd.

'Do you know a youth named Myrddin ap Madoc?' he said.

'I know him, yes, but he is no longer here. He went back to Dyfed in the spring. Why?'

Taliesin feigned nonchalance. 'One of his kin told me he was living in the town. I thought perhaps to hear him sing.'

He looked out over the river, listening to the rhythm of wavelets splashing against the side of the diving stone, relieved that he would not have to face Gwenddydd's brother. Though the other youths were his own age, they seemed young and over loud. But he felt contented, away from Talhaearn's all-seeing eyes, for once able to relax and laugh.

Owain dropped the empty flask onto the ground and unstrapped his dagger belt, throwing it down beside the flask, then leapt to his feet.

'We are here to swim!'

Following his lead, his companions pulled off their tunics and breeches, leaving them scattered in a bright array on the grass, and ran naked towards the river. Owain dived first, his body slicing the water's surface, making scarcely a ripple. Taliesin was next to step onto the warm stone, feeling the pull of the river, a craving in his blood drawing him towards its depths. As he dived, the chill of the water hit him, a jarring shock, then exhilaration.

He surfaced close to the prince, shaking wet hair from his eyes.

'Race you to those reeds,' he said.

Owain waited for the others. 'The winner gets my dagger. If I win, Taliesin and Ysfael must sing a heroic song for me tonight.'

Taliesin began the race swimming underwater, making swift progress, eyes open, noticing the play of light above him. When he emerged he was already ahead, and though the others were now gaining on him, he managed to hold the lead until he reached the reed bed.

'Fine swim.' A large red-haired youth clapped him on the shoulder.

'The dagger is yours.'

Taliesin turned to Owain. 'And the heroic song is yours.'

They began to swim again, and again Taliesin dived, going deeper than before, weaving easily between trailing weeds, seeing the life-energy surrounding them, then moving out into the central channel. The water felt smooth around his body, his natural element. He no longer had legs and arms, but salmon tail and fins. There was no effort, only freedom. His thoughts focussed on the life of the river, on the cool flowing currents, outside time.

Eventually, he skimmed upward, startled by shimmers of sunlight, his lungs suddenly aching for want of air. He surfaced and took a long breath, feeling drunk and wild, more drunk than at the previous night's feast. He could see the others a long distance away, staring at him. Owain's face was very pale.

'Thank God.' He began swimming towards Taliesin with powerful strokes.

Taliesin watched in bewilderment, wondering what was amiss. How could anything be wrong when each breath of air felt like an elixir flowing through his body? His flesh tingled, and every pulse beat as one with the rippling currents.

Owain reached him and laughed with relief. 'I feared I'd have to explain the loss of his chosen apprentice to the Master Talhaearn.' He hesitated, awe in his eyes. 'I did not think it possible for a man to hold his breath under water so long.' Then he grinned. 'You owe me that song!'

Taliesin grinned back, and together they clambered up the bank, warmed by the sun.

'Who has a flask of wine?' Owain called brightly. 'Let us have more wine.'

chapter three

The day was hazy and hot. Taliesin sat back against a grassy hillock, shaded from the sun, and was drifting between dream and waking when he heard a woman's voice. At first he thought the voice was in his own mind, then it came again, sharper, more urgent.

'Cybi.......Cybi......you little........Come here now. Now! Where by the saints are you? Cybi........Cybi.'

Taliesin opened his eyes and sat up, dazzled by the brightness. When his vision adjusted he saw a young woman walking in his direction, looking anxiously to either side, her tangle of curls catching the light as she turned. He thought she seemed familiar. Then he remembered she was the girl Owain had winked at in Caer Liwelydd. She wore a plain dress, dusty and faded, and as she drew nearer he noticed that her feet were bare. For a second she seemed unnerved by his presence, then called out a greeting.

'I'm sorry to trouble you,' she said, coming to a halt several paces away, 'but have you seen a child? I have lost my little brother.'

Taliesin shook his head. 'I've seen no one......How old is he?'

'Only three.'

He smiled reassuringly. 'Someone so small cannot have gone far.'

'I fear Cybi could. I must have been dozing, and he wandered off.'

'No doubt he is simply hiding.' Taliesin looked round, then back at the girl's sun-bronzed face. 'We'll soon find him.'

'What if he has fallen in a ditch? Or tripped and knocked his head on a stone, or........'

Taliesin raised a brow. 'Are you always so optimistic?'

The girl sighed and gave a reluctant smile, then started to walk, glancing over her shoulder as if she expected Taliesin to follow. Instead, he moved to the top of the hillock where he was more clearly visible, and sat down again, producing a bone pipe from the pouch at his belt.

The girl stopped with a look of exasperation, but Taliesin had already begun to play - a tune that filled the balmy air, carrying far in the stillness. After a moment's uncertainty the girl knelt near him, tense and alert. Once more she searched for any sign of Cybi, and before long saw him running through the grass. She relaxed, but remained seated, listening as Taliesin played, the tune so intoxicating that she did not want it to end.

As Cybi got closer he slowed to a walk, ambling nearer, slower and slower, until he stopped opposite Taliesin, watching him with round blue eyes. He stood unusually quiet, paying no heed to his elder sister.

Eventually, Taliesin lowered the pipe and looked back at the child.

Cybi sucked his lip and pulled at the side of his crumpled tunic, then took a deep breath. 'Are you an angel from Heaven?'

The girl threw her head back and laughed, but Taliesin continued looking into the child's eyes.

'No, I'm afraid not. I come from the kingdom of Gwynedd, many day's ride in that direction.' He pointed with the pipe before beginning another tune, and again Cybi chewed his lip, listening intently. When the tune ended, Taliesin spoke softly to him. 'If I were to give you this magical pipe, would you be good from now on and do as your sister tells you?'

The round eyes became yet rounder, then Cybi nodded wildly.

'Here you are then.' Taliesin handed him the pipe, and he blew a shrill discordant note, jumping with delight.

'Say thank you,' his sister prompted, still laughing.

But, instantly forgetting his promise, Cybi began running away. The girl got to her feet to give chase, and took him firmly by the hand. Taliesin strolled after them, falling into step beside her. She was tall, with a womanly figure, unlike Gwenddydd's girlish slenderness, and her expression was bold, worldly. But he felt no awkwardness with her.

'I think I should say thank you, even if Cybi will not.' She held on to the struggling boy.

'I had nothing better to do than charm a child out of the undergrowth.'

The girl met Taliesin's eyes. 'I'm Mair. My father's a bondman who farms in the valley. We came out a long way from our dwelling today. I dislike straying too close to Pen Beirdd Talhaearn's settlement. Strange things take place there.'

'Do they?' Taliesin remained straight-faced. 'What manner of things?'

'There is talk of unexplained lights and the wailing of spirits. And at night he shape-shifts into the form of a wolf, so people say.'

'I see.'

Mair frowned. 'I think you are laughing at me....... Forgive my questions, but you are Prince Owain's comrade, are you not? Yet you do not seem like a warrior.'

'No.' The corner of Taliesin's mouth curled into a smile. 'I am here to study under Master Talhaearn.'

'I knew you were mocking me......' Mair caught her breath.

'I transform myself into a mouse at sunset.'

'Oh God, when will I learn to hold my tongue? I'm sorry.' Taliesin noticed a momentary look of fear. 'So you're a bard,' the girl continued in an undertone. 'I should have known. I have never heard anyone play the pipe as you did.'

Another shrill blast tore the air.

'I have never heard anyone play the pipe as Cybi does.'

Mair laughed, a full rich laugh, as they walked side by side across the pasture.

'You will have to teach him to play it properly,' she said. 'You have a way with children.'

In the pale dawn light, Taliesin and Ysfael stood with Talhaearn, apart from the crowd which had gathered beside a field of oats ripe for harvest. The gathering looked towards the east, where a rosy glow stained the horizon, then at the man with grizzled hair who waited at the centre of the field, gripping a sickle with both hands, knotted muscle taut on his flexed arms.

The colour in the sky grew brighter, more vibrant. The eyes of the crowd moved from the man to the sky, and back to the man. The light intensified. Finally, a ripple of excitement passed through the gathering as a blood red arc appeared on the horizon.

Standing motionless as the reaper in the field, Rheged's chief bishop watched with the people. Then, stepping forward, Abbot Segnius raised his hands, his voice loud in the silence.

'May God our Father bless what we are about to gather.'

The harvester glanced at Talhaearn, a flicker in his eyes betraying that it was not Segnius to whom he answered. Facing east again, as the sun cleared the horizon he grasped a handful of stalks, slowly raising the sickle. He swung it, severing them with one swift stroke, and, like a warrior at his moment of triumph, held the sheaf up to the sun, the sickle in his hand flashing scarlet so it seemed that the blade was stained with blood.

In his mind Taliesin heard Cadfarch sing,

'Corn falls to the sickle,

between earth and sky,
a life to give life.......'

He recalled the mystery of the sacrificed god, the sacred king, his blood spilt on the land, for the land. And, each year, the great wheel revolved, season vanquished season, death took man and beast, but the spirit lived on, reborn - as the tale of Llew told: the bright lord slain through the betrayal of Blodeuwedd, the wife Gwydion had created for him from spring blossoms,

'Skin, milk white,
speech of honey.'

The harvester turned three times sunwise, beginning to chant the reaping paean, which was taken up by the people. Chanting, men came forward wielding sickles, blades catching the early rays. More joined them, field by field, a wave filling the valley.

Taliesin was not present at the festivities which began after noon. In the remoteness of the grove, with a dozen initiate bards he performed the ancient rites for abundance, rites of earth and sun and seed. He missed the games, and seeing Owain ride with the men who raced the clan's horses into the River Idon for purification.

The contests continued until darkness fell. And as the harvest moon rose, its face so close it seemed to touch the earth, Taliesin and his master joined the assembly of Gwyl Awst gathered on the hillside beyond Caer Liwelydd. A feast was set out in the open, with cakes baked from the first harvest and freshly picked bilberries; with fish, boar and ox, and the finest wine and mead. Urien stood before the assembly, magnificent in a purple cloak fastened with a gold and garnet brooch, a golden torc about his neck, his tunic richly ornamented. To his right stood Owain, clad in scarlet, and to the king's left Abbot Segnius, with his heavily jowled face and hard glistening eye.

The Abbot held his hand over the platter in front of him as he spoke. 'In the name of God, I bless the fruits of the harvest. May he grant us freedom from want. Let us thank the Lord for his bounty.'

Urien inclined his head. Then, tall and proud, he looked out at his people gathered below. 'We have great reason to rejoice and give thanks,' he proclaimed. 'For our children, our clan, our land - a land that will be returned into the hands of the Britons.'

He paused as a cheer rang out across the moonlit hillside.

When it faded, once more he addressed his people. 'There is further cause for celebration. I have received news today that my kinswoman, the Lady Gwenddydd, daughter of Lord Madoc Morfryn of Caerfyrddin, is to wed King Rhydderch of Ystrad Glud - a union of the dynasties of Coel and Dyfnwal.'

Another cheer followed, roaring in Taliesin's ears. His body had turned cold and he felt unsteady. For a moment he had the illusion that Gwenddydd was beside him. It was followed by blinding anger. At her? Himself? Rhydderch? All he knew was that he wanted to cry aloud, to strike out, to escape the pain, somehow.

Yet he stood still and expressionless, surrounded by Urien's bards, the king himself and Prince Owain not ten paces away, the gathering like a human palisade restraining him, while above them the moon, growing in brightness, cast long shadows across the land. With his inner vision Taliesin saw a slender figure walking away between the orchard trees. Walking away from him. But he had chosen bardcraft, he had accepted the trials of Ceridwen, taken her hand. He had believed that the memory of Gwenddydd could no longer move him.

> 'Skin, milk white,
> speech of honey.
> The wife of another.....'

As he forced himself to control his emotions he had begun to shake, not realizing it until Talhaearn leant towards him.

'Taliesin, are you ill?'

'I'm simply.....tired,' he whispered, fearing his voice would crack.

Talhaearn looked at him with concern, but said no more as the feasting began.

Each time the wine jar was offered Taliesin held his cup out to be refilled. He knew that since his initiation he could not tolerate large quantities of wine, but welcomed the pain he would suffer. As the wine jar was offered for a sixth time, Talhaearn waved it away. The Pen Beirdd's voice was dark.

'Think......You cannot sing if you are insensible. And eat something.'

Though Taliesin no longer dreaded Talhaearn's anger, he complied. This was the first time he was to perform before Urien and his warriors, and somewhere in the back of his mind he remembered it was the moment he had anticipated all his life. He took a bite of freshly baked oatcake, sweetened with honey. Yet in his mouth it seemed dry and tasteless. It felt like a lump in his throat when he swallowed, and he drained the remains of his wine, knowing Talhaearn would prevent him from having more until he had performed.

That time did not come for a long while, when the moon was past its zenith and the company growing uncouth. As Taliesin bowed before Urien, he felt dazed but not drunk. Silently he invoked Ceridwen's guidance, then looked at the faces around him. He knew the company would be curious about Talhaearn's new apprentice, but they were only faces, soulless faces.

Singing unaccompanied, he began, staring across infinity, the hollowness inside him gradually filling with the spirit of the Awen.

'Arianrhod of the Spiral Caer,
dawn gives birth to the sun,
the noble son born
in Math's royal hall.

His mother denied him,
bright Llew......'

For an instant Taliesin was distracted, struck by an older pain.

'Three curses, Arianrhod laid:
without name,
without weapons,
without mortal wife.....'

When the song ended, again he felt empty and desolate, not registering the awed silence, scarcely hearing the shouted praise that followed. But he saw that Talhaearn now stood with the king, and knew it was his chance for escape. He returned to his place as Ysfael stepped forward, and waited until attention was no longer on him. Then, slowly he began making his way through the laughing, jostling company, moving further and further from the royal clan.

He continued down the hill onto level ground where the bondmen and common people of the town were celebrating. All he wanted was to be alone, to walk the land, and as he edged through the crowds he lowered his head, cursing his height which made him conspicuous.

The smell of roast ox filled the air, mingling with the odour of ale and sweat. Caught up in the mass of people close to the fire where the carcass turned on a spit, Taliesin watched the dripping fat turn the flames to blue. Then a clear voice called out beside him.

'Taliesin! Why are you not at the king's feast, at the bardic contests?'

He looked down at Mair's upturned face. Her cheeks were flushed and her forehead moist with perspiration. His first reaction was anger at her easy familiarity, the intrusion into his private anguish.

'I've had enough of the feast,' he replied flatly. 'I'm taking a walk.'

He was about to continue when she spoke again, her voice lilting, blending with the pipes and drums as a frenzied dance leapt and spun towards them.

'I'll come with you.'

Suddenly Taliesin knew he could not bear to be alone after all. He felt out of control, afraid of himself. He gave no reply, but did not try to prevent her from following him to where the crowds finally thinned. The music and shouts faded into the distance as they continued walking, heading towards the Idon, along the edge of pastureland where grasses grew tall. Neither spoke.

Only as the river came within sight did Mair break the silence between them.

'I'm tired,' she sighed. 'I've been dancing since dusk.'

Though when Taliesin looked at her, she did not appear tired. Her eyes shone, and she was smiling at him. He sat beside her amongst the grasses, the fading moonlight reflected in her face. Instinctively he touched her cheek, his fingers slowly tracing the curve of her neck, her smooth shoulder. She continued to smile.

Gripping her shoulder more firmly Taliesin pressed his mouth to hers, his pulse beating heavily. Mair reached up, holding him as she let herself fall back with a breathless laugh, pulling him with her. He looked down at her, her eyes brighter still, then his lips were on hers again, his tongue tasting ale and berries.

His hand caressed her thigh, moving higher, beneath her dress. He felt her breathing quicken as she loosened the belt that held his breeches, her other hand in the small of his back, pulling him closer. Taliesin knew for certain then that he was not the first. Not that it mattered. Nothing mattered any more. His heart was pounding, the energy rising in him like liquid fire. Anger and pain transmuted. As the fire filled his loins, his life, strength, energy were drawn to one centre of awareness. Locked in the physical. Then, at the moment of fiercest intensity, he felt his consciousness released, flying into a thousand fragments, more than himself, outside himself. As the sky and the stars, he merged with Mair, the warm body of the earth.

A light drizzle blurred the outline of the trees in the grove as Taliesin stood at the door to his roundhouse, the damp seeping through his clothes, plastering his hair to his temples.

He had last seen Talhaearn standing with Urien at the feast, today he was nowhere in sight. Taliesin assumed his master had ridden from the settlement at dawn, and hoped he would remain absent all day. He could not face doing any work. Yet worse was the thought of being questioned about his behaviour, or why he had left the gathering without explanation.

His head throbbed, and he felt an aching emptiness deep inside. The previous night with Mair seemed strangely unimportant. He had imagined he would feel very different to this. At least she would expect nothing more of him.

It was Gwenddydd, not Mair, who was constantly in his thoughts. She would be marrying a man over twice her age, sharing his bed, bearing his children. In vain, Taliesin tried to blot the knowledge from his mind. The pain in his temples intensified and he felt physically sick. Could he find some way of speaking to her? The idea was madness. He would be risking everything. Achieving nothing.

He turned abruptly, entering the darkness of the hut, where his hand closed around an oak bough propped against the wall. He had found it earlier in the year, intending to make it into a staff in due time. Now was that time.

Frowning in the poor light, a knife in his hand, Taliesin sat on the ground by the door and began to carve, something he had not done since he left Braich y Dinas. He tried not to think, just to keep on carving, directing all his energy into the task. He worked intuitively, with no pattern or plan. And, as the hours passed, sinuous animal forms twisted up the length of the staff. Climbing and descending the pole that linked Upperworld with Underworld, they manifested the shape of Taliesin's emotions - liberating them.

chapter four

Standing at the centre of the grove Taliesin faced his master, noticing the remote metallic light in his eyes.

Talhaearn raised a hand, and exhaled over the three pebbles in his palm before casting them into a cauldron of water. Then softly, almost inaudibly, he began to hum, a vibration deep in his chest. Taliesin echoed the sound, keeping his mind focussed.

As the vibration strengthened, vapour rose from the cauldron, thickening, blocking out the sunlight. The birdsong which had filled the grove was silenced and all movement ceased, a chill stealing the seasonal warmth.

Soon Taliesin could no longer see Talhaearn, but only hear his voice through the gathering mist, through the swirling shapes that rose up amongst the leaves and branches. And, in the gloom, he saw luminous tendrils flow from his own lips, the power of his chant spiralling upward.

Down in the valley the harvesters stopped singing. Some rested their sickles on the ground and exchanged glances, suddenly and inexplicably uneasy, sensing a foreboding of winter though the sky was clear, the late summer sun warm on their skin. Mair took an empty ale flask from her father, who was overseeing the work, and placed it in her reed basket.

'We'll return when the bread is baked,' she said.

She hitched up her skirts, then led her younger sister Megan across the stubble towards the track.

'Do you sense something eerie, Mair? Do you think it's........?' Megan tilted her head in the direction of Talhaearn's settlement, out of sight far beyond the rise.

'I'm certain it's nothing to concern yourself over.'

'You are usually the first to question when such things.......'

Mair cast her a warning glance, but Megan spoke again.

'You never did say where he got that.' She pointed at Cybi, leaping ahead of them waving his new pipe over his head like a trophy. 'He claims that an angel gave it to him, an angel with silver hair and skin.'

Mair laughed, but it rang hollow in her ears. 'He does have a way for telling tales. I think one of the shepherd boys made it.'

And what was Cybi's 'angel' doing now? She shuddered, getting a self-satisfied look from Megan. Angel! Or demon? God, if her father knew what she had done. This time it was not with a youth from the village, who could be compelled to wed her, but with a stranger from another kingdom. She realized that she scarcely knew him. All she really knew was the feel of his body against hers, and the expression in his sea green eyes, eyes that looked as if they had seen things no mortal was meant to see. But, outweighing her anxiety, she felt a sense of triumph, of pride that she had lain with a nobleman. She had that secret to warm her own heart, though she dared not tell her companions or sisters in case word reached her father.

Taliesin felt the chill seep through his flesh, touch his bones. He saw the barrier of light that encircled them as his voice blended with Talhaearn's. Then, as the mist touched the upper branches of the trees, the pitch of the chant altered. Gradually, the swirling forms and chill receded, sucked in towards the cauldron. A haze shimmered in the clearing, a silvery halo above the cauldron, wisps of vapour..........

After a short interval a bird sang a clear note, followed by another, and sunlight dappled the earth at Taliesin's feet. As he steadied himself, he watched Talhaearn raise his staff and bring it down with a thud.

Sensing that all had returned to normal, Taliesin stepped forward and removed the stones from the water, wiping them on the side of his tunic before handing them to Talhaearn.

'That is enough for today.' His master placed the stones in a box of yew wood. 'Tomorrow you alone will raise the druid mist.'

Galloping hooves shook the ground as Taliesin and Owain rode across Urien's land to the north of the Wall. There was a sharpness in the air, heralding the start of autumn, though both horses and riders were hot from exertion. Eventually, they came to a halt overlooking Merin Rheged, the horses blowing steam as they stamped and snorted.

Taliesin gazed at the grey waters, and at the Wall that stretched from west to east, no longer a barrier between kingdoms, recalling the first time he had seen it with mortal sight.

When Owain spoke, he turned.

'Have you heard the news that Ceawlin has finally been acknowledged king of the West Saeson tribes?'

Taliesin nodded. 'Talhaearn told me. And that the Dumnonians have had to fight fiercely to hold them back. Now the foreigners are united amongst themselves they set their sights on our territory again.'

'Of the three battles fought, two have been our victories.'

'I wonder if Glinneu has won glory,' Taliesin said under his breath, almost to himself. 'The last time I saw him, he was soon to leave for Dumnonia.'

Owain straightened in the saddle. 'I envy him. Father insists I am too young to go on the cattle raids into Manaw, or to fight at his side in battle. But soon I will be on the field, my deeds remembered in bardic song.' His eyes were bright. 'Father thinks there will be much action in the spring. Though, as I'll still be only fifteen, I suppose I will be confined here.'

'You'll be fighting years before I'm fully trained or permitted to go anywhere near a battlefield.'

Owain appeared thoughtful. 'It is said that Talhaearn knows secret arts to aid the warriors. Is that so?' He lowered his voice. 'Do you know such arts?'

At first Taliesin gave no reply. In the months since his initiation, he had begun to master a dangerous knowledge he could not discuss with Owain, and with it came the knowledge of what he was capable, which at times filled him with terror. When he did answer, his voice had none of his friend's bravado, but a quiet maturity.

'There are powerful weapons besides sword and spear,' he said. 'When I fight for Ynys Prydein, it will not only be through recounting the deeds of others.'

Owain looked at him with undisguised awe. 'In ancient times no king would address the assembly until his druid had spoken. I understand why. Though, now, most bards do not have Master Talhaearn's druidic power.'

'Most kings do not have your father's power.'

'That is true.' Owain's youthful face was eager. 'Perhaps when I am king you will be my Chief Bard, when the Britons have reclaimed those kingdoms that are ours by right.'

He spoke bravely, but Taliesin felt a twinge of apprehension. Not wanting to risk giving insult, he forced himself to reply before Owain noticed anything amiss.

'Yes.....Perhaps that is our destiny.'

Owain glanced at the dagger at Taliesin's belt, its hilt catching the sunlight. 'I am pleased it is you who wears my dagger,' he said.

* * *

As autumn drew on, Taliesin's training intensified. He was discouraged from going to Caer Liwelydd or from riding with Owain, though on three occasions he had managed to meet Mair while Talhaearn was away. Those meetings - laughing and holding her close, lying with her on the warm earth - anchored him to the world. Her companionship gave him some sense of stability as dimensions merged in a storm of disorientating experiences. But by Calan Gaeaf Talhaearn rarely left their settlement, and Taliesin had had no outside contact for weeks.

On a bitterly cold afternoon he was exercising Gwyn not far from the woodland when he saw Mair approaching, wrapped in a threadbare cloak. He jumped from Gwyn's back, smiling and reaching for her hand.

'Mair, it's good to see you.' He glanced over his shoulder. 'But Talhaearn is in the grove, we may be observed.'

She did not return the smile. 'What does it matter if we are observed? We're simply talking.'

Leading Gwyn, Taliesin began walking beside her. He thought she looked well, and despite the cold her skin had a radiance it had never possessed before. She was almost beautiful.

'How's Cybi?' he asked. 'And Megan?'

'They've nothing to complain of.'

There was a long silence. It seemed odd. Mair was not usually sullen.

'Are you cold?' Taliesin said eventually, reaching out to her again. 'Perhaps we could light a fire to warm ourselves, and......'

'And nothing.'

'What in Heaven's name is the matter with you?' He felt a growing uneasiness. 'Is something wrong at home?'

'At home and everywhere else. At least it soon will be.' Mair stopped and met his eyes. 'I only came here because there is something I must tell you,' she said. 'I should have done so

214

sooner, I suppose, but I hoped I was wrong........that it would all be all right.'

Taliesin frowned, his concern over being seen by Talhaearn replaced by a greater anxiety.

'I haven't had my monthly courses for two moons now.' Mair continued to face him. 'But I had to be certain......I had to……..'

Taliesin felt a shock like diving into the chill waters of the River Idon. 'What! What are you saying?'

'You know very well what I'm saying. I am with child, your child.'

Bewilderment, fear, hope, confusion........There was no point in questioning. She was obviously sure.

'But.......' He struggled for words. 'Oh God......I never thought about.....'

'My father would kill me if he discovered. He would kill you for certain.' Mair's voice faltered. 'But no one will ever know. There's a woman in the town who has skill with herbs. I'll go to her as soon as possible.'

'No!' Taliesin took her arms so violently that she flinched. 'You mustn't. You cannot take the life of an unborn child.'

'It is easy for you.' Mair spat out the words. 'You are not the one who'll have to raise it, to suffer the disgrace, and my family can ill afford another mouth to feed.'

Taliesin felt a sense of desperation, and a pain rooted in his earliest memories. His grip on Mair's arms loosened, though he did not release her.

'We could be married.' His voice was barely audible. 'Then there would be no disgrace.'

Mair stared at him. 'Sometimes, Taliesin, you are so naive. Perhaps it is the result of living alone with a......no matter.' As he stepped back from her Mair spoke again. 'You are from the royal clan of Gwynedd, I am just a bondman's daughter. And you are the apprentice of the Pen Beirdd himself, with a brilliant future. Would you sacrifice that?'

Dismayed by her rationality, Taliesin was unable to curb his emotion. 'You think you have the right to take a life.' He raised his voice. 'Only the gods have that choice.' When he saw the tears welling in her eyes his tone softened. 'I swear I won't let you suffer hardship.'

'But you can't help. You have no money of your own, nothing.'

'Some day I may have.' Taliesin struggled to remain calm. 'Until then I know my family will be understanding.'

'It's hopeless, you are just making false promises.' Mair was shouting at him through her tears. 'When it's too late to...... to.......you'll go back on your word.'

Without replying, Taliesin put his arm around her and drew her close, expecting her to push him away. Instead, she pressed her face against his shoulder, crying bitterly, and an instinctive sense told him that she did not really want to do the thing she suggested.

'Listen, Mair,' he said. 'There's something I've never told you, but if I do then perhaps you'll understand.' They began walking, still pressed close to each other. 'Though you believe I'm of the royal clan of Gwynedd, the truth is that I am of no clan, I may be no more than a bondman's child too. Elffin ap Gwyddno is only my foster-father.'

Mair turned sharply, and wiped her eyes with the corner of her cloak.

'He saved me when I was an infant, after my natural mother rejected me...... She placed me in a coracle and set it adrift out to sea.' Taliesin looked at Mair, his voice hoarse. 'She must have thought like you, once she knew she was carrying an unwanted child. But at least she gave me the chance of life.'

His eyes burned, and his throat ached so he could barely speak. 'Would you deny our child that?'

Mair was shaking. 'It's impossible to imagine that you had

not lived, that we had never met.' She collapsed against him, crying again. 'I must think. I cannot give you an answer now.'

The fire at the centre of Talhaearn's hall pushed the darkness out to the perimeter, amongst the skulls and horns and skins. Outside, fog lay over the land, so dense it was impossible to see from the hall to Taliesin's roundhouse. And with it, the fog brought a stillness from the Otherworld, a thinning of the veil for those who had the knowledge to pass through.

Across his shoulders Talhaearn wore the skin of a wolf, its teeth threaded on a cord around his neck, yellow in the flickering light. Taliesin sat cross-legged opposite him, clothed in his usual long-sleeved woollen tunic and breeches, and over the tunic a fur-lined jerkin to protect against the cold, which even the fire could not banish.

He watched Talhaearn remove the tightly fitting stopper from the vessel in front of him, and on his outstretched palm hold out pieces of fungus, sun-dried and carefully preserved. Red and white, the colours of life and death.

His voice was low. 'From the ancestral darkness into the light of present life, from the light of the present life to the ancestral darkness, sacred time and sacred space combine.'

His eyes met Taliesin's in an unspoken question, and Taliesin nodded. He took what the master offered in silence and, concentrating on his intent, made the declaration.

'Without fear,
I loosen the bonds of the physical.
In the realm of spirit,
I am the traveller,
I am the seeker.'

He placed a piece of fungus on his tongue and chewed,

trying to ignore the musty taste, his attention focussed on the journey ahead. Though for a moment his concentration lapsed. He had not been able to see Mair since she told him her news, because every day Talhaearn watched him like a hawk, driving him mercilessly. And he wondered suddenly if he was about to meet with the soul of his unborn child, denied incarnation. Perhaps he should have confided in Talhaearn, asked to go and see Mair before taking on this ordeal. But it was too late to turn back now, and he would have to face whatever the gods ordained.

As Taliesin finished ingesting the sacred drug, his master repeated the teaching he had heard often before. 'You will encounter helpers and challengers. Be alert, always, take nothing for granted, use your discretion. Danger and glamour are close companions.'

Taliesin listened calmly. And, with Talhaearn, he began to chant a low droning note, a note that filled his body, flowing with his blood.

He lost track of the passage of time as by turns they chanted and meditated, until he began to experience a creeping nausea. The ground lurched beneath him like a coracle in a storm, and relaxation gave way to agitation, his breathing becoming shallow and rapid. From knowledge gained through years of training he worked to control it, fighting back the nausea.

He sat up straight, palms flat on the ground to keep his balance, watching the shadows pulsing, drawing closer and retreating, bringing the skulls and skins with them, grossly enlarged. Then his attention focussed on Talhaearn. His features were blurred, dissolving. Taliesin saw a row of bared fangs. Yellow eyes with slit pupils stared at him. He noticed the grey skin of a wolf, the alert ears, the long jaw, and again the eyes. For a moment his heart beat with sickening speed. Then the face of the wolf again became the face of his master, and the fear subsided.

As Talhaearn threw a handful of dried leaves and berries of nightshade onto the fire, Taliesin heard a hissing voice that seemed to have no source.

'The gateway is open. The journey begins. When you have found your way through, seek me by the whitethorn tree beside the mound.'

Thick smoke rose from the fire and Taliesin watched tendrils of fog seep around the edges of the door, filling the hall. Where the fog hung most densely it guarded a dark entrance.

Though he journeyed to seek the wisdom of the ancestors, as he stepped through the gateway it was a vision of his own descendants that he saw, and in that moment of clarity it seemed that the ancestors and the descendants became one.

chapter five

It had been a cold night, and the clearing was ghostly in the pre-dawn light as Taliesin walked towards the trees.

The winter in Rheged had been the bitterest he could remember, with snowfalls that covered the ground for weeks and biting winds that penetrated through the cracks between the timbers of the hall. Isolated, with snow and ice separating them from life beyond their settlement, he and Talhaearn had missed the Christmas festivities in Caer Liwelydd, bringing a disappointment bitter as the weather.

During the worst of the blizzards Ieuan could not reach them, so Taliesin himself had had to dig a path between the buildings. After journeying in the world of spirit, each day he chopped firewood, to his mind living more like a pauper than the Pen Beirdd's apprentice. Rations dwindled, and as winter dragged on he could scarcely imagine that he would ever be warm again. But beyond all hardship and disappointment lay the knowledge of Mair's decision. They had met before the snows set in, and her promise that she would keep their child filled the short dark days with hope.

Though the tracks were again passable, Taliesin had not seen her since early December. He walked quickly to fight off the cold, wishing he was back in the warmth of his bed, but too restless to sleep. And as he walked, he tried to convince himself that the gnawing unease he felt was caused by nothing more than loneliness and the chill of winter.

When he reached the ridge he stood still and faced east where a faint mist hovered over the horizon, the sky above him lightening to blue. He watched until the sun emerged from the mist, red as the garnet gems on the brooch at his shoulder, remembering another sunrise six moons ago, with the community gathered in the valley beside fields that were now black and unyielding.

The sense of awakening, of new life, was held in the silent moments as the sun rose. It cleared the horizon, red light reflected on frost. Then a dark shape swooped between Taliesin and the skyline, silhouetted in front of the sun. Shaken, he pressed his palms to his eyes, trying to stay calm, to understand.

When he finally looked up, he could no longer see the raven, but he knew it had meaning. Fear that something was amiss with Mair and the child was his first thought, and as if to escape it he began running, back to the still dusky woods, not stopping until his lungs ached.

Later, inside his roundhouse, Taliesin crouched in front of the hearth at its centre. Staring into the embers he tried to use the spirit sight, but found it impossible, the sight barred by anxiety. He tried once more, then stoked the fire into life and sat back, attempting to devise some way that he could speak to Mair. Though there was a risk of discovery, he had to know if all was well. He rejected plan after plan, growing increasingly tense, so deep in concentration that he gave a start when Ieuan entered with a bowl of broth and a dish of oatcakes. The boy placed the food beside him, and was leaving when Taliesin spoke in an undertone.

'I would like you to deliver a message.'

'Whatever you wish.'

'Do you know Mair, eldest daughter of Gruffydd who farms in the vale?'

Ieuan grunted.

Taliesin rose, and went to search for a sprig of dried rowan amongst the plants of power he had gathered. Handing it to Ieuan, he said,

'Give this to Mair. Wait until she comes from the dwelling alone and say nothing more than 'noon tomorrow'. Be certain that no one else sees what you do.'

Ieuan, who had shown little interest until then, was now smirking. The boy's expression irritated Taliesin and he felt his anger kindle. With an effort he managed not to give in to it.

'I'll show my appreciation when I know you've done as I asked.'

'It'll be done.' The smile still hovered on Ieuan's lips as he turned towards the door.

* * *

'I have been in many shapes,
Before I attained a congenial form.
I have been a narrow blade of a sword.......
I have been a drop in the air.
I have been a shining star.
I have been a word........' [6]

Talhaearn nodded, indicating for Taliesin to stop reciting. He exhaled the breath he had taken to complete the verse and looked questioningly at his master. Though he felt none of his usual inspiration, he was sure he had made no error.

Talhaearn met his eyes. 'If you would rather be elsewhere, do not let me detain you.'

Taliesin tensed. So Ieuan had betrayed him. Or did his master read him as he read the stars and the signs of the land?

'Do you think I am completely unaware of your feelings? ' Talhaearn's voice was firm, but not harsh. 'You are clearly in distress. Would you like to tell me what is preying on your mind?'

At first Taliesin simply wanted to get up and leave, saying nothing. How could he possibly admit what had happened? But it could not remain a secret for ever, and he was beginning to find the pressure intolerable. If Talhaearn knew, perhaps it would ease. At least he would not have to make excuses or slip away from the settlement like a fugitive.

In the silence he listened to the crackle of the fire, struggling to put his thoughts into words. None seemed right. Whatever he said, he would appear stupid and reckless. Talhaearn did not hurry him. It was his own sense of urgency, with noon drawing ever closer, that finally made him speak out.

His voice was little more than a whisper. 'In the summer I met the daughter of a bondman. We.....saw each other several times.' For a moment he thought he could not tell Talhaearn after all. That he must invent some lie. Then, scarcely knowing what he was saying, he forced the truth from his lips. 'Now......now she is with child, about six months gone.'

He waited, frozen, remembering when he was a boy at Braich y Dinas expecting the bite of Brother Docmael's cane, the threats of hellfire.

'The gods are uncompromising teachers. Their laws cannot be denied simply by ignoring them.' The calm of Talhaearn's voice only made Taliesin feel worse. Anger would at least have been predictable.

'Who is the girl?' the bard asked.

Once more Taliesin fought to conquer his reticence. 'Mair.......Gruffydd's daughter.'

'I take it he doesn't know who the father of his grandchild is?'

'I haven't seen Mair for a long while. She may have told him.'

'Gruffydd can be a violent man, often in conflict with his neighbours.....Have you thought about what you'll do?'

Taliesin saw only concern on Talhaearn's face.

'I wish to go home and speak with my foster-parents. I've promised Mair that she and the child won't go hungry or want for anything.'

Talhaearn inclined his head. 'I'll arrange for you to pay a

223

visit to Braich y Dinas as soon as possible. Until then I would advise you to keep away from Gruffydd. I doubt he would venture to come here.'

Taliesin paused, afraid to speak but knowing he must.

'I gave Mair a coded message,' he said. 'I have to see her. I've had a sign, and I fear for her.'

'Very well, you'll gain nothing from bardic practice when your thoughts are on other matters.' Talhaearn's tone hardened. 'I have been lenient. However, if your work suffers you will find me less sympathetic. And if you are ever careless in this way again you risk everything.' He gave a gesture of dismissal. 'Now go.'

Taliesin stood, and moved slowly towards the door, wrapping his cloak about his hunched shoulders.

He mounted Gwyn and rode westward through watery sunlight, pressing his heels into the horse's sides. As he galloped across the grazing lands, he knew by the angle of the sun that he was late, that it was already past noon.

The rowan tree beside which he and Mair had met in the last days of summer was concealed by the embankment of an ancient fortification. Dread grew in Taliesin's mind the nearer he came to the place, not wanting to reach it, afraid Mair would not be there, then certain of it. He began to wonder why he had been so open with Talhaearn. If the child was lost no one need ever have known.

He slowed his pace where the land began to rise, then came to a halt. While Gwyn snorted and stamped, fretful after the forced gallop, Taliesin looked at the cloaked figure below him, trying to gather his thoughts.

'Why do you stare so?' Mair called out. 'It was you who sent the message!'

At last the tension eased. Taliesin was glad to be cut by a tongue that was sharp as ever, to see her defiant gaze fixed on him.

'Are you well?' he asked, dismounting and leading Gwyn to where she stood beneath the leafless tree.

'I've never been better, no thanks to you.' To his surprise Mair reached up and touched his cheek. 'You have lost weight, I thought only monks mortified the flesh.' He shrugged and Mair laughed, throwing her cloak open. 'I cannot say the same for myself.'

Taliesin looked at her rounded belly, faced by a reality he could scarcely comprehend. After a winter spent thinking of little else, now he found it hard to believe that his child rested within her body. That in less than three moons he would be a father.

'It seems you have not only lost weight, but your voice as well.' Mair took his hand and placed it against her. 'Here, feel. The little one kicks all the time.'

At first Taliesin felt nothing except the regular rhythm of Mair's breathing and the warmth of her hand over his. Then, a faint stirring. A moment later, a stronger movement. Mair's face was blurred by the tears in his eyes as he smiled at her. She returned the smile, and still clasping his hand kissed him as she used to in the summer. Eventually, she stepped back, her expression anxious.

'Why did you send the message?' she asked.

'I was concerned for you.......both. It has been a harsh winter.' Taliesin spoke tenderly, through his joy remembering the confrontation he must still face. 'Very soon now I'll go to Gwynedd and speak with my family,' he said. 'By the time the child is born you will be provided for.'

Mair sighed. 'Father has been questioning me, but I've told him nothing, and in the end mother asked him to let me be.'

Taliesin looked at her. 'But you do not regret your decision?'

'No, I do not regret it.' From the tone of her voice, he knew she spoke true. 'And I should have trusted you'd keep your word.'

Spring had finally melted the winter frosts, and the door to Taliesin's roundhouse stood open as he bowed his head over his harp, its notes drifting across the settlement.

Talhaearn had ridden to Caer Liwelydd several hours earlier, and though Ieuan was somewhere close by he made no sound. Beyond the music, the woodland was strangely still. No birdsong, no rustle of wind. Though Taliesin knew that Mair and the child were safe, he was often plagued by a fear that would strike without reason, a fear which haunted him that morning.

He began to sing, stumbled over the words of the refrain, and began again. But his spirit was unable to resonate with the music, leaving him detached and unmoved. With a sigh, he stopped playing, questioning whether he should go out onto the land, take time to think away from the confines of the settlement. But, though Talhaearn had given him more freedom recently, the workload had not lightened. And he knew he must prove his dedication, now more than ever.

Reluctantly, he resumed his practice, and was beginning to find inspiration, to bring the song to life, when he heard the sound of hoof beats in the clearing, followed by Talhaearn calling for Ieuan. Moments later he glanced up to find the boy standing by the door.

'The master wants to see you in the hall,' he said curtly.

'Now?' Taliesin wondered why Talhaearn was sending for him when they had arranged to work in the grove at noon.

'I'm only repeating the message.'

As he placed his harp to one side and rose, Taliesin felt apprehensive. Was Talhaearn less accepting over Mair than he first seemed? Or perhaps Gruffydd had discovered who was responsible for his daughter's condition and had threatened violence.

In the hall, he found Talhaearn at the hearthside. There was no fire, only smouldering embers, but he had not summoned Ieuan to lay more wood nor to bring refreshment after his journey.

'Will you sit down,' he said in a low voice.

The apprehension Taliesin felt turned to fear when he looked at the master's face, seeing the gravity of his expression.

Talhaearn waited until he was seated.

'There is no easy way for me to tell you what I must.' He spoke with disturbing gentleness. 'As you know, I have just returned from Caer Liwelydd. There, I met with a messenger sent by Lord Elffin.' He continued, more gently still. 'Your brother Glinneu has been slain whilst fighting in Dumnonia.'

Taliesin lowered his eyes, disbelieving. Glinneu, with all the fire of the rising sun. Brave. Ambitious. Black wings dimmed the horizon, the memory of a raven at dawn.

He found it impossible to reply, to voice the half-formed questions that arose in his mind.

'The man told me that Glinneu was in the heat of the battle, that he showed great courage,' Talhaearn said quietly. 'Shortly before the Britons won victory he received a head wound, and died on the field, without lengthy suffering.'

Taliesin swallowed hard.

'He so wanted to go to Dumnonia, it was.........' Words seemed empty and foolish, and his voice faded to silence. He got to his feet. 'At the moment, I need to be alone.'

'Of course. But if you wish to speak later.'

Taliesin's throat tightened, and he said no more before making his way to the door, ignoring Ieuan, who stopped and stared when he passed him.

Taliesin felt the sun's warmth on his back, and it seemed like a mockery. He gazed down at the spring grass, speaking almost to himself.

'There'd always been conflict between us. But the last time I saw him we were beginning to find some understanding. Perhaps we could have become close.........'

Mair rested a work-hardened hand on his arm. 'I can only imagine how it feels to lose a brother.'

'I should not trouble you with this, you have worries enough.'

She shook her head. 'I would be grieved if you did not share your sadness with me.'

'Glinneu lived to be a warrior. All his life he longed for glory. Now he cannot hear his praises sung in the halls of Gwynedd and Dumnonia.'

Taliesin turned to Mair, feeling remote from her, and from all he had come to be a part of, separated from the sense of oneness he had experienced since his initiation.

'You will be going home?' Her question was tentative.

He nodded. 'I was to go back anyway. And I will tell them......I will find some opportunity.'

He shrank from the prospect of facing his foster-parents, explaining his situation and asking for support at such a time. When they were grieving, mourning their blood son, the hero, he who was only a foundling was to burden them with shame. The more Taliesin thought about it, the heavier the weight became. But he had to do as he had promised, for Mair and the child, or know himself to be a coward.

'When will you go?' she asked.

He tried to keep his voice steady. 'Before the end of the week, to be there for the burial. I don't know how long before I'll return.'

'I'll miss you, as I missed you all winter.'

'The spring seems to have become like winter too,' Taliesin said under his breath. 'How many more must die just to keep what is ours?

CHAPTER SIX

It rained throughout the journey back from Gwynedd, turning the tracks to mire and draining all colour from the land. To Taliesin the ride seemed endless and exhausting. He found it hard to imagine that it was the same route he had taken only a year ago, inspired by all he saw.

As he dismounted and strode across the clearing towards Talhaearn's hall, the door opened and Ieuan stood there unsmiling, dark hair casting his face into shadow. He looked as if he wished that Taliesin had never returned.

'I'll see to the horses,' he muttered with no word of greeting, and stamped past him through the mud.

Accompanied by the attendant who had escorted him from Gwynedd, Taliesin stepped across the threshold into the glow of firelight and watched Talhaearn rise from his seat by the hearth, his movements easy as a youth's. After so long away Taliesin was struck by his presence, the power that filled his slight frame. And he realized how he had missed his master's quiet strength at a time when he most needed it.

There was a look of empathy in the grey eyes that met his. 'I'm glad to have you back.'

Taliesin smiled faintly. 'I have two homes now.'

He removed his wet cloak and sat down, glancing round the hall, though in two moons nothing had changed. He imagined it had been the same for years before he came here as apprentice, and would remain so many years after he had left. All changes were beyond the physical.

He drank the sweet mead offered, and, while Talhaearn made conversation with the attendant, sat silent as the first time he had arrived, having no heart to speak; and before long he excused himself and left for his quarters. There, in the gloom

230

and damp, he lay on his bed, staring into nothingness.

He longed to see Mair immediately, to put his mind at ease. And he wanted to tell her that she need not worry for the future. That he had fulfilled his promise.

Lying in solitude, listening to the rhythm of the rain on the roof, he heard again the abbot's words as Glinneu was laid to rest, and the keening, the praise, Cadfarch's elegy in his brother's honour. He saw again the love in his grieving parents' eyes when he returned home from Rheged, and their look of calm acceptance when he found the courage to speak of the child soon to be born. Yet, as the days passed, a sense of guilt had come to dominate Taliesin's every waking moment. Though he had been glad to see his family, to walk and ride with Henwyn, and to share Cadfarch's wisdom, talking as men, as bards, he found no peace whilst he remained at Braich y Dinas. The more he felt loved, the greater the burden became. Nor could he confide his thoughts to anyone, not even Cadfarch.

It was only an awareness that he was no longer alone that brought him back to the darkened roundhouse. Raising his eyes, he met those of the spirit woman who had once told him she was his guide, silently asking her to explain what he could not, to guide him now.

But he found no comfort in her words. 'Look within yourself, Taliesin,' she said in a low voice. 'You have taken the initiation and must follow your own guidance, as all initiates must. I cannot help you.'

Angry and desolate, he turned from her, shutting her out, longing only for the forgetfulness of sleep.

Over the following week the skies cleared, and the weather grew warmer as the days lengthened. Able to work outside again, Taliesin and Talhaearn sat by the lake, its water sparkling where the sun struck the wavelets. After a while Talhaearn began to converse silently in the Secret Language of the Bards. Then, resting a hand on the flat surface of a stone scoured by wind and rain, he spoke aloud.

'The rocks wait through the aeons, storing power, retaining all impressions like bardic memory. Nothing is impenetrable, nothing is entirely solid. The foundation.......'

He stopped, facing Taliesin.

'The foundation lies in the past.'

Taliesin's focus sharpened. The teaching seemed to be aimed at him like a weapon, to draw not blood, but emotion.......from a stone. Though he wanted to look away, he found he could not, as if paralysed by Talhaearn's gaze.

It was Talhaearn who broke the trance, picking up Taliesin's staff and raising it, the eagle that crowned it silhouetted against the sky, clutching a salmon in its talons. Eagle and salmon - the double wisdom of the clearest mind and the deepest intuition. Taliesin understood what he was being told. He had carved the meaning into the wood himself in the days after Gwyl Awst, after he heard about Gwenddydd and.......He had made a dedication, a sacrifice, he was on the true path, and he carried the symbol with him always, so he would never forget why he had made that sacrifice. But he could no longer touch the inspiration, no longer feel the flow of the Awen. He felt that his power was slowly seeping from him.

His thoughts found expression in Talhaearn's words. 'In such a condition of mind I cannot expect you to undertake challenging spirit journeys, it would be too hazardous.'

'I.....I know.' There was a helplessness in Taliesin's voice.

'I am not asking you to tell me anything, to disclose that which is the concern of you and your family. But matters cannot continue as they are. Nor need you suffer like this. If you are to help yourself there is one journey you must take, one man you must communicate with.......in spirit.'

As Talhaearn spoke, a flock of birds rose from the lake with shrill cries. A brisk wind stirred the surface, ruffling Taliesin's hair. And on its breath he whispered,

'Glinneu.'

Again there was stillness, as the waters beside them settled.

'It will not be easy or painless, but we must all resolve the past before we try to conquer the future.' Talhaearn gave one of his rare smiles. 'Let us walk, healed by the sun and the earth, and by the gods who can teach you far more than I could ever hope to.'

As the light in the sky faded towards dusk, Taliesin and Talhaearn took their evening meal in the woodland close to the settlement. When they had finished eating, they remained outside drinking wine, but spoke little. During his time with Talhaearn, Taliesin had learnt the richness of silence. His eyelids felt heavy after working throughout the day, mastering control of the elements, and for the first time in a long while he felt a sense of peace that allowed him to relax, to give in to the tiredness.

The bird chorus dwindled as the evening star grew brighter, glinting through the trees to the west. Taliesin reclined, gazing at the pattern of leaves above him. He lay without blinking until his vision unfocused and in his mind he heard Cadfarch's elegy for Glinneu, spoken in the familiar warm tones of his first master's voice,

'Spirit of fire, was Glinneu,
A flame in the heat of battle.
Fierce blaze of courage.'

Still, Taliesin felt calm. He no longer sought to shut out

233

the words, and with them the memories. Though the past could not be undone, his inner conflict had eased now he was certain that Glinneu had not died resenting him, nor believing there was resentment in Taliesin's heart.

'Bold as the sun at noon,
Bright sword in combat.
An eagle, swift to strike.'

Cadfarch's voice fell silent, replaced by the sound of footsteps a long distance away, running, urgent footsteps. Taliesin sat up and listened more closely, wondering if he had slipped over the threshold of sleep and been dreaming. He glanced at Talhaearn, who had begun to replace the strings of an aged harp, carrying out the intricate work by the light from an oil lamp on the ground beside him.

Again, Taliesin listened, until at last he felt he had to speak.

'Do you not hear anything?'

Without raising his eyes or pausing in his work, Talhaearn replied, 'Do you not feel anything?'

Taliesin frowned. The day's lessons were over, he had no patience left for solving riddles. As Talhaearn selected a new piece of gut and began to secure it, he looked round for Ieuan. Seeing no sign of him, he picked up the wine cups, and was about to go and refill them himself when he paused, gazing into the darkness of the woodland. He was certain now. The sound of approaching footsteps was clearly audible.

Soon a boy of around ten years of age appeared from between the trees, no longer running, but walking hastily. When he reached them he bowed before Talhaearn, and it was only as he straightened, the lamp illuminating his features, that Taliesin noticed his resemblance to Mair. As realization hit with a rush of hope and confusion, he questioned how he could have been fool enough not to have known earlier. How intuition and the spirit sight could have failed him at such a time.

'My respects to you, Pen Beirdd,' the boy muttered nervously, breathless from his run. Still catching his breath, he turned. 'Are you …..Taliesin?'

He nodded. Then he felt a stab of fear. 'Is Mair all right?'

'Her.....your...baby is born. A girl.' The boy looked at him with the same awe as he had looked at the master.

Taliesin dropped the cups with a clang, and was on his feet in an instant. 'But is Mair all right?'

'Yes.....my lord.'

'And the baby, is it....she....healthy?'

'She is. She cries loud enough.' Mair's brother lowered his eyes and began to fidget, as if anxious that he had spoken too freely.

Taliesin breathed out with a laugh. 'Thank the gods. Can I see her now?'

'Mair asked….that I fetch you….my lord.'

Talhaearn rose, retrieving the cups. 'What are you waiting for?'

But Taliesin hesitated, recalling the tales he had heard of Gruffydd. 'Your father.......am I welcome in your home?'

'Father was pleased with the sacks of grain. He.....he won't be angry now.'

Hurriedly, Taliesin fetched his cloak against the night chill, fumbling with the brooch as he fastened it, his hands shaking and clumsy. Everything seemed altered. He felt intoxicated, his emotions swinging between elation and disbelief.

Somehow he managed to harness Gwyn, and, with the youth behind him, rode west along the woodland path, between the trees where darkness had already fallen. But once they reached open ground there was still enough light to make out the way, first across pastureland where cattle grazed, raising their heads as they passed, then skirting fields of oats, still unripe.

Lost in his thoughts, Taliesin glanced up at a sky glittering with stars. Above, shone the northern star, guide to seafarers, with the celestial dragon curved about it. And nearing its setting, Caer Arianrhod. He let his spirit travel, spiralling into that semi-circle of stars until he could see that the stars were seven halls of rainbow glass, roofed in silver.

Beside the largest, he glimpsed a figure with pale hair. At first he thought it was his guide, the spirit-woman, but the figure was smaller, slighter. She became blurred against the dazzling background of light within the hall, shifting shape into a bird which rose into the air and circled sunwise. A white raven - Branwen. Not a bird of ill omen, but a sign of hope, bright with the blessings of the Otherworld. Three times it circled, the sound of its wings whispering its name.

Then Taliesin was again riding along a dark and stony path, an earthly, rather timid, voice in his ears.

'We're almost there.'

He felt unsteady, gripped by a nervous anticipation that made it difficult to think clearly.

Forcing himself to stay calm, he shook Gwyn's reins, urging him on.

They rode faster now. The ground rose slightly as they crossed an area of rough grassland, until from the top of the slope a huddle of buildings came into view - wattle and daub, with thatched roofs. And by the door of the main dwelling a lamp had been placed, a beacon in the gathering dusk.

The boy jumped from Gwyn's back and ran on ahead, while Taliesin approached at a steady pace. Beyond his inner turmoil, he heard the barking of dogs, and watched a full-figured woman emerge from the house and take up the lamp. She waited for him to reach the yard, then came forward as he dismounted, the dogs leaping at her heel. By the light from the lamp, he could see that her face was brown and lined from working in the fields, old beyond her years.

It was she who spoke first. 'Taliesin.' There was no bitterness in her voice. 'I am Tegla, Mair's mother. She'll be pleased you're here.'

'Is all well with her?'

'She's a strong healthy girl. So is the baby. Come in. Our home is only a simple one.'

The boy took Gwyn's reins, and Taliesin followed Tegla into a roundhouse filled with people, the air close and smoky. A dozen adults were gathered around the hearth, while the older children played on the floor. The younger ones, including Cybi, were already asleep in a corner.

Silence fell as they entered, even the children stopped their games, all eyes fixed on Taliesin. Men with ale cups in their hands stared at him grimly, and he could only guess which one was Gruffydd. But none spoke.

'Come,' Tegla urged.

In an area that had been separated from the living quarters by a hide curtain hung between posts, Mair lay on a pallet bed. She looked pale and tired, but smiled when she saw Taliesin. As he took a step forward, he heard the curtain fall behind him, and the rumble of conversation resumed on the other side.

He gazed down at the tiny puckered face in the crook of Mair's arm, the baby's head covered with downy hair so fair it was almost white. Without taking his eyes from the child, Taliesin sat on the edge of the bed, feeling as if he could never look away again. She was so small, so vulnerable, yet radiant, untouched by the world with all its pain and grief.

'Do you want to hold her?' Mair whispered.

Taliesin met her eyes, then gently took the child from her arms. As she was moved, the baby woke and began to whimper, but after a moment settled again, and, nestling against the folds of Taliesin's tunic, fell asleep.

Feeling the child's warmth, listening to her soft breathing, an image flashed across his inner sight, of a coracle caught between the poles of a salmon weir. The tale of his rescue by Elffin was his earliest memory, almost as if he remembered the event itself, though he was only newborn, the same age as the infant he now held. It was a memory that had always brought pain, the knowledge that he was an outsider, not of the family at Braich y Dinas. But that day everything had changed. For the first time in his life he looked at one who was his kin. The tiny girl in his arms was a part of him - his own flesh and blood.

Branwen. The white bird which had circled above him three times. He knew now that he had been given the child's name, and that she was the figure he had seen in vision.

'She is so.........perfect,' he said under his breath. 'I cannot find the right words.'

'And you are supposed to be a bard.' Mair grinned.

Reluctantly, Taliesin returned Branwen to her and reached into the pouch at his belt, removing a richly engraved bracelet. He slipped it onto Mair's wrist, then kissed her.

'I didn't expect a gift.' She lay back, dreamily admiring the silverwork. 'I've never owned anything like this.'

Taliesin kissed her once more, then kissed the child's brow before getting to his feet.

"I'll come back soon,' he said. 'As soon as Master Talhaearn gives me leave from my studies.'

chapter seven

In the glen below Penmaenmawr Mountain, Taliesin sat with Henwyn on the banks of the stream, close to the place he had often escaped to as a child. Afternoon sunlight slanted through the trees and, though the nights were drawing in and the first leaves had begun to turn, the days were still warm.

'We're glad you could come home for our wedding,' Henwyn said. 'I imagine you don't have much time to call your own. Training under Talhaearn Tad Awen is reputed to be more arduous even than a warrior's training.' He glanced at the blue spirals tattooed on Taliesin's arms. 'People here still allude to the Initiation, though officially it no longer exists.'

'That is not something I can speak of.' Taliesin cast a pebble into the rushing waters. 'But Talhaearn is generous with his wisdom. You and Alarch must meet him. Come and visit me when you're able to travel.'

'Perhaps next year.......I'm keen to visit Rheged, to witness its glory. Throughout the summer, we've received news of Urien's victories over Bernicia.'

Reaching into the saddle-bag that lay on the ground beside him, Taliesin took out an apple and cut it cleanly in two, handing the other half to Henwyn. 'It has been a summer of celebration in Caer Liwelydd,' he said. 'But though Urien holds the enemy back, Elmet has suffered defeat. As I left, I heard that Aelle had taken Efrog, and he continues to advance westward.'

'With matters as they are, it's unlikely Dyfnarth can attend the wedding.' Henwyn sighed. 'And Alarch says you must go back directly after the feast. We have a lot to catch up on before then.'

Taliesin inclined his head, thinking of his daughter, whom

he missed more with each day that passed. When she was grown he would show her this glen, the ancient ring of stones, the hermit's beehive hut........'Why don't we ride to the strand tomorrow?' he said, recalling a winter's afternoon many years ago. 'Does Beulan still preach there?'

'He has many followers.' Henwyn grinned. 'Though I doubt any are initiated into the Old Ways!'

Taliesin bit into the apple, then rested his elbows on his knees and gazed into the woodland on the far side of the stream as he used to when he was a boy. Though he was seventeen, a man and a father, in Henwyn's company sometimes he felt as if nothing had changed since he lived with his foster-parents at Braich y Dinas.

He let his thoughts drift, but as a cloud passed across the sun and he was no longer dazzled by its brightness, he noticed a figure walking between the trees in the distance. The woman was tall and slender, and wore a gown of pale green that merged with the green of the foliage. Moving with animal grace, she appeared and vanished from view as she made her way past low-hanging branches and patches of fern.

Taliesin sat up straight, struggling to see more clearly. Though he was neither dreaming nor in trance, he realized that he looked at the being he knew as his guide, no longer in spirit form, but a woman of flesh and blood. And with the realization came fear.

'Shall we also ride into the valleys tomorrow?' Henwyn turned towards him. 'Taliesin? Do you hear me?.........By God what's the matter?'

Taliesin tore his attention away from the woman. 'I'm sorry.'

'Don't apologize. Tell me what you saw. Is there danger?'

He shook his head. 'It's nothing. A trick of the light.'

'I was ready to reach for my sword!' Henwyn glanced in the direction Taliesin had been gazing, finding nothing out of the ordinary, then threw the apple core into the undergrowth with an air of frustration.

Taliesin, too, glanced back across the stream. But the figure was no longer there. There was no sign that she ever had been. He questioned if perhaps he had seen in spirit vision after all, though deep down he knew he was deceiving himself, avoiding a truth he could not face.

'Yes, let us ride into the valleys tomorrow,' he said boldly, trying to recapture the childlike joy he had felt only moments earlier.

The family and their guests had gathered around the hearth, the aroma of mead blending with wood-smoke as talk filled the hall.

His cup empty in his hand, Taliesin listened to snatches from one conversation, then another, none holding his attention.

'Aelle plans a sound strategy, I'll say that for the barbarian. He's got brains, and that makes him a threat.' Gwyddno emphasized the word, striking the table with his fist. He scarcely seemed to have aged. His broad, grim face had been the same for as long as Taliesin could remember, his pessimism an elixir of youth.

'Gwallawg is a match for him, a brave leader.'

'But too slow to act. He must organize his forces, move swiftly.'

'.......I'll be making good elder wine this year, the berries are heavy on the trees already.'

'........a storm may be on the way. The sea birds are flying inland.'

'......but the dice was weighted. The man's a cheat, and I'll prove it.'

'Taliesin, you are very quiet.' It was Alarch's voice, close beside him.   'Henwyn said you seemed distressed this afternoon and I told him not to worry, but now I do.'

He looked at the circle of faces around them, young and old, firelight and shadow flickering across familiar features. Then he met his sister's eyes.

'It was a long journey from Rheged, I'm simply tired.'

'D'you think I'll believe that? I know you too well.' Alarch lowered her voice. 'My own joy is mixed with deep sadness that Glinneu is not with us to share our celebrations......I know things were never easy between you, nor were they always easy between him and myself. Too alike.' She gave a little laugh. 'I even miss the arguments. Strange, isn't it? To miss being mocked for childishness and vanity.......And now it seems that Dyfnarth cannot leave the fighting in Elmet.' She rested her hand on Taliesin's arm. 'But I'm so glad that you are here. And I do not want to see you unhappy.'

'Coming home brings back memories. I will be all right in a few days.'

Alarch took the mead flask and refilled his cup.

'We're all eager to hear your tales of life at Urien's court. We are isolated here and you are at the heart of everything, singing in the hall of the man they say is the new Arthur, living amongst heroes and great warriors.'

Taliesin took a draught and looked at her, thinking how young she seemed, her head filled with fantasies. 'It's not quite like that,' he said dryly.

'Now at least you're smiling. I hope you have your songs and poems prepared for our wedding feast, songs in praise of my beauty and virtue! Not every bride has the Pen Beirdd of Ynys Prydein's apprentice for a brother.'

'I hope Henwyn knows what he's taking on.'

Alarch grinned. 'Why, the most desirable woman in all Gwynedd, of course.'

Taliesin grinned back.   Then, from across the hearth he

noticed Eilonwy watching them. She looked weary, worn down by grief, her hair now more grey than dark. But she smiled as Taliesin met her eye, a mother's warmth that still gave him comfort. Though Branwen was his only flesh and blood, this was his home, his family.

He drank again, the mead like sunlight in his throat.

'Here is one who can tell us the truth of the campaign in the north.' Gwyddno's words rose above the clamour, and Taliesin turned towards the company as talk dwindled, drawing breath to speak in the voice of a bard.

It was growing late when Taliesin and Henwyn cantered through the gates to the fortress, their cloaks spattered with mud from the valley streams. A group of Henwyn's warrior apprentices loitered near the hall staring, and Drych frowned and cursed under his breath when he saw his son Collen with them, aware that he copied all Henwyn did.

'The world is not a racecourse,' he said, taking the reins as the riders dismounted. 'And to think you're soon to be a married man.'

Henwyn raised a dark brow. 'You bet on me last time I raced, and weren't sorry for it.'

Drych frowned again. Then gave a warning nod as he caught sight of Alarch approaching, lifting the hem of her gown clear of the dirt underfoot.

'So you're back at last,' she confronted Henwyn. 'Did you forget we were to begin planning the feast today?' Turning to Taliesin, she spoke with the same note of impatience. 'You have a visitor.'

'Rhys?' he asked hopefully.

'It's a woman, a.........priestess.'

'Indeed!' Henwyn laughed and took Alarch's hand. 'So you punish our lateness with jests.......Forgive us, cariad.'

243

She did not share his laughter, but looked at Taliesin as if trying to resolve an unanswered question. 'You had better hurry,' she said. 'She has been waiting many hours.'

He felt the sweat cooling on his forehead.

'I cannot see anyone like this.' There was an edge to his voice, and instinctively Alarch gripped Henwyn's hand more tightly. 'She will have to wait a while longer.'

It was so long before Taliesin appeared at the entrance to the hall that Elffin was about to go and search for him. Now he approached slowly, clothed in a rich blue tunic and amber breeches, his hair fastened at the nape of his neck and bound down its length with blue cord. Trying to keep his own feelings concealed, he noticed the tension on his foster-parents' faces, how they seemed awkward and uneasy. Then his gaze fell on the visitor seated by the fire. As she rose, Elffin rose too.

'Taliesin, this is the Lady Finllian.'

She wore the same gown as she had the previous day in the woodland, of a fine shimmering cloth, with a silver girdle that matched the band about her brow, over hair the colour of his own. Seeing her face to face, in the flesh, for the first time, Taliesin knew beyond doubt who she was, and in that instant all the pain of his childhood was reawakened, the hurt he had fought so long to conquer.

Without speaking, he turned, striding towards the door through which he had just entered.

'Taliesin!' It was Elffin's voice.

His father hurried after him, reaching him as they crossed the threshold to the courtyard.

'At least talk to her.' He spoke quietly, gently encouraging.

'I have nothing to say.'

Elffin sighed, his eyes clouded. 'Listen, this is something that must be faced or it will haunt us for the remainder of our lives. We cannot avoid the truth.'

'Why can't......she.......leave us alone. She has shown no

244

interest in me all this time. She has no part in my life.'

He took another step, and Elffin spoke more firmly.

'I'll only ask you once more. Come back, if not for your own sake, for mine, for your mother's.'

Taliesin gave a bitter laugh, and Elffin grimaced, realizing what he had said, the words that slipped so easily from his tongue after seventeen years.

'You need never see her again after today.'

Taliesin looked out across the darkening courtyard, trying to calm himself. He longed to continue walking, to find refuge in Cadfarch's house and seek his counsel, or to re-saddle Gwyn and ride from the fortress alone. But he could not go against his father's wishes. And, with an acquiescence that took all his resolve, went with him back into the hall. He was filled with confusion, frightened by the intensity of his feelings, but held his head high, telling himself he was not the one who should lower his eyes in shame.

Reluctantly, he sat down at the hearthside, keeping a distance between himself and the still, pale figure of their visitor.

She faced him, meeting his stony gaze.

'You know who I am.'

It was a statement, not a question, and Taliesin noticed a slight tremor in her voice. So she felt less composed than she seemed. That was as she deserved. He did not trust himself to reply, but simply inclined his head.

'Perhaps nothing will alter how you feel, but I ask that you hear me.' Finllian's expression could have been mistaken for tenderness, a possibility Taliesin refused to consider as he forced himself to listen. 'I have travelled much,' she said, 'to distant lands.......but I have been with you in spirit.'

Taliesin saw that her eyes were green-blue as the sea. 'Why did you tell me only that you were my guide?' he asked. 'Did I not have a right to know the truth?'

245

'I feared your anger would shut me out, that I would no longer be able to communicate with you.'

Quietly, Elffin and Eilonwy got to their feet, leaving them to speak alone. Taliesin scarcely noticed, as he remembered when he first held his daughter in his arms, feeling a love so powerful it bordered on pain, sensing the Otherworld still close in a child so young. He would rather sacrifice his own life than lose Branwen. It was beyond his understanding how the woman who had borne him could have abandoned him to almost certain death. It hardly seemed worth listening to an explanation, because there was none that would make any sense.

But when Finllian spoke again, it was not to offer excuses.

'You are dedicated to Ceridwen,' she said.

Her words startled him, though he fought to conceal it.

'You know that her demands are high.'

'A price I willingly pay.......She spared me when my companions were falling sick and dying from the pestilence.' The moment Taliesin had spoken he wished he had not, realizing that he had forgotten himself and replied as if Finllian possessed natural human feelings.

'She saved you because you are her son.'

Again, Taliesin was startled, a dozen questions tugging at his mind.

'I will try to tell you everything, all that belongs to you, your inheritance.' Finllian hesitated. Then, in a low voice, she began,

'I was born and raised near Viroconium in Powys, of the royal clan. My paternal grandmother was sister to King Cynan Garwyn's paternal grandmother. For as long as I recall, I knew myself to be different from other girls; I saw and experienced things they did not, and was often frightened. At the age of twelve this drove me to confide in a friend of my mother's, a woman I believed could help me. I found I had been right to

246

trust her, and she trusted me in return, telling me that she was a priestess of the Old Faith. And she offered to instruct me, in secret, without the knowledge of my family.'

Taliesin looked at the being of his visions sitting beside him: solid, breathing - the human woman whose callousness had left scars of self-doubt and alienation that remained with him still. Her presence in the hall of Braich y Dinas seemed an impossibility. In the place where he had heard Cadfarch recount the genealogy of his foster-family, he now listened to the tale of his own blood-line, his own story.

Holding his gaze, Finllian continued. 'At sixteen I was married to a man twenty years my senior. Our marriage took place at an inauspicious time, the dark year when Arthur was killed at Camlann, when fear and foreboding hung over the land. I was thrown unprepared into a new life in Gwynedd. The marriage was a dynastic alliance, no more, and I found my husband harsh and often violent. I missed my home, my family, my spiritual teacher........'

She faltered, and looked down, taking a sip of wine. Still, Taliesin said nothing, waiting quietly until she found her voice.

'In the first three years of marriage I bore a son and a daughter.......Though I communicated with the Lady Ceridwen in spirit, seeking her wisdom, it was only when I visited Powys that I could work with my mortal teacher, who was then ageing and sick.

'In my twentieth year, while my husband was away I returned home to see her, leaving my children in the care of my husband's sister. It was the start of the harvest, but the yield was poor and we knew there would be famine over the winter. Our people had been stricken with pestilence and the enemy was gathering strength, taking advantage of our weakness. With Arthur dead there was no true leader. Contact with the old gods was forgotten, and where it was not forgotten, it was forbidden. The desperation of my people, the sickness of the land, reflected my own suffering. And I knew that my teacher, the priestess who had guided me since early womanhood, was dying.......When she asked if I would agree to perform the Great Rite, I could not refuse. I was willing to do anything that might help the land and people I loved.' Finllian spoke under her breath. 'During the rite the presence of the Lady Ceridwen filled my being, so I was no longer myself but a vessel for her power, a channel for its manifestation in this world.'

Disbelieving, yet knowing he must believe, Taliesin stared at her. He recalled Ceridwen in all her terror and beauty, the bitter-sweet love of his goddess, his mother. Finally, he found the courage to ask,

'And my father?'

'He was a priest of Beli, a nobleman, a warrior. I was not told his name, nor did I ask it. I met him only once, and knew him only as the embodiment of his god - lord of the solar fire, source of life-giving energy..........

'After the rite I returned to Gwynedd, uplifted by a sense of hope, and glad that my husband was to be away for another two moons.......Then I discovered that I was with child, and knew the child could not be his.'

There was no change in Taliesin's expression as he sat motionless, trying to summon the strength to face what he had always thought he wanted to know. Now, though he no longer wished to hear it, he was imprisoned by his duty to Elffin; and by Finllian's gaze, that sickening look of concern as she slowly broke down his defences.

Her voice remained gentle. 'When my husband learnt of my condition, he consulted someone, the bishop I think, who said that my child would have forbidden powers, and in his madness he interpreted this as a threat to himself........Shortly before you were born I fled, but was certain he would seek me out and find some way to harm you.' Though there were others in the hall, Taliesin was aware only of Finllian's words dragging him into the darkness of her guilty conscience. 'I was alone and exhausted. I could think of no answer but to place you in the hands of the gods, trusting you to their mercy. And I believed they would show mercy, that your birth had been no accident, but Ceridwen's will.

'Many years passed, when I searched in spirit and was unable to find you, until I feared that I had been wrong.........But in time our link was renewed, and at last I found solace in the knowledge that you were healthy and well cared for.'

Taliesin turned away. His mother? No. She was not the one who had nursed him as an infant, who had comforted him, disciplined him; who loved his weaknesses as she loved his strengths. Eilonwy was the only earthly mother he would ever accept. The only mother he could ever love.

His voice was flat. 'Where is my.........father....... now?'

Finllian shook her head. 'I would tell you if I knew, but he was not from Powys and returned to his own kingdom after the rite, to continue fighting the outer battle.'

The fire glowed brighter in the gathering dusk. A horse whinnied in the courtyard and Drych shouted at a stable boy - reminders that life continued as before.

Taliesin forced his question from between tight lips.

'Why did you not come here sooner?'

There was a brief pause.

'My husband died at Gwyl Awst........Though I had not seen him for many years, while he lived I feared for you at his hands.'

Finllian finished her wine and placed the goblet on the table beside her. 'If you wish it, I'll never seek you out again. You've made your own life. But......I hope, I pray, we may get to know each other better.' She rose with a rustle of her grown, the unfamiliar shimmering fabric. 'I leave the decision to you.........Taliesin.'

The echo of his name lingered. It filled his head as he

listened to her footsteps receding, followed by other voices, entreaties and farewells. He remained where he was, not looking up as she left, feeling drained, empty even of anger. He waited alone until Elffin came quietly to his side and sat with him, his presence solid and reassuring as it had always been.

chapter eight

For five years, since Branwen's birth, the northern Britons had held their territory against the Angles, and the bards sang of Urien's victories over Ida of Bernicia and Aelle of Deira. But each year news came from the south that the enemy shadow was cast further west across Dumnonia towards Mor Hafren.

In the heat of late summer, as another battle season drew to an end, the royal hall was filled to capacity, the company growing loud and restless with anticipation. Through the closed doors of a private chamber, the clamour reached Taliesin's ears, yet he felt only a deep sense of peace. He stood straight-backed while an attendant pinned a jewelled brooch at the shoulder of his robe; his arms, with their tattoos showing the spirals of life, relaxed at his sides.

When the man retreated, Taliesin glanced at the elder bards who flanked him, then nodded his readiness. With his escort he headed out into the courtyard, and at a measured pace crossed the short distance to the hall. The roar of voices, of laughter, grew louder with each step. But as the doors were opened, the noise faded into silence and the gathering turned to face him. Soft harp music began to play, followed by pipes, welcoming the new master bard into the company of his peers.

Without looking to either side, Taliesin moved towards the circle of robed figures at the centre of the hall, his gaze directed beyond them to Urien: grizzled hair resting upon broad shoulders, the golden torc of kingship around his neck shining in the torchlight.

Approaching the king, Taliesin walked a path between the elite of Rheged, conscious of the unity that bound his people. Finllian sat amongst those at the royal table, and he noticed the look of pride in her eyes, and a warmth that he was gradually

251

allowing himself to accept. He had long since conquered his self-destructive bitterness. Seeing her closeness to Branwen, he realized he had been wrong to think her cold and selfish. He had watched her comfort Branwen when she was hurt, laugh with her, listen patiently to her tales, showing her the love she had been unable to give him.

The pulse of a single drum accompanied Taliesin into the circle, echoes of a circle in the woodland long ago, so long ago that he felt he had been little more than a child. Yet every trial, every journey, remained in his memory. His initiation had marked the beginning, the awakening, in secret. Now he was to receive formal honour, a culmination that was at the same time but another turn of the spiral.

The drumming ceased as he bowed his head to Urien. Then, taking up the harp that was brought by an attendant, he ran his fingers across the strings, hearing the notes echo through the worlds, over the bridge he had crossed many times.

Taliesin stood on the threshold now, and sang.

'Nine waves
beyond the shore,
I see the plain of honey.
Sweet golden mead
flows from its fountains.
And a tree of bright aspect,
glorious to behold.
Three fruits upon it:
nuts, apples and acorns........'

His voice filled the hall, the circle of bards singing in harmony. No guest at the feast tables spoke, nor raised a wine cup. And as the last note lingered, the drum was struck once. Their trance broken, the company looked away from Taliesin to watch the delicate dark-haired woman who entered, robed in white and gold, a silver branch in her hand, each step she took creating shimmering music. She was followed by Talhaearn Tad Awen, walking in time with her, carrying a cloak of bird feathers over his outstretched arms.

Taliesin focussed on the woman, aware only of her. As if she had come from the Otherworld, she was no one he had ever seen in the hall or in Caer Liwelydd.

She entered the circle and stopped, speaking in a sweet melodious voice,

'A branch of the apple tree from the Glass Isle
I bring, like those we know;
Twigs of white silver are upon it
Crystal grows with blossoms.' [7]

Taking seven paces, she stood before Taliesin, and as the bards began to chant, placed the branch in his hand, bells softly chiming.

'He who bears the branch of silver knows the secret of the Awen, commands the hearts of the company, holds the key of truth.'

With the faintest of smiles, she turned and left the way she had come, by her arts melting into invisibility. The attention of the company was now centred on the circle, the chant soaring as Taliesin faced his master.

He sank down onto one knee for Talhaearn to place the cloak of power across his shoulders: white swans' feathers at the neck, below it, the plumage of many-coloured song-birds.

'Taliesin,
enter now the invisible door,
flame in the fire of bright knowledge,
bard amongst bards.'

When Taliesin rose, their eyes met, speaking silent words, and in that moment of great joy he experienced sorrow for what now lay in the past. He watched Talhaearn withdraw to become part of the circle, he himself standing alone at the centre, for the first time in twelve years no longer an apprentice.

He felt the power of the feathered cloak about his shoulders, the smoothness of the branch in his hand, silver bells answering every movement. The strength of the sacred land beneath his feet, and of all who loved and fought for it, filled him as he spoke in a deep rich voice,

'I am bard, I am truth-teller.
I am shield, I am see-er.
I am maker, I am the mead of comradeship.'

He stepped forward, and the circle of bards widened to accept him, adding their voices to his,

'Seven score muses
There are in the inspiration of song;
Eight score in every score
In the great abyss of tranquillity,
In the great abyss of wrath,
In the depths below the earth,
In the air above the earth........' [8]

* * *

Taliesin heard women's voices and got to his feet, carefully laying aside the Latin manuscript he had been reading. A breeze cooled his face as he waited by the door to the roundhouse, glancing at the smaller building beside it, which for the last six months had been occupied by Talhaearn's new apprentice, an eager youth of fourteen.

Before long Branwen ran across the clearing towards him, waves of deep gold hair falling to her shoulders. She was followed by Mair, whom Taliesin now saw only when she brought Branwen to the settlement, and, strolling at Mair's side, her sister Megan.

Taliesin crouched down and his daughter jumped into his arms, laughing.

'Good day, my jewel.'

Blue eyes met his. 'We saw lots of birds on the way........swans and seagulls.'

He assumed a tone of wonder. 'How many did you see?'

She began counting on her fingers as he stood, still holding her.

Mair frowned. 'You spoil the child. Then she makes mischief when we go home.'

'I was not expecting you, I was soon to ride for town.'

Ignoring Branwen's demands for attention, Taliesin looked at Mair, noticing the anxiety in her face, which had become fuller and heavier since he first knew her.

'Is something wrong?' he asked.

'I need to talk with you. It's important, so if you do not have time......'

Taliesin led the women into the roundhouse and indicated a bench near the hearth.

The moment he put her down Branwen began to tug at the hem of his tunic. 'Father, tell me a story.......father.'

'Be silent,' Mair snapped. 'We must speak alone. Megan can take Branwen for a walk.'

Taliesin nodded, then sat down, eye to eye with his daughter. 'I will tell you a story when you return. But now you must go along with Megan and not complain.'

The small slight figure in front of him looked back determinedly, mouth set, so he felt like laughing, recognizing his own stubbornness in her. Mimicking her expression, he waited until her frown melted into a smile and she took Megan's hand.

He closed the door behind them, and poured Mair a cup of mead. After taking a drink himself, he turned to her.

'Is it money?'

'No, not that.' Mair smoothed her work-stained dress. 'I don't want an argument, nor for you to judge me. It is about Branwen.......God, I find it hard to speak, especially when you look at me so. It reminds me of when......' She drained her cup in one draught. 'For some time I have known a man, a tradesman in Caer Liwelydd, and he now wants to be wed.........Taliesin, I am still young, I do not want to live all my life without the comfort and support of a husband. But he is unwilling to raise your child. He is a Christian and it makes him angry when Branwen says she sees spirit beings and speaks with the trees. He scolds her, though I tell him it is only childish fancy.' Suddenly Mair seemed near to tears. 'I.....I find myself having to make a choice between him and Branwen.'

With an effort Taliesin curbed the anger that followed his disbelief at what she was saying.

Controlling his voice, he spoke in an undertone. 'You have never mentioned this man before.'

'It is not that I don't care for Branwen, I swear........You think me selfish, but you don't know how it is.'

'Perhaps not.' Taliesin hesitated. 'But what are you expecting? That I will offer to raise her?'

Mair shrugged helplessly.

'And if I have no solution? Will you refuse the proposal of marriage?'

When he received no reply, Taliesin lowered his eyes, knowing then what her answer was. And in the turmoil of his thoughts, he felt Branwen's rejection with the pain of his own abandonment. In his daughter he saw the carefree child he could have been, and through her he had experienced a second childhood that had helped heal his past.

'I am leaving Rheged for Powys in under a month,' he said with forced calm. 'I shall be accepting the position I have been offered at the hall of King Cynan Garwyn, as one of the royal bards. Even if I can find a way to take Branwen with me, it will distress her to be parted from you and all that is familiar.'

'She'd be parted from you when you leave.' Mair's eyes flashed, her words cutting deep.

Taliesin's voice also cut like ice. 'You began this by saying you did not wish to argue. If I too speak my mind, you may hear more than you anticipate.'

Mair sighed. 'But Branwen is not my responsibility only, though I have raised her.'

Taliesin reached for the mead flask and refilled both their cups, trying to get beyond confusion and futile anger, to find some way forward. But he could not gather his thoughts. He pictured Branwen running at Megan's side, talking brightly, observing everything with childish delight.......

Putting the flask aside, he faced Mair. 'I need time to consider. Though I have other matters to attend to, Branwen's welfare is of first importance.'

Mair met his eye, and found words to cut him once more. 'Of course. Before even the King of Powys.'

As Taliesin placed Finllian's green cloak around her shoulders, she looked at the rolled manuscript on a chest beside the silver branch.

'What is this? Your memory failing?' She raised a brow.

Taliesin gave a short laugh. 'I do not intend to be outdone by Abbot Segnius and his kind.......There is something to learn from their writings, but, unlike those who follow the new faith, I recognize how foolish it would be to commit our most sacred lore to parchment where it would stagnate and die.'

Together they walked out into the autumn mist, passing Ieuan carrying firewood, his squat muscular frame making even the heaviest work appear easy. He greeted Finllian reticently, then began to stack the logs beneath the eaves, a reminder of the coming winter.

It was not the weather to be outside, yet Taliesin felt trapped by the walls of the roundhouse, and by the walls of his own mind, which pressed in on him with the unresolved dilemma over Branwen's future. As he and Finllian headed towards the River Idon, crossing open pasture, their feet sank into the wet turf, and cattle loomed half-seen from the mist.

After some time, Taliesin broke the silence. 'I wish to talk to you about Branwen.'

'It cannot be easy, knowing you will see her so seldom once you leave for Powys.'

He felt on edge, uncertain how to begin. 'Of course the thought of separation troubles me,' he replied carefully, 'but there is a more immediate concern.'

Finllian turned sharply. 'She is not sick or hurt is she?'

'No, but I fear she may soon be hurt, deeply.'

'Whatever makes you say such a thing? Mair is a good mother, is she not?'

Taliesin continued walking, staring into the greyness. 'I thought she was, until recently. But now, at the worst possible time, she tells me there is a man whom she wishes to marry. Apparently he is unwilling to take on another man's child, and from the way she speaks of him I think it best he has no part in Branwen's life.'

Finllian shuddered, and wrapped her cloak more tightly about her shoulders.

'When did you first learn of this?'

'Two days ago. And I've thought of little else since. My preparations for taking up the post in Powys have fallen by the wayside, though neither King Cynan nor Mair will wait while I search for an answer.'

Below them the river snaked towards Merin Rheged, lead-grey and sluggish. Finllian came to a halt, watching it through a break in the mist.

'It does not take me a moment to find an answer,' she said softly, 'though you may already have considered, and rejected, it in view of.......of the past.'

She turned to Taliesin. 'The last few years in Caer Liwelydd have brought a happiness I never thought possible. My days of travelling are over. I would not surrender what I've found here, nor leave those who rely on me. People come to me for healing, and there are a few of the Old Faith with whom I can work.'

He listened, afraid to hope, while around them the land lay still and silver.

'No one could be dearer to me than Branwen.' Finllian spoke again. 'I would do anything to ensure her welfare.......I have a secure home in a place she knows, where she can be with her own class, others of royal blood. And she is sensitive. My gifts, and yours, are developing in her. She needs someone who can offer guidance.' Her voice had become fainter, tinged with uncertainty. 'It would grieve me if you refused to leave her in my care, but I would understand...... I've scarcely been an example of motherhood, and am in no position to criticize Mair.'

Taliesin met Finllian's eyes, as he felt the burden of anxiety begin to lift. 'But I will not refuse,' he said in a low voice.

She smiled, so like Branwen that it startled him. Then he smiled too, without reserve. 'I prayed you would suggest this, so I did not have to. I feared you would be the one to refuse.'

Finllian shook her head. 'I sacrificed the chance to raise you, I will not do the same with Branwen.......Now you must think of your own future, your first position as bard.' She paused. 'Your gifts are unique. And this is but the beginning......'

Lost in thought, Taliesin gazed at the line of the Wall to the north, sections of stonework highlighted where the sun had broken through. A desolate country, so often cold and grey, but a place he had grown to love. He wondered if it would again be his home. Or would he remain in Powys, the kingdom of his own clan, no longer without blood kin but part of a web of kinship that he had never imagined he would know.

Rays slanted through the clouds over the estuary as he looked at the land he had walked in all seasons, familiar with each cairn, each rock, each wind-bent tree; the land with whose spirit he had spoken. Its elements were absorbed into his own being, a deep knowing that he would carry to Powys, as Braich y Dinas and Deganwy lived with him still.

Part Four

Rheged Arise

Rheged arise,
the spawner of kings,
I have watched over you
even though I am not one of yours.
Blades and spears in battle wheeze;
men moan
behind their shields......... 18

chapter one

It was late in the season for travelling. Beneath lowering cloud, Taliesin and the two warriors who rode with him were nearing the end of their journey from Powys. The sky cast its shadow over the land, purple as the late-flowering heather on the hillside, as the riders left the mountains and lakes of Llwyfenydd behind them and continued north into the heart of Rheged.

For five years Taliesin had been at the side of his king and kinsman, accompanying his warband against the advancing Angles, raiding cattle across the borders of Wyeland and Gwent. And rising in rank to take the bardic chair, he had sung before the company in the feast hall, celebrating Cynan's courage and generosity. A generosity that was unbounded for his Chief Bard - pure-bred horses with silver trappings, garments of the finest cloth, brooches and armbands of gold; most prized of all, Cynan's parting gift - the bay stallion Nerth, which now carried him back to Rheged.

Cynan had been grieved to see him go, but forgave even that, pressing him to visit in the spring. Though he left praise and honour behind, his own clan and kin, Taliesin had not considered long when he received Urien's summons. Rheged stood firm as the foundation of British resistance, more powerful than ever, and it was Branwen's home, where he could watch her grow, be a father not a stranger.

Frowning into the twilight, at last he picked out the silhouette of the woodland surrounding Talhaearn's settlement, dark as he had first seen it in a summer storm. Each year the master withdrew further from the company in the hall, and no longer rode with the warriors into battle, working in secret for the protection of Ynys Prydein, and in training those who would carry the Bright Knowledge. Though Taliesin was but twenty-seven, the youngest man to hold the office, Talhaearn passed on the mantle of Chief Bard to him as chosen successor, to take over his duties in the outer world.

A band of warriors were gathered around one of the great oak tables in the feast hall. Taliesin had heard them return earlier in the day, the clamour of horses and voices echoing from the courtyard as he sat alone in his quarters, resting after his journey. Now, laughter and curses were loud in the smoky air, and the mead flask was passed once again, celebrating the success of their foray into Bernician territory, their spoils heaped against the far wall.

As Taliesin reached the table, a dark-haired man in rich attire turned towards him. He had a hard face, gaunt and weathered, the right side scarred from jaw to cheekbone. But the look in the deep-set eyes, the arrogant bearing, were unchanged.

He got to his feet, clasping Taliesin's forearm in greeting.

'I have been awaiting you……..Will you drink with us?'

Unable to refuse, Taliesin took the seat offered, accepting the meadhorn that was placed before him. Thinking back, he realized it was six years since he last saw Dyfnarth, years that had taken their toll, with hard fighting, and grief at the death of his wife and the son she bore, after only ten months of marriage. The uproar resumed, horns of mead downed in answer to challenge or toast, fists thudding against the table as the next oath was sworn.

Dyfnarth leant forward to be heard above the shouts of his comrades. 'I'm honoured to drink with the Chief Bard of Rheged,' he said in an undertone.

Though Taliesin suspected sarcasm, he could not be sure of it, and replied evenly. 'It will be my honour to recount the deeds of Urien's champion.'

He raised his meadhorn towards Dyfnarth, feeling grim satisfaction to see his own suspicion reflected in his brother's eyes. But Dyfnarth, too, raised his meadhorn and, after he had drunk, inclined his head towards the heap of spoils.

'We encountered an enemy warband; obliged the bastards by taking their weapons.........and their lives. Earlier, we surprised a settlement, sparing only women and children. The Anglian scum show no such mercy.'

'I saw their work on the borders of Powys. The slaughter.......and their treatment of those they'd not killed...... Death came to them as a blessing. Like a sickness, the barbarians spread across the land, but a sickness can be cured, with the right medicine.'

'And a sword through the skull is not the only medicine?' Dyfnarth laughed. 'We heard that victory was assured whenever you rode with Cynan's men. It's what they used to say of Talhaearn.'

'No one can ensure victory. But I will fight, by the same means as Talhaearn. And I will preserve the memory of our victories for the next generation.' Taliesin took another draught of mead. 'Rheged is still strong.'

'Strengthened by men such as us.'

Again, Taliesin listened for mockery, but again could detect none.

'You were in Elmet for many years. What brought you to Rheged?' he asked.

'Urien can make better use of my sword than Gwallawg. I cannot fight under a weak leader. His courage fails and he shrinks before Aelle of Deira. My skills were wasted in Elmet.'

A draft fanned the flames of the fire, and bold voices rang out as the door to the hall was flung wide. Amongst the warriors who entered was a tall, broad-shouldered man in a crimson cloak, his black hair braided at the temples.

Seeing Taliesin, he called out. 'God be praised, you're back.'

Owain crossed the hall with swift strides.

'So we've re-captured our prize fish.' He glanced at the jewelled dagger that had once been his, still at Taliesin's belt. Then, laughing, they embraced like brothers.

Space was made at the table, and as the prince sat with Taliesin, drinking and exchanging news, Dyfnarth observed their closeness.

When Taliesin finally rose to leave, he spoke in a tone of comradeship.

'We must go hunting......Tomorrow at noon?'

Taliesin knew the words were for the ears of others - the first time in his life that Dyfnarth had publicly sought his company or shown pride in acknowledging him as foster-brother. Telling himself it mattered neither way, that the clanless boy in Gwynedd no longer existed, he inclined his head. Then he walked with Owain from the hall, talking as they went.

After many hours in consultation with Urien, Taliesin was thankful to leave the smoky hall, to breathe cold air that carried the bitter scent of the sea. Caer Liwelydd, with its noise and bustle, often became a maelstrom that seemed to threaten his reason, waging war on his senses. His advice was in constant demand, but without time alone he could not fulfil that demand.

As he headed towards the stables, he saw Finllian crossing the courtyard with a younger woman, dark as Finllian was fair. A stranger who had recently come to Caer Liwelydd as attendant to Owain's wife Penarwen, who was soon to bear their first child.

At that moment Taliesin wanted only to get beyond the

town walls, to speak with no one, but knew he could not avoid them without giving insult.

Finllian met his gravity with a smile, and turned to the olive-skinned woman beside her.

'Let me introduce you to Lady Nefyn, widow of the renowned warrior Cadog, who was slain fighting the Bernicians two years past..........Nefyn, my son Taliesin.'

She nodded her greeting. 'I've seen you perform, and long before that heard your name on the lips of all who'd been guest in Cynan's hall.' Her gaze was direct, black eyes in an oval face framed by curls that had escaped the jewelled clasps in her hair. 'Your songs last night had power.'

'Thank you.' Taliesin met her gaze. 'I take it that Caer Liwelydd pleases you?'

He sensed her appraising him, like fruit for a feast, though her reply was formal. 'It pleases me very much, the hospitality and fine entertainment. And I'm glad to see how the market and its traders flourish even in these times.' She glanced at Finllian. 'I have already been introduced to your daughter, who sang for me.'

Taliesin smiled. 'She is never slow to seek an audience.'

'My sons are the same. Gwilym is twelve, Einion just nine. They remain at our fortress of Dun Anarawd in eastern Rheged. Though I've not been long in Caer Liwelydd, I feel sure it will come to be like a second home.'

'I find it to be so. Rheged is where I undertook the greatest part of my training - under the Master Talhaearn - and I was glad to return.'

'To stay?'

Taliesin inclined his head, conscious that his tension and need for solitude had begun to ease. 'If it be the will of the.......of God.'

* * *

269

The sun was sinking towards the west by the time Taliesin rode from town. At first he thought of Nefyn, recalling their conversation, but gradually the voice of the land drove out all other thoughts, its spirit alive to him as it had always been.

He did not slacken his pace until the expanse of the estuary lay in front of him, grey waters burnt crimson in the sun's path. The mountains of Galloway on the far shore drew his eye as he sat astride Nerth, a bitter wind stinging his cheeks and tearing at the folds of his cloak. They appeared to loom nearer as the sun sank lower, Beli's fire descending into the waters of life.

Taliesin leapt from Nerth's back, and left the horse free to graze. Still looking out towards the west, he regulated his breath, then began a low chant.

> 'Beli Mawr, hear me.
> Sun Lord, hear me......'

As each breath circulated through him he became a part of the sun and wind, the sea and mountains. Yet, he felt an overwhelming grief: the ache of his people, who were no longer whole, whose spirits were closed to the wisdom and divine being of their land. In their hopelessness and separation they had grown weak, allowed Ynys Prydein to be taken and abused by the enemy.

He remembered the destruction of the groves on Ynys Mon. That had been the start of the decay. Remembered Ceridwen's voice, the voice he had first heard when he was no more than a boy. He was one of the few who could turn the tide.

> 'Beli Mawr, hear me.
> Sun Lord, grant me
> warrior spirit......'

Red sun reflected on the waters. In its path the head of a dragon reared from the depths, jaws and nostrils blazing fire, rising in a cloud of vapour. Its flashing tail encircled the shores of Ynys Prydein.

Taliesin felt the searing heat, the flames flowing over and through him, dragon's eyes like white hot iron melting his, in answer to his chant. He stood without moving, welcoming the exhilaration of fear, of pain, drinking in the energy like wine.

'Victory must be earned.' The words burnt in his mind. 'The faint-hearted perish.'

Amidst the fire, like an isle of cool silver, he saw the cauldron with its pearly rim, Beli's claws upon it, sword-sharp and deadly.

Three ravens circled downward. Above the cauldron they became one, transformed into the smiling face of Ceridwen, hideously beautiful.

'Your song must feed the Britons, as I have fed you from the sacred vessel,' she whispered. 'There is still life in the land, courage in the warrior heart........Feed it.......feed it.'

His body trembling, Taliesin exhaled the sacred breath. A gust of wind whipped across the land, almost unbalancing him, and he blinked the mist of vision from his eyes. The waters of Merin Rheged toiled grey as lead, and only a thin line of crimson was visible now, smeared across the tops of the mountains. The glory had faded, replaced by darkness, the onset of night.

Beside him, Nerth whinnied and raised his head, scenting rain on the air. Taliesin took the reins, but instead of making his way back to Caer Liwelydd he began walking westward, gazing at the troubled sea.

In Bernicia Ida's son Aethelric now held the throne, crueller and greedier than his father. With his brother Theodoric, he posed the greatest threat Rheged had ever faced. First there was winter, but in spring the assault would come.

Both sides would give food to the ravens, blood sacrifice to Ceridwen. And over the winter Taliesin would work, with Talhaearn and alone, to be prepared - a warrior with spirit power, strong as any who carried the sword beside Urien.

Holly and ivy decked the pillars in Taliesin's quarters: garlands hung by Branwen after they roamed the frosty woodlands together gathering boughs. The frost had been followed by days of icy rain, which kept the community indoors and saturated the air with a dampness no hearth-fire could dispel.

Nefyn continued speaking as Taliesin rose to refill their goblets, feeling a chill as he left the fireside.

'Gwilym and Einion are to stay with me over Christmas,' she said. 'I've spoken of you and they're keen to meet you.'

Taliesin handed her one of the goblets, then sat beside her on a couch draped with coverings woven in vibrant colour. Nefyn took a sip of wine and leant forward, reaching her hands out to the fire's warmth, jewelled rings glinting, her profile silhouetted against the red light.

'They are strong and bold, especially Gwilym.' There was pride in her voice. 'He craves to be a warrior, to fight the Angles and avenge his father's death, yet I cannot help but dread the day when he takes up arms.'

'That time is several years away.' Taliesin spoke gently. 'We can only live for the present.'

'Which brings challenge enough, I know, and joy.' Nefyn stared into the flames. 'The tides of fate are strange. By blood my mother's family are not of this land, though she was born here and feels as much for the cause as any Briton. One of my ancestors came north with the conquerors to command the fort where Caer Liwelydd stands. For generations they made certain to marry others of Roman descent, and to maintain a connection with the great city, until my mother met a British chieftain.........Perhaps some day it will be the same with the Angles and Saeson. They will be united with the Britons by blood.'

When Taliesin replied, there was an edge to his voice. 'In some cases that may happen, but I believe that eventually we will succeed in ridding our land of them. That is the only way peace can be restored.'

Nefyn sighed and sat back, taking a mouthful of wine. 'We grow too serious. After resolving to live only for the present, we speak of both past and future. Meanwhile this moment passes us by.'

Taliesin, too, sat back, stretching his legs towards the fire.

'We have little enough time together,' Nefyn said, 'with your many duties.'

'There's a composition I should be working on now, for the season. It must be completed within the week.'

'Your songs and tales are a jealous rival.' Placing her goblet on a carved wooden chest beside Taliesin's harp, Nefyn turned to him. 'May I? Or do you not allow others to play it?'

The question was unexpected, and he smiled. 'Were it anyone else I would refuse.'

Nefyn returned the smile, and holding the harp like a beloved child began to pluck a simple tune, her body taut with concentration.

In time she relaxed and played more fluently, then struck the wrong note, followed by another, and stopped, laughing.

'I fear I'll never make a bard. I'll torment your ears no more.'

She handed the instrument to Taliesin who took up the tune where she had left off, playing lightly, the music flowing through him, vital as the flow of his blood, as the warmth of Nefyn's companionship. During his years in Powys, with the women who shared his bed he had never allowed himself to cross the barrier which would have brought emotional

273

closeness. But with Nefyn he had begun to feel differently.

Her skin glowed like bronze between the open folds of her gown, her eyes bright in the firelight as she faced him. Gradually, he began to weave the notes into a deeper, more complex melody, watching her expression change with the music.

chapter two

The Britons were encamped in Gwen Ystrad, where the River Idon flowed narrow and fast, close to its source in the mountains which cut the sky to either side of the valley. Since first light, cloud had swept in from the east, driven by a March wind that bit his flesh as Taliesin stood at the water's edge, gazing towards the enemy camp on the far bank. Though he had spent a troubled night and risen at dawn, his mind was clear, every sense heightened. For the first time he would be with Urien's forces as they rode into battle - a time he had long anticipated.

Turning his back on the rushing waters, he walked through the camp, greeted by warriors who sat by smoky fires, readying their weapons. As he passed, he noticed a change of mood, like a brightness striking through the chill northern spring, a look of hope on hardened faces. Amongst the warriors were men from the south of Rheged, lords and their warbands fighting under Urien against the encroaching power of the Bernicians.

As the moments passed, activity in the camp increased. And above the sound of the river, the valley filled with the snort and stamp of horses, the rattle of harness, men calling to each other.

At his master's approach, Nerth raised his head and whinnied, blowing steam in the damp air. Taliesin placed a hand gently on the horse's nose, and fed him the remains of an oat cake that he himself had no appetite for. Already many of the Britons were in the saddle, preparing to advance. Dyfnarth wheeled his horse at the centre of his men, a spear held aloft as he addressed them, dark hair, lank from moisture, streaming across his shoulders, the scar on his cheek starkly visible.

Tension escalated. As Taliesin mounted, moving forward with the company, Owain rode to his side, clothed in crimson, the round shield he carried emblazoned with his device of three ravens on a crimson ground.

'The hour has come for the enemy to pray,' he said, reining in.

When Taliesin turned, Owain saw the steely light in his eyes, deadly as a blade, and knew he would sooner face sword or spear than the strike of that power. It was something he could never fully understand, yet it brought him confidence, hope of victory.

'I am sent to remind you to stay well back.' He glanced towards Urien's distant figure. 'And to remain where you are visible, for British morale and to un-nerve the enemy.'

'So I am to be like some gilded battle standard. Honoured by being stuck in the rump of the advancing host!'

Owain laughed uneasily. 'As your comrade, I ask you not to put yourself at risk.'

Without further word, he dug his heels into the sides of his black stallion and accompanied the warriors who were making their way through the mud of the valley.

Heeding Urien's message, Taliesin remained behind the lines, watching from a rocky outcrop clear of the action: a still figure clad in a white cloak trimmed with silver, his face and hair almost as white. With him, four lesser bards watched, still and silent as he.

In the rushing water, the rough earth, the outline of mountains softened by mist, he saw the body of the Great Queen, the sacred land whose spirit bore the burdens of her people, his people. And Ceridwen, her golden beauty savage and terrible, poured the elixir from her cauldron through him, into the heart of Ynys Prydein.

The battle was joined at the ford, the advance led by Urien, strong as a man half his age. Battle cries and the blast of war-trumpets echoing from the rocks, Rheged's horsemen rode through the shallow waters, an answering yell rising from the Bernicians.

In a rain of death, British throwing spears struck the enemy ranks. Screams and yells mingled with shouts of challenge and fury as the Angles retaliated, as spears fell amongst the Britons and scramasaxes slashed man and horse.

Above the field of battle, Taliesin began a low chant, summoning the spirit of the red dragon: the divine energy, the strength and courage that would fill the warriors who struggled to free the land. Inhaling the sacred breaths, he channelled the power, seeing the enemy surge forward - bold warriors, many of gigantic stature, fighting on foot against the British cavalry. Did they sense the presence of his gods, bright and deadly on the battlefield, as he sensed theirs - Tiw, and Woden the slayer, master of the sacred runes. No battle was fought on one level alone.

As the warriors closed in, the action became a tangled mass of movement. Sometimes Taliesin would glimpse a scarlet shield, Urien's purple cloak, then again they were lost in the throng.

At the ford, the river gushed red with blood. Bodies were thrust against the rocks, and wounded men writhed in the water.

Taliesin remained where he was stationed, overlooking the action, until he felt the touch of an unseen hand on his shoulder.

'Go forward.' The din of battle became the voice of Ceridwen, hollow as death. 'Go forward. There is danger to one close to you.'

He ceased to chant, his mind wracked with conflict. Urien's message had been clear. Yet he could not put the king's words before those of his goddess. Cynan had never restricted him in this way. With the Lord of Powys, his own judgement had been unquestioned.

He flicked Nerth's reins, uttering a brief command. As the bay moved in answer, stepping between the other bards waiting on horseback, one of them turned, a man of around Taliesin's age who had come with a warband from the southern borders of Rheged.

There was a restlessness, an eagerness about him that reflected his own mood.

Thinking that his support would aid his task, Taliesin addressed the man in a tone of encouragement. 'Accompany me if you wish,' he said. 'We can do little here.'

Keeping their eyes on where the clash was fiercest, they rode towards the ford, the other bards remaining on the crag, holding the chant.

As they crossed the river, the battle energy hit Taliesin like a stone in the chest, taking his breath. Chaos, rage, pain........vivid as the cold red water that frothed around Nerth's hooves. And he felt the power of Beli ignite his spirit, the fire of the red dragon coursing through his veins.

Thrusting-spears gleamed in descending mist, dripping blood. A man staggered after a blow and fell, pulped beneath the hooves of a dozen leaping horses. Swords severed flesh and bone. With a yell of triumph, an Angle struck through the neck of the Briton who faced him, swift as a wood-cutter felling a tree.

Exchanging a glance with his companion, Taliesin continued, taking up a position on the far bank, on higher ground that enabled him to survey the battlefield. Close to the action, with pockets of fighting around them, for the first time the bards had to look to their own safety. While the other man remained watchful, Taliesin sought out king and comrades, until a flash of scarlet caught his eye, and he saw Owain locked in combat with a Bernician swordsman. As the prince lunged at the enemy, a second Bernician raised his spear, aiming at

Owain's unguarded back. Taliesin felt the white fire burn behind his eyes, though he could afford no error. The shock as the energy passed through his body would leave him too weak to strike again.

Suddenly Owain's horse reared, kicking the swordsman in the chest and knocking him to the ground. Owain turned, deflecting the spear-thrust before plunging his blade in deep at the second Bernician's throat. Exhaling, Taliesin earthed the energy he had built, and watched Owain's advance, afraid his comrade's life lay in danger, though in strength, in skill, he was unequalled.

The bards held their horses in check, following the tide of battle, and as the enemy rallied, the Britons falling before them, Taliesin heard Urien's voice raised above the tumult,

'For the glory of Rheged, stand firm.'

The king was close to him now, riding to meet with the Bernician chief Aethelric. Noise hammered in Taliesin's ears - the clash of metal on metal, hooves striking stone, shrieks of death. Each breath he took was filled with the reek of hot iron, of blood and sweat.

As Urien charged, a spear pierced his horse's chest. A fountain of red spurted over the Angle, who was already bloodied, and the horse screamed and stumbled, Urien leaping clear, sword in hand. Aethelric lunged, but Urien was quick. He dodged, and while Aethelric was unbalanced struck him in the side, though his chain mail took the full force of the blow. Again, Aethelric's sword was raised; again, Urien leapt clear. Swiftly, he lashed out, launching his attack, giving no ground. The Angle met the onslaught with his shield, his blade sudden and sure. Urien pressed forward - leaping, slashing........

Only once the Bernician chief was too slow. Urien's sword bit into his arm and he dropped his shield, falling as the next thrust caught him on the thigh. But before Urien could finish his work, the Angles formed a wall around their leader, and with a yell another took his place.

Outnumbered, and finally tiring, Urien and his men fought bravely. Taliesin focussed his intent, and was ready to unleash the white fire when the Angles came under surprise attack, confronted by British reinforcements under Dyfnarth's command, warriors who took the brunt of the assault from the king.

With a sign, Taliesin indicated for the other bard to join him in summoning the spirit energy to their aid, and from his vantage point Dyfnarth's strategy was plain. The Britons were cornering the foreigners in a gully, like hunters cornering a wild beast. The press of men was so dense he could no longer pick out Urien's figure. Only Dyfnarth remained within sight, fighting an Angle who brought down his horse with an axe blow, and thrust a blood-soaked knife at his throat. Outwitting him, Dyfnarth plunged his sword beneath the man's shield, slicing through flesh and sinew so the enemy fell to the trampled earth. Without pause, Dyfnarth turned to meet a fresh assault, showing no sign of exhaustion. It was only when he faced a stocky warrior with streaks of fire in his beard that at last he seemed to have met his equal. With his sword, the man struck at Dyfnarth, each time meeting Dyfnarth's blade.

Once more the Angle raised his sword. At the same instant another ran at Dyfnarth's side, scramasax unsheathed. With no time for thought, Taliesin concentrated the power, building it to intensity, dagger points slashing his brain, almost blinding him, a furnace roaring in his ears. The scene before him froze in burning silver as he released the energy.

Immediately, the pain was gone, his senses restored, though he was left weak and vulnerable. As he steadied himself, he saw both Bernicians paralyzed, eyes wide and staring. His sword fell from the red-beard's hand. The other man stumbled, scramasax plunging harmlessly into the earth. For a second Dyfnarth hesitated, bewildered. Then, leaping forward he cut the Anglian warrior through the neck with one driving thrust.

Before Taliesin had the chance to recover his strength, he heard a cry, and span round to see the gleam of a spear in flight. Lying flat across Nerth's neck, he swerved, feeling a rush as it passed, so close it tore through a fold of his cloak. As the Angle who had cast it stepped back, Taliesin rode at him, Nerth's hooves striking him in the face as he fell. The man moaned, writhing helplessly, then lay still.

Taliesin gripped the reins, trying to calm Nerth, and turning, saw a robed figure lying on the ground. While the battle raged at the entrance to the gully, he dismounted and crouched beside his fallen companion. The other bard was still conscious, though his robe was wet with blood, his breath coming in shallow gasps as the life-force ebbed from his body. Taliesin rested his left hand on his arm, with his right, tracing a symbol of blessing on the bard's forehead. Fighting his own despair, he spoke with deceptive calm,

'Great Mother of Life, take the spirit of your son into your care. As the sun sets in the west and rises in the east, so are we born again in the eternal cycle of being.'

The man's breathing became shallower, grating in his throat, his eyes clouding. Taliesin stayed at his side, shutting out the clamour of battle, careless of his own safety. Though he had saved Dyfnarth's life, he thought only that he should have ridden from the crag alone, placed no one else in danger.

Remaining alert, he travelled in spirit to ease the man's untimely journey across the threshold to the Blessed Isles. He continued to guide him even after he no longer breathed, white eyes gazing beyond the chill mist that swept through the valley.

In the camp, fires were lit, as cries of pain and death jarred the stillness.

'I must speak with Prince Owain.' Taliesin addressed the warrior who walked with him across ground churned to mud by the tramp of man and horse.

'Have you not heard?' The warrior's voice was low. 'He has been wounded.'

Taliesin felt a tightness in his belly. 'Grievously?'

'I do not know, my lord. I received the news from another.'

Haunted by the face of the dying bard and oppressed by the suffering around him, Taliesin hastened through the camp, in his exhaustion fear taking increasing hold.

Outside Owain's tent two warriors leant on their spears. They straightened as he approached, and the elder man bowed his head in respect,

'My lord, I have instructions that you may enter.'

With a silent prayer, Taliesin pushed the tent flap aside, finding his comrade lying on a pallet bed, Urien's chief physician Iorwerth attending him. Owain's face looked drawn, but his eyes were bright as they met Taliesin's.

'A glorious victory,' were his first words. 'Aethelric is wounded. And our losses are few compared to the foreigners whose blood pollutes our earth.'

He cursed as Iorwerth began to bind his knee, where a Bernician sword had slashed through to the bone. Grinning against the pain, he spoke boldly.

'I'll live to fight another day, and to enjoy the victory feast. There are those in greater need of Iorwerth's skills than I.' Then, noticing the blood that stained Taliesin's cloak, he forgot his show of fortitude. 'By God, you are not hurt are you? I saw that you did not remain on the rock.'

'I am unharmed. This is the blood of another.' Blood that stained Taliesin's conscience, allowing him no peace. The voice of reason told him that Urien and Owain did not torture themselves for each warrior who was slain under their command, fighting of his own free will. As the bard who had

282

ridden with him had made his own choice. Yet he could not reason away the guilt.

Avoiding the question in Owain's eyes, he turned to Iorwerth. 'If there is anything I can do to assist you with the wounded, I have some skill.'

Mead horns were put aside, food forgotten, as Taliesin's voice filled the hall, strong in praise of Urien.

> 'He keeps the chiefs at bay
> and scythes them down.........
> The defender of his tribe
> against the foe
> whenever they come
> like calamitous waves over the land.' ₉

Many who had been wounded the previous day listened - Owain, seated with his father, others, more severely wounded, lying on mattresses by the hearth. All attention focussed on Taliesin's blue-robed figure, the torc around his neck catching the firelight. Those who had suffered grievous injuries, those who had seen comrades slaughtered, heard his words and found courage.

Nefyn sat at the royal table, gold at her throat and wrists, Taliesin's gifts. She noticed how he spoke not only with his voice but with his body, knowing the power of movement, and of stillness. Not once did she take her eyes from him. Though most were flushed from heat and mead, his skin retained its silvery pallor. She felt a jealous pride, aware that other women envied her. In under a year she had emerged from obscurity amongst the windswept mountains to the heart of Rheged, to Urien's table and the bed of his Chief Bard. Yet she was angry that he had scarcely found time to speak to her since he returned from Gwen Ystrad.

He looked towards the king as he recited.

'On the entrance of the ford
I saw bloodstained warriors,
their weapons abandoned
before a grizzly lord.......' [10]

Only when Taliesin's performance ended did the company find release into the present. For a moment, silence, before the reaction broke, more tumultuous than Urien remembered even under Talhaearn. After the fight he had been weary, now he felt that he possessed the vigour of a young man, that the future lay bright before him and his people.

As another bard stepped forward and Taliesin resumed his place, Nefyn herself refilled his meadhorn, dismissing the attendant who came to serve him.

Beneath the table, she clasped her hand on his thigh.

'Thank God, or perhaps I should thank your gods, that you returned safely from Gwen Ystrad.'

Taliesin rested his hand over hers but did not look at her. Sitting back, he watched the bard who had begun to sing, so she saw only his aquiline profile.

'I have heard rumours......reports. They say you took part in the conflict, risking your life by riding into battle to slay the enemy without physical weapons.'

'Is that what they say.' Taliesin spoke flatly. He took a draught of mead and reached for a piece of dried fruit from the silver platter in front of them.

'It is what they believe. What I believe.' Nefyn lowered her voice. 'Rheged loves you, Taliesin.'

Finally, he turned, and in his eyes she saw a depth of emotion that struck to the depth of her own feeling. He gave no reply, and simply inclined his head in the direction of the bard who was performing.

'Let us listen to this man's words,' he said softly, 'as he listened to mine.'

The weather had grown warmer, and flowers were in bloom on the hillsides where cattle grazed. Branwen carried a bunch of meadowsweet in her hand as she ran ahead, tall and narrow as a sapling, barley-coloured hair shining in the sunlight. Nefyn wore a chaplet the girl had made and, for once, no jewels except the ring of interlaced gold and silver that had been her first gift from Taliesin.

'My complexion will become brown and leathery like a peasant's,' she said with a brisk laugh. 'And I shall blame you for having lured me out of the shade.'

'You should thank me instead. The sun grants you its warmth, its life-energy, in celebration of summer.' Taliesin looked at the expanse of land around them. 'Surely it's better to be here than confined with a host of irritable and sweaty townspeople.'

'If you put it so. At least you have escaped Urien. I half expect a messenger to ride up at any moment with a request for you to return and settle some dispute.' Nefyn fell silent, frowning as she followed the direction of Taliesin's gaze to the eastern horizon. When she turned back to him there was a note of challenge in her voice. 'Prince Owain has gone raiding into Manaw again......Did you wish to ride with him?'

He put an arm around her waist, drawing her to his side. 'What do you imagine?'

'Probably you are wondering if they've crossed the border yet, how many head of cattle they've taken.......hoping that you can go next time and compose a poem to glorify the adventure.'

Taliesin laughed, then kissed her. No longer walking, Nefyn returned the kiss, wishing that Branwen was elsewhere.

Or that they were in the comfort of their own chamber, with a soft bed, and costly wine to share after making love.

When they moved apart, she glanced in Branwen's direction and saw her turn away as she knelt amongst the long grasses.

'Do you forget we're not alone?' she said with a smile.

'You wanted a reply to your question. Or perhaps you are still unconvinced.'

Nefyn shrugged and leant closer. 'I may be, or maybe not.'

'Have no concern over Branwen.' Taliesin kissed her again. 'She knows I'm human. And Finllian taught her the ways of the world many years ago.'

'Soon she will be following your example, be warned.'

He raised a brow. 'And Gwilym will follow yours.'

They continued walking, listening to Branwen's song. Finally, she stopped and waited for them to catch up, carrying not only the flowers but her shoes. She glanced at Nefyn, then looked up at Taliesin with mischief in her eye.

'Would you like me to pick more flowers, father?'

He remained straight-faced. 'I think you have plenty. Finllian won't know what to do with them all.'

'Then I will give them to Princess Penarwen. She's unhappy because Owain is away. I know how sad she must feel........I'm so pleased you are no longer living in Powys.'

With a lively step she walked beside him, chattering and laughing. And though he knew it was time they turned back, for a long while he could not make himself, wanting to hold on to those moments of happiness when it was almost possible to forget that their land was in turmoil, Anglian raids increasing as the days lengthened; that before nightfall he must sit with the elders in council to debate alliance with Elmet, and a burden he had grown accustomed to would weigh heavy on his shoulders once again.

They delayed so long that the sun was losing heat by the

time they reached the town gates, and a chill had crept into the air as they made their way through the streets of Caer Liwelydd, dark in the shadow of the houses.

Leaving Branwen in Nefyn's care, Taliesin went directly to the hall, his mood still uplifted by the joy of the afternoon. Though the elders had not yet assembled, he sensed a heightened atmosphere. Pouring himself a cup of mead, he took a seat by the hearth, where Owain came to his side.

'Discussing alliance with Elmet seems of little importance now,' the prince said, meeting Taliesin's gaze.

Taliesin frowned. 'I have been from town since noon, and have only just returned.'

For a second Owain hesitated. 'I assumed you knew.' He took a draught of mead, then spoke eagerly. 'Father has received a message from Ystrad Glud. Rhydderch wishes to visit Caer Liwelydd over the feast of St John, bringing his wife and son. He seeks reconciliation.'

Taliesin said nothing, his mind empty of words. Misreading his silence, Owain continued,

'This news is indeed unexpected. There's been bad blood between the clans for as long as I recall. But Queen Gwenddydd is our kinswoman, descended from the sister of my great-grandsire. Perhaps it is she who has persuaded Rhydderch to lay aside past grievances for the sake of their son. When he inherits the kingdom he will welcome strong allies.'

Taliesin forced himself to reply. 'Rheged, too, needs strong allies, and Ystrad Glud is growing in power.'

He got to his feet, knowing that somehow he must face the discussions that lay ahead, remaining clear in thought, objective in advice - over-riding his own feelings for the sake of Ynys Prydein.....as he had once before.

chapter three

It was mid-afternoon when the herald strode into the hall.

Watched by a company impatient for news, he bowed before Urien. 'My lord, the party from Ystrad Glud have been sighted from the gatehouse.'

The king drained his mead-horn and rose from the table, turning to Taliesin.

'May God be with us.'

He spoke firmly, standing resolute and proud amidst the glorious display of his wealth. Yet Taliesin saw that the strain of the past weeks was beginning to tell. Not within living memory had the clan of Dyfnwal been offered hospitality by the descendants of Coel. Since the messengers were despatched to Ystrad Glud, preparations had been under way, everything done to ensure the guests could find no excuse to take insult. But Gaulish wine and lavish gifts could not guard against word or act, and Urien's decision to accept the offer of reconciliation had roused anger amongst a faction of his own clansmen - a fire that smouldered close beneath the surface.

Under a heavy sky, the welcoming party waited in a courtyard thronged with people. At intervals, muted talk broke the silence. Spots of rain fell. Men shifted restlessly, glancing towards the road. Then, a murmur of excitement. One by one, heads turned, attention focussed on the retinue which advanced along the straight thoroughfare leading from the gates of Caer Liwelydd; indistinct at first, no more than a silhouette. Anticipation mounted as it drew closer - a vast company..........To the fore, the outriders of the warrior escort, spears held high in salute, shield bosses and harness gleaming bright; following in procession, a host of richly clad attendants who parted into crescent formation as they entered the courtyard.

Taliesin watched as the royal visitors came within sight, slowly making their progress towards where he stood with Urien; and, in the dignified woman who approached, he glimpsed the girl he had once known - in another kingdom, in another life, it seemed. Head held high, dark hair coiled in braids above a gold coronet, Gwenddydd rode at her husband's side. She appeared at ease, and turned once to smile at the slender auburn-haired boy who rode with them. Rhodri, who had been born a month after Branwen. In his veins flowed the blood of Coel and of Dyfnwal, and Taliesin knew that if there was to be hope for the future, a permanent end to generations of feuding and bitterness, that hope lay with him.

Rhydderch dismounted first, agile despite his years, and helped Gwenddydd from the saddle. Though she looked at Urien, she was conscious of Taliesin standing to his right, robed in sea green and gold, his height dwarfing the warriors gathered about him. An outsider who had risen to become one of the most powerful men in Rheged.

He remained outwardly impassive as Urien faced his guests, speaking boldly.

'Lord Rhydderch, Queen Gwenddydd, the hospitality of Caer Liwelydd is yours.'

Urien clasped Rhydderch's forearm in greeting, as a cheer rose from the assembled clansmen.

Rhydderch's voice, too, was bold. 'This is a propitious day, when the people of Rheged and Ystrad Glud meet in friendship.'

Despite the rain, which was now falling steadily, Urien addressed the company in praise of Rhydderch. As he listened to the speech he had composed for the king, and discussed over many hours of consultation, Taliesin became increasingly tense. Yet this was what he had worked for throughout his life - to achieve a position of high standing where he had the power to make his voice heard in the service of Ynys Prydein, to fight for the sacred land. This day, when the kingdoms of the north stood at the brink of alliance, was the accomplishment of his own wishes.

Again, cheering resounded in the courtyard, three hundred voices raised in celebration. Taliesin waited. And as the uproar faded, with measured paces he came forward to greet the Lord of Ystrad Glud, trying to think of the future, not the past. Addressing Rhydderch, he found himself looking at a kindly, intelligent face, the face of a strong and deeply spiritual man. In his words he found encouragement, the reflection of his own hopes. But though they spoke at length, Taliesin's attention was divided, straying to the still, blue-cloaked figure beside Rhydderch. After weeks spent trying to reconcile himself, he knew he was unprepared for the moment when he would meet Gwenddydd.

Perhaps it was he who prolonged the conversation, giving himself time, but finally he stood before her. As he inclined his head, his eyes met hers. Her gaze was steady, and possessed the gentle confidence he remembered. He feared to seek more, to see beyond her barrier of composure.....and rational thought was slipping from his grasp. Images held in memory merged with the present, time and place held in precarious balance. He forgot her husband, the elite of two kingdoms who looked on, and a core of emotion he had buried so deeply that he had almost forgotten its existence suddenly lay unprotected.

The company watched the Chief Bard of Rheged and the Queen of Ystrad Glud greet each other as strangers, keeping a respectful distance; heard his words, courteous and formal.

'My lady, may your stay in Rheged be a pleasant one.'

'I am sure it will.' Gwenddydd's tone echoed his, carefully neutral. 'We are keen to hear you sing tonight, your reputation has travelled far.'

Drenched by the rain, Taliesin's body felt clammy beneath

his costly robes. With an effort he maintained concentration as he went to speak with others of Rhydderch's clan, aware that all he did was judged. He would not be the one to jeopardize the alliance he had argued for at the council of elders, anticipating a time when the kingdoms of Ynys Prydein stood side by side against the Anglian enemy, no longer tearing at each other's throats.

The feast began at dusk, and continued all night until the dawning of the holy day of St John. Though he seldom attended the services that Bishop Segnius held for Urien, out of respect for the pious Rhydderch, Taliesin was amongst the congregation at the royal chapel that morning.

The bishop's voice reverberated in the candlelit darkness, yet Taliesin scarcely listened, responding automatically as the psalms were chanted. It seemed incongruous to him to worship inside when the sun was at the height of its yearly power, and when St John himself had preached in the open air, laying the foundations for the coming of Christ. He looked at Segnius' grey-robed figure, and from the corner of his eye saw Gwenddydd - head bowed, her pale face deep in reflection like her husband's - her nearness unsettling him. Was she in reality now so devout a Christian? The girl who possessed the sight, who communed with spirits and was herb-wise like the priestesses of the Old Faith. He longed to speak with her alone, but knew it was impossible, that she would always be in the company of her husband, her women. And he was Chief Bard, the servant of Rheged, a bridge at the centre of a fragile alliance.

After the service, Taliesin lingered in the sunlit courtyard, finding a moment's respite in Owain's company. As the crowd began to thin and he headed towards the hall, he noticed Gwenddydd and Rhydderch talking with a slight, dark man who had not been in the chapel, nor at the welcome feast, and who still wore dirt-stained travelling clothes.

His face the usual mask of formality, he stopped to offer his greetings.

Gwenddydd responded with a smile, less reserved than she had been the previous day.

'Lord Taliesin,' she said brightly, glancing at the dark man beside her, 'my twin brother Myrddin, Chief Bard to Lord Gwenddoleu of Arderydd.'

Taliesin turned to him. 'I'm glad we have the opportunity to meet, and on such an occasion.......I believe that you were once at Urien's court.'

'That was many years ago.' Myrddin appeared uncomfortable and continued hurriedly. 'I undertook most of my training in Dyfed, and Lord Gwenddoleu is now my patron, my chieftain. As one of his warband, I cannot stay long in Rheged. We live under constant threat of raids, from the foreigners and from the men of Manaw attempting to plunder our cattle.'

The group began to walk, Myrddin speaking animatedly. His eyes, of so dark a blue they appeared black, glinted like a troubled flame, and there was a nervousness about him, in the movement of his sinewy hands, the abrupt changes of expression.

Before they reached the hall, Rhydderch interrupted his flow of speech. 'The queen and I are tired after many day's journey,' he said. 'We wish to rest. If you will excuse us, Lord Taliesin.'

As they left, Taliesn noted the angle of the sun. It was just past noon. At mid-afternoon Urien expected him in consultation, and he must prepare the work he would recite that evening before the guests. He must also make time to speak with Ysfael, to organize the bardic performances. But even as the weight of responsibility pressed on his mind, he addressed Myrddin.

'Can I offer you some wine?' he asked. 'Unless you, too, wish to rest?'

Myrddin laughed. 'There is opportunity enough for rest in the grave.'

In the silence of his chamber, Taliesin filled a silver goblet for his guest, then sat down on the opposite side of the hearth, conscious that he was with the one person in Caer Liwelydd who knew that he and Gwenddydd were not strangers.

Myrddin glanced towards the closed door, then spoke in an undertone. 'Soon we shall see the result of this new friendship between Rhydderch and Urien. An alliance of old enemies brings many trials.'

Taliesin remained on his guard. 'With resolve, all trials can be overcome. There is much to be gained on both sides.'

'I can only view the situation from an outsider's perspective. I am not Rhydderch's man, simply his brother-in-law.' Myrddin's quick grin spoke more than his words. 'And I suspect it will take more than an ever changing pattern of alliances to drive the foreigners out. As an initiate, I believe you understand my meaning.'

Taliesin took a draught of wine, and laid his cup on the table beside him.

'After the victory at Gwen Ystrad I knew that the cauldron is not beyond the reach of our people. Many in Rheged still feel the power of the Awen; still revere the spirit of Sovereignty.'

Myrddin's narrow face was animated. 'Urien is a true king. Though baptized, Talhaearn ensured that he was wed to the land, as he arranged the rite for Urien's father Cynfarch many years before. Not so with Rhydderch, nor will it be with Rhodri........if he has a kingdom to inherit when the time comes. The Great Queen is not a mistress to be trifled with.'

Taliesin sighed. 'The enemy's increasing hold over our land is a result, as much as a cause, of separation.'

'The Britons must drink of the cauldron as they once did,

revive the sacred tradition. Only then will the red dragon drive out the white.' Seeing the recognition in Taliesin's eyes, Myrddin paused, then looked at him quizzically. 'I noticed you were in chapel with the others.'

Taliesin replied evenly. 'I seek the similarities between the old and new faiths, not their differences. The festival we celebrate today, under whatever guise, has been honoured since the days before the great druid priesthood.' He thought back to his own past - Brother Docmael, Beulan, Cadfarch - then continued in a low voice. 'I was raised a Christian by my foster-parents, but though I no longer regard myself as such, I find no conflict in my soul........It is to the Lady Ceridwen that I have dedicated my life.'

'I wield my sword in the name of Llew, the many-skilled, the light of all true kings. And, if needful, under his guidance use more subtle means to overcome the enemy.' Myrddin's eyes were bright in his pale face. 'Many times I have summoned the fog of concealment.'

Taliesin gave a faint smile. 'Two summers past, the course of battle was against Cynan's men when the advancing Saeson saw fire fall from a clear sky, setting the waters of Afon Hafren ablaze......They retreated like frightened children, granting us victory.'

'I heard reports of it. My Lord Gwenddoleu would be glad to offer hospitality to such as you. In his lands you'd not have to maintain a facade of Christianity.'

Taliesin drained his goblet, uncertain if he should voice what was on his mind. But despite the risk in dredging up the past, he could not keep himself from asking,

'And Gwenddydd? Has she wholeheartedly embraced her husband's faith?'

Myrddin did not seem surprised, nor disquieted, by the question. 'Her attitude to matters of faith is akin to your own,' he replied without hesitating, 'though, of course, she has less opportunity to follow her own path, nor is she an initiate.'

'She once studied herb lore, and used the gift of spirit sight.'

'Since she married she no longer discusses such things with me. She says she has more pressing concerns, such as the running of her household, the duties of a queen, of a mother.'

Taliesin leant forward to refill their goblets as Myrddin continued.

'As I said, you must visit the fortress of Caerwenddolew.........Do you enjoy riding? Cattle raiding?'

Taliesin's glance was met with a wicked smile.

'I think Gwenddoleu may be planning to test the alertness of the men of Ystrad Glud, in preference to Manaw. Rhydderch has some fine cattle.'

Unsure if Myrddin spoke in jest, Taliesin raised a brow, feeling a growing liking for him.

'Ah.... Tonight when I sing, I shall praise Rhydderch's great wealth, the splendour of his herds, and of course his famed generosity.'

Myrddin stopped, and became suddenly serious. 'If you wish, we could work together on a composition before I leave in three days time. An alliance of bards, of initiates. That is where hope for victory lies. And were we to combine our powers in rites concealed from the once-born........'

Taliesin faced his guest, his voice low. 'Concerning the deep, we will bring it to the common source of rivers.' 11

The golden serpent ring Myrddin wore gleamed on his forefinger as he wove the ancient signs, replying silently in verse. Then, speaking aloud, he said, 'Rhydderch does not have to know, only to reap the rewards. And no doubt take credit for the outcome.'

'I'd be honoured to accept your invitation to Caerwenddolew, as soon as my duties here allow.' Taliesin rose, crossing the room to a locked chest. 'I have a copy of a manuscript that may interest you. Though the man who wrote it is a cleric, by the name of Gildas, he has much to say with a bearing on our current situation.'

'Yes, I have read some of his works.' Again, Myrddin's eyes shone with an elfin light. 'Perhaps we, too, should scratch our creations on parchment. To ensure we are remembered.'

chapter four

Three boys rode at a gallop beneath the walls of Caer Liwelydd, taking turns to cast spears at the stump of a dead tree, their shouts ringing out in the summer evening.

When Rhodri's spear struck the target once again, his companions cheered. The thrill of the contest filled them, beyond rivalry, combined with pride at riding with the visiting prince, at having his company to themselves away from the other boys at the fortress.

Rhodri wheeled his horse around, his sensitive face framed by fiery hair, while Nefyn's two sons held their own excited horses in check.

'Fine shot, Lord Dyfnarth could do no better,' Gwilym called out as Rhodri pulled the weapon free and returned to his comrades.

On the road from town, Taliesin reined in and watched. It was a week since the celebrations to mark the northern alliance began, and each day he had welcomed Rhydderch and Gwenddydd into the hall, sealing the peace between clans. Had he ever truly imagined that seeing her would be this hard? When they parted they had been but fifteen. For years they had lived separate lives. And he thought he had found happiness with Nefyn, that he had accepted what could not be altered. But now everything seemed unclear, his certainties undermined, and he felt an ache that even Nefyn's love could not ease.

He dug his heels into Nerth's sides, and closing his mind to regret, rode on in the direction of Talhaearn's settlement. The master had come to Caer Liwelydd to witness the oath of alliance, but had since returned to his own hall, leaving his former duties to Taliesin. As he headed along the overgrown path to the clearing, finally he felt a measure of peace. This was the place which had been his home for so long, the place where he had crossed the bridge from boyhood to manhood, where he could find rest from the pressures of his role at court.

One of Talhaearn's two apprentices was seated in the shade of the larger roundhouse and turned at his approach.

'Good evening, my lord.' The youth got to his feet as Taliesin dismounted. 'The master is in the hall with my comrade, who is trying to understand the Secret Language.'

Taliesin raised a brow. 'Trying.......and not succeeding?'

'He has been finding it difficult.' The apprentice went to place the three wooden staves he had been casting back in their leather pouch, but Taliesin extended a hand, and instead the boy laid them in his palm.

'The alder trees in the first line, they made the commencement.' Taliesin spoke with an undulating rhythm. 'The hazel is the judge, his berries are thy dowry.......The oak tree swiftly moving, before him tremble heaven and earth, stout doorkeeper against the foe.' [12]

The boy gazed up at the Chief Bard who, despite his formidable height and knowledge, looked back with a kindly expression.

'Meditate, and the trees will unlock their secrets.'

As he returned the staves, the door to the hall opened.

'Taliesin! There is only one such voice.' Talhaearn crossed the clearing, no less agile with advancing years. 'I did not expect to see you here while Urien entertains the Lord of Ystrad Glud. A Chief Bard's time is precious as gold.'

'I managed to escape those who seek to enrich themselves.' Taliesin paused. 'I hope I do not disturb your work.'

The master ignored the question as if it did not warrant an answer. 'Come into the hall, we have some fine elder wine, made by the apprentices last year.'

Taliesin followed him through the door, for a moment

unable to see clearly after the brightness outside. As his eyes adjusted, familiar forms emerged from the gloom. Stone and skull, horn and antler were there as they had always been, the wolf-skin still hanging above the carved chest. Then he noticed that two boys had risen from beside the hearth as he entered. The second, a stranger.

As an apprentice went to fetch them wine, Talhaearn beckoned the boy forward.

'My most recent pupil - Bedwen. He has been with me but a week.'

Taliesin looked at an intense face sprinkled with freckles. 'Are you from Rheged?' he asked.

'No, Gwynedd, my lord.'

'Myself also. There is no sight more inspiring than the peaks of Eryri in the first glow of dawn.'

The boy's startling blue eyes brightened with the memory. 'I left my home and kin to study under Master Iestyn, but he became sick, and died in the spring.'

After Taliesin had taken the cup that was brought, Talhaearn turned to the boys with a gesture of dismissal. The door closed behind them and Taliesin sank down onto one of the benches, suddenly realizing how exhausted he was.

He looked across the hearth at Talhaearn. 'Bedwen is exceptionally promising?'

It was many years since the Pen Beirdd had trained three apprentices at one time.

'His previous master once studied with me. He was concerned about the boy, whose gifts are matched by his wild nature. When Iestyn's health began to fail, I assured him that I would take Bedwen on. A strong will can be an asset.........and he'll not be my first wilful apprentice.'

Their eyes met as Taliesin took a draught of wine, while outside in the clearing he could hear the boys speaking in excited undertones.

Humour lingered in Talhaearn's eyes. 'The position of Chief Bard brings great privilege. When alliances are forged he must live without sleep or solitude, and be answerable to all.'

Taliesin sighed, thinking how Talhaearn knew nothing of the strain he was under, nor the reason for it. 'I confess I'll not regret it when the guests leave,' he said, 'though I'm heartened by what we've achieved, beyond expectation. And I was glad of the chance to meet Rhydderch's brother-in-law, Myrddin ap Madoc - an interesting man.'

Talhaearn nodded, but Taliesin noticed a reticence. 'I knew him when he was a youth, around Bedwen's age. For a short time he lived with his kinsmen in Caer Liwelydd.'

As he listened to the boys' voices fading into the distance, Taliesin wondered why Talhaearn had not taken someone so gifted as apprentice. When the master said no more, he himself spoke. 'We worked together before he returned to Arderydd, and intend to do so again. His powers could be an asset to our cause.'

'Perhaps. That will become clearer as your work progresses.' But again Taliesin noticed Talhaearn's reticence.

The company had begun to assemble for the farewell feast, and in the torchlit courtyard a crowd of young people gathered about Rhodri, who smiled with easy confidence as his companions vied for his attention. Twelve-year-old Branwen stood between two other girls, though she took no part in their conversation, and they talked across her while she gazed at Rhodri, a distant look in her eyes. Taliesin noticed it with discomfort - a further reason why he would only rest easy once the visiting party returned to Ystrad Glud. Yet he dreaded the emptiness he anticipated when Gwenddydd left.

He turned away and entered the hall, joining Rhydderch's bards. Over the hours he had spent with them during the visit, contesting and debating, listening to song and tale, he had found them to be empty shells, divested of power. Though they were skilled in technique, the Awen no longer flowed through their words.

The atmosphere was already heightened by the time the king and his royal guests made their entrance. As the roar of acclamation died down, Urien raised his meadhorn.

'We feast tonight in honour of King Rhydderch and Queen Gwenddydd, and Prince Rhodri - heir to Ystrad Glud; and all our noble comrades and allies. God grant you peace and prosperity.' He drained the meadhorn, the company following suit. Immediately, it was refilled by the attendant who stood at his shoulder. 'From this hour the swords of Rheged and Ystrad Glud are wielded side by side against the enemy. May the bond between our kingdoms grow in strength and lasting friendship, allied to my sons' lands: Prince Owain's realm of Galloway and Prince Elffin's realm of Aeron.'

Once more, the company drank deep, then Rhydderch rose to speak, his voice softer but resolute.

'We thank Rheged for your hospitality. Mid-summer has been bright, like the brightness of the Britons' enduring courage.' He looked at those gathered before him. 'God's blessing upon our cause.'

The feast began, talk and laugher filling the hall.

'Maybe in future we can forge an alliance with Lord Gwenddoleu as well,' Ysfael whispered close to Taliesin's ear.

He took a mouthful of mead, then gave a bitter laugh. 'I think not, while we are allied with Rhydderch.'

An attendant served him a fine cut of pork from an engraved platter, but he ate little, conscious of the ever-changing tides of loyalty amongst the clansmen. Despite fine words, the new friendship was fragile. And there were those who would have preferred to make alliance with Gwenddoleu, though his wealth and strength of arms were dwarfed by the power of Ystrad Glud.

Rhydderch's Chief Bard was first to perform in celebration. Many bards of the highest skill sang, and many toasts were drunk, many oaths sworn, before the company heard the words they had come to expect.

'My lords,' Urien's voice rose above the clamour, 'lend your ears to the Master Taliesin, Chief Bard of Rheged.'

As he got to his feet, silence fell. He turned first to Rhydderch, then Gwenddydd. When he addressed them, only he knew that he spoke not for the people but for himself.

'My lord, my lady, your visit to Rheged will be long remembered.'

Gwenddydd smiled, but Taliesin sensed the tension behind the facade. Slowly, he moved to the centre of the hall, between the great oak tables, the torc at his neck flashing in the torchlight. Pausing, he held the company's attention, fuelling the fire of their anticipation until, in a clear voice, he began to recite.

'In the hall of the men of Rheged
there is every
esteem and welcome,
offering of wine
for jubilation,
fair lands.....
riches a-plenty
and gold, gold.' [13]

At last, forgetting his own conflict, he felt the Awen pour through him, driven by his love for Ynys Prydein, for Rheged, his respect for Urien.

'Kings bellow
for fear of your onrush:
battle's goader,

country's defender,
defender of country,
goader in battle.
Constantly around you
is the pounding of horses
and the drinking of mead........' 14

The elite of Ystrad Glud and Rheged listened.   Past
enemies seated together, united in spirit. At that moment they
were one, and as one would win victory - a moment warriors
from two kingdoms would recall as they rode into battle. Each
verse Taliesin recited, the power grew stronger.

Finally, his praises ringing loud, he faced the royal table.
Again, he saw Gwenddydd smile, the tension gone, and he
knew that she, too, felt the power of the Awen.

Such was the bounty of Urien's hall that both food and
drink were still plentiful when dawn tinted the sky above Caer
Liwelydd, and the bondmen rose to begin their day's labour.
After Taliesin had entertained the company, he was called
before Rhydderch to receive gifts of gold and silver, and of
jewels. The warriors and their women, hot and drunk but past
tiredness, looked on, awed at the generosity of the northern
king. When it seemed there could be no more to give, an
attendant clothed in white entered, bearing silver horse-
trappings and two richly ornamented goblets.

'Lord Taliesin, please accept these gifts from me.' Rhodri
spoke with dignity, his young face calm but joyful. 'It has been
an honour to hear you perform.'

As the guests went to take their rest, the prince approached
Taliesin, less formal now.

'I'll be sad to leave Rheged,' he said. 'I've made many
comrades, and there is good sport here.'

'At which you are skilled.' Taliesin spoke warmly, seeing
something of Gwenddydd in her son. 'The other boys will be

sad too, though when you go there'll be no one to put them to shame at spear throwing.'

The prince flushed slightly. 'I'm sure I don't deserve such praise. But some day I hope to earn the praise of the bards.'

'You have earned it already,' Taliesin replied. 'Come to the hall before you leave tomorrow and you'll have a eulogy from the Chief Bard of Rheged.'

Rhodri's eyes gleamed. 'My lord.....' Overwhelmed, he was at a loss for words. 'Thank you.'

With the boy's delighted voice still ringing in his ears, Taliesin turned towards the courtyard, his own mood lightened. He liked Rhodri, not simply for who he was, and wanted to please him, to give him his own gift. But he could not fool himself into imagining he did not also wish to please Gwenddydd.

A single lamp was lit in the chamber, illuminating Nefyn's body as she sat on a stool, working a comb through the spirals of her hair. She had her side towards Taliesin, who lay on the bed in semi-darkness, and assumed his eyes were on her.

When she looked round and saw that he stared into the shadows beneath the rafters, she felt foolish, then angry. 'You've been distracted ever since the visit from Rhydderch and his clansmen,' she said, 'though two full weeks have passed since they left.'

Taliesin sighed, scarcely listening.

'The influence of the king's weird brother-in-law, no doubt.' Nefyn gave a derisive laugh. 'There's something unsettling about him, and he forced his presence on you for the duration of the visit.'

At last, she had Taliesin's attention. He spoke softly, but with an edge to his voice. 'Do I make a point of insulting your companions?'

'I'm not aware that I have any companions who openly worship Pagan gods, much less claim to be the incarnation of one.'

'I was not aware that you listened to gossip.' Taliesin raised himself onto one elbow and reached for the goblet that stood on a chest by the bed. 'But, of course, it's an infallible source of wisdom.'

Nefyn's eyes flashed anger, and she turned her back on him, looking at her own image in the mirror she held. Watching her now, Taliesin drained the goblet before lying down again. But it was not long before she put the mirror aside and, picking up the oil lamp, carried it to the chest. She sat on the bed and met Taliesin's gaze.

'Are you lying there thinking of metaphysics, of starlore, treelore, herblore......' With each word she moved closer, her expression a combination of mockery and tenderness. 'Demons and spirits, and guardian beasts, and prophesies for the coming two thousand years. How exciting it must all be. How can such as I ever imagine......'

Her lips were almost touching his. He could feel her breath as she spoke, and smell the scent of her body.

'I'm sure there's nothing in Heaven or on earth that someone such as you cannot imagine,' he replied, taking her by the waist and drawing her down beside him.

For a moment she lay still, then clasped his face between both hands, kissing him fiercely. When the memory of Gwenddydd came to his mind, he blocked it out. Nefyn was no less beautiful, no less desirable than she had been two moons ago. And she was here, with him now, her skin warm against his nakedness. As he returned her kiss, he told himself that he loved her, that nothing had changed.

chapter five

As Taliesin rode between Owain and Dyfnarth, the March wind stung his eyes, forcing him to alertness after an uncomfortable night in the open. Huddled beside the fire, with only his cloak for protection against the bitterness of the young year, he had not slept. But discomfort was the penalty for freedom, for arguing against Urien, who had tried to dissuade him from leaving the safety of Caer Liwelydd.

The sun broke through the clouds as the raiding party crossed the mountainous border between Gwenddoleu's kingdom and Manaw Gododdin. Continuing north-east, they descended into a river valley sheltered from the wind, where the sun's warmth could be felt for the first time. They made good headway on the softer ground, riding through squally showers broken by spells of brilliant sunlight, and around noon stopped to rest the horses.

While Dyfnarth surveyed the land, Taliesin led Nerth down to the water's edge and, looping the reins over the horse's neck, left him to graze. As he took a draught from his mead flask, he looked back towards Arderydd, recalling his visits to Myrddin. During the seasons when it was possible to travel, he had made the journey many times, and found welcome at Gwenddoleu's stronghold above the River Lludd.

He had seen Gwenddydd only once since her stay at Caer Liwelydd three years earlier - when he visited Alclud as Rhydderch's guest - and prayed they could now live without the strain of meeting in a constant exchange of royal hospitality.

He turned at the sound of Owain's voice.

'The weather is deteriorating.' The prince glanced in the direction they were bound. 'Do you think it wise to hold to our plan of taking the higher route? There's less chance of being surprised, but we risk losing our bearings if we're caught in a blizzard.'

Taliesin looked up, noting the direction of the wind, the formation of the clouds, using his spirit senses, his knowledge of the elements. As he continued to look upward he spotted a hawk riding the air currents, no more than a speck over the distant peaks, and pointed it out to his comrade.

'Follow his example,' he said. 'There'll be no blizzard.'

Owain swung round. 'We waste time lingering here,' he called to his men. 'The adventure has not yet begun.'

With each mile covered they moved with greater caution. During the afternoon they followed a series of rugged passes overshadowed by low cloud. Only as daylight began to fade did the land become less harsh, with an isolated hut or settlement, and on the rough pasture long-horned cattle grazed, thin after the winter, but highly-bred and valuable. When a hilltop fortress came into sight against the skyline Owain headed towards the shelter of a copse and reined in.

He gripped the hilt of his sword as he spoke. 'We rest here 'til nightfall.......Soon the Lord of Manaw will be the poorer and we the richer.'

The men dismounted, and Owain strode across to where Taliesin stood with Dyfnarth, tethering his horse beside Nerth. Already the air was growing chill, and Taliesin hunched his shoulders and wrapped his cloak more tightly about him.

'Your thoughts must be with Penarwen,' he said, talking to hold off the tiredness.

'Yes, the child is due at any time. It may even be born while I'm away. With three sons, I know Penarwen hopes for a daughter, a companion for herself.' In the wintry half-light the vapour rose from Owain's breath. 'She is saddened that Nefyn will not be accompanying us when we move to Din Carreg in the summer.' He paused. 'Though her choice cannot have been a difficult one.'

'You will be missed by all in Caer Liwelydd.'

'We cannot remain with my father's household for ever.' Taliesin noticed a sudden edge to Owain's voice. Then, as quickly, it was replaced by the old enthusiasm. The prince glanced towards Dyfnarth. 'The doors of my hall will always be open to my comrades. You must both visit.'

The short twilight passed, and the wood was cast into blackness, temperatures plummeting. The men paced to and fro, drinking mead from leather flasks, taking turns on lookout - alert for any sign of movement. But all remained peaceful.

Occasionally the lowing of cattle or the shuffling of an animal in the undergrowth broke the silence. Still, they waited.

Owain took a mouthful of strong wine, for warmth, and walked to the edge of the trees.

'No sign of anyone.' He spoke in a charged whisper. 'Let us move now, before we freeze to death.'

In the gloom and stillness, they made ready. At first they stayed under cover, advancing steadily. The men knew their orders, and the lowland route they would take back towards Rheged once they had what they had come for. It would be many hours before they could stop with stolen cattle in their possession.

Taliesin rode beside Owain as the party moved out into the open. He noticed that the skies had cleared, though the night was moonless, and above them Caer Arianrhod shone brightly.

Dividing into two groups, with silent precision they began to round up the cattle. Riding in a wide sweep, the men circled the animals. The next arc brought them nearer. With each sweep, the arc decreased. Gradually, they mustered the beasts into a tighter mass. The strays were herded in. Then, Owain gave the signal, and steering their prize, the party turned south.

His heels pressed to Nerth's sides, Taliesin felt his heart pound as the earth shuddered beneath galloping hooves. Horses and cattle veered across the meadow, plunging through darkness, the raiders drunk on the speed of their flight.

Suddenly Dyfnarth's voice yelled above the din. 'We are pursued!'

Taliesin glanced over his shoulder, seeing a band of warriors riding hard in their wake, silhouettes racing across the pastureland like hounds scenting a quarry.

Soon the first spear whined through the air, a hand's breadth from Owain's shoulder. Another struck the ground by Nerth's foreleg. Their pursuers were gaining on them, sending an iron rain into their midst. One of the herd was hit, and fell with a shriek.

Riding alongside his comrade, once more Taliesin glanced over his shoulder at the men closing in, swords upraised as they shouted their challenge, and knew that escape would require more than swiftness or skill at arms.

At first he found it impossible to circulate the sacred breaths, to focus, whilst racing across a dark, unfamiliar landscape, but failure meant a fight to the death........and they were outnumbered. He thought of Branwen, of Nefyn, of all he had to loose. Then he called upon Manawyddan, the beat of hooves like a drum in his head.

A spear fell in his path, a second to the side, wide of its mark. Behind him a man cried out. But he closed his mind, focusing again, summoning the elements of air and water, starting to concentrate the power. He continued riding at speed, though it was blindly, trusting Nerth's senses, his instinct to follow the herd.

The power intensified, drawing strength from sky and sea.

As Taliesin felt the energies coalesce, the night rang with sounds of confusion - curses, yells, the terrified whinnying of horses. Aware of his surroundings once more, he turned, relief becoming triumph. Between the men of Rheged and of the clan Gododdin lay a wall of mist, blotting them from sight, the distance that separated hunter from hunted increasing with each stride.

Shortly after the raid in Manaw, Taliesin and Dyfnarth received word from Elffin of Gwyddno's death, and together they travelled to Gwynedd for the burial, to mourn with their kin at Braich y Dinas.

Winter lingered long that year, but frost and ice gradually gave way to gentle showers and light winds as the days lengthened. Cattle were driven between the cleansing fires at Calan Mai, before being herded up to higher pastures, and the people danced and feasted to celebrate the start of summer. Calan Mai was also the time when Taliesin's birthday was celebrated with great rejoicing throughout Caer Liwelydd. And in recognition of his service as Chief Bard, Urien made him a gift of rich pastureland around the shores of Llyn Glas to the south-west of the town.

The year waxed, the season of growth becoming the season of strife, with clashes between Angle and Briton on Rheged's eastern border. After generations of fighting each other, Rheged and Ystrad Glud directed their combined might against the Bernicians, the alliance strengthened with each victory. Even in defeat there was optimism, born of comradeship.

At the height of the year, Taliesin was amongst the bards from across the kingdom assembled on a sacred hill overlooking the River Idon.

Light and shadow flickered across their robed figures as they gathered about a fire of oak wood, Talhaearn's apprentices feeding the blaze with golden furze so it burnt fiercely. The undulating waves of the Alban Hefin chant rose into the night, punctuated by the beat of a drum struck by Bedwen. Seated beside him, Taliesin saw the dedication on his face, heard his fine voice harmonize with the others. Not for the first time, he noticed that when the youth worked the bardic rites, channelling his rebellious energy, it brought power to the work. No longer restless and wilful, briefly he found peace.

Beneath a sky that never fully darkened, the initiates watched in vigil. Taliesin gazed at the vastness of that sky, and, carried on the rhythm of chant and drum, his spirit journeyed, spiralling upward as a star amongst stars, freed from the bonds of time.

Through eternity, the ever-circling wheel span. The hub of the wheel was burning gold, revolving in sparks of white fire, of crimson fire, blinding in brilliance. Taliesin felt its strength as his own strength. His spirit bathed in that energy, to carry for the land and his people. The turning tide of the year drew closer, and he sensed it like a breath exhaled across the spinning earth.

On the beat of the drum, he returned to dew wet ground in the hour before dawn. He continued to sit in meditation, watching the brightness increase. A soft glow creeping across the horizon.

As the light intensified, Talhaearn crouched by the fire and filled a bowl with water gathered from the hollow of an ancient oak. Clasping the vessel between sinewy hands, he stood straight, raising it first to the west then the east.

He matched his voice to the rhythm of the drum.

'Dew of life -
gift of the mother,
dark mother,
earth mother.
In the vessel of the waters,
the tomb and the womb,
we are born once,
and twice,
and thrice.'

In turn, each man came forward, and with the consecrated water traced the symbol of the three rays on his brow. Then, forming a crescent, they faced east. Moment by moment the horizon glowed brighter until, like burnished bronze, the sun rose, shimmering through the mists, and with it rose the chant of the Awen.

Around the base of the hill dozens of figures now danced with ecstatic leaps, singing and piping. They circled clockwise as the growing light flowed across the land, igniting the tips of branches and grass blades. The dance quickened to a point of frenzy, pipes shrill in the clear air.

As Taliesin stood apart from the other bards, the dancers glanced upward, still whirling and leaping. He waited, motionless, then raised his arms, and with a cheer the people raced up the slope. At the summit, men and women, youths and maidens bowed to receive his blessing before they approached the fire, taking smouldering branches from the blaze - the solar gift of health and fertility.

Bedwen's expression was tense when he entered the chamber. He stood stiffly in front of Taliesin, his face framed by light brown hair that hung straight to his shoulders.

'My lord.'

Taliesin laughed softly. 'There's no need for formality. We've been acquainted long enough.' He got to his feet, putting his harp aside. 'Shall we take a ride? The weather is fine and there's something I should like to show you.'

'To show me, my lord?'

He could see the confusion, the disappointment, in Bedwen's eyes. He had come to see the Chief Bard expecting news, not simply an invitation to ride. But he did not question further, and handed Taliesin his cloak.

They stepped out into the mellow sunlight of late summer,

and crossed the courtyard to the stables, where an attendant saddled their horses. The main street of Caer Liwelydd was almost deserted at that hour, and the townsfolk they passed moved respectfully out of their path.

Beyond the walls, Taliesin directed Nerth along the Roman road, riding south. Above them the blue of the sky was unbroken, though heavy cloud was building to the west, and the land lay in its shadow. Taliesin engaged Bedwen in easy conversation, making no mention of bardic practice or of where they were heading. After some distance he turned right from the road, still without explanation, and continued down a barely visible track overgrown with grasses and wild flowers.

Moving at a steady pace, he drew Bedwen's attention to the cloud formation ahead. Looming over the estuary, it rose in a myriad shapes, from the darkness at its base to the bright glow at its summit.

'What do you see?' he asked.

The youth gazed at the cloud, deep in concentration, saying nothing for a long while. Then his pale cheeks flushed, and he would not look at Taliesin.

'I see.......ambition realized.' Bedwen paused. 'The element of earth is important, like the base of the cloud. A bard must not lose contact with the stability of the earth. Then the mind and spirit can climb, facing dark and light. Everything shifts and changes, but the brightness grows always more powerful.'

Taliesin nodded. 'Let us then continue towards that portal, forgetting nothing, even when the darkness disorientates, or the brightness seems too dazzling.'

They rode on in silence, as long grasses flicked against the horses' legs and swallows swooped low overhead. But Bedwen was too tense with expectation to be lulled by the drowsiness of the day. His senses alert, he looked into the distance, and spotted a new, unfamiliar shape on the horizon.

As they drew nearer, the sounds of men at work were

carried on the air: shouts, and axe blows splitting wood. Reflected in the still waters of Llyn Glas, and sheltered from the east by a stand of white birch, the walls of a rectangular hall were in place, though it was still unroofed. Behind it, work had already begun on the stables and three roundhouses.

When he saw Taliesin, the foreman approached with a bow-legged swagger.

'My lord, good afternoon. I hope you're well pleased with what meets your eye.'

Taliesin studied the half-constructed buildings, trying to mask a tide of emotion, disbelief that he looked upon the hall, the lands, of the boy who was born an outcast, with nothing. 'Very well pleased,' he said in an even voice. 'Things have progressed quickly since I was last here.'

'My men are hard-working, and loyal in your service, my lord.'

Taliesin rode forward, in his mind seeing the finished settlement, the place where he would at last be able to provide a home for his daughter, and where Finllian could live and carry out her healing work in peace.

Eventually, he turned to Bedwen. 'Master Talhaearn and I have been discussing the matter of your studies. He feels he cannot give sufficient time and attention to three apprentices, along with his other duties.' He glanced at the lake and the gently sloping pastures where his cattle grazed. 'How do you feel about continuing your training here?'

When he turned back to Bedwen, the youth's face was transformed by a smile, his blue eyes startlingly bright.

'You'll take me as your apprentice?'

Taliesin inclined his head. 'For my sins........It will be an interesting experience for both of us.'

CHAPTER SIX

'So you intend to live out there?' Nefyn's eyes blazed. 'Constantly?'

Taliesin sighed. 'No, of course not. My duties in Caer Liwelydd mean I'll be here as often as at Llyn Glas.'

'You never said you planned to live in that God-forsaken place. It's miles from noble company, nothing but peasants and cattle.......and the ever-present Bedwen. Perhaps I should join Penarwen in Galloway after all. I only remained here as one of Morfydd's attendants so I could be near you.'

Taliesin fastened a gold torc about his neck. 'I have no time for this now. I am late for a consultation with the king and Bishop Segnius. We can discuss things tomorrow.'

'And when you do happen to be in town it'll be like this. I'm surprised you don't share Urien's bed, or perhaps Owain's.'

Trying to stay calm, Taliesin reached for his cloak and headed towards the door.

'Don't turn your back on me.' Though Nefyn got to her feet, he did not stop or look at her. When she next spoke it was in an undertone, barely audible. 'Arrogant bastard.'

Taliesin's breath caught in his throat as he felt a vulnerability he had known so often as a boy, which even now had not lost its hold. He knew that Nefyn wanted him to rage back at her, that she sought a way to claim his attention, but he continued walking, shutting out the hurt, attempting to compose himself for a meeting he had no stomach for, least of all now.

When he arrived in the hall the elders were already assembled close to the hearth, though many of those who usually met in council were absent. Dyfnarth was away on the border, leading his men in early raids against the Deirans, and

Owain and his younger brother Elffin had returned to manage the affairs of their own kingdoms beyond the Wall.

As Taliesin took his seat on the bench the men nodded their greetings. All but Segnius, who looked at him with undisguised contempt. He paid no heed and, accepting the cup brought by an attendant, turned as Urien spoke.

'Today I received news of the deteriorating situation between Ystrad Glud and Arderydd.' The king's expression was grave. 'It has gone beyond threats. Rhydderch draws up plans to attack Gwenddoleu, dragging Elmet into the dispute.' Urien drained his cup and set it down in front of him. 'There will be war.'

His words were met by the rumble of voices. Only Taliesin remained silent. No longer distracted by his argument with Nefyn, which now seemed as nothing, he felt concern for Gwenddydd and Myrddin. His comrade had never trusted Rhydderch. How could he himself have so misjudged him? He had believed him to be wise, reasonable, a leader who sought peace, not aggression.

Without waiting for the uproar to die down Urien raised his voice above it. 'Rhydderch accuses Gwenddoleu of murdering his cousin Cynlas, as Maelgwn slew Elgan thirty years ago, which he declares is un-avenged. He will accept no compensation, except in blood.' Urien's fists were clenched as he leant forward, the firelight playing on his grizzled hair. 'Queen Gwenddydd is from the clan of Coel, but Gwenddoleu, too, is my kin.'

'My lord, the man is a Pagan, a sinner who has not accepted the word of the one true God.' Segnius' tone was dark. 'He is dangerous, and through his lack of faith condemns the souls of his own people. King Rhydderch acts on this knowledge. The murder of Cynlas is not the only reason why he musters his troops.'

'That is no cause for us to support Ystrad Glud.' It was a

man named Tewdr who spoke, a veteran warrior whose face was heavily scarred, the lid closed over the empty socket of his left eye.

'Is it not?' Segnius rounded on him. 'May the Lord forgive you.'

'It would create more internal divisions in Rheged.' Tewdr's voice remained calm. 'Gwenddoleu is a Pagan, yes, but as the king said, he is a descendant of Coel. Many in Rheged feel kinship with him.'

The bishop snorted. 'Pagan idolatry is not confined to Gwenddoleu's lands........I see you take no part in this conversation, Lord Taliesin.'

Taliesin addressed those gathered before him. 'It is my belief that we have enemies enough without adding to the strife amongst our own people.' He faced Segnuis. 'If you want to wage war on Paganism, let us consolidate our forces against the foreign invaders. If we fail to drive them from Ynys Prydein we will be slaughtered, or enslaved and compelled to practice their faith......With no exceptions.'

Urien's youngest son Riwallon stifled a chuckle.

'There are those amongst us who would not have to be so compelled.' Segnius' face was flushed, and he locked eyes with Taliesin. 'A man may be judged by those he keeps company with, men such as Myrddin ap Madoc, and Gwenddoleu himself.'

'I would take it as the highest compliment to be judged by my association with Myrddin,' Taliesin replied dryly. 'He is renowned for his learning.'

'And known to be a sorcerer, a practitioner of evil arts. Am I then to assume, Chief Bard, that you condone such arts?'

'You may assume whatever you wish, Brother Segnius, I have no jurisdiction over your thoughts.' Taliesin met his gaze squarely, knowing that the others at the table savoured the confrontation as they would one to one combat between champions on the field of battle.

The bishop rested a hand on the cross at his breast. 'God will not grant us victory over Angle and Saeson when men of rank deny him. His punishment extends to a whole people. Only a fool would risk having such guilt on his conscience on the day of judgement.'

Finally, Taliesin sensed discomfort amongst the elders. 'As you often remind us, God is just,' he said quietly. 'What kind of justice is it to punish a whole people for the sins of the few?'

Segnius drew breath to reply, but seeing the fire in his eyes Urien intervened.

'This is not the time for religious speculation. If a messenger arrives from Ystrad Glud, we must be ready with an answer.'

Segnuis turned from Taliesin to Urien. 'My lord, we are sworn allies of King Rhydderch. There can be only one answer.'

Urien shook his head, and once again voices were raised in debate. At first Taliesin said nothing, debating instead within his own mind, questioning his instinctive response, weighing it against the words of the council. As the uproar subsided, he spoke in a measured tone.

'Should Rheged's unique position not be used to advantage, rather than seen as a quagmire in which we are trapped?' He paused, reading the faces of the elders. 'As we have bonds of kinship with both sides, surely we must at least attempt to bring about a reconciliation.'

Urien sat in thought, arms folded across his broad chest. This time there were no murmurs, no argument.

Eventually, the king looked up. 'I see the sense in this. If all are in agreement, messengers will be sent to both parties at dawn tomorrow, inviting them for negotiation.'

At the close of a long day Taliesin stood in the doorway of his

318

hall, looking out across the still waters of Llyn Glas. He drew in a deep breath, grateful to be away from the noise and odour of Caer Liwelydd, grateful too that Nefyn was with him, that they had made their peace. When she saw the hall furnished with carved benches and richly woven hangings, and attendants came to serve them fine wine, she no longer complained about its remoteness, though he knew she would sooner have stayed in town.

Listening to the silence, Taliesin gazed at the reflection of the birch trees which sheltered the settlement to the east, their branches in new leaf. He let his thoughts drift until a distant movement caught his attention, and he looked up to see a horseman riding at a gallop from the direction of Caer Liwelydd.

He watched the approaching figure, an intrusion on the still landscape. All else remained as before. A faint ripple stirred the waters of the lake. Herds grazed in the fading light. Though Taliesin was now denied the tranquillity he craved.

He continued to watch the figure draw nearer, riding hard along the rutted track towards Llyn Glas. The man only slowed his pace as he reached the settlement, when the sound of hoof beats brought Nefyn from the hearth to Taliesin's side.

The messenger reined in before the hall, his cloak blood-stained, his horse's flanks gleaming with sweat.

He spoke wearily. 'My lord, I bring news from Arderydd. Shortly after noon today the men of Ystrad Glud marched on Caerwenddolew and met the men of Lord Gwenddoleu on the plain below the fortress.'

Taliesin felt Nefyn grip his arm, as he struggled to think clearly. This was so sudden. All afternoon, while they had been in their inner chamber enjoying rare moments of privacy, the battle had been raging without his knowledge.

'What is the progress?' he asked in a low voice.

For one insane moment he wondered if Rhydderch had

been slain, questioned what repercussions the Lord of Alclud's death would have on his own life. But he dismissed the thought, thinking instead of Myrddin fighting for his patron and for what remained of the Old Faith.

With growing tension, Taliesin listened to the messenger's report. 'King Rhydderch's forces were joined by warriors from Elmet, warbands under the leadership of Peredur and Gwgri, my own lord, and another under Dunawd the Stout. The first clash took place below the southern ridge, where Gwenddoleu's ally, Dreon, defended the ground against us. After a bitter fight Dreon was slain, and the men of Ystrad Glud and Elmet advanced towards the stronghold, meeting the main force of Arderydd. The fighting continued until sunset, when Lord Gwenddoleu fell.'

Nefyn's hold on Taliesin's arm tightened.

'Have his men then surrendered?' he asked. 'And Rhydderch's declared victory?'

'The battle is not yet over.........Greatly outnumbered, Gwenddoleu's warriors made for the fortress, concealed by fog, which descended unexpectedly.' Taliesin nodded, remembering how Myrddin had bragged of his power to raise the druid mist. 'King Rhydderch's forces have surrounded Caerwenddolew, prepared for a siege. I cannot say who has taken over command, but the men of Arderydd swear they will fight to the death or die of starvation.'

Taliesin swallowed hard. 'Do you have news of Myrddin, Lord Gwenddoleu's Chief Bard? Is he with his comrades in the fortress?'

'I have no news of him, my lord. Not since I saw him on the field of battle. After the warriors of Arderydd retreated, I left to bring word to King Urien, then rode here at his request.'

A breeze sighed through the stand of birch trees and a cow lowed in the pasture beyond, familiar sounds that seemed dislocated.

'This is a dark day for our people.' Taliesin saw that the man in front of him was stooped with exhaustion, his lips dry and cracked. 'Will you come into the hall for refreshment?' he asked. 'And to rest the night before returning north?'

'Your offer is generous, but in the circumstances I......'

Before he could protest further, Nefyn stepped forward.

'We will be insulted if you deny our hospitality. And there is nothing more you can do until morning.'

'Then I thank you, my lady.'

The man dismounted, turning at the sound of approaching footsteps and youthful voices. Bedwen, who had been visiting Talhaearn's settlement, walked briskly between the trees, accompanied by one of the other apprentices. He began to call out a greeting, then stopped when he saw the stranger.

Taliesin faced the boys. 'Let us go inside,' he said quietly. 'I have received grave news.'

Bedwen remained silent, though the meaningful glance he cast his companion did not escape Taliesin's notice.

Days passed, and the messages from Caerwenddolew reported no change.

The moon reached its fullness and began to wane, and still the siege dragged on. Rhydderch had not asked for assistance, but each day Urien expected a request for the help he could not give. He could not use the might of Rheged to crush the remainder of Gwenddoleu's force, men of courage who refused to surrender after the death of their lord, his own kinsman.

Taliesin stayed in Caer Liwelydd, meeting in council with the elders. And, in the feast hall, night after night he sang in praise of battle glory, to inspire the noble company and lift the darkness that lay over Rheged. But his words rang hollow in his own ears, as he thought not only of Myrddin but of Gwenddydd - torn between loyalty to her husband and love for her brother.

Bedwen, too, stayed in the town, and each morning came to Taliesin for teaching. Though working with his apprentice was often a challenge, he welcomed it. For those few hours the demands on his attention left no space to dwell on the situation in Arderydd.

It was an overcast day, and the light was dim as they sat beneath the window. When Taliesin gave a nod to indicate that he was ready, Bedwen closed his eyes. The youth sat still and focussed, then slowly he began to speak, describing the visions which took shape in his mind, crossing the bridge between them.

'A lake.......three lakes.........about a fort of glass. I stand in the fort of glass. There are circles around it, three rings of fire. Before it flows a fountain......'

He was interrupted by a rap on the door, and an attendant's voice called from a place that seemed far distant.

'My lord.'

Taliesin sealed the inner gateway, grounding the energy that flowed through him. He had given instructions not to be disturbed unless the matter was urgent. Taking a moment to regain his bearings, he rose and spoke softly to Bedwen.

'Take your time, make sure you return properly.'

He unbolted the door, keeping hold of the wooden bar to prevent it from opening fully, and faced the man who stood outside.

'I apologize for interrupting, my lord.' The attendant's expression was anxious. 'But I have been sent by the king.'

'Is there news of Myrddin?' Taliesin kept his voice low for Bedwen's sake.

The man shook his head. 'I bear no news. I was sent to summon you.'

* * *

As Taliesin entered the hall with Bedwen at his heel, he found Urien and the elders seated at the royal table. Amongst the warriors assembled around them, Dyfnarth stood grim and silent.

The king raised his eyes, blood-shot with weariness. 'We have news at last, though it is news that brings no comfort.'

Taliesin took a seat, while Bedwen stood like stone behind him. Waiting........as the fire crackled and spat in the hearth.

Finally, Urien spoke, jaw muscles taught. 'Rhydderch has taken the fortress of Caerwenddolew,' he said gruffly. 'Our messengers report carnage, with no survivors amongst the defenders.'

Taliesin looked back at him, sick with despair, his voice a hoarse whisper.

'Myrddin.......Myrddin is dead?'

'His body has not been found. He may have escaped, but against such odds.......' Urien drew a calloused hand across his chin and sighed. 'That is not all. Though Rhydderch is the victor, victory has cost him dear. In the final battle his only son and heir was slain.'

Taliesin lowered his eyes. He wanted to argue with Urien, declare he must be mistaken. Rhodri had been only fifteen. What madness possessed Rhydderch in allowing him to fight? In his mind he saw an eager youth listening to his song of praise. Now that song would be an elegy.

He knew the gaze of the elders was on him as he sat in silence, his thoughts with Gwenddydd, feeling her pain as his own. Was there no end to the grief, the folly? Did the old gods punish the royal clan of Ystrad Glud for denying them?

His voice burned with anger. 'This sacrifice of a young life is not only Rhydderch's loss, but a loss to all Britons. The battle was ill begun and ill ended. It is hard to conceive of anything more futile.' Glancing at the elders, he got to his feet. 'By your leave, my lords.'

Those who saw his eyes noticed a metallic light they would not soon forget. Then, staring bleakly ahead, he strode towards the door. Bedwen remained where he was, watching his master's departing figure, knowing that Taliesin would ride for the hall at Llyn Glas and that it was not his place to follow.

chapter seven

Accompanied by an attendant, Taliesin headed north across Arderydd, passing the distant fortress of Caerwenddolew. Now an empty shell, a shrine to the memory of the men who had fallen. Continuing northward, the road wound along valleys green with summer, overshadowed by heather-covered slopes and gaunt peaks that cut the sky.

Throughout the journey he questioned whether he had been right to accept Rhydderch's invitation, a doubt that deepened as he drew nearer to Ystrad Glud. The message had been brief, giving no explanation. It had angered Urien, and to see Gwenddydd again seemed foolish, but he had found he could not refuse, nor prolong his delay, in case she was in need of help.

After a day spent following the course of Afon Clud, the travellers approached the royal fortress, set high on a rock where the river widened out towards the firth. Sunset silhouetted the ramparts against a crimson sky, but Taliesin saw no beauty in it. To his eyes the colour was the red of spilt blood, a symbol of the waste and futility that had its source in this place.

Only now did he send his attendant on ahead so Gwenddydd and Rhydderch would have warning of his arrival, though not sufficient to prepare a welcome feast. Alone, he rode up the steep track to the stronghold, weary from travel and oppressed by doubt. He had never thought to visit Alclud again, and shrank from the prospect of accepting Rhydderch's hospitality: speaking amicable words to the man responsible for the slaying of Gwenddoleu's warband, drinking his mead, performing in his hall. As the fortifications loomed above him, and the waters swirled about the base of the rock, once again he asked himself why he had come.

When Taliesin reached the stronghold he was admitted with royal honour. Armed keepers opened the heavy oak gates and attendants waited to escort him to the hall. Crossing the courtyard he tried to put all misgivings aside, telling himself that anger, and sentiment over Gwenddydd, were equally futile. If he could bring nothing positive to the situation his journey had been wasted.

As the Lord of Alclud rose to greet him, it struck Taliesin how Rhydderch had aged since they last met. Though not young, he had always been strong and upright, a warrior still. Now he appeared like an old man, sunken in face and body, his shoulders stooped.

'Thank you for coming in answer to our message.' The familiar soft-spoken voice sounded strained.

'I wish that my return to your kingdom was under happier circumstances.' Taliesin turned to Gwenddydd. 'My lady.'

She nodded acknowledgement, pale and unsmiling.

Still facing her, Taliesin spoke again. 'There could be no nobler or braver youth than Rhodri. I remember him with fondness.'

'I know he had great respect and fondness for you.' Gwenddydd's response was carefully controlled. 'He was so joyful when you composed the song in his praise.......Perhaps you will sing it for us during your visit.'

Rhydderch indicated a couch draped with richly embroidered cloth, and Taliesin accepted the horn of mead that was brought to him. He took a long draught, relieving a dryness in his throat that was not only from lack of refreshment on the road.

'When we heard from you, we did not think you would come,' Gwenddydd said.

Taliesin looked at her drawn face, the torchlight deepening the shadows beneath her cheekbones, and replied quietly. 'I am sorry for my vagueness. I was unsure when I would be able to leave Caer Liwelydd.'

'Of course. We understand the demands made on someone in your position. It cannot be easy to make time for travel.'

'Perhaps we should not have troubled you. But this is an invitation made in friendship, in our time of sorrow.'

As Taliesin sat opposite his host, he detected a darkness in the king's voice that was more than grief.

Rhydderch continued. 'We were touched by your message of condolence. But Urien has sent us no communication since........since our son was slain.' His tone hardened. 'Many would regard that as an insult.'

Taking another draught of mead, Taliesin tried to frame his reply. He felt too exhausted to deal with such matters now, when a misplaced word could have consequences that affected the destinies of kingdoms.

'My lord, no insult was intended,' he said evenly. 'Like all in Caer Liwelydd, Urien is deeply saddened by your son's death.'

Rhydderch sighed, turning away.

In the silence that followed, Gwenddydd laid a hand on her husband's arm and leant towards him.

'Do you not think we should discuss this when we are all rested? We will have time enough to talk at length another day.'

The anguish on Rhydderch's face betrayed the war he waged within, but he managed to retain self-control, and spoke courteously.

'I apologize, Lord Taliesin. The queen is right. It grows late and you have had a long journey.' He summoned an attendant to bring more mead. 'Please dine with us. I hope you will find the entertainment of my bards to your liking.'

The following day dawned wet, and heavy rain hammered on

the chapel roof as morning service was conducted by Cunotigern, abbot of the newly consecrated foundation on the banks of the Clud. Afterwards, Taliesin broke his fast with the royal company, though Rhydderch scarcely touched the food set before him, and once closing grace had been said left to consult with his cousin Neithon, heir to Ystrad Glud since Rhodri's death.

Taliesin remained in the hall, drinking wine with Gwenddydd and Cunotigern, their conversation safe and impersonal. Finally, the abbot drained his goblet and rose.

'I must return to instruct my novices. I hope you will visit us, Lord Taliesin, and accept our simple hospitality.' He smiled at Gwenddydd. 'Glas Chu, as we affectionately name it, is a place of deep peace.'

They watched his departing figure, saying nothing, but before the silence became prolonged, Gwenddydd spoke. 'It brings me consolation that you are here.'

Taliesin turned to her, seeing a beauty undiminished by grief.

'You have been in my thoughts and prayers since the message reached us.' He lowered his voice. 'Words cannot express what I feel, especially the formal words of condolence you must be weary of hearing. But I want you to know the depth of my sorrow.'

'I do know,' she replied softly. 'Your words, though you describe them as formal, are not empty like so many........ At present I'm unable to see beyond each day, the future seems not to exist. Yet there must be a future, there must be hope, however remote.'

Hearing the bleakness in her voice, Taliesin felt his throat ache, pain burn behind his eyes.

'Rhodri pleaded to ride with his father,' Gwenddydd said, hoarse with the tears she could not shed. 'He insisted that now he had reached manhood he would not stay behind like a coward.......Eventually Rhydderch relented, though he made Rhodri promise to remain at the rear of the advance. In the first clash he did as he was told, and he camped with the warriors below Caerwenddolew throughout the siege. But when the final onslaught came, he broke his promise and rode forward.' She paused, then spoke under her breath. 'No doubt you think me a poor mother.'

Taliesin met her eyes, overcome by a sense of helplessness, a longing to ease a suffering that could not be eased. And, always, he and Gwenddydd must face each other across an invisible barrier. He could not even rest a hand on hers in compassion.

'You cannot blame yourself,' he said. 'Rhodri may have been young, but he was bold, with a mind of his own. He was the warrior he always wanted to be.'

'Fighting a battle that should never have been fought.' Gwenddydd sighed. 'Every day I think of all who lie beneath the earth. I am not the only mother to have lost a son, not the only woman to grieve. How many mourn lost husbands and brothers?'

She gazed across the hall. Though no one was with them at the table, women were gathered about the hearth, spinning, and attendants moved to and fro. Unhurriedly, she drank the remainder of the wine in her goblet, then got to her feet, speaking so her words might be overheard.

'Let us return to the chapel......to pray for those who have been taken from us.'

Not until they were alone, seated on a cold stone bench, did Gwenddydd speak again.

'I have news of Myrddin,' she said in a low voice. 'He lives, thank the saints, though.........'

By the poor light from one small window high above the altar, Taliesin looked at her bowed head.

'He suffers from a sickness of the mind,' Gwenddydd

whispered. 'I fear Rhydderch, too, is sick, an obsession that knows no bounds. Until.......until our loss he was always gentle and wise.'

Taliesin's lips tightened. 'No one could claim it was wise.......or Christian........to attack Caerwenddolew.' Angry at himself, his tone softened. 'I'm sorry, I speak too freely.'

Gwenddydd stared at the golden cross upon the altar, the sound of the rain loud in the silence. 'Perhaps this obsession was always with him,' she said eventually, 'this desire to destroy the remains of Paganism amongst our people. He never liked Myrddin, and only tolerated him for my sake. Now he wants his blood, though he hides it from me. He blames Myrddin for Rhodri's death, because he fought beside Gwenddoleu, and sends out bands of armed men in search of him.' She turned to face Taliesin. 'You are Myrddin's closest comrade. I believe that you, and no other, can help him.'

Before he could reply, she continued.

'It was I who encouraged Rhydderch to summon you. He had been raging against Urien for sending no message, so I used that as a reason. I know I have placed you in a difficult position, but.......I would do anything to help my brother.'

Taliesin recalled sitting late into the night conversing with Myrddin, the times they had shared mead and laughter in Gwenddoleu's hall, celebrated the rites of the Old Faith with the Lord of Caerwenddolew. 'I too would do anything for him,' he said. 'And perhaps I can assist in the other matter as well, to ease relations between Urien and Rhydderch.'

Gwenddydd took a slow breath. 'At the dark of the moon, I had a vision of Myrddin. He spoke to me, asking my forgiveness. And I saw the place where he stood - at the top of a mountain, with a spring surrounded by hazels........He had once visited such a sanctuary in Coed Celyddon, and I sent out a loyal attendant to discover if I had seen true or if it was all delusion.

'After many days search the attendant came upon him, and observed him in secret. The man says that Myrddin raves like one insane, addressing a companion only he can see.' Her voice faltered. 'He must be helped before it's too late, brought back to where he can be cared for, though he cannot live openly in Ystrad Glud.'

Taliesin spoke softly. 'There's no certainty he'll respond to my persuasion,' he said. 'But if you wish me to try.'

He saw the gratitude in Gwenddydd's eyes. And a look he remembered from when they parted in Deganwy, before the long years of separation. For the first time since then they were alone - he could have laughed at the irony of it - in a chapel. Dismissing the words he wanted to say, he clung to practicality.

'It'll be safest if I go to Coed Celyddon on my return journey. My attendant can be trusted to keep his own counsel.'

'I will give you directions. The sanctuary is not easily found.' Gwenddydd smiled faintly. 'Thank you, I know the extent of what I ask.'

'It is no more than Myrddin would do for me.' Taliesin returned the smile. 'We must live in hope, for that is a gift which can never be taken from us unless we relinquish our hold on it.'

Near the border between Arderydd and Galloway, Taliesin and his attendant turned off the metalled road which ran through Coed Celyddon, riding beneath a tree canopy so dense the forest was cast into twilight. The track they followed soon dwindled to nothing, overgrown with bramble and ivy, with no sign that anyone had ever passed that way. Twice they came up against a barrier of underbrush and had to retrace their path, the hazel mountain close yet unreachable. And, though they had travelled since dawn after spending the night in the open, it was past noon before they came to the place Gwenddydd had described.

At the foot of a steep incline, Taliesin left his attendant in charge of Nerth and went on alone. The trees thinned out as he climbed, until the leafy canopy which had sheltered him became a floor of green far below and the sun reflected off bare rock, glaringly bright. Sweat ran down his face and back, though he kept up an even pace, gathering his light cloak about him as he felt his skin begin to burn.

Half way to the summit he paused to catch his breath, and took a drink of wine. Shielding his eyes, he looked towards the distant peaks, his memories of Ystrad Glud overlaid by the gravity of the task he had undertaken. All remained unknown. He had no knowledge if Myrddin even remained on the mountain. It was almost a full cycle of the moon since Gwenddydd's attendant had made this journey. Within days he would be back in Caer Liwelydd, bearing Rhydderch's words to Urien. Would Myrddin then be with him? Or was Gwenddydd to suffer yet further sorrow?

Tying the flask to his belt, Taliesin began to climb again, entering a gully where loose stones skidded under his feet and boulders jutted from hard earth. In the eye of the sun, he pressed on, increasing his pace as the slope gradually grew less steep.

Despite the heat he took no rest, and did not slack until he emerged from the gully onto a plateau where the rush of water reached his ears in the hot silence. Once more he looked at the land below, from horizon to horizon, then began to walk swiftly, guided by the sound of the water. He came first to an outer circle of whitethorn. Within it, a semi-circle of hazel bushes stood in guardianship around the spring: a place of power, where healing flowed from the depths of the earth. Myrddin, in his sickness, had been drawn here to find solace, though the only sign of human presence was a simple wooden cup that stood on a slab above the spring.

Taliesin crouched beside it, in the shade of the hazels, and let the cool water flow over his hand. Then, sitting back on his heels, he traced the sign of the three rays on his brow and spoke in an undertone,

'Lady, I ask your blessing, that the wounds which divide our people be healed.'

He filled the cup, pouring a libation onto the earth before drinking. As he leant forward to fill the vessel for a second time, a hoarse voice made him start.

'Who dares drink the sacred waters without........'

He raised his head, dazzled by a beam of sunlight that slanted through the thicket. Through the glare he met eyes that were familiar, yet those of a stranger, darting nervously from side to side above a dark matted beard.

He straightened, and getting to his feet without averting his gaze, saw recognition dawn.

'Taliesin.'

'I come in friendship.'

Myrddin ran a filthy hand across his mass of tanlged hair, staring at Taliesin as if uncertain whether he was in the flesh or an apparition.

'This may be a trick,' he said with sudden ferocity. 'You have used your powers in Rhydderch's service. He has sent you. His men follow, ready to take me captive.'

Taliesin kept his voice even. 'It is no trick, I am alone but for an attendant who waits in the forest.' He held out the cup of sacred water. 'If I lie, may the earth open and swallow me, the sky fall and crush me, the seas rise up and overwhelm me.'

The dark eyes that stared at him cleared, and he glimpsed the man he knew. 'Then I must believe you.'

Taliesin replaced the cup, and from his pack handed Myrddin a piece of salt beef and a hunk of bread, which he took without thanks and ate greedily. Taliesin waited, and when Myrddin had finished eating offered him what remained in the wine flask.

As he returned it, Myrddin frowned. 'Why have you come? If not to betray me?'

'In the hope that we can speak in the spirit of comradeship, as we once did.'

'I have no comrades except the animals of the forest. My comrades are dead.' Myrddin's voice cracked. 'Gwenddydd hates me. All in Ystrad Glud want my head, as they condemn my soul to their Hell.'

'That's not true,' Taliesin answered gently. 'Gwenddydd does not hate you. It was she who sought you out, without her husband's knowledge, because of her concern for you. And my own feelings of friendship are unchanged. I want only to help.'

Myrddin turned away. 'I am beyond help, you waste your time here.'

'At least let us talk a while, then I'll leave if you wish it.'

Taliesin moved into the shade of the thorn bushes and sat down, thinking they could not continue to stand opposite each other like adversaries. After a brief hesitation, Myrddin followed his lead, though he remained tense, unsteady hands clasping and unclasping the hem of his tunic which was still stained with the blood of battle.

For a while they remained silent, listening to the murmur of the spring. When Myrddin spoke, it was more to himself than to Taliesin.

'I cannot escape. Wherever I look I see the boy's face, eyes staring, blood seeping from between purple lips. Each night I fear sleep. I see my own comrade's sword raised, plunging into Rhodri's belly, tearing through flesh.' He drew his knife from its sheath and began playing with it like a child's toy, his fingers caressing the sharp blade. 'The cry of agony echoes across the mountains, and it becomes my own cry.......My Lord Gwenddoleu is dead, though he speaks to me from beyond the grave, calling for revenge upon Rhydderch. A host of dead

334

warriors rise from the earth below the fortress, riding from the Underworld with Arawn, grey-cloaked, white-faced, summoning me to ride with them.'

He turned, as if remembering Taliesin's presence, and glared at him, a dangerous fire in his eyes. Then, as swiftly, he became composed again. 'I saw the sword raised........I should have put myself in front of Rhodri, taken the death blow myself.'

Taliesin fought to save himself from being dragged into the mire of Myrddin's despair.

'Rhodri was slain in the heat of battle,' he said, 'when a second divides life from death. Now, in the days of cold grief that follow, you have too much time to think on what might have been. No one, least of all Rhodri, is to gain by your self-torment. And as long as you remain here it is not only you who suffers, but Gwenddydd, who cares deeply for you.'

Myrddin shook his head. 'Gwenddydd blames me for her son's death. She has no love for me.'

'So you say, but those are not her words. She would have you return to society where you can be in the company of men.'

'To be despised. No, I will not inflict my presence on another so long as I live.'

For the first time, Taliesin felt hope fading. Once he began to speak with Myrddin, he had believed that he could make his comrade understand he need not suffer alone. But he now realized that though Myrddin was sick in mind and weak in body, his strength of will was undiminished.

'How long can you live this way?' he asked firmly. 'Food is plentiful in summer, but what when there is no fruit, no game? What will happen when the snows come and you have no shelter?'

'Then my ordeal will finally be at an end.'

The detachment in Myrddin's voice filled Taliesin with sorrow, a sorrow that was replaced by anger. 'Would you throw your life away?' he said. 'Your bardic inspiration, your gifts of healing and prophecy? Is this how you honour the gods who endowed you with the power to help your land, your people.'

Myrddin frowned, and averted his gaze. 'I have done all I can for my people, I can do no more. I cannot even help myself.'

'Then allow others to. Return with me to Caer Liwelydd.'

Myrddin sprang to his feet, so suddenly that Taliesin recoiled, thinking he would strike out. He watched his comrade stagger backward, eyes wild and unfocussed, still clasping the knife in a shaking hand. Avoiding doing anything that might antagonize him, Taliesin sat tense and alert, until with a cry Myrddin cast the knife into the ground, the blade barely missing Taliesin's arm. A second later Myrddin flung himself down beside the spring, splashing his face with the cold water.

When he looked up, his eyes were as cold.

'I'm asking you to leave and not seek me out again,' he said. 'I'll never return to Caer Liwelydd except in my coffin.'

Taliesin remained seated, unable to accept that he had failed, questioning whether he should make one more attempt to reason with Myrddin. The thought of Gwenddydd's disappointment when she received his message almost drove him to try again. But he told himself that doing so was futile, and he risked pushing his comrade beyond the border of sanity.

Slowly he rose, and retrieved his pack from the ground.

'May Llew watch over you.' He looked at Myrddin, who continued to kneel by the spring, eyes downcast, water dripping from his hair and beard. 'You have my friendship, always.'

He paused, waiting for a reply, but received none. Then, reluctantly he turned, and walked several paces before glancing round. Myrddin had not moved, and already seemed to have forgotten his presence. Finally, knowing there was no more he could do, Taliesin headed back towards the gully.

chapter eight

The streets of Caer Liwelydd were crowded, and in the forecourt of the royal hall a band of warriors were dismounting after a foray across the Bernician border. Outwardly all remained unchanged, though behind it Taliesin sensed a despondency that had taken root during the time he had been away.

He found Urien seated at the high table with Tewdr, his veteran comrade-at-arms.

'It is over four weeks since you left. Rhydderch must have been good company.' The king's tone was gruff. 'How goes it with my noble ally? Does the good Christian congratulate himself on the murder of my ungodly kinsmen?'

Taliesin sat down, accepting a cup of mead, but he placed it in front of him, untouched. 'I sought to keep the peace with the Lord of Ystrad Glud.'

The tension on Urien's face eased. 'I bark like an old dog that can no longer hunt down its quarry. Take no notice of my snarling. I'm glad you're back, and with your head on your shoulders.'

As Tewdr left them to speak alone, Taliesin turned to the king.

'On the road I heard rumours of defeat at the hands of the Deirans.'

'You heard true.'

Taliesin lowered his eyes. Still, the enemy advanced whilst his people fought amongst themselves. There'd be no victory over the foreigners until men like Rhydderch conquered their lust for vengeance. No victory until........He was jolted back to the present by Urien's words.

'Your brother was wounded in the battle, shoulder wound

that turned bad. I thought to send for you.'

The news drove other thoughts from Taliesin's mind, and he looked sharply at Urien. He tried to keep his voice even. 'And now?'

'He recovers well. The danger is past.' Urien paused, a glint in his bloodshot eyes. 'Kywere's care would speed any man's recovery. She's scarcely left his bedside.'

He took a drink, wiping his moustache with the back of his hand. 'What news from Alclud?'

Taliesin made an effort to focus on the crisis that had preoccupied him for so long, to put concern for Dyfnarth aside until he could see his foster-brother. 'The situation remains unstable,' he said slowly. 'Rhydderch cannot find peace within himself, and looks in all directions, seeking a target for his anger......I was greeted with the declaration that you had insulted him by not sending condolences at Rhodri's death.'

There was a moment's silence. Then Urien sighed. 'Rhodri died too young. But Rhydderch's a fool to expect condolences when his son was on the field to slay my kinsmen ....He should offer me condolences.'

Taliesin met the king's gaze. 'When he continued to dwell on the matter, I told him that the man who bore my message of sympathy failed to discharge his duty in full.'

Urien's expression darkened, then he gave a hollow laugh. 'You're wily as a fox. I'd be happy to watch Rhydderch burn himself out in rage, but we cannot afford war with Ystrad Glud.' He clenched his fists. 'Though the alliance is broken.'

Taliesin spoke under his breath. 'There are many in Rheged who'll be glad.'

'A curse on friendship with the descendants of Dyfnwal!' Urien turned and shouted over his shoulder. 'Bring us more mead.........Taliesin, why are you not drinking?'

Taliesin raised his cup. 'To future alliances that will forge peace between kingdoms.'

He downed the mead in one draught, and the attendant refilled both cups. Once the man had retreated out of earshot Urien leant forward, lowering his voice. 'But you did not ride north because of old men's insults........Does Myrddin ap Madoc still live?'

Taken off-guard, and surprised by Urien's shrewdness, Taliesin hesitated.

He inclined his head. 'He has been found alive, sheltering in Coed Celyddon, but his mind is disturbed. I've visited him, and he'll not listen to reason.'

Urien grunted. 'Mad? One so brilliant.'

Taliesin recalled how Talhaearn had once described Myrddin, likening him to a tree with branches reaching into the heavens but with roots not anchored deeply enough to hold such weight, though Taliesin had always been reluctant to believe that the seeds of disturbance were sown long before Arderydd.

He realized that Urien was looking at him, brow furrowed, and replied to his unspoken question.

'The trauma he has suffered is beyond his endurance. 'Madness', if you will call it that, was the only refuge. If Rhydderch's men do not capture him, he can survive for the present, but when the weather turns he will die of exposure.' Taliesin paused, praying he did not misjudge Urien. 'My lord, with your leave, I'll return to Coed Celyddon after Alban Elfed and offer him hospitality in my hall for the winter.'

The king's response was swift. 'Nothing will give me more pleasure than to shelter an enemy of Rhydderch's.'

Taliesin smiled faintly. 'Should I get Myrddin to accept, and it may prove impossible, there's no reason for Rhydderch to know of his whereabouts.'

'I will know. That is enough. Myrddin's a fine man, I'd not have him suffer any more than you would. And he could be of use to us if he recovers.'

340

'No doubt.' Taliesin helped himself to a piece of stale bread that had been left on a platter, and sat back, grateful that he had Urien's support. 'Tell me news of the battle with the Deirans,' he said. 'I heard only confused fragments.'

Urien took another draught. 'At first the gods favoured us, and we had the strategic advantage. But two of our chieftains fell, then Dyfnarth received a spear wound......That was when the tide turned.   We were driven back, giving Aelle and his scum an easy time of it, Rheged's energy drained.......You want reasons? The slaughter at Caerwenddolew. The loss of an ally. The lack of Owain and Elffin at my side.' Urien stopped, looking squarely at Taliesin, who had no doubt what was to follow.   'Had   you   been   there   the   outcome might.......would......have been different. I ask that you do not travel north again until the battle season is over.'

'I make no plans to.' Taliesin knew he had been away too long, and it was not only on the battlefield that he would stem the tide of despondency.

Urien glanced at the half eaten bread in his hand. 'What lord allows his Chief Bard to eat like a peasant? You will dine with me on the finest meats before you visit your brother or ride out to your lands. We will speak of hunting, of cattle-raiding, of gaming. Tonight, at least, there'll be no more talk of Anglian vermin and treacherous allies.'

Unsteady from a night's drinking, Taliesin opened the door to his chamber, expecting cool darkness and welcome rest after his journey. But he found the place lit by oil lamps and Nefyn seated on a couch by the hearth, wearing only a translucent white gown and an array of jewels that glistened like her eyes.

She watched him as he crossed the room, throwing his cloak onto a bench without retrieving it when it slid to the floor.

'You're drunk.' Her lips curled into a smile. 'I have never

seen you this drunk.'

'Urien downed two cups to each of mine, yet could have speared an ant at twenty paces.'

Nefyn continued smiling as Taliesin sank down beside her. 'Everyone knows Urien can outdrink a man half his age. I hope I've not been waiting all this time in vain.'

Taliesin glanced at the cup in her hand and at the empty flagon on the table, realizing that she was scarcely more sober than he. She looked lazily back at him, then moved close and slid under the arm he put around her.

'I missed you,' she whispered. 'And you choose to spend the best part of your first night back in the company of Urien, with his hairy hands and mead-drenched moustache.'

Taliesin laughed, holding her against him. Her body felt soft and supple through her gown, vital as her presence. He told himself that he must have missed her too, though in Alclud he rarely thought of her. For a month he had been caught up in a chaos of grief and confusion. And amidst it there were the times he had sat alone with Gwenddydd, conversing in undertones, always chaste as brother and sister.

But now he was with Nefyn, with all her brilliance and warmth and flashes of anger. There was no longer need for restraint. His kiss was urgent, driving out the conflict, the darkness of mourning.

When they drew apart, she spoke teasingly. 'I feared you'd be tired after your journey.'

'Perhaps we should rest.' Taliesin exaggerated the weariness in his voice and got slowly to his feet. 'There's much to do tomorrow.'

Then suddenly he turned, and lifted Nefyn into his arms as he stood to his full height, making her cry out in surprise.

He spoke close to her ear. 'You will see how tired, how drunk I am.'

She laughed, and kissed his neck as he carried her towards

342

the bed.

'This place has been insufferably dull,' she said. 'Next time you go anywhere, take me with you.'

Dawn had broken before Taliesin fell asleep, Nefyn's head on his shoulder, her hair soft against his cheek. Only a few hours later he was up again, dazed and heavy-limbed.

As he crossed the courtyard a fine summer rain began to fall, refreshingly cool on his skin. He tried to still the throbbing in his temples, to look forward to the peace of his own household, but he could not leave for Llyn Glas until he had seen Dyfnarth.

'Who is it?' At the sound of his footsteps a woman's voice called out from behind the hide curtain that divided the chamber.

'It is Taliesin. I can return later if you wish.'

'Come in, for God's sake, and be done with formality.'

Relieved to hear his brother's voice, clear and brusque, he pushed the curtain aside. But Dyfnarth's appearance renewed his concern. He lay propped against a pile of pillows, his gaunt face grey as parchment, his left shoulder heavily bandaged.

Taliesin greeted the woman who sat at the bedside, then turned to his brother. 'Urien told me you'd been wounded. How is your health?'

Dyfnarth scowled. 'How is yours? You are yet paler than usual.'

After a barely noticeable pause, Taliesin replied evenly. 'The journey from Alclud was arduous, nor were the weeks I spent north of the Wall the easiest of my life.'

'I understand you were on an errand of diplomacy, my lord.' Kywere addressed him. 'We've been anxious about events in Ystrad Glud and what they may lead to.'

She rose from her seat and looked at Dyfnarth. 'I'll leave

you to talk in private.......Don't overtire yourself.'

'Do you see an infant? Or a man in his dotage?' Dyfnarth fixed her with a stare. 'I'll be on my feet within a week.'

Kywere winked at him. 'I look forward to it.'

She grasped the curtain, then turned and let it fall, leaving them alone.

Taliesin waited until he heard the outer door close behind her. 'I would have come last night but.....'

'........there were more pleasing things to do.' Dyfnarth gave a crooked grin. 'Help yourself to wine, I'm in no position to play the host, and bring me some. Kywere dilutes what she gives me so it tastes like poison........No doubt you know of our defeat?'

Taliesin went to a table where goblets and a flagon stood in readiness, speaking as he poured. 'We've suffered defeat before, but this has laid Urien low, it seems to have sapped his confidence, his energy for the fight.'

'He grows old, and there've been quarrels with Owain and Elffin. He wants them under his command and cannot accept that they're lords in their own kingdoms, commanding their own men.'

As Taliesin returned with the wine, Dyfnarth struggled to sit up, grimacing with pain.

'Damn this.' He forced the words from between clenched teeth. 'Bloody foreign filth........the bastard deserves to be........skewered by a British sword like meat on a spit.'

Taliesin would have offered help but stopped himself, knowing it would be taken as an insult and provoke another in return. As he looked at Dyfnarth, his mind filled with boyhood memories of the elder brother who had once seemed invincible, his strength matched only by his cruelty.

He handed him a goblet and sat down on the seat Kywere had left, talking about other matters before Dyfnarth suspected pity.

'I return with news of Myrddin ap Madoc,' he said. 'Though he was missing, presumed dead along with his lord and comrades, he survived the battle of Arderydd. He is now in hiding from Rhydderch's men, and sick.'

Dyfnarth drank the wine in long gulps, but his expression was attentive. 'He was wounded during the battle?'

'Not in body.'

'A pretty way of putting it, a bard's way. I never took the man for a coward.'

Taliesin ignored the remark and continued. 'I shall visit him again and offer sanctuary at Llyn Glas.......It is with Urien's accord.'

'Of course. A new weapon for him to wield against Rhydderch.' Dyfnarth met Taliesin's eyes, speaking pointedly. 'And Myrddin is his blood kin.'

Once more Taliesin ignored the remark, wishing he had always known that Dyfnarth's words showed not strength, but weakness.

The wind soughed across Llyn Glas, rustling the leaves of the birch trees and gusting through the open door to the hall.

Bedwen sat opposite Taliesin, outwardly calm, though Taliesin could feel the intensity of his apprentice's gaze as he unstopped the container on the floor between them.

From it, he removed pieces of dried fungus, then looked up, meeting Bedwen's eyes.

'Here lies the sacrament, gateway to the seven senses, bestowed by the gods.' He extended his hand. 'To accept the gift is to accept the truth, the path that must be followed to its end.' As he spoke, Talhaearn seemed to stand at his shoulder, intoning the words that he echoed. Throughout the generations, from master to apprentice, until the apprentice became master, the bright knowledge was passed on. 'From the

345

ancestral darkness into the light of present life, from the light of the present life to the ancestral darkness, sacred time and sacred space combine.'

He inclined his head, and Bedwen took what he held, speaking softly.

'Without fear,
I loosen the bonds of the physical.
In the realm of spirit,
I am the traveller,
I am the seeker.'

As Bedwen chewed the fungus, Taliesin resealed the vessel, then reached for his harp and began to play.

'The words of the bards are energy made manifest, at the threshold of being.   Gwydion's incantation transcends the boundary of matter. The forest awakens to his summons.......'

Bedwen stared at Taliesin's face, at his jaw and cheekbones cast into sharp relief by the fireglow.

'Hear the call of the birches, the trees whose name you bear.' Taliesin lowered his voice, synchronising it with the sighing of the wind through the branches until they became one. Bedwen responded only with his eyes, showing that he understood. 'They speak of beginnings, all beginnings: of the start of the combat at the root of the tongue, of another at the base of the skull. Each tree gives us the weapons to fight and win, through the sound, the spirit of the letter, the sacred word - bedwen, cerdinen, gwernen, helygen........onnen, draenen wen, derwen, celynnen, collen.........'

Taliesin and Bedwen sat in meditation. And when the drug began to take effect, Taliesin rose and led his apprentice from the hall into the gathering darkness. Through the twilight, clouds scudded across the sky, driven by the wind which stirred the waters of Llyn Glas into a frenzy of wavelets.

To Bedwen's dazed eyes his master seemed tall as the birch trees that swayed behind him, the wind rippling the fabric of his cloak. As he watched, he saw the folds become birds, their song more entrancing than the song of any mortal bird. Only the birds of Rhiannon could create such music - music to carry the spirit to the Otherworld.

He looked down to see his master's figure reflected in the lake, broken into a thousand fragments by the wavelets. The birds flew around him, rising from the water, dissolving into it, crossing between worlds.

Through the chorus, and the maze of his own thoughts, he heard Taliesin's voice.

'Enter the gateway, Bedwen.'

Though he spoke to his apprentice, he spoke also to the trees. Bracing himself, Taliesin stepped through first, through tingling air, sparkling white filaments, walking between the birches, which began to glide forward. He heard Bedwen's gasp of awe behind him, signalling that he too had passed safely across the threshold.

The trees surrounded them, vibrating a note that seeped into the mind, that hovered on the tongue like a taste, making the throat ache to respond. As the darkness deepened and rain lashed against their faces, Taliesin raised his arms, his voice merging with the sound. Bedwen felt it assault him with maddening beauty. It made him want to scream, to fight. Then, scarcely aware of what he did, he echoed the note, the syllable that Taliesin intoned, absorbing it from the trees and returning it to them.

The clearing had become a vast spinning disk, a great wheel on which Bedwen struggled to keep his balance. He watched Taliesin crouch on the still hub of that wheel and take up the Ogham staves that had been placed there, then walk the circumference laying them out around the rim, twenty spokes joining them to the centre - one gleaming bright, the path they had already trodden.

'Draennen wen.'

Bedwen thought Taliesin spoke. Or was it the voice of the wind? Of the trees?

The wheel ceased spinning as he picked up the stave with a single line carved to the left of its central ridge. Dagger sharp, he felt something stab into his palm and, with a cry of pain, dropped the stave. Stepping back, he saw that he had been clasping the branch of a hawthorn bush. Every bough upon it was frothy with white blossom, but he focussed only on the thorns as they slashed at him, moving nearer. And a new note filled the air, bitter-sweet like the scent of the flowers. It was too powerful, too resonant, it stirred him too deeply. Bedwen tried to shut it out, to fight off the assault, forgetting his master's presence. He believed he had been abandoned to struggle alone. He felt angry, then frightened...........and finally, defiant. Still, the branches slashed, rending his flesh, blood dripping onto the earth.

'Bedwen, do you not remember?' A steady voice reached him through the tumult.

Taliesin saw what was happening. He saw the thrashing branches, the thorns, but would not intervene. Then he saw Bedwen pause in his frenzy, beginning to chant, though at first he was off key and the assault continued. Eventually, a delicate harmony filled the grove, and from the midst of the tangled branches a figure took form: white skinned, lips red as hawthorn berries, as blood, her hair entwined with leaf and blossom.

'Lady Blodeuwedd.' Bedwen gazed at her, his body shaking. 'I give thanks for your gift.'

The note faded as the image faded, as if washed into the earth by the rain. From all around the hub of the wheel came a ferment of sound, ascending and descending, straining to break through an unseen barrier.

Bedwen glanced up at Taliesin's eyes, green-blue like the waters of Llyn Glas. He felt disorientated, exhausted, yet knew he had undertaken to follow the path to its end and would not fail.

He longed for a moment's rest, but Taliesin turned from him, speaking in an undulating whisper.

'Gwinwydden.'

The wheel span again, or was it only he who was spiralling downward? Seeking support, Bedwen reached out, and felt a tendril twist around his arm, constricting the circulation. His pulse throbbed in his hand, like the beat of a drum. Another tendril took him around the chest. For a while he fought, then he realized he must stay calm, and at that moment became aware of a new note manifesting in his throat, brushing against his lips, demanding to be freed, as he longed to be freed. Without prompting he uttered it, and was released, plummeting downward once more, spinning and twisting.

He did not try to resist, but let himself fall through his own life, through the lives of his ancestors, to the conquest of Ynys Prydein, the rising of the first land, the creation of the stars; through aeons to a nothing that contained all existence.

Then, again he spiralled, forward now, to his birth and his second birth as an initiate, until the note faded and he took a choking breath. He wiped the rain from his eyes and looked up at his master, no longer tired or afraid, but filled with inspiration and the strength to tread each successive path.

Through the darkness three paths glowed, then four, then five, six, seven........notes, colours, seasons, creating paths in his head, on his tongue.

'............ysgawen, ffynidwydden, eithin, grug, aethen, ywen.'

Taliesin's chant grew slower, softer, and Bedwen realized that rain no longer stung his cheeks, the wind no longer tore at his clothes. Not knowing how he came to be there, he lay beside the warmth of the hearth, his mouth parched, his stomach queasy.

ChapTER NINE

Rain came in sudden squalls, lashing across the fells as Taliesin climbed, the trees of Coed Celyddon obscured by the mist that filled the valley. He could scarcely recognize the place he had visited in the summer, dazzled by a fierce sun. Now, after the last deluge, muddy water streamed down the slope, making the going slow and treacherous.

Many times he lost his footing. Again, his boot slipped and he went down onto one knee, the hem of his cloak dragging in the mire. Steadying himself, he heaved the pack he carried onto his shoulder, then continued, struggling to find a secure foothold on the slippery track.

The climb seemed longer than he remembered, but eventually the slope began to level off. Soon afterwards he reached the spring, flowing faster after the autumn rains. As before, he crouched beside it and touched the sacred waters to his brow before offering them back to the earth.

He took a drink and replaced the wooden cup on its ledge, noticing that the sky had darkened, clouds building up from the west before the next squall. The wind stirred the thorn bushes, but there was no other movement. Looking for any sign of his comrade, Taliesin walked further onto the exposed plateau at the summit of the mountain, where a few stunted trees and shrubs grew between outcroppings of rock. He stopped and surveyed the area, then, with the full power of his voice, called out Myrddin's name.

A distant echo was followed by silence. The name rang in his ears like a mockery of his hopes. He waited, gazing across the plateau, and after a moment called again. But before the echo died he was struck by the full force of the downpour and, pulling his cloak around him, took what shelter he could beside a clump of bushes that grew in the cleft of a sharp incline.

As the rain increased, accompanied by a rising wind, Taliesin edged further back, pressing against the rock, impatient for the squall to pass so he could continue his search. And if it bore no fruit here? He tried to think ahead, to plan whilst the weather delayed him. Should he ride north to Alclud? Scour the forest surrounding the mountain? There was only one certainty - he would not give up while he had a chance of finding Myrddin. His thoughts had begun to drift, when from the corner of his eye he glimpsed a grey form moving through the rain. Not human, but animal, slinking close to the ground. He tensed, suddenly alert.

The form was still now, the yellow eyes of a wolf staring at him, its body old and emaciated. Remaining calm, Taliesin showed neither fear nor confrontation. For years, training under Talhaearn, he had worked with the wolf spirit. But this animal was different - something in its stance, its gaze, gave the impression of a domestic hound, not a wild beast.

As he waited quietly, a second form emerged, stooped and walking with painful effort.

'Myrddin,' Taliesin whispered, looking from animal to man.

'Myrddin? Who.......who are you?' The voice was hoarse and tremulous.

'The wolf, you've tamed it?'

'Tame! What is tame? Not the land, nor the storm, nor the thorn tree.'

Myrddin limped away through an almost solid wall of rain, as if oblivious to it, the wolf loping at his side. Reluctantly, Taliesin stepped from his shelter, and followed several paces behind until they reached a shallow cave gouged from the rock.

The squall passed as suddenly as it had struck, and in the lull that followed, as rivulets trickled across the plateau, the two men faced each other. Taliesin, richly clad and clean-shaven, hair bound in a single braid that reached to his waist. Myrddin, crouched in the cave, looking back with the face of a corpse, half-hidden by a dark matted beard. His body, too, was skeletal, inadequately clothed in the ragged remains of the tunic and breeches he had been wearing when he fled Arderydd, his cloak lost. Through his own sorrow, Taliesin was thankful that Gwenddydd was not there to see what her brother had come to.

The wolf lay down beside its master, fixing Taliesin with a wary eye. Cold and wet, he pushed strands of damp hair from his forehead, not knowing how to begin, what to say that would mean anything to his comrade. Myrddin appeared to gaze through him as if he watched something or someone only he could see, making uncoordinated gestures, clasping at the invisible.

When he spoke, it was in a hollow, disembodied voice that was not his own.

'Blood falls from the skies, crops blacken.........Seven mighty lords are struck down, infants ripped from their mothers' bellies.........Suffering, untold suffering.........so the shining one may seize power again.' 15

Taliesin crouched opposite him. 'Tell me, who will seize power?'

He laid his pack on the ground, untying the leather drawstring that fastened it.

'The Man.........of Bronze.' Myrddin's words were choked in his throat and he doubled over, coughing. When he recovered, his eyes burnt with feverish brightness. 'The Man of Bronze.........and over five generations he will guard the gates of Londinium astride his brazen horse.' 15

Seeing how Myrddin's condition had worsened since the summer, Taliesin realized that if his task had been hopeless then, it was doubly hopeless now - yet more urgent. Though hardened to cold and hunger, to pain, Myrddin could not survive in the wilderness for much longer.

Warily, Taliesin offered him a piece of salt beef, thinking the wolf would attempt to snatch it. But the animal lay still while Myrddin took the food and ate with little appetite. As he refastened his pack, Taliesin questioned if there might be any sense, any genuine prophecy in his words, or were they simply the ravings of one who was starved and sick?

'Who is the Man of Bronze?' he asked in an undertone.

Myrddin threw the meat in the direction of the wolf, and began speaking maniacally.

'Famine.........fields stripped bare. Corpses scattered across the sacred island. The few who are spared flee, and plant their seed in foreign soil..........' [15]

He doubled over again, coughing, then weeping into his hands as a chill wind blew across the mountain. Taliesin shivered, feeling the chill seep through his bones.

'Myrddin,' he said, speaking softly. 'Do you recall Caerfyrddin in Dyfed? The house of your father Madoc?'

Though the instant the words were uttered, he wondered if it was cruel to try and bring his comrade back to sense, away from the refuge where he felt nothing but a universal sorrow, where he no longer existed as the sole survivor of Arderydd, blaming himself for his nephew's death. For a moment Taliesin saw a flicker of understanding in his eyes, night blue like Gwenddydd's, then again it was lost.

Myrddin rested a hand on the wolf's head, and the animal rolled onto its side, exhausted as the man who had befriended it. Like him, it had lost its proud spirit. Taliesin knew that its power, its life force, was slowly ebbing. Shutting out the present, in his mind he saw Myrddin at the hour of his greatest prestige, clad in the many-hued robes of a master bard, holding the company at Caerwenddolew in thrall with his song. Saw him as noble companion to his lord, a golden torc about his neck: astrologer, adviser, strategist in battle.

He began to recite, softly at first, a poem of his own they had performed together in those happier times, when he was guest at Gwenddoleu's fortress.

'The first word from the cauldron, when was it spoken?
By the breath of nine damsels gently warmed.' [16]

Taliesin's voice grew stronger, increasing in volume, and as his voice rose he raised his eyes, meeting Myrddin's and holding his gaze, projecting the images of joy, of a past glory that could be again.

'Is it not the cauldron of the Chief of Annwn.........
With a ridge round its edge of pearls.......' [16]

Myrddin returned his gaze, sitting quietly now, and after a while Taliesin saw his expression begin to clear. Still, he continued.

'A sword bright flashing to him will be brought,
And left in the hand of Llyminawg.
And before the door of the Underworld a lamp is burning.' [16]

He was no longer speaking alone. He was no longer with a stranger. The eyes that met his were fully comprehending, though the voice that had once been rich and powerful grated, scarcely above a whisper.

'Am I not a candidate for fame, to be heard in song?
In the four-cornered Caer, the Island of the Strong Door,
Where twilight and darkness meet together,
Bright wine is the drink of the assembly.' [16]

Their voices echoed from the rock wall, resonating, then slowly fading. The silence that followed seemed yet emptier than it had before, and Taliesin knew that he must follow up the advantage he had gained before pain drove Myrddin back across the threshold where he could not reach him.

But it was Myrddin who broke the silence.

'I told you never to return.'

Taliesin could find no clever words, only the simple truth. 'I have worried since I last came here. This is no place for a man of your rank, for any man, to live.'

'It is the place I have chosen, and not for you to judge, however noble the intention.'

Taliesin removed the stopper from the flask he carried and took a draught of strong mead, glad of its comforting warmth. He handed the flask to Myrddin, and while he drank took more food from his pack: bread, cheese, honey cakes and dried fruit.

'Has anyone else been here?' he asked.

Myrddin lowered the flask and shook his head, tangled hair falling across his eyes.

'Rhydderch cannot find me.'

'Rhydderch is no longer searching. Abbot Cunotigern counselled him against it, and he has finally come to realize that his time will be better spent holding back the enemy than hounding his own brother-in-law without cause.'

'Without cause! Night after night I am denied rest!'

Myrddin returned the flask, and Taliesin took another draught before speaking, his voice firm but gentle.

'You have no shelter and scarcely any food, though the leanest months still lie ahead, and you need a physician. Will you not accompany me back to Caer Liwelydd? It'd be with Urien's blessing. He awaits your arrival.'

'I......I cannot live in company. Do not try to persuade me, you waste your breath.'

A gust of wind lashed at Taliesin's cloak, and he saw the

sky lowering again, clouds massing over the distant mountains. The forest below had vanished into the mist which separated them from the world where men worked and loved and fought.

Paying no heed to Myrddin's words, Taliesin spoke again. 'Why continue to punish youself for something of which you are blameless? You will be welcomed, honoured.......'

'Then it will be a lie and a mockery.' Myrddin glanced down at the wolf sleeping at his side. 'I fed him when he was injured and unable to hunt, and he has been a loyal companion.........But he is old and will not survive the winter.'

Taliesin frowned. 'Nor will you, Myrddin. You know that, as I do. Consider again.......for Gwenddydd's sake.'

He received no reply.

'Do you wish to see her? She would come if you asked.'

'Can you all not leave me alone?'

Hearing the finality in his comrade's voice, Taliesin was forced to accept that once more he had failed. As the first drops of rain struck the ground, he unclasped the gold and garnet brooch at his shoulder and removed his heavy cloak, placing it across Myrddin's back.

'I'll return for it within the month,' he said. 'May the gods be with you.'

The brooch still in his hand, he began to walk away, this time not turning.

'My comrade lies cold in the clay, over two hundred of our men with him.'

Taliesin saw the despair in Urien's eyes and a look akin to triumph in Segnius'.

'It is the punishment for sin. Have you not read Gildas' works? He warned the Britons of their sins over thirty years ago. We reap what our fathers sowed, as our children will reap what we sow.'

Urien sighed loudly. 'Sin......sin.....such talk does not win battles, Brother Segnius. We need a new strategy. We cannot end the season in humiliation. The people of Rheged are tired and grieving, they need hope to see them through the winter.'

As Taliesin listened, unable to put Myrddin from his thoughts, Myrddin's sickness became one with the sickness of Ynys Prydein - weak and wracked by internal conflict. He recalled Gwyddno's tales of the warlord Arthur Pendragon, whose strength of leadership had held the Angle and Saeson hoards at bay. In the past Urien had been glorified as a second Arthur. He was the hero of Taliesin's youth, his name on the lips of every bard. But he was no longer young, and his power was in decline.

'My lord,' Dyfnarth spoke out. 'We have to consider alliance with Elmet. It has been discussed before. Now is the time to act. And harder training throughout the winter, or our men grow soft.'

There were nods, murmurs of agreement round the table. Even in defeat, Dyfnarth was respected - Rheged's champion.

'I will think on the matter with Elmet.' Urien drained his cup and rose.

Taliesin rose too, wanting to return to his hall before darkness fell. As he crossed the courtyard, his mind preoccupied, he became aware of someone beside him.

'Sin.' The word jarred in his ears and he turned to see Segnuis' heavy-jowled face. 'The king is blind to your conduct. He must be warned.'

Taliesin continued walking. 'My conduct?' he asked icily, not slowing his pace.

'It is an abomination to have relations with a woman outside holy wedlock.'

When they reached the stables, Taliesin raised a hand to unlatch the door, his sleeve falling back to reveal the tattoos that spiralled about his forearm. He met the bishop's eye, and laughed derisively. Then, without giving him the satisfaction of a reply, called out for an attendant to saddle Nerth.

Looking across Llyn Glas, Taliesin watched the birches sway in a rising wind. Their leaves were yellowing, and in the woods and hedgerows the wild fruits had been gathered, but still Myrddin was sleeping in the open on the hazel mountain, or perhaps in the forest below, the haunt of wolves less tame than the one he had befriended.

'Father?' There was concern in Branwen's voice.

She came to his side, barley-fair hair blowing around her face as she clung to her shawl, fighting to stop it from being taken by the wind. Taliesin thought how she seemed so much a part of this place, in her simple blue gown with no ornaments, her feet bare. But the following summer she would be leaving his settlement. She was fifteen, no longer a child, and betrothed to the eldest son of a chieftain from Penrhyd.

'You seem troubled,' she said. 'Do you wish me to leave?'

He smiled at her. 'Your company is a cure for most troubles, my jewel.'

Branwen laughed. 'It must be years since you last called me that.'

'How is your mother?'

'Busy as always, and usually ill-tempered. I dare say I'd be the same with six children in that small house. And with such a man for a husband. I think he has no speech of his own, every word he utters is a quote from the scriptures.......of the direst kind.'

Her remark reminded Taliesin of Segnuis. The bishop was trying to drive a wedge between himself and Urien. If he succeeded, the rift could only sink Rheged yet further into the mire, an easy prey for the land-hungry Bernicians.

'Sorry.' Seeing his expression, Branwen clapped a hand

across her mouth, the playful gesture tinged with uncertainty. 'I should hold my tongue, but it has a will of its own and runs away with me.'

'Say what you please to me.' Taliesin's tone was gentle. 'Though with others a little more thought might be wise.'

Branwen nodded, a confidential smile on her lips. She held her shawl more tightly around her shoulders, her expression growing serious. 'Llawdoc is downcast,' she said. 'He had such dreams of glory, but this year, since he took up arms, there's been defeat more often than victory. Is that what lies on your mind?'

Taliesin hesitated. She had no knowledge of his attempts to help Myrddin. 'That, and other matters,' he replied quietly. 'But Llawdoc has many years in which to achieve glory, and Rheged will see glory again........All is well with you and he?'

Branwen's smile returned. 'I could not be happier.'

'Then I, too, could not be happier. He will be a husband worthy of you.'

Taliesin saw her shiver, as another gust whipped across the lake.

'We have stood here too long,' he said. 'You are cold, and I have important work to attend to.'

She took his arm, and in deepening twilight they walked towards the settlement.

The hall was dark but for the faint red glow from a dish burning dried belenos herb. Bedwen drummed softly as Taliesin lay on a bull's hide, taking controlled breaths until awareness of his surroundings, of his mortal body, faded.

In his spirit body he descended the tunnel between worlds, journeying to the shores of a great ocean. The rhythm of its waves pulsed in his head as he watched darkness rolling into light, light falling away into darkness. And, riding the waves, a glass boat moved slowly towards him. It had neither oars nor sail, and a solitary figure stood at the prow, swathed in a cloak so only her face was visible - white as death.

He continued to wait, listening to the drumming of the breakers. The boat drew nearer, nearer still, until it came to a rest. But when Taliesin met the eyes of his initiator they were empty reflections, offering no welcome. In silence, he stepped on board, remaining standing as the vessel turned, heading out from the shore, into the mists, the glancing light.

Journeying westward, they made their way beyond the setting sun, into a peace where Taliesin felt neither grief nor conflict. The rhythm of wave, the lap of water, carried him, and, looking to the horizon, he saw the crystal barrier that bound it, refracting spears of colour across the ocean.

It seemed to him that the boat no longer moved. That the barrier spiralled inward, closing around them, hard and bright. But as it touched the prow, crystal melted into shimmering haze, enveloping the vessel. Taliesin felt an intoxication, energy tingling along his spine. Light shifted - maddening in its brilliance. Then there was release. Once more the boat was in open water, rising and falling to the beat of his own heart.

The tidal pull sucked them onward until a second barrier rose on the horizon - a dark mass that came no closer though they sailed with increasing speed. Movement and time collided and dissolved. The darkness slipped over the rim of the world. Then, it was all about them, a living shadow born from itself. Dead weight pressed against Taliesin's eyes, filled his lungs. Unable to see, to breathe, he turned his focus inward, his intention a lifeline to a drowning man. He no longer had awareness beyond that intention, until even the power of thought was taken from him. Only then did the pressure begin to ease, his senses returning.

He breathed again, drawing each breath deep into his lungs, knowing that soon the gift of air would be stolen once more. The clear water around the boat grew opaque, smoke billowed into cloud and ocean. Red flickered against the horizon as they headed towards a ring of fire so vast it blotted out the sky. There was but one course, and no mercy for cowardice.

Surrounded by flames, Taliesin stood fearless, feeling no heat, only purification, clean and deep. Like the three rings of protection he had cast around his mortal body before journeying, three rings guarded the eternal isle.

Out of fire and smoke, the sea rose in a great wave that carried the boat on its crest. Roaring echoed in Taliesin's ears, spray lashed his face. The wave rolled landward, thundering, spitting, and in self-destruction hurled its body upon the shore.

Taliesin staggered as the boat struck, and for a moment grasped the stern, dazed and unsteady. Then, regaining his balance, he looked up at golden crags that pierced the sky, watching the eagle that circled above the precipice.

Finally, he faced his goddess.

'Your task is not an easy one,' she said. 'The tide has turned. But if you are strong enough to carry the Awen back, against the tide, there remains a chance for Ynys Prydein.'

Taliesin stepped from the boat, and without effort began to climb, his footfalls matched to the rhythm of the waves that pounded the shore far below. At the cliff top he paused, looking out to the ocean, at the three barriers he would have to pass through a second time before his spirit could re-inhabit his mortal body. Telling himself that he did possess the strength, the courage, to carry the Awen back, he turned inland, where golden rock met emerald grass. All care slipped from his mind as he headed towards a hall that lay within a palisade of living trees, each branch laden with apples. The walls of the hall were gleaming silver, its roof white birds' feathers, and harp music and bold voices spilled from open doors.

Within, the noble company sat around a circular table

decked for a feast: jewelled goblets overflowing with mead, platters heaped with food that was never depleted. As Taliesin entered, heads turned towards him, hands and voices were raised in greeting. He glimpsed a gentle-faced, auburn-haired youth drinking and laughing with his comrades. And he knew that if Myrddin ceased punishing himself, allowed himself to journey, he too could have seen.

Though he longed to talk with Rhodri, with Glinneu, with all those from whom he was parted in life, Taliesin was not there for himself, nor for Myrddin or Gwenddydd. With an effort of will he continued walking until he stood before a strong man in his prime, clothed in purple and scarlet, a torc of twisted gold about his neck.

Bowing his head, Taliesin spoke. 'My Lord Arthur, I pay my respects.'

'You are welcome, Taliesin. Join our feast.'

He accepted the seat of honour, but when he left the meat and fruit untouched, Arthur nodded.

'It is true you must return to the outer world, your task lies there. But first, will you entertain us?'

Taliesn took the harp that Arthur's queen, Gwenhwyfar, placed in his hands - its frame carved with oak leaves and inlaid with gold. As he began to play, its music evoked the brightest joy and the deepest despair. He opened himself to the Awen, receiving it like an empty vessel receives liquid, words pouring from his lips. He sang for moments, or aeons, not knowing the passage of time, until the song departed, leaving him warmed and lulled, as if he had drunk heady mead or made love.

Whilst praise rang out, the king motioned for him to rise, and, laying the harp aside, Taliesin went with his host from the table. As he passed Rhodri, the youth addressed him.

'Each time you sing my eulogy I hear it, though the gateway of death now separates us........Tell those I've left that I have found peace.'

Taliesin looked kindly at the face of Gwenddydd's son. 'Your name is remembered with honour.'

Beyond the hall, he walked at Arthur's side until they came to a grassy plain encircled by hills. In the centre stood a stone, a lone sentinel engraved with ancient symbols. The king stopped, facing Taliesin.

'You were expected,' he said. 'And I know why you've come.'

He unsheathed his sword, Caliburn, and laid it on the flat top of the stone, resting his hand over the blade. Though, in the world, it lay rusting amongst the votive offerings at the bottom of the lake where Bedwyr had cast it, here it shone in the sunlight, gleaming bright. Taliesin placed his hand beside the king's, feeling the cool metal of the sword and its underlying heat, the power waxing, igniting a fire in his skull.

Arthur's voice burnt like that fire. 'There will be victory before winter's rest. Take courage, and Rheged will arise in triumph.'

chapter ten

Clothed in an amber robe, a silver torc shining at his throat, Taliesin stood at the centre of the hall where the company were gathered. For half his life he had shared their joy and their pain. He waited, allowing himself time to remember. Then, driven by love for the kingdom that he had made his home, he spoke.

> 'Rheged arise,
> the spawner of kings,
> I have watched over you
> even though I am not one of yours.
> Blades and spears
> in battle wheeze;
> men moan
> behind their shields.......' [17]

He looked towards Urien, seeing not a grizzled warrior but the figure of Arthur Pendragon, with the sword Caliburn between them on the sacred stone. In the stillness, he heard the king's words, words that became his own. Then the vision faded into the worn features of an ageing man. Urien sat straighter as Taliesin recited the great victories he had won since the days when Taliesin himself was only a boy, inspired by tales of Urien's valour as he fought under his father Cynfarch.

When he sensed the despondency begin to lift, he turned from Urien and strode amongst the warriors - the ranks who would ride before him onto the field of battle - his voice low and clear.

> 'I know that a war is being mooted,

and the amount I say
will be annihilated........' [17]

His words brought a chill, then fierce optimism. Rheged's
men knew the power he wielded: certain and deadly, a power
that had not been lost with the druids who once guided the
destiny of Ynys Prydein.

Again, he addressed them, his tone lighter, drawing them
back from conflict.

'I got drunk on the mead
of the bold darer......
My king has scattered gifts happily.
The country's good men are useless
alongside Urien.' [17]

As he spoke the final lines, Taliesin met the eyes of the man
who had become both lord and comrade, the shouts and
applause which filled the hall not for himself alone. Though the
weather was turning, the battle season had not yet ended.
There was still hope for a victory that would warm the spirits
of Rheged over the long northern winter.

The third time that Taliesin climbed the hazel mountain, his
attendant climbed at his side, an icy wind gusting in their faces.
The track was frozen hard, and once they cleared the tree-line
stray flakes of snow began to fall from a pallid sky.

Taliesin reproached himself for leaving it so late in the year
- it was past Calan Gaeaf - but to follow his own wishes would
have meant disregarding Urien's. When the king led his men
east against the Angles he had demanded the support of his
Chief Bard, and many believed that without Taliesin there
would have been no victory. In defeating the enemy, Rheged

had won back its confidence, its honour, celebrated with mead in the brightness of the torchlit hall.

Now, as the rock-strewn slope stretched above him, Taliesin recalled that hour of glory - how he had feasted with his comrades, sung of their courage, knowing that Myrddin starved in Coed Celyddon. He walked briskly, and in silence, the air stinging his throat with each laboured breath. Snow came in thicker flurries the higher they climbed, and Taliesin was beginning to feel the strain of the demanding pace he had set, yet he could not afford to give in to tiredness and waste the precious moments of daylight that remained.

Only when he reached the spring did he pause. Removing the wooden cup from its ledge, he made the offering and took an icy draught. Then, standing amidst the snow that whisked around the hazel bushes, he spoke aloud,

'As the waters flow and the earth receives, as day follows night, by divine blessing may all who suffer find peace.'

He went to replace the vessel, but his attendant held out a hand for it, and echoed his words before drinking.

Taliesin looked at the man's weathered face, feeling the respect of spiritual kinship.

'Take what shelter you can until I return,' he said. 'I think it wisest if I go on alone to the cave. Lord Myrddin may become distressed by your presence.'

The man bowed his head. 'The gods grant him mercy.'

Turning into the teeth of the blizzard, Taliesin made his way onto the plateau, able to see only a few paces ahead and slowed by patches of ice. Finally, he reached the incline where he had first encountered the wolf, though there was no sign of the animal, nor of Myrddin. Resting a hand against the rock, he edged his way around it, but was forced to stop, blinded by a flurry of snow.

Stepping back, he shielded his eyes, waiting until the wind dropped. As visibility improved, he moved clear of the rock and looked towards the cave.

Immediately, he began to run.

Curled in a foetal position, Myrddin was covered by the cloak that Taliesin had left on his previous visit, his face half-hidden by a tangle of black hair streaked with white. When Taliesin crouched beside him, he scarcely recognized his comrade in the skull-like features, veins showing blue beneath grey flesh. There was no sign of movement, no vapour to indicate that he breathed. Offering a silent prayer, Taliesin pressed his fingers to Myrddin's neck to feel for a pulse.

He expected nothing, and was startled when he stirred, coughing weakly.

Gently raising him, Taliesin managed to make him swallow a little mead from his flask, though most drained into his beard. He made another attempt, but concern over the rapidly deteriorating weather, and the need to bring his comrade to safety, made him reluctant to delay any longer.

He secured the flask at his belt, then lifted Myrddin into his arms, his wasted body light as a child's, his bones sharp through cloak and clothing. Walking with care, Taliesin headed back towards the spring, brutally conscious of the distance that lay between them and Rheged - the hard journey that must be endured before his comrade reached warmth and the attention of Urien's physician.

His attendant came forward as they emerged through the falling snow, the relief in his eyes quickly replaced by fear.

'He lives,' Taliesin replied to the unspoken question, feeling Myrddin stir again, fighting for air.

The man offered to take him, but Taliesin refused his help. And as they made the treacherous descent, he spoke continually to his comrade in the hope that he would remain conscious, that he might find reassurance in the sound of another human voice, giving him the strength to cling to life.

By the time they reached the horses, early darkness was

drawing in. The howl of a wolf broke the silence of the forest, and Taliesin wondered what had become of Myrddin's companion. No doubt it was long since dead. Myrddin had said that the animal would not survive the winter. Taliesin looked at the sick man he held, telling himself he should have defied Urien and returned sooner, whatever the consequences. Had he lost courage with age and high rank? Grown afraid to follow his conscience? To speak his mind? Once, he would have ridden north without question.

Myrddin lay in the hall at Llyn Glas, his thin body piled with furs.

The king's physician, Iorwerth, glanced at Taliesin, then led the way from the bedside, speaking in an undertone.

'I'm concerned about the lung fever, but he has resilience. Few men would have survived under the conditions in which you found him..........Rest and adequate nourishment will be the most effective medicine.'

And the will to live. Taliesin did not voice the thought, nor that he intended to send for Gwenddydd. He could not let her continue to suffer in ignorance now that her brother had been found, and seeing her might be the one thing that would give him that will. Though it would not be easy for her to leave Alclud. The truth must be kept from Rhydderch, lest he be provoked into sending his warriors south.

Taliesin turned to Iorwerth. 'Thank you for attending Lord Myrddin without delay.'

'My skills are at your command, Chief Bard. I'll return tomorrow. There should be some improvement by then.'

As the physician walked out into the bitter afternoon, Taliesin sat by the hearth, knowing that he should see Bedwen, and consult with Urien, but he had no stomach for other matters while his comrade remained dangerously ill. Over the coming days everything in his power would be directed towards Myrddin's recovery - his earthly wealth and position, and the spirit-healing that lay beyond Iorwerth's skill.

Muffled voices, and occasional soft laughter, drifted from the inner chamber of the hall as Taliesin waited, a manuscript unread on his lap and a goblet of wine untouched at his side.

He raised his eyes when the door opened, and watched Gwenddydd cross the room with silent steps.

'I've left Myrddin to sleep,' she whispered.

She sat down on the couch, and accepted the wine he poured for her.

'He is so much stronger than he was a week ago,' Taliesin said. 'Iorwerth is pleased with his progress.'

Gwenddydd raised her goblet and took a small disinterested sip. She had grown thinner since he last saw her and looked weary.

'You've done so much. Time and again. If it were not........'

'You risk giving me an exaggerated sense of my own importance.' Taliesin smiled, finally able to relax now his comrade was recovering.

Gwenddydd sighed, managing a faint smile in return. 'Myrddin has accepted that I do not hold him responsible for Rhodri's death. And it brings me such happiness to see him.' Briefly, her expression lightened. 'I never thought I would, this side of the threshold, and I feared that he'd go to his grave believing I hated him. He says Urien has offered him a piece of land to the south, in a valley with an apple orchard.......It means a great deal, after he lost everything, everyone except us. To have nowhere to go, no foundation to rebuild your life upon.......' Her voice trailed away, and she took another mouthful of wine. 'The place is far from any settlement, which also pleases him. He still feels unable to tolerate company.'

'For the present, yes, but he knows that he is not alone.'

'When I received your message I sought Cunotigern's advice. I was afraid to be the cause of yet more strife, though I longed to see my brother. It was Cunotigern who told Rhydderch that Myrddin had been found. He has a way about him that calms even the bitterest anger.' Gwenddydd paused, her hands clasped in the folds of her gown. 'Rhydderch and I scarcely speak.......not since Arderydd.'

Taliesin wondered why she was telling him this. He would rather have remained in ignorance, believing that she and her husband had at least found some reconciliation. Stifling his instinctive reply, he tried to lead the conversation down a path where his own feelings would not be laid bare.

'Great trouble can strengthen a bond,' he replied gently. 'I know the years cannot be retraced, grief healed, but with time......'

'No.' Gwenddydd spoke in a whisper. 'The future is a void. I am unable to think ahead.'

She continued facing him, and after a moment Taliesin reached out, taking her hand. Despite her words, he expected her to withdraw it, to move away, but her fingers closed around his. Even after the passage of years he had not forgotten her touch - easing a loneliness that was always with him.

The warmth of Gwenddydd's hand became the warmth of her arms, of her body held close. It was sweetness, honey-mead, tainted with a deadly poison. But Taliesin's dazed mind could not find the strength to break free.

Naturally as breathing, they kissed lightly, echoing their first kiss. Then that past was lost to the present. Gwenddydd's lips parted as Taliesin pressed his mouth to hers, her hunger answering his.

He felt her hands grip his shoulders, move down his back, as they lay together on the couch. Breathing hard, he drew her closer still, with the urgency of long separation. Holding her,

371

feeling the rise and fall of her breasts, the smoothness of her skin, he was beyond thought, beyond conscience.

Then, through his need, the intoxication that burned through his body, the voice of Ceridwen screamed at him. He saw the blood of the battlefield, his own blood as the ravens feasted on his flesh, the cauldron shattered, belching venom into the sacred land.

Thrown back to cold awareness, he became still, and releasing himself from Gwenddydd's embrace sat up, cursing his folly. Desire turned traitor, now he felt only pain.

Turning away, he leant forward, his head in his hands. He heard the rustle of Gwenddydd's gown as she got to her feet, but did not move, feeling that he never wanted to move nor speak again, to face the world with its grief and injustice.

Gwenddydd stayed at Caer Liwelydd a fortnight longer, riding out to Llyn Glas to see Myrddin, though she was always accompanied by an attendant and avoided being alone with Taliesin. They addressed each other with polite formality, the Queen of Ystrad Glud and the Chief Bard of Rheged. But when she left, Taliesin felt an ache, like a sickness, and swore that he had seen her for the last time.

As the months passed his mood lifted a little, as winter melted into spring, grey mist and snowfalls giving way to sunlight and green pastures. And with the improvement in the weather Myrddin went to his own dwelling, half a day's ride to the south.

'At last we're no longer all huddled together like dormice. It gets tedious when the roads are a mire, with few visitors to bring news and fresh company.' As they walked arm in arm amongst the birch trees, Nefyn looked up at Taliesin, a challenge in her eyes. 'I wish to travel more.'

'Travel grows ever more dangerous as Angle and Saeson

raid further west with each passing summer.'

'Unless you're Chief Bard!'

Taliesin raised a sardonic brow, in no mood to be provoked. 'Where do you wish to go?'

'So you don't intend to argue over it?'

'Not unless you want me to, to compensate for the lack of other entertainment here.'

Nefyn's black eyes glinted and she tightened her grip on his arm. 'I long to see new kingdoms, meet new people ....together. We are too often apart.'

'Would you like to visit Gwynedd? See Rhun's court at Deganwy, and Braich y Dinas where I was raised?'

She nodded. 'You know I would, I'd like nothing more. But can Urien spare you?'

'I think so, for a while.' There was mystery in his voice.

Silent and puzzled, Nefyn allowed him to lead her to the edge of the lake, where he spread his cloak on the grass between two birches. Taliesin sat beside her, gazing at the far bank, trying to erase the final doubts..........The past must be cast to the waters. He could not live out his life in regret and guilty conflict. The future lay ahead: challenges, new beginnings.

Eventually he turned, a vague smile on his lips. 'If you wish it, you could travel to Gwynedd and meet my foster-family.........as my wife.'

Nefyn stared, then laughed suddenly, wildly, and kissed him hard, a kiss he returned with tenderness. It was she who drew back first, though only a little.

'I never imagined,' she said. 'But when? When?'

Holding her, seeing her joy, Taliesin replied softly.

'Soon. In the early summer.'

Once more, he told himself that the future lay bright ahead, a future with Nefyn. He would neither see nor think of Gwenddydd again, except as a part of his youth, long since passed.

Part Five

Earth to Spirit

Earth to spirit,
spirit to earth.
Our blood is your mead,
Ceridwen, cauldron-keeper.
Breathe, breath of life....

CHAPTER ONE

Looking from the corner of her eye, Nefyn watched eleven-month-old Afaon crawl towards the door which stood open to let in the sunlight. When he reached it she went after him, swinging him into her arms and bringing him back to where Taliesin sat.

His birth had been an unexpected joy in Taliesin's thirty-fourth year, the same year as a son had been born to Branwen and Llawdoc. But joy was tainted by uncertainty over the future. Though Rheged's power kept the Bernicians at bay, there had been news of defeat at Deorham in the south. The towns of Glevum, Corinium and Aquae Sulis were all taken. Lands that once linked the Britons of Dumnonia and Powys now lay in the hands of the Saeson chief Ceawlin as the enemy closed in, captured territory pressing against Cynan's eastern borders.

Taliesin smiled at his son, who struggled to free himself from Nefyn's hold. The child's hair was dark and curly like his mother's, but he had Taliesin's fair skin and green-blue eyes, and he was tall for his age, larger and stronger than Dyfnarth's son Maeglor, who was two months older. As he looked at him Taliesin felt a sense of pride, and a longing to remain here with his family, to walk the land together in the brightness of summer.

Turning to Nefyn, he spoke softly. 'I must leave for Caer Liwelydd before noon, when the warband rides north. We make camp tonight amongst the hills.'

Nefyn released the struggling infant and frowned. 'So soon?'

'Messengers have been sent to Owain, confirming where we join forces with the men of Galloway.'

Nefyn swallowed hard. 'I'll go with you to town, and stay there while you're away. Wine and song have always been better able to distract me than fields and flowers.'

Taliesin got to his feet as Afaon crawled across the threshold, fetching the boy back himself, laughing at his kicks and shrieks of defiance.

Noon approached, and Taliesin made ready to travel. After instructing an attendant to saddle the horses, he filled a cup of mead and stood by the empty hearth, pack and cloak on the bench beside him. Only the knowledge that he was soon to see Owain weighed against his reluctance to leave. They had not met for over a year, not since his son's birth and, if the gods willed it, after the battle they would drink and share news in the warmth of comradeship as they had always done.

When the sound of footsteps intruded on his thoughts, he turned to see Bedwen walking hastily from the courtyard. His apprentice was approaching his twenty-first summer and his narrow face had gained firmness, though it had lost none of its intensity.

Bedwen waited until he stood opposite Taliesin before speaking. 'Master, there is something I wish to ask of you.'

'Can it not wait? We are leaving at any moment.'

'That is my reason for coming here. I ask to ride with you, to be at your side as Rheged engages the enemy.' There was no hesitation, no flicker of self-doubt.

Taliesin sighed. 'We have been through this earlier, and my answer remains the same.'

'I would learn from the experience,' Bedwen said, undeterred. 'It would give me the chance to practice my skills. I possess the power already, and it's but a year until my training is complete.'

'You make my argument for me - the field of battle is not

the place for practice, however advanced. I never accompanied Urien's warriors while I was studying under the Master Talhaearn, nor did I expect to.' Taliesin drained the mead cup and laid it aside, glancing at the door to the inner chamber as he heard Nefyn's voice. For him the discussion was at an end, but Bedwen remained where he was, tight-lipped and resolute.

'Have you no confidence in my ability? Do you fear I may make a dangerous error? I swear that......'

As the door opened, Taliesin reached for his cloak.

His tone cut like flint. 'In arguing with me you already make a dangerous error. Power is nothing without discipline and self-control. Say no more, and I will forget we had this discussion.'

The young man turned on his heel and strode angrily from the hall, watched by Nefyn and Afaon's nurse, who carried the sleeping infant. Nefyn looked at his departing figure with amusement, then went to Taliesin and took his arm.

'He follows his master's example,' she said dryly. 'No doubt he will achieve greatness.'

The sun rose through the mist, clearing the mountains at the first clash between Briton and Angle. Long hours of daylight followed, long as the fight, but by dusk ravens flew over Argoed Llwyfain and the enemy retreated.

After burying their dead the Britons returned to camp, exhausted and mourning lost comrades, but victorious. Amongst the drunken company Taliesin lay by a smoky camp fire, and resting his head on his pack gazed up at the deepening blue of the sky. As the evening star brightened he remembered the night he had sat at Talhaearn's settlement and seen it shine between the trees, not yet aware that Branwen had been born. Now she herself was a mother. The darkness he had experienced before leaving the previous day was replaced by hope. He thought of watching Afaon grow, as he had watched Branwen grow, strong and free of spirit. Until he, too, fathered children. Children who still had the chance to live in a land that was their own.

Owain, seated beside him, held out a wine skin and Taliesin raised himself to drink. He had missed Owain's companionship over the past year, and decided then that he would accept his comrade's invitation to visit the stronghold of Din Carreg. Nefyn would be delighted. They could travel to Galloway in around three months time, after Alban Elfed, once the battle season was over.

As he passed the wine skin back, the firelight glinted off the hilt of the dagger at his belt.

'You still have the prize you won from me,' Owain said, grinning.

'I'll give it to Afaon when he's older, with the tale of how I acquired it.'

Owain laughed. 'So the Chief Bard of Rheged commemorates my defeat! I trust you'll also immortalize today's victory with your words.'

Alone in his quarters, Taliesin paced to and fro, speaking aloud as he worked on the composition he would perform before the company. That night in the feast hall, those who had been at Argoed Llwyfain would hear again the clash of blade against blade, as Anglian gore flowed red in their sight and the odour of blood on hot metal filled their nostrils. And generations of his people, far distant in time and place, would re-live the fight as he had witnessed it.

Theodoric 'Fflamddwyn' of Bernicia stood on the field before him, squat and muscular, with ruddy face and golden beard. In a guttural accent he hollered the challenge,

'Have my hostages come,
are they ready?' 18

The call was answered by Owain.

'They haven't come.
They don't exist.'

And Urien shouted,

'If there's to be a meeting for a parley,
let's raise our banners above the mountain,
let's lift our faces up to the edge,
let's raise our spears above the heads of men.......' 18

A knock at the door made Taliesin start, caught between realities.

Giving a curt reply, he looked round and saw one of his own attendants from Llyn Glas standing at the threshold, his expression grim.

'I apologize for the intrusion, my lord, but Lady Finllian has sent me to summon you.'

Taliesin waited for the man to continue, his mind dazed.

'There was a fire yesterday.......It started amongst the birches, though the hall was spared.' The man hesitated. 'Young Bedwen's been absent since, missing all night.'

Anxiety gripped Taliesin as the news took hold. 'Was anyone injured?' he asked, fully back in the present.

'No, thank the saints. Only Bedwen was nearby.'

'And he is unharmed?'

'Yes, my lord. I saw him walk away.'

Though his fear eased, Taliesin felt shaken. He wanted to ride out to the settlement immediately, to deal with the crisis himself, relieve Finllian of the responsibility that should be his, but his duty as Chief Bard must take precedence. He must celebrate Rheged's victory beside Urien, recount the glory........and the sacrifice of those who had not returned.

He faced his attendant. 'I cannot leave Caer Liwelydd now,' he said firmly, masking his uneasiness. 'I will be at Llyn Glas in the morning.'

As Taliesin approached along the track, he saw the scars left by the fire: the charred birch trees and smoke-blackened palisade. The blaze had been so close to the buildings it could have destroyed everything, and he thanked the gods no one had been killed or maimed. His concern now was for Bedwen.

In the hall, he took a seat beside Finllian.

'Forgive me for not coming yesterday,' he said, trying to read her eyes.

'Perhaps it is I who should apologize, for troubling you at such a time.' Though she appeared calm, he could hear the strain in her voice.

'You look weary,' she observed. 'This is a sorry welcome home. And I fear you'll be wearier still before the matter is settled.'

'You know what happened.' It was not a question.

'I did not see how the fire started. But yes, I know.'

Taliesin turned away, gathering his thoughts. 'Where is Bedwen?'

'He was gone for two days after the disaster, but he's back now, awaiting your return. For hours he's been walking across the pastures. He seems to have accepted that escape is no answer, that he'll have to face the consequences.'

'I would that I myself did not have to face them.' Taliesin spoke under his breath.

'What will you do?'

He shook his head. 'May Ceridwen guide me.'

The tone of his voice made Finllian frown, and she laid a hand on his arm. 'Surely you don't blame yourself?'

Taliesin gave no reply, and she did not pursue her question.

'Shall I send one of the men to fetch him?' she asked.

'No, I'll go.'

Quietly invoking Ceridwen's wisdom, Taliesin left the settlement, and skirting the lake made his way south.

When he eventually caught sight of Bedwen his apprentice was no longer walking, but seated on a solitary outcrop of rock. He remained motionless, staring at the ground, and only got to his feet once Taliesin reached him. His vivid blue eyes had lost their vitality but he stood straight, holding his head high, not with a look of pride, rather of forced courage.

'Master.' Much was said in that word.

Taliesin sat down, and indicated for Bedwen to do the same. For a moment there was silence between them, then Taliesin spoke, his voice neutral.

'Can you tell me what happened while I was at Argoed Llwyfain?'

Again there was silence, and Bedwen gazed beyond Taliesin towards the horizon. He drew breath to reply, but could find no words. Only a breeze rustling the long grass broke the stillness.

Taliesin did not hurry him, containing his own anger, resolved to make no judgement until he had given his apprentice a chance to explain.

Finally, in a detached, expressionless voice Bedwen began. 'I performed the rite for summoning fire spirits, to destroy the enemy. I thought to work with you at a distance because I was not permitted to be with you in body.' Bitterness replaced the detachment. 'Because you doubted my powers.'

'Then you must be satisfied at having demonstrated them so conclusively.'

Bedwen's jaw muscles tightened but he said nothing, and Taliesin continued, speaking evenly.

'I was not disputing your powers, nor your ability. I told you that it has never been the practice of a master to take his apprentice onto the field of battle. Your failure to accept this, to show restraint, has put your progress into question........It saddens me that an initiate of your experience chose to work with the wrong-motivation, raising chaotic forces that in your state of mind you were in no condition to control.'

There was another long silence, then Bedwen looked directly at him.

'It will never happen again.'

But his expression was stony, and Taliesin heard no note of remorse or apology. It was clear that Bedwen laid the blame at his door for refusing his request, still believing it was because Taliesin had doubted him. Though he was mistaken. There had been no serious doubt before. Now, the trust and mutual respect they had built up over the past seven years had been shaken to its foundation. Taliesin felt hurt, disappointed.......and angry at himself. Perhaps he was to blame, for not devoting sufficient attention to Bedwen's training, for taking on too much, trying to do everything, be everything.

As his hand rested on the warm surface of the rock, he felt the strength of it, drawing its stability into himself. He paused in thought, letting reason over-ride impulse.

'Three days ago you reminded me that in a year your training would be complete.' His voice held calm authority, an authority that could not be challenged. 'From today the length of your apprenticeship will be at my discretion, depending on your future work.'

And Bedwen did not argue. He inclined his head, then got to his feet and once more began to walk across the pastures, in the direction of Merin Rheged.

* * *

For a week Taliesin stopped all instruction with Bedwen, to allow emotions to settle on both sides. But a fortnight later the tension had not eased. Neither spoke, except to discuss their work, and instead of being able to give more attention to Bedwen as he had hoped Taliesin found his presence constantly in demand as Urien prepared another campaign against Fflamddwyn. After a period of respite, the Angles were again sacking villages within Rheged's borders, burning fields of ripening grain and raiding cattle.

His cloak draped across his shoulders, Taliesin stood beside Afaon's wooden cradle. As he looked down at the face of his sleeping son and listened to the child's soft breathing, he was touched by an overwhelming sense of peace. Time ceased to pass and, in that moment, the thought of the Angles plundering and killing seemed vague and remote. He stood for a long while, then turned and walked quietly from the room.

In the main chamber, Nefyn rose from the couch at the hearthside. She wore only a light shift, and her eyelids were heavy from rising early.

'I might as well be wed to a warrior.' She sighed. 'It's under a month since you went with Urien to Argoed Llwyfain.'

'Do you not want a future for Afaon? For his descendants?' Taliesin met her eye. 'You know there's a price.'

'Noble words!' Nefyn gave a hollow laugh, then took his hands. 'May God watch over you.'

He kissed her, holding her to him, and when he left did not look back. Nefyn remained by the hearth, twisting the ring he had given her on their wedding day, unable to face lingering on the threshold until he was no longer in sight.

At the head of Urien's warband, Taliesin accompanied the warriors through the quiet town. It was barely light as they advanced beyond the gates, following the great wall towards

387

the Bernician border. Man and horse - a shadow moving swiftly across the land.

The terrain grew rougher, the slopes steeper, vegetation more sparse, and by sunrise they had made good progress from Caer Liwelydd. As the sun blazed above the horizon, a flash of brilliance glanced off hilt and spearhead. Then, like a dowsed fire, it was blotted out. Cloud built from the west and a chill wind blew across the fells.

Throughout the morning Taliesin rode with Urien and Dyfnarth, saying little as he dwelt on the unresolved rift with Bedwen, believing that what had happened was a mark of his own failure. Then he would picture Afaon's tranquil face. Only a child could sleep in such peace, knowing no conflict. While he was on the field of battle, his son would laugh and play as usual, unaware.

Around noon they rested briefly, then continued along a ridge overlooking scrubland, alert for surprise attack. But none came. They made camp that night in heavy rain, and it was only on the following day that they began to see the devastation: wasted fields and mounds of charred wood that had once been British settlements, the bodies of the villagers lying where they had fallen, with no one left alive to bury them. Still there was no sign of the enemy, only of their works.

The scouts who had been sent on ahead returned to report that the Angles were close. Soon there would be no more waiting, no more opportunity for thought. As Urien issued the final commands Taliesin looked at Dyfnarth. Not for the first time, he saw a grim anticipation on his foster-brother's face that was more than desire for victory and the need to drive the enemy from their land.

Under a grey sky, Urien led the men of Ynys Prydein onto the moor where Fflamddwyn's force was gathered amidst the heather and bracken. As the Britons came within sight, the Angle bellowed out the Bernician war cry, a roar that echoed from the throats of the enemy host.

Urien unsheathed his sword, holding it high.

'For the glory of Rheged, victory,' he yelled in answer, and a great clamour of shouts and the blast of trumpets arose from the ranks behind him.

The king glanced at Taliesin, but no word was spoken, and as the warriors advanced he and Ysfael dropped back. They took up position on an ancient cairn, watching their comrades pass, crushing heather blossom beneath hooves, the tide surging onward, gaining momentum.

Bold challenges accompanied the first clash, followed by cries of death as men struggled and fell in the heat of the onslaught.

Looking out across the moor, at the dark mass which heaved like the clouds that rolled overhead, Taliesin began to circulate the sacred breaths. The power flowed through him until he felt his sense of separation dissolve. His spirit joined with the warriors' spirits, part of a greater whole - the spirit of Ynys Prydein. One, not only with the warriors, but with the villagers who had died defenceless in their settlements, and with generations past and future.

With spirit sight Taliesin saw the red dragon above the field of battle, its being merging with the Britons who fought beneath it. Wings spread, it spat fire, breathed venom upon the foreigners who desecrated the sacred land.   It fed upon rage and death, and in the path of its vengeance the enemy faltered. The tide turned against them, and rank upon rank, they fell before Rheged's advancing cavalry.

Watching with Ysfael, Taliesin followed the action, seeing Urien where the fight was fiercest. Around the king and his warband the earth grew slippery with blood, and on heather crushed to pulp the wounded lay, crying out in their agony.

Holding the focus, allowing himself no distraction, Taliesin turned fear and grief to battle fury, directing the power.

The afternoon wore on, and the sky darkened above the moorland. The stench of blood filled the air and ravens circled overhead, black as the heavens.

In desperate fight, Fflamddwyn stood firm, then started to press forward. Strong and thick-set, he was visible at the head of his force, cutting swathes with his gleaming long-sword, reaping horse and man. Inspiring his followers to slaughter. Taliesin watched him cleave the shield of a British warrior. Then, raising his own shield with its iron boss, the Bernician rammed it into the warrior's face, smashing his skull.

As the setting sun burst from beneath the cloud cover, bathing the moor in a lurid glow, the fight raged. On a battlefield that appeared awash with blood from a gash in the sky, still Fflamddwyn advanced.

Spears flashed red, close to the cairn. An axe struck the ground, making Ysfael's horse start in fright. And though he brought the animal under control, he did not resume his chant. With each moment the conflict intensified, savage light and shadow playing on the warriors' faces.

Finally, Ysfael turned to Taliesin, unable to keep silence any longer. 'Retreat,' he yelled. 'Placing ourselves in danger is to disregard royal command.'

'You go,' Taliesin called in reply. 'It will confuse the enemy if we separate.'

Ysfael veered to one side as a spear whined through the air.

'The heat and gore have turned your head.' His voice rose above the tumult. 'Don't risk your safety.'

Taliesin remembered when he first met Ysfael, coldly confident, the elder of the master's pupils, while he himself was only a novice in a strange kingdom. He hesitated, then edged Nerth alongside Ysfael's horse, though he went with reluctance.

As they rode, Taliesin looked over his shoulder, and when he glimpsed Nefyn's son, Gwilym, facing a warrior twice his stature, he reined in, ignoring Ysfael's shouts.

He watched Gwilym use his agility to outwit the foreigner and, moving swiftly, strike the Angle's right arm with his sword, cutting deep. The moment the enemy's weapon spun from his useless hand, Gwilym made a final thrust up under his chin, and the man fell, spluttering blood.

The red light was fading from earth and sky, casting the field into a gloom which confused the senses, but again Taliesin hesitated, seeking Urien in the thick of the fight. Afraid for his king, he refused to retreat further until he knew the Lord of Rheged lived.

He had begun to narrow his focus, believing he saw a familiar bull-like figure, when he heard Ysfael yell out and thought the other bard had been struck. An instant later he felt a sharp pain across his stomach and slumped forward, clutching the wound, warm blood seeping between his fingers.

Through the ringing in his ears, once more he heard Ysfael's voice. 'Taliesin, look out! To your right.'

Nerth shied as a calloused hand gripped the bridle, accompanied by a word of triumph in an alien tongue. Taliesin felt other hands take hold of him, hauling him roughly from the horse's back, paralysed by pain and unable to resist.

CbAPTER TWO

Torches blazed around the hall, throwing fiery light across the faces of the elders. For a night and a day they had been in council.

Urien hunched over his meadhorn, jaw muscles taught. 'The messengers I sent with an offer to trade hostages have not returned. No doubt murdered by the barbarians.' He glanced at the men around him. 'Now we can do nothing but wait in the hope that our spies bring news of where Taliesin is held.'

'Wait......and pray for his safety.' As he got to his feet, the one-eyed veteran Tewdwr looked narrowly at Segnius. It had not escaped his notice that he had made no contribution during the discussion. 'We will add the strength of our prayers to those of the holy brothers,' he said, still looking towards the abbot.

One by one the elders left the table, until only Talhaearn remained with Urien. Despairingly, he faced the man whose advice he had first sought on the day he underwent the rite of kingship, though recently he had come to rely on Taliesin - an adviser actively involved in the affairs of the kingdom. But Urien still had faith in the master's wisdom, which had not diminished with years or with retirement from public office. Though he was aged, seventy-seven summers, his lean frame was supple and his mind sharp as ever.

Urien gave a harsh laugh. 'I speak as if Taliesin lives. But the foreigners fear his power, the power that gives us the advantage in battle. If they've not already killed him, they won't hold back for long.' He stopped abruptly, and leant forward. 'You know something?'

'I know he does live.'

'Keep nothing form me.'

Talhaearn met the king's eyes. 'By the ancient arts, Lady

Finllian and I have succeeded in finding him. I have seen the fortified settlement where he is held and may be able to direct your men, though the route is less clear.'

For a moment Urien's expression lightened, then he lowered his brow. 'I asked that you keep nothing from me.'

The bard hesitated, and when he spoke there was a tremor in his voice.

'The Angles torture him, though he is already wounded, defying him to use his powers to save himself.'

Urien clenched his fists. 'Damn them to Hell! I'll lead the rescue myself. The land will swim with their blood for this.'

Talhaearn's tone remained calm. 'My lord, nothing will be gained by you risking your own life. The people need you here. Taliesin's capture has brought them insecurity enough.'

Urien struggled to swallow back his fury. 'I cannot find peace until Taliesin is here in this hall, not until his torturers are dead.' He brought his fist down on the table. 'Tomorrow a band of Rheged's finest warriors ride into Bernicia. There will be no more delay.'

It was shortly after daybreak when Dyfnarth stood before Urien, the expression in his eyes dark as the king's mood.

'My lord, allow me to lead the men. It is my due as Taliesin's foster-brother, I have no other brother since Glinneu was slain.'

Urien looked at his kinsman, seeing a warrior in his prime, straight-backed and lean, arms muscled like iron. By comparison he felt old and flabby, remembering his former vigour. He knew the task was arduous, a task for a younger man. Taliesin's life was not something to be gambled with for the sake of his own pride, and Talhaearn had been right, it would further destabilize Rheged if he himself were killed.

He nodded gruffly. 'I agree to your request. The master

will give you all the information you need.'

'I will not fail.'

Urien stared at Dyfnarth. 'No, you will not.'

Watched by a silent gathering of townspeople, Dyfnarth's warriors rode through the gates of Caer Liwelydd and followed the wall east as they had done only a week earlier. Amongst the assault party was Urien's third son, Riwallon, and a young physician from Hibernia named Credan, who had trained under Iorwerth. He, alone of all the company, did not bear arms.

The layout of the Anglian settlement was imprinted on Dyfnarth's mind, as Talhaearn had described it, together with landmarks they must pass on the way, though the information was often vague. Never before had he led his men into enemy territory with only a vision to guide him, and he continued to question whether theirs was an act of courage or insanity. If he failed, he knew he would die at the hands of the Angles, spared from disgrace, but if he succeeded there could be no greater glory.

The late summer sun burned his skin as they headed into the hills, the horses lathered with sweat. At first, riding hard, they travelled openly across Rheged, covering a good distance before evening. Only as the heat of the day faded, and the sun dipped towards the horizon, did they stop to feed the horses and prepare themselves for the crucial hours ahead.

While his men rested, Dyfnarth stood on the bank of a stream, feeling in no need of rest. He looked at Riwallon's bearlike figure beside him, seeing a younger reflection of Urien.

'We enter Bernicia at nightfall,' he said. 'Then head south-east through forest.......' Again, doubt flashed across his mind. He prayed Talhaearn's information was sound, not simply the delusions of an old man. But he left the treacherous thought unspoken. 'God knows how far we must travel before we reach the broken pillar stone. This is like riding into battle blindfold.'

Riwallon's voice was confident. 'The enemy do not fear blindfolded men. By taking Taliesin to an obscure settlement deep within their territory the Angles fool themselves....... We'd have no chance of storming a major fortress.'

Dyfnarth grunted. He waded through the shallow water and walked briskly along the far bank, reviewing his plan of attack, searching for any point of weakness. When he finally returned to camp he forced himself to lie down, aware that he must conserve his strength, be capable of making decisions quicker than a spear-thrust, or risk everything.

In gathering dusk the men remounted and travelled on, into land now held by the Angles. And as they reached each ford and deserted British farmstead, each cairn or pool, Dyfnarth's confidence in Talhaearn grew.

They entered the great forest at dawn and halted briefly to get their bearings, then once more they pressed on, conscious that every delay meant less chance of finding Taliesin alive. Noon passed, followed by long hours of daylight, though it was drear and shadowy beneath the leaf canopy, and they had no landmarks to guide them. The warriors spoke in undertones, recounted tales of battle, and ate as they rode, pausing only for the horses to drink from a muddy pool. Dyfnarth remained silent and irritable, fresh doubt taking hold as he questioned if they had missed the way amongst the confusing monotony of trees.

The sun was low on the horizon before the forest finally thinned out, bordering scrubland where the sight of a lone megalith, cracked and fallen, told Dyfnarth their journey was almost done.

He reined his horse in, frowning into the distance, then addressed the men behind him.

'We wait here until dark, there's insufficient cover to

continue now.' He raised a hand and pointed. 'Beyond that ridge lies our goal. Less than a league distant.'

He led the way through dense undergrowth, caressing the hilt of the sword which had sent countless Angles to their deaths. He was here not only to free Taliesin, but because Rheged demanded vengeance for the Chief Bard's capture. The more Angles his men could kill, the greater Urien's satisfaction.

Twilight lingered - the sky too bright, the land too clearly lit, for them to cross open country. And, despite a sense of urgency, Dyfnarth's judgement subdued his impatience. As the moments dragged, he strode along the forest edge, constantly vigilant. Again he stopped, and glanced up at a sky studded with stars, then scanned the ground to the ridge. Stepping back into the shadows, he turned to Riwallon.

'We waste time......I'll give the order to advance.'

He felt his muscles tense, the familiar fire burn in his blood, as the hour when he would lead the assault drew nearer, though he knew that when it came he must act with cold precision.

The prince nodded. 'This infernal waiting saps the energy.'

Relieved to move at last, the warriors rode out from the shelter of the trees, making for the ridge which hunched against the skyline. At their head, Dyfnarth remained wary, angered by the vulnerability of their position. Lashing the reins, he dug his heels into his horse's flanks until the animal broke into a canter.

He kept up an even pace, then once more dug in his heels. They were over half way across the scrubland with no sign of the enemy. But though they had not been set upon, there was a danger that the Angles had received warning. If he and his men had lost the element of surprise, they rode to their deaths.

As they drew nearer to the ridge, Dyfnarth spotted an overgrown hollow at its base and headed towards it. He looked across the scrub to either side, then came to a halt and dismounted.

Holding his horse's bridle, he faced the men. 'I'll go up on foot,' he said. 'See how the land lies.'

'Let me go in your stead, my lord.' The youngest warrior stepped forward. 'The risk is......'

But before he finished speaking, Dyfnarth threw his reins to the youth and made for the slope, cutting a path through the undergrowth with his sword. Using root and rock for a foothold, he began to climb, scarcely slowing as the incline steepened. Near the summit he crouched low, then got down on his belly, half-expecting to find nothing beyond the ridge but more empty wilderness, to learn they had been sent on a fool's errand. He hauled himself forward, raising his head, and exhaled.

On the next rise was an enclosed settlement, its cluster of wooden buildings protected by a palisade, the gates hidden from view on the far side. Dyfnarth lay motionless, watching for any movement, noting the angle of approach, the height of the defences. Taking a final look, he edged back, and once he was clear of the skyline got to his feet, and scrambling, then running, descended to where his men waited.

Losing no more time, they rode across a narrow valley, through darkness which had deepened as night wore on. All seemed uncannily still, and Dyfnarth questioned if the Angles lay in wait, luring them into a trap. Uncertainty fuelled his hatred of the enemy. If he was to die, he would die fighting, deal out slaughter to the foreign scum before he fell.

He reached the rise first and tethered his horse to a stunted tree. The men followed his lead. No word was spoken. And at his signal, his plan became action.

The Britons surrounded the palisade, divided into four groups with rope and grappling hooks. The enemy heard only the hoot of an owl. Then, swift and silent, four men scaled the defences, shields slung over their backs, pausing at the top to cast throwing spears at the guards by the gate. The Britons dropped down easily inside the palisade, swords drawn, the next four joining them before the alarm was raised.

A sudden blaze of torches lit the enclosure as men rushed from buildings, armed but wearing only linen tunics and breeches. In the confined space, amidst flickering light, Briton and Angle met in a chaotic and desperate fight.

Dyfnarth raised his shield to ward off the strike of a thrusting-spear, then wheeled round, feeling the snap of ribs as his sword sunk into the Angle's chest. The man staggered, and Dyfnarth struggled to drag the blade out, ducking as a second warrior came at him from the shadow. The enemy sword whirled above his head, dripping blood. Finally, he worked his own sword free, confronting a man with yellow hair and beard, eyes gleaming in the torchlight. In the clash of iron against iron, the flash of sparks, Dyfnarth knew he fought for his life.

Catching the enemy in an unguarded moment, he slipped past his shield, slicing his neck with one stroke like a knife through butter. Confident he had dealt the death blow, Dyfnarth's concentration wavered, until he felt the sting of honed metal against his forearm. Infuriated, he struck out, partially severing the man's head. He laughed wildly at the sight, in pain and triumph.

Blood trickled over his wrist, but he was able to hold his sword, and he turned in search of fresh combat. Only then did he realize that the fighting had almost ceased. On the beaten earth of the enclosure lay the wounded and dying, and within seconds the four Angles who remained standing threw down their weapons in surrender.

At spearpoint, they were herded into a storehouse and forced to kneel, their hands bound.

'What shall we do with them, my lord?' One of his men addressed Dyfnarth.

He looked coldly at the captives, wiping blood from his

sword before sheathing it.

'Kill them.'

He spat in their faces and walked away.

Beneath the palisade three Britons who had been wounded were being treated by Credan, the rest were on their feet, awaiting orders. Dyfnarth glanced at Riwallon, then back at the men.

'Search the buildings,' he yelled.

Though his arm still bled, he left it untended. His only thought, to find where Taliesin was held, hoping he had not been slain once the enemy knew they were under attack. With two of his men, he made for the largest building, taking a torch from a sconce by the entrance. The men separated, moving to either side as Dyfnarth strode down the central aisle. Sacks of provisions and bedding emerged from the gloom, each time bringing a shot of hope, quickly dashed.

In rage and frustration Dyfnarth overturned a bench that stood in his way, scattering meadhorns. He cursed, kicking the debris, then stopped. A yell from the courtyard made him look round. And with the torch still in his hand, he ran for the door and headed towards a low hut where the warriors had gathered.

Their expressions were grave as they made way for him to pass. Steeling himself, he held the torch high and saw a man lying on his side close to the far wall, his silver-fair hair unmistakable. Without speaking, Dyfnarth hurried to him.

Taliesin's face was like wax beneath the dirt and a week's growth of beard, and blood had trickled from the corner of his mouth. As Credan knelt on the ground to tend him, Dyfnarth heard a faint rasping breath that made him recall the death rattle of comrades who had fallen on the field.

Carefully, Credan turned Taliesin onto his back, and after a moment raised his eyes.

'I'll do as much as I can,' he said in an undertone.

Riwallon went with the warriors from the building, though Dyfnarth remained, holding the torch steady while Credan took instruments and dressings from his pack and laid them on a cloth. But as he began to cut away Taliesin's blood-soaked tunic, Dyfnarth tensed, the light wavering. He regretted his decision to have the captives killed as too merciful when he saw Taliesin's body, bruised black and covered by deep gashes, and as Credan finished cutting away his tunic it revealed an open sword-wound.

Seeing his condition, Dyfnarth felt certain he could not survive, and knew he would be the one who must travel to Gwynedd to break the news of his death to their ageing parents.

Finally, he spoke. 'What are his chances?'

'They would be better if we did not have a long journey ahead. His right arm and many ribs are broken.......injuries consistent with being struck by a heavy weapon.' Credan lowered his voice. 'I pray for his sake that he lost consciousness early on........I cannot tell what internal injuries he has suffered, but there is danger from infection of the blood, and a splinter of rib bone may have punctured his lung.'

Dyfnarth squinted into the flickering light, looking at Credan. 'Then there is no chance...........that is what you're saying.'

'I never say such a thing, Lord Dyfnarth, not while a man lives, but he cannot travel like this. I will have to make an incision and remove the fragment of rib that has been displaced.'

He fell silent, and Dyfnarth watched as he operated, quickly and competently. There was a time when he would have felt no grief at Taliesin's death, but he had come to respect the bastard his parents had taken in, the strange boy who had no interest in warrior games, but who won the praise of all who heard him sing. Bitterness and jealousy had been transmuted into pride at acknowledging the Chief Bard as foster-brother, knowing that Taliesin's fame reflected on himself. The journey back would be dangerous for them all, slow and dangerous, but even if Taliesin died before they reached Caer Liwelydd, Dyfnarth did not regret having risked his own life to free him.

When the physician had finished binding Taliesin's wounds, Dyfnarth summoned his men to bring the litter they had constructed from wood and hide found at the Anglian settlement. As they placed it on the ground, Credan addressed them in his soft-spoken voice.

'Have a care, even the slightest movement may cause further harm.'

And crouching beside the men, he helped them lift Taliesin.

Dyfnarth stood on the threshold, staring out at a scene of carnage. His command rose above the moans of the dying.

'Let us get out of this Hell hole!'

chapter three

Leaving Taliesin's closest kin at his bedside, Iorwerth crossed the courtyard to the hall. The atmosphere was sombre, and he found Dyfnarth with Urien, drinking in silence. By the time he reached them the king was on his feet, and meeting Iorwerth's eye he fixed him with a gaze that left little room for words.

Even after half a lifetime of tending the sick it had become no easier to see that look of guarded hope and know he must destroy it. His expression remained detached, a mask he had assumed over the years to keep his own feelings from increasing the burden of those who suffered.

'Talieisn's condition is very grave, my lord,' he said. 'I suggest you send for one of the holy brothers.'

He saw Dyfnarth move uneasily, though he said nothing, and it was Urien who spoke.

'Are you telling me that........?'

The question was choked by despair.

'I fear he will not survive another night.'

'No! He stands at the heart of Rheged, of all British kingdoms, wielding a power that cannot be held by the sword alone. He is still a young man, destined to be Pen Beirdd of Ynys Prydein after Talhaearn.'

Iorwerth tried to keep his voice even. 'I know, but he is mortal, like you or I.' He looked towards Dyfnarth. 'It would be unwise to wait too long before summoning someone who can provide spiritual comfort.'

For a moment Urien stood frozen, then he turned abruptly, shouting to one of the attendants. 'Send for the Master Talhaearn......Make haste.'

* * *

Talhaearn pulled the door to behind him and offered a quiet greeting to the three women who sat with Taliesin. There was no anxiety in his eyes, only kindness, and they felt the profound sense of peace that had entered with him.

He went directly to the end of the chamber, where Iorwerth stood beside a table laid out with tinctures and salves, and waited as the physician resealed a vial of Roman glass. Only when he had finished did Talhaearn address him.

'The king sent me an urgent summons. I have no wish to intrude on your province.'

'You do not intrude.' Iorwerth lowered his voice. 'Lord Taliesin is beyond the need of medical care.'

Replacing the vial, he returned to the bed and took Taliesin's wrist. The women sat very still, watching, each alone with her thoughts.

After a few moments Iorwerth spoke softly.

'His pulse is irregular, and growing fainter.'

Nefyn leant forward, covering her face, and Finllian put an arm about her shoulders and held her, concern for her becoming one with her own grief. Feeling a strange sense of unreality, Branwen reached for her father's hand, her vision blurred by tears as she recalled her earliest memories of sitting on his knee, entranced by the magic of his voice and of the tales they shared.

As if from a great distance, she heard Iowerth's words. 'Should you need me, I will be in the adjoining chamber.'

When the physician had left, Talhaearn stood at the bedside, looking down at Taliesin's ashen face. He could still see the wilful youth who had arrived from Gwynedd long ago, possessing a power he had never encountered before, a power that he had often felt exceeded his own - his spiritual heir, the son he had never had in the flesh.

He laid a hand on Taliesin's brow, cold beneath his palm, the other over his heart.

'Taliesin, if you hear me.........I journey to meet you. I ask only that you wait until then, until we have met once more.'

But even as he spoke, Talhaearn's spirit-sense told him that Taliesin was already so weak there was no time to undertake the journey needed to reach him. He could not begin until the fading life-force had been strengthened. His voice fell into a low chant, barely audible. Each breath was an inflowing stream of energy that filled his ageing limbs with the vitality of youth and poured from his hands like water from a spring in sunlight.

His palm still resting over Taliesin's heart, he continued to chant, closing his mind to the grief that surrounded him. The improvement was only slight, but at last the life-force he felt had stabilized.

'Earth to spirit,
spirit to earth,' he intoned the sacred words.

'Our blood is your mead,
Ceridwen, cauldron-keeper.
Breathe, breath of life
to your son, cauldron born.'

Turning away, Talhaearn unrolled a bull's hide decorated with a web of interlaced animal forms and spirals, and wrapped it around himself before lying on the ground close to the bed.

He placed one corner of the hide over his face, shutting out the light, and lay motionless, circulating the sacred breaths. Slower.........slower......in time with his steps.

Ancient yews formed an arch above Taliesin, the berries on their boughs like drops of life blood, their trunks the twin pillars that flanked a dark entrance deep into the belly of the earth. He had waited in this place, beyond time, since he left

404

his mortal body, no longer able to endure the pain. But only now did he feel ready to begin the final journey.

Raising his right hand, he traced the triple sign of the Awen to open the gateway.

'Without fear,
I break the bonds of the physical.
In the realm of spirit,
I have sought,
I have found.'

He stepped across the threshold and entered the tunnel, moving effortlessly downward as he had countless times before. Yet there was a new freedom. The silver cord that bound him to the world was weakening, and soon would be severed. He would continue his work from beyond the great sea, beyond the three rings of power. Those who wished to seek him, who possessed the knowledge, could find him as he had found Arthur Pendragon.

Eventually, he saw brightness ahead, the shimmering reflection of the moon on water. Waves broke, the sound resonating within the tunnel, then lapped over the rocky rim to bathe Taliesin's bare feet in purification.

He stood with the darkness behind him as the moon sank in the west, casting a silvery track across the water. And along that path of light he watched the glass boat move silently towards the shore. At its prow Ceridwen awaited him, hunched and white-cloaked.

The boat glided to stillness at the entrance to the tunnel, and she held out her hands, clasping his.

'My son, stay at my side, where the cauldron is always full, the barley always ripe, the hazels sweet. Where the power of song turns the world on its axis.'

Without resisting, Taliesin allowed her to guide him into

the boat, and once he was aboard she released her hold, staring into his eyes.

'Are you prepared to confront the three barriers? When the first ring is passed, this time there will be no return.'

Taliesin forced himself to think of the world he had left, to accept that he would be parted from Nefyn, leaving her a widow, and that Afaon would grow to manhood not knowing his father. Never again would he sit in council with the king in the great hall of Caer Liwelydd, nor ride at Owain's side across the fells.

For a moment doubt held him back. Then he remembered that his mortal body was broken, a useless cage where his spirit would be trapped, through which it could no longer work. Here he moved with ease, breathing freely, filled with the radiance of inspiration. He would live on beyond the threshold, until the time when his spirit was called to pass through the dark tunnel into another body. In truth there were no barriers, no limits.

Returning Ceridwen's gaze, he gave his reply. 'Lady, I am prepared.'

He saw her smile faintly, as a great weight fell from him. The boat began to move once more, journeying westward along the silver track. Inevitable as the turn of tide and season, it followed its course, drawn towards the timeless isle.

The moon sank lower, swallowed by the ocean, its reflection dissolving into the blackness of eternal night. And at the prow of the boat a small flame now burned, lighting their way.

Taliesin looked onward to the future. His music would fill the feast hall where Arthur sat as host; with him he would hunt the white stag instead of raiding cattle from Manaw. As Arthur himself had said, the battle was not lost. The Great Queen still reigned in the land of Ynys Prydein, a divine strength that would nourish her people if they remained open to the bardic wisdom - generation upon generation.

The waters were smooth as a dark mirror, and Taliesin experienced peace such as he had never known. His mind freed from doubt, he gazed into the night, standing silent at Ceridwen's side. The boat sailed on through tranquillity, until a faint glow divided sea from sky in a ring about the horizon. He watched the line of brightness expand, tracing a decreasing spiral, fluid waves of light radiating upward. Though they approached the first barrier, still he felt only the peace of certainty. But as the boat entered its force-field, he heard a distant call and turned, suddenly restless. Ceridwen, too, raised her head, looking to the east.

From out of the darkness, there came the beat of wings, the rush of air. A shadow hovered above them, curved beak and talons cut in silhouette. Then, swiftly the eagle swooped to alight on the prow, feathers gilded by the spirit-flame, eyes luminous and unmistakable: the eyes of bird, wolf, initiate, master.

Ceridwen laughed, harsh as a raven's cry. 'Are you prepared, Radiant Brow?.......For the hardest test of all.'

Taliesin remained motionless as the boat moved rapidly towards the barrier through which he would pass and never return. In silence, he gazed at Talhaearn Tad Awen standing at the prow, now in human form, wrapped in the hide cloak of a spirit traveller.

The master bowed before Ceridwen. 'Lady, I ask your indulgence.'

She inclined her head, and slowly he stepped forward.

'Taliesin, consider again.' Talhaearn's voice was calm, though the pull of the vortex intensified. 'The hour has not yet come for you to work from beyond the threshold, your task lies in the world of men. You are the king's strength, the Awen that sustains him, my heir.'

Taliesin said nothing. He had travelled too far to return.

He had made his decision.

Unrelenting, Talhaearn spoke again. 'It is not the will of the gods that you leave the flesh before your time.' He glanced at the shrouded figure who watched them. 'Your king, your land, your people summon you to continue your work.'

'In a body that is damaged, robbed of power?'

But even as he replied, Taliesin felt the weight returning - a weight he thought had left him for ever. He could see Nefyn's grieving face, Afaon asleep in her arms. He felt Urien's rage, Bedwen's guilty confusion.

Talhaearn met his eyes. 'You have never been a coward. You will return to pain, yes, but in time you will be healed.'

Certainty gave way to doubt, as Taliesin's resolve began to weaken. Was his decision to leave the flesh the decision of a coward, driven by fear and selfishness? He had not thought so. If Talhaearn was wrong it would be selfish to return, to live out his days as an invalid, a burden Rheged could not afford to bear. Then he thought of his children, his grandchild, the land of Ynys Prydein solid beneath his feet, the changing seasons........

The crack of glass cut through his thoughts as the boat rebounded against the outer barrier. Suddenly the hesitation was gone, replaced by fear. He knew that soon it would be too late to reconsider.

He turned to Ceridwen. 'Forgive me, Lady, I was mistaken.'

She threw back her hood, her face more beautiful than imagination. And, as she smiled, he felt a madness, a passion intoxicating as wine.

Her voice was honey. 'My gifts are beyond all desire.'

Another crack of glass broke the glamour, and Taliesin took a step away from her.

'My place is not here, not yet,' he said.

'Stay or go as you please, you have always been mine.'

Ceridwen was still smiling.

With an effort, he took another step back and faced Talhaearn. Standing straight and steady in the heaving boat, he focused his attention, growing lighter. His arms extended, transformed into mighty wings. His body was cloaked in golden feathers, his talons and beak dagger points, sharp as his vision, and he saw Talhaearn's form begin to shift, ready for flight.

The boat struck again, glass splintering. Taliesin braced himself, then rose into the air, soaring over the ocean. The beat of his wings propelled him towards the dawn, towards the eye of the sun that opened above the horizon.

As the sun climbed higher, brightness saturated sea and sky, burning through him. His flight ceased to be easy and joyous, and many times he longed to dive into the water and find escape in its cool oblivion. But Talhaearn remained with him, always ahead, his presence giving Taliesin the courage not to surrender. Fire and air flowed over his wings, as aeons of ocean passed and faded.

Finally, they began descending towards the shoreline, plummeting downward, the glassy waters rushing to meet them; then gliding, levelling their flight, in sight of the tunnel where waves broke in a meeting of elements. Talhaearn was consumed by its darkness. The tunnel drew nearer, filling Taliesin's vision, then darkness was all around, the entrance receding into the unseen distance behind him.

For a moment he experienced relief. But relief became constriction, walls squeezing the air from his lungs, pinning his wings against his body. The pulsing of the tunnel itself now propelled him onward, no longer in control of his progress. The constriction intensified. There was an instant of numbness, of stillness, then release.

Disorientated, Taliesin reached out to steady himself, aware only that he had resumed human form. Then, feeling the dry bark of yew beneath his hand, he realized that once more he stood between the pillars of the archway.

Again, he had a choice. To go forward, taking the last step, or retreat for ever.

Through a veil of mist he saw a wounded man lying on a bed draped in costly coverings, his face ghastly as the face of a corpse. Taliesin stared in disgust, conscious of the spirit-energy that flowed through him, scarcely able to believe that the man he saw was himself. He could not take that step. He had come so far, but the final step was impossible.

Paralysed by indecision, he looked at the women seated at the bedside, and at the figure who lay on the ground, wrapped in a bull's hide. The figure began to stir, then pushed the hide from his eyes and slowly raised himself until he was seated. As Taliesin watched his master, knowing that Talhaearn had risked his own life for him and the sacred land they served, his choice was made.

He stepped into the mist, which appeared soft and silvery, to find himself thrown against a wall of pain, each breath he took a dagger thrust into his chest. In desperation, he tried to cry out, but could not draw in enough air. He felt utterly alone, frightened as he had never been, when a hand was placed gently on his shoulder.

'It's all right. Lie still, do not try to speak.'

Taliesin recognized the voice as the first he had heard when his spirit crossed the threshold to incarnate in this life, the hand as the first that held him. He half-opened his eyes, seeing only a blur like the mist he had stepped through, and closed them again, longing to retreat back to where he was free.

Another hand was placed under his head, raising it, and a bitter liquid touched his lips.

'Drink this, it will ease the pain and bring sleep.'

Talhaearn got to his feet, the hide still draped across his shoulders. Turning to Finllian, he met her eyes in a look of

410

empathy and silent prayer.

chapter four

Bedwen sat in the shadows of the hall, sick with anxiety, as he tried to overhear Urien's words.

The king drained another meadhorn. 'Damn Fflamddwyn. Damn all foreign scum. A warrior expects wounds in open combat, but to be bound and tortured........'

Iorwerth nodded. 'You should look to your own health, my lord. You need rest.'

'Ha, I'm well enough. And will be yet better when I face the Bernician bastard on the battlefield.' He looked around for another full flagon. 'It has been almost a week and there is scant improvement. You are certain that Taliesin will recover? That he will regain his former strength?'

'Allow me to worry over such matters. You have concerns enough.'

'You do not answer my question. Is it because you cannot?'

Urien found what he was searching for and replenished his meadhorn, staring over the rim with blood-shot eyes.

'It is my opinion that Lord Taliesin will recover. But I cannot assure you that he'll be able to resume the demands of his role as Chief Bard. Not if his lung is permanently damaged.'

'God!' Urien downed the mead and turned away, his raised voice making Bedwen start, the knot in his guts tightening.

When he saw that Iorwerth was leaving the hall, he leapt to his feet and pushed past a group of youths who were gathered by the door, ignoring the curses that followed him. He caught up with the physician in the courtyard, and fell into step.

'Surely it's possible for me to see Lord Taliesin now.'

Iorwerth slowed his pace. 'I'm sorry, but not yet, he is still very ill and not to be troubled.'

Bedwen bit back the first words that came to his lips, determined not to justify the reputation he knew he had gained. Instead, he replied with courtesy.

'I'm concerned. I intend only to offer my good wishes.'

'Then I will convey them on your behalf.'

Iorwerth's icy manner roused first anger, then alarm. No one would tell him the truth about his master's condition. And he was denied the opportunity to see him, the one thing that would put his mind at ease.

'Lord Taliesin is out of danger, is he not?'

'As I said, he's still very ill.' Iorwerth stopped at the gates to the enclosure. 'You must be patient for a few more days. I'm sure you understand.'

'Yes, I understand.' There was a sting in Bedwen's reply. 'I apologize for having troubled you.'

Taliesin opened his eyes, his thoughts dulled by the drugs that Iorwerth administered to deaden the pain. He questioned if it was merely hallucination, the sight of Gwenddydd sitting beside the bed, her figure haloed by lamplight.

She spoke softly. 'I tried not to wake you.'

Taliesin looked back in silence, remembering how they last parted. Why, then, was she here? If he had been given a choice he would have avoided her, not wanting her to find him as he was now - a helpless invalid.

With an effort, he drew in enough breath to speak in a hoarse whisper. 'I never thought to meet again.'

There was a brief pause. 'Nor I.' He noticed the shadow that passed across Gwenddydd's face. 'I have been in Rheged two weeks,' she said. 'At the full of the moon I rode south to visit Myrddin, and when my retinue entered Caer Liwelydd I heard........' Her voice caught in her throat. 'I heard you were dead.' Again, she paused. 'I had not intended to remain this

413

long, it displeases Rhydderch. But I could not go back without seeing you, and waited until your physician would permit you to have visitors.......I hope it is not against your wishes.'

Though Taliesin could scarcely move, somehow he found the strength to hold out a hand to her, and she took it without hesitation.

Neither spoke for a long while, united in a closeness unchanged by what happened before their separation three years earlier, the parting he had believed was final. Simply to have Gwenddydd at his side brought Taliesin comfort, and he realized he had been foolish to imagine he could live contentedly by forcing the thought of her from his mind. The knowledge that she had come to him, twice forgiving his rejection, gave him courage to continue fighting the pain and the lingering terror. Not a fear of death, but a dark pool at the edge of memory, where he knew he would drown if he stepped across the brink.

'Afaon is already walking, the other day he took five steps. Gwilym and Einion were both sixteen months before they walked.' Nefyn smiled. 'Their childhood seems like another life now. It makes me feel old.........And Afaon and Maeglor are growing fond of each other, like brothers.........'

She looked over her shoulder at the sound of footsteps entering the adjoining chamber, and voices debating in undertones. Taliesin followed the direction of her gaze.

'Will you go and ask Bedwen to come in. I'm aware that Iorwerth has been sending him away. He seems to think I cannot cope with seeing my own apprentice.'

'You must avoid all exertion.'

'I intend to speak with him, not engage in single combat.'

Nefyn raised a brow. 'Small difference where Bedwen is concerned.'

She looked at Taliesin, feeling a sense of relief. He was only able to lie still, dependent on others, but there had been a change over the past week. She noticed a vitality that had not been there before, and at last he had begun to converse, to turn his attention outward to the world.

'Very well, have it your way.' She sighed, getting to her feet. 'I'll leave you to talk alone for a while.'

Taliesin watched Nefyn pass Bedwen on the threshold, exchanging a brief word, too softly for him to hear what was said. Then slowly his apprentice approached the bed, his expression tense, as if he was uncertain how he would be received.

Taliesin indicated the seat Nefyn had left. 'Please sit down.'

Bedwen did as he was asked, placing his cloak beside him, though he did not relax. 'I'm glad to see you, Master. Each day I've prayed for your recovery, as all in Caer Liwelydd have been praying.' He glanced towards the door, then turned back to Taliesin. 'I wish to talk, and would have come sooner if Iorwerth had not prevented it.'

'You would not have got much sense from me.' Taliesin's voice was calm. 'I too wish to talk.'

Bedwen hesitated, apprehension etched across his features. 'I've had opportunity enough to consider my actions, what the consequences could have been......Perhaps, in my confusion, I wanted to incur your anger.........Are you still angry?'

Had he been able to, Taliesin would have laughed, instead he gave a wry smile.

'Do I appear angry? Recent events have put life in perspective........for both of us.'

Bedwen nodded quickly. 'Of course. I must have been the last thing on your mind.'

'That was not my meaning.' Taliesin held his gaze. 'You

have great potential, or I'd never have agreed to undertake your training. And, from the start, I felt we could work together because I saw myself in you.'

He paused to get his breath. Though he found it a strain to talk, he had to let Bedwen know that he understood. 'Each of my masters cautioned me against acting rashly,' he said in a low voice. 'Yet I thought I knew better, and at the battle of Gwen Ystrad I risked not only my own life but that of another.......When the bard I led into danger was slain, his death haunted me. Even now I reproach myself, knowing that if I had stopped to consider before encouraging him to accompany me he would still be alive.'

In Bedwen's eyes there was a look of dawning realization.

His voice was faint, but unwavering. 'I am truly sorry for what I did.'

When his apology met with silence, he continued. 'After I learnt that you had been captured, I feared I would never have the chance to say those words.'

Taliesin felt a tightness in his throat. 'Let us not dwell on the past. We must look forward.'

Finally, he saw Bedwen begin to relax, his confidence returning. And when he spoke again, his expression was lighter. 'I have been thinking a great deal about the future, questioning my vocation. When my training is complete, and I accept that it may not be for a while, I would like to concentrate on teaching rather than seek a post in a noble hall.'

Taliesin took a moment before replying. 'You say you've considered your decision at length.......Now I, too, need time to think.'

Bedwen inclined his head. 'I'd value your advice when I next visit.' He reached for his cloak, aware that Taliesin was tiring, and recalling Nefyn's warning. 'If you wish, I could bring my harp. It must grow tedious lying here.'

Even before his apprentice reached the door Taliesin

closed his eyes, exhausted and in pain, but he felt that a great weight had been lifted from his shoulders. He knew he had not failed after all.

The colour of Gwenddydd's gown reminded Taliesin of the summer sky, a sky he had not seen for many weeks. Though he was strong enough to sit up and his wounds were healing, he was still confined to his bed.

Gwenddydd crossed the chamber with a faint chiming of jewels, more than she used to wear. She kissed Taliesin and sat down, not on the chair as usual but beside him.

'Is Myrddin not with you?' he asked.

'He had some important matter to discuss with Ysfael.' Gwenddydd smiled, taking his hand. 'Is my company not enough for you?'

'Your company..........is everything.'

Her smile faded. 'I wish I never had to return to Alclud, there is nothing there for me any more.'

'You need not go back yet. Make some excuse.' Taliesin met her eyes. 'I'd find it intolerable being trapped here day upon day, while life continues beyond these walls, were it not for your visits.'

Gwenddydd frowned. 'Don't speak so, you only make things more difficult for me.......and what of Nefyn? She must wonder why I visit so often.'

'Until now Myrddin has accompanied you.' Taliesin sounded dismissive, masking his uneasiness. 'And today Nefyn is away. She has gone to see Branwen and Llawdoc, and my attendant will say nothing.'

'I hate deception.' Gwenddydd got to her feet. 'I do not wish to talk of it. '

She went to the table and returned with a silver goblet, which she held to Taliesin's lips, then retook her seat beside him.

'I heard Bedwen perform in the hall last night,' she said with forced brightness. 'He may upset some of the royal company, but his talent is beyond compare.'

'Did you know that he comes to play for me? He seems to have matured, no longer a prey to every passing emotion, and he dedicates himself to his work.'

'Because of your encouragement, because you understand him in a way no one else can.' Once more Gwenddydd raised the goblet so Taliesin could drink, and took a sip herself.

'Perhaps.' He sighed. Since he had been bed-ridden, the insecurity of his boyhood, and a self-doubt he thought he had long since conquered, would often trouble him. He spoke in an undertone. 'When I began working with my master Cadfarch, for the first time I knew someone who saw the world as I did, one person who did not think me strange. But no mortal teacher can do more than point the way. Only those who teach from beyond the threshold can offer true wisdom.'

Gwenddydd laid the goblet aside and turned to him. 'Those who guided your spirit back to this world?'

'It was Talhaearn who guided me back.' Taliesin's voice faltered. 'There have been many times when I did not thank him for it.'

At first Gwenddydd said nothing, conscious of the trauma he kept locked within. She longed to help him, to break the isolation, though she knew what she risked.

'Forgive me if I intrude,' she began. 'But if ever you wish to speak of what..........you suffered in Bernicia.......'

Immediately, he looked away, over-shadowed by the horror of the memories.

'Taliesin, I'm sorry,' Gwenddydd whispered, cursing her stupidity. No, it was the enemy that she cursed, the barbarians who had succeeded in breaking a man who had been the strength and inspiration of kings. Moving closer, she held him, her head against his shoulder. And after a moment, he put his arm about her. She looked up, hesitating, restrained by uncertainty, then her lips met his with the same gentleness as she held him.

For a second he did not respond, then his arm tightened about her waist and he returned the kiss with an intensity that answered her own longing. Though in joy there was pain. She had overcome rejection, seen Taliesin fight back from near death. She wanted only to remain with him.

As Taliesin's lips moved to her neck, kissing her softly, neither saw the door open, nor close again in silence.

chapter five

The afternoon was unusually mild, and Taliesin lay on a bench beside Llyn Glas, watching swallows dive for the insects that hovered above its waters. It was almost Alban Elfed, the time when he had intended to visit Owain's fortress in Galloway. Now, he could not say how long it would be before he could make that journey.

Finllian and Bedwen had accompanied the litter which carried him back to his own hall to convalesce, but he was there without Nefyn. More than a week after he left Caer Liwelydd, still she had not joined him. Though he felt hurt, he was not surprised. He had noticed that the loving concern she had shown when he first began to recover had turned to detachment. And he questioned whether his dark moods, his inability to break through the barrier that often closed around him, were the cause of her continued absence.

He made an effort not to dwell on it. Each day he could breathe more easily, and thanked the gods for every breath drawn deep into his lungs, finally, unreservedly, grateful that he had returned from beyond the threshold. The bitterness he had felt towards Talhaearn for not allowing him to die was long past. As a breeze disturbed the glassy surface of the lake, a flock of birds rose from the birches, and he raised his eyes to the sky, sharing their flight, free from thought, from the dragging weakness of the body.

Only the sound of Finllian's voice broke his trance.

'Taliesin, you have a visitor.'

He sat up slowly and glanced over his shoulder, feeling a moment's disappointment to see that it was Myrddin, not Gwenddydd. His hair and beard, which had once been dark, were now grey, and he appeared older than his thirty-seven years, but the strained expression was gone and his movements had lost their agitation. He had also begun to leave his isolated settlement to perform as a bard in his native kingdom of Dyfed and for Urien's son Elffin in Aeron.

Refusing the offer of a seat on the bench, he sat on a fallen trunk opposite Taliesin, his lithe figure framed against the blue-green of the lake behind him.

'You seem much improved,' he said. 'Better each time I see you.'

Taliesin tried not to betray doubt. 'Iorwerth hopes that by Alban Arthan I will be able to resume at least some of my duties as Chief Bard.' He managed to keep his voice steady. 'I know it is many months ahead, but time has changed its meaning for me of late.'

'I found it to be so too.' Briefly, Myrddin's expression clouded, before he shook off the burden of the past, continuing on a new note. 'Gwenddydd still delays her return to Alclud.' His gaze was penetrating, and he gave a wry smile. 'Have a care, Rhydderch may be old but he is no fool, and soon I'll not be here to act as a bridge. I have plans to travel.'

'To Dyfed?' Feeling awkward, Taliesin led the subject away from himself and Gwenddydd.

'A short distance further.' He noticed the elfin gleam in Myrddin's eye. 'No, I intend to journey not only across land, but many miles beyond the sea........I would have left sooner had you not been so ill, and now I cannot delay. I must sail before the autumn storms set in.'

'Surely the seas are infested with Angle and Saeson?' Taliesin frowned. 'You take a great risk in leaving Ynys Prydein.'

'A calculated one. This has long been my ambition and perhaps in a few years the door will be permanently closed, depending on the fortunes of the enemy. I will not shut it in my own face. First, I will cross the Narrow Sea to Llydaw, to enjoy the hospitality of our own people; to converse......' he smiled, 'and contest, with bardic colleagues. Then, when it is again possible to sail, I embark on the long voyage around the Iberian Peninsular into the Middle Sea and thence to the cities of the east. Llew will guide me to the place I seek, a place that has been described to me by learned men of many faiths, and that I have seen in vision.' With glazed eyes, he stared beyond the green pastures and hills of Rheged. 'Across a barren wasteland, by the banks of a river the traveller reaches a city, Harran, where initiates have carried the arcane knowledge of Aegyptus that was ancient even when our ancestors conquered Ynys Prydein. Like every bard, they are versed in the power of symbol and number, once encoded in the architecture of mighty temples.'

Taliesin looked closely at his comrade. Though he appeared rational, he wondered if Myrddin had again lost his reason. To think of undertaking such an expedition was madness. Then he wanted to laugh at himself. He had journeyed beyond the three circles of the threshold; this was but an earthly voyage.

Instead, it was Myrddin who laughed. 'Forget your fears, my mind has never been more balanced. You, of all men, must understand the desire to seek knowledge at whatever cost.'

Taliesin hesitated, recalling the early memories brought into focus by days of enforced idleness. 'I was a boy of nine summers when I first slipped through the veil,' he said. 'All that was familiar dissolved into an alien world of stone-built cities and domed palaces. I heard the names of Alexander and Absalom, Nimrod and Troy, which meant nothing to me then. Though I've journeyed to distant kingdoms many times since, unlike you, I do not have the freedom to travel there in the flesh. I know beyond doubt that my life's work is here, to fight for this land, the sacred tradition. It is Ceridwen's will. And I cannot leave Nefyn and Afaon.'

Myrddin bit back the words 'and Gwenddydd', saying, 'I do this in order to further my work here. With Llew's blessing, I shall not be away from Ynys Prydein for ever.'

'If you're attempting to arouse my envy, you have succeeded.' Taliesin answered lightly, but when he spoke again his tone was thoughtful. 'Perhaps there is a tide of change that affects us both. I've not considered distant travel, but I have begun to question whether it is time for me to seek another patron. I've been Chief Bard for eight years.'

Myrddin nodded. 'Becoming fixed in one place can only stifle inspiration.'

'I tell you this in confidence, but I may go to Din Carreg to take up an offer Owain made in the past. I've reached no decision yet, and it depends upon many things, but my sickness, and the possibility that I would never recover, has made me realize that time and choice are not infinite.'

'Then you do truly understand my motives.' Myrddin grinned. 'Despite the look you threw at me.'

Taliesin glanced to the west, as the sun dipped below the horizon and a chill wind blew across the pastures. 'Let us go inside,' he said, 'and raise a toast to the future.'

He got stiffly to his feet, but shook his head when Myrddin offered his arm. 'Will you stay and dine with us?'

'I'm afraid I cannot, I am expected in Caer Liwelydd and there is much to do before I leave.'

They began making their way between the trees, then crossed the courtyard to the hall.

'I was surprised not to find Nefyn and Afaon here with you.' Myrddin turned as they reached the entrance. 'I assume you know that there is sickness in town?'

Short of breath, Taliesin rested a hand on the doorpost for support. 'What manner of sickness?'

'An outbreak of the flux. It has already claimed several lives. Were he my son, I would not let Afaon remain in Caer

Liwelydd.'

Still breathless and weak, Taliesin hesitated. He could not understand what possessed Nefyn to gamble with their son's health. He also knew that to have her at Llyn Glas meant he would see no more of Gwenddydd.

'I will send a message immediately,' he said. 'Would you carry that message for me?'

'Of course.'

He allowed his comrade to push the door open and assist him, no longer having the strength to walk unaided.

It was three days later that Nefyn arrived with Afaon, accompanied by his nurse and two attendants, one of the men leading a spare horse laden with luggage. Taliesin watched their approach as he sat by the lake, then went to the gates to meet them, relieved to see that his son looked happy and showed no sign of sickness.

Nefyn's greeting was off-hand, Taliesin's expression icily accusing.

'What prevented you from coming sooner?' he asked. 'You put Afaon at risk by your delay.'

'We need to speak in private.'

Nefyn dismissed her attendants, and led the way to their chamber. There they stood facing each other, Nefyn still in her travelling cloak.

'I am not staying,' she said. 'I'm taking Afaon to the safety of Dun Anarawd.'

Taliesin stared at her. 'Why, by the gods? It's half a day's journey away.'

'Gwilym and his wife will make us welcome.'

'And I will not? This is your home, far enough from Caer Liwelydd to be safe.'

'The sickness is not my reason for going.' Nefyn's reply cut like a challenge.

Seeing her distress, Taliesin moderated his response. 'Still you give me no explanation......And I wish you to stay, to be with you and Afaon.'

Nefyn's eyes narrowed. 'Though you'll not be without company, will you? I'm surprised you want me here at all, sending that snake-tongued Myrddin with your message.' She spat out the words. 'But I should expect you to choose a comrade whose capacity for deceit matches your own.'

Taliesin frowned, though he knew what he was about to hear.

'Give me credit for some intelligence, though you have no care for my feelings.' Nefyn continued under her breath, emphasizing each word. 'The saintly Gwenddydd, said to be more devout than any other woman in Ynys Prydein, and tragic, which further sanctifies her in the people's hearts. And you, the immortal Chief Bard of Rheged, returned from the dead........to your lover's arms.' Her voice faltered. 'If they knew the truth! You and she were lovers in Deganwy, weren't you? Many years before you met me. How long ago was this relationship consummated? Rhydderch is old, and you had a fatherly fondness for Rhodri.'

'You are being ridiculous.'

'Better that than a liar.' Finally, Nefyn vented her anger. 'When I think how I wept for you, prayed for you. And you only married me for convenience. The whole thing has been a mockery.'

Shaken by what she said, Taliesin met her gaze. 'That is not true,' he replied. 'I care deeply for you. And I've never lied. I do not deny that Gwenddydd and I were acquainted when we were young, but I swear we've never been lovers. Rhodri was Rhydderch's son.........This summer, she visited me only because I was gravely ill.'

Nefyn lowered her voice, hurt softening the anger. 'I saw

425

you........holding each other........Since then many things have become clear. Even if you had not been ill, you and she would have been drawn back to each other, time and again, as you always have.' She got briskly to her feet. 'I cannot be with you, knowing you long for her. That is why I am going home.'

Taliesin sat with his head bowed. For a moment he thought to plead with her, to promise that he would never see Gwenddydd again. But he found he could not speak those words.

Nefyn remained standing, still and silent, until he raised his eyes.

'What of Afaon?' he asked in an undertone. 'Will you admit me if I ride to Dun Anarawd to see him?'

'You have made your choice. You cannot expect to have everything.' Nefyn took a step back.

Taliesin gave no reply, nor did he go with her from the chamber. It would only upset Afaon if he came to say farewell. He could not imagine never hearing his laughter again, never watching him play, nor seeing him grow to manhood. Though he could not stop her now, he would not let Nefyn separate him from his son. Perhaps, once she had spent some time cloistered in Dun Anarawd she would return. If not, as soon as he was able he would ride north and demand to see Afaon.

The week after Nefyn left, a messenger brought news of Eilonwy's death. She had been ailing for over two years, becoming thinner each time Taliesin returned to his childhood home, and he was filled with sorrow that he had been unable to visit her during the last months. Even now, he was too weak to accompany Dyfnarth on the long journey to Braich y Dinas to see her laid to rest.

As the nights lengthened and the weather started to become unpredictable Myrddin sailed for Llydaw, and

Gwenddydd was finally forced to return to Alclud. In the days that followed, Taliesin found the remoteness of his own hall oppressive. The silence gave him too much time to think, to question his past actions and to crave the company of those he was separated from by death or distance.

On a grey afternoon he rode back to Caer Liwelydd, the first time he had been in the saddle since his capture. He arrived tired and aching, and went directly to his chamber, but could find no peace. The town quarters he had shared with Nefyn were desolate as the hall he had left. He glanced at his harp standing unused in one corner, then filled a goblet with wine and brought the full flagon to the couch at the hearthside.

As he drank, he thought of Afaon. Since his son's birth he had never been parted from him for so long. And he feared for his welfare. Perhaps he had sickened with the flux since Nefyn took him away. Even if he thrived, the boy must be pining for his father, for his home, for Maeglor, unable to understand why he had been dragged from all that was familiar.

Taliesin drained the goblet and poured another. The following day, when he was clearer in thought, he would attempt to use the spirit sight. He had delayed too long, and he had to be certain that all was well at Dun Anarawd. Nefyn had found the surest way of punishing him, but Taliesin's anger was directed at himself, not her. Because nothing could stand against his feelings for Gwenddydd, he had allowed them to destroy the happiness of his family.

He lost count of how many times he refilled the goblet. Only when there was no wine left in the flagon was the edge of his grief blunted, and the pain of his body eased as he slipped into the oblivion of sleep.

When he woke the fire had died down. The chamber was in darkness and bitterly cold. It took him a moment to realize he was back in Caer Liwelydd, then memory returned, bringing with it a chill more bitter than the chill of the advancing

427

autumn. He got unsteadily to his feet, and without troubling to light a lamp or stoke the fire made his way to the bed.

Betraying no sign of the troubled night he had spent, Taliesin stood straight as an attendant smoothed the folds of his robe and pinned a gold dragon brooch at his shoulder. Bedwen waited quietly until the man had finished, then stepped forward and handed Taliesin his staff. They walked side by side across the courtyard, but once they reached the hall Bedwen fell back to let his master enter ahead of him.

As he crossed the threshold Taliesin watched the company rise to their feet. Mead-horns were held high and shouts thundered from the soot-blackened beams to the beaten earth of the floor. Taken off-guard, he felt overwhelmed and confused. The people's joy at his return kindled an emotion that threatened to reignite his grief and a fear that had lain dormant since his captivity. He wanted only to remain numb, safe.

With an effort, he maintained self-control and took his place at the king's side, the faces in the hall before him merging into a blur. The shouts had subsided and silence fell, the company watching him. Waiting. Taliesin blinked to clear his vision, gripping his staff for support, thinking he would be unable to speak. Then, regulating his breath and calling upon the courage of Beli, he addressed the assembly, surprised at the steadiness of his voice.

'You do me honour by the warmth of your welcome.' As he relaxed he began to distinguish individual faces in the crowd, speaking to each one as he spoke to the whole. 'But the honour is mine, to be once again amongst this noble company. I thank you for your messages and your prayers.' He turned towards Urien. 'With all my power I serve my king, none greater in courage and generosity. I serve this land, sacred and bounteous. For the glory of Rheged.'

The hall echoed the battle cry, and meadhorns were raised again as Taliesin sat down and the feasting began. One by one the bards came forward. Only Taliesin himself did not perform. Still short of breath, and with no strength in his right hand, he could neither recite lengthy verse nor play the harp.

Sitting passive and expressionless, he listened to his own words on Bedwen's lips.

> 'Sing a brilliant song
> Of boundless inspiration,
> Concerning the man who is to come
> To destroy the nations.........' [19]

Taliesin fought not to show the frustration he felt. It was harder than he had imagined to see Bedwen standing in his place, while he was unable to give voice to the Awen. Imprisoned, it built like a storm in his mind. But he resolved that by Christmas he would no longer be forced to sit idle. He would push himself to the limit, until he won back the gifts his torturers had stolen.

> 'And his swift devastations,
> And his ruling leadership,
> And his written number,
> And his red purple robes,
> And his assault against the rampart.' [19]

Bedwen's performance was delivered with the skill of a master bard, flawless as his spirit work and control of the elements had been over the past month. And, above all, he had gained control over himself. If he continued to progress, Taliesin knew that he could not reasonably deny him the achievement of the silver branch in the spring.

His song ended, and as shouts of praise filled the hall Bedwen turned to Taliesin. The cheering grew louder, more insistent. It rang in Taliesin's ears as he looked back at Bedwen, again seeing himself in his apprentice. Through him he had relived the mistakes and illuminations of his own training, learning for a second time. But only now, when Bedwen's apprenticeship was almost over, had the tension between them resolved into a deeper level of understanding.

Taliesin cursed as he plucked yet another wrong note. He was about to begin again, then hesitated, and with a sigh put the harp to one side. His fingers were clumsy as a new apprentice's, even after long and tedious hours of practice. The barbarians had done their work well. Massaging the aching muscles of his right arm, he gazed across the chamber at the richly woven rugs, the costly vessels and carved chests bronzed by the fireglow. Meaningless symbols of wealth. More meaningless yet if he had lost the gifts that had earned them.

He turned at the sound of a single knock at the door, hoping that whoever it was had not heard his pitiful attempt at playing. Nor had he any desire for company.

'Yes?'

Impatience made his voice harsh, and the attendant who appeared hovered anxiously on the threshold.

'My lord, I apologize for disturbing you so late, but the matter is urgent. Lady Kywere wishes to see you.'

Taliesin's first thought was of Dyfnarth, who had not yet returned from Gwynedd. 'Do you know what it concerns?'

'I know only that Iorwerth has just attended the infant Maeglor.'

Immediately, Taliesin got to his feet, imploring the gods that his fears were unfounded - fears transferred from his own son, whom he now knew to be safe, to his brother's.

Neither man spoke as they crossed the deserted courtyard, the torches that blazed outside the feast hall sending billows of smoke into the night sky.

In the quarters she shared with Dyfnarth, Taliesin found Kywere leaning over a wooden cradle, another woman at her side. As he entered she turned, a look of relief in her eyes. She whispered a word to her companion, who remained beside the cradle, then walked with Taliesin to the hearth, speaking in an undertone.

'Thank you for coming. With Dyfnarth away, you are my closest kin here.' Kywere's voice was strained. 'Iorwerth says it is the flux that ails Maeglor.......Yesterday there was no sign of anything amiss, and when he fell sick this morning at first I thought it some harmless childhood ailment. But he worsened so quickly, burning with fever and........God, I wish Dyfnarth was here. Why is he not back? Perhaps he too is sick.'

Pale and unsteady, she took a seat at the fireside, and Taliesin poured two goblets of wine. Again, he thought of Afaon, feeling for Kywere in her suffering. And Dyfnarth? When he finally did return it would be to find his son ailing, or worse. His first wife had died in childbed, along with the son she bore. It seemed too cruel a fate should he lose a second child.

Sitting down opposite Kywere, Taliesin spoke with a confidence he did not feel. 'Maeglor has always been strong and healthy. There's a good chance he'll recover, as many have.'

He noticed that Kywere's hand shook as she clasped the stem of her goblet. 'But Iorwerth says he cannot be certain.'

Taliesin took a mouthful of wine, trying to find words of reassurance. 'Maeglor could not be in better hands.........My own life is testimony to that.'

Kywere met his eyes. And through her fear, he saw her look at him in a way that had become familiar since rumour spread that he had survived death itself.

'There is always hope,' he said softly, 'though no one can promise you certainty.'

'I know it's foolish, but I want to hear someone tell me that all will be well. I so want to believe it.'

'Would you like me to stay for a while? We can sit quietly in prayer.'

'I would find that a comfort.' Kywere looked towards Maeglor's cradle. 'But the hour is late.'

'My concern is not timed by sun or moon.' Taliesin gave her an encouraging smile.

chapter six

A flurry of dead leaves and dust followed Taliesin through the door to the feast hall. Inside, under the heavy beams, it was dark even after the dimness of the autumn afternoon. Torches had not yet been lit, but the glow from the fire illuminated the faces of the men gathered around it, Dyfnarth's amongst them. So at last he had returned.

As Taliesin reached the hearth, his foster-brother got to his feet and Taliesin clasped him in greeting.

'I'm glad to see you back.........How is father?'

Dyfnarth shook his head. 'He cares for nothing since mother's death. I could not leave Gwynedd until I'd dealt with matters at the fortress: stores near empty, the bondmen not paying their dues. He asks that you visit him as soon as you are able.......' He stopped abruptly. 'I have been away too long. Why in God's name did I not take Kywere and Maeglor with me, away from the sickness?'

'We all believed the danger was past, you cannot blame yourself.'

'Why in God's name..........' Dyfnarth slumped on a bench, staring at the ground.

Taliesin sat beside him as the other men resumed their drinking.

His voice was calm. 'Though we've seen no improvement yet, tomorrow Maeglor may show signs of recovery. Iorwerth's medicines must be allowed time to take effect.'

When Dyfnarth gave no response, Urien spoke.

'My grandchildren who sickened with this flux are back to health,' he said. 'Take courage.'

* * *

That evening Taliesin watched Dyfnarth down horn after horn of mead, until he could no longer sit upright and fell against Tewdwr's shoulder. The veteran warrior hauled him to his feet, and in the silence that followed dragged him to where he could sleep, though Taliesin knew that the drunken oblivion would be all too short. He had been to see Kywere and Maeglor a few hours earlier, and what little hope he had had was dwindling. The sick boy seemed so small, lying in Kywere's arms whimpering helplessly, unrecognizable as the bright child who used to play with Afaon.

Taliesin left the hall early and went to his chamber, missing Nefyn at his hearth-side and in his bed when he most needed her companionship. It was a long time before sleep came, and then it was shallow and disturbed.

In the half-light before dawn he woke from a dream in which he watched Maeglor wade into the sea, the waves lapping over his head as Kywere called out his name, screaming for him to return. Even when Taliesin was fully awake the keening continued from somewhere in the distance. Then, as he sat up, all became quiet.

He waited for the ache in his ribs to ease before he pushed the fur covers aside, shivering as his bare feet touched the floor. He splashed his eyes with icy water from a basin and dressed hurriedly, throwing his cloak across his shoulders, not troubling with a brooch.

Outside, a dense mist hung over the courtyard. There was no breath of wind, the only sign of life a scavenging hound that wandered through the greyness. Taliesin was close to the hall when the keening began again. He paused and offered a silent prayer, seeing Maeglor taken from the sea into Ceridwen's arms. The mist seemed to thicken about him, the chill seeping into his heart, and scarcely aware of his actions he continued walking. As he reached the door to Dyfnarth's quarters it opened, and he stepped back, trying to focus his thoughts.

It was Iorwerth who stood at the entrance, his expression drawn and weary.

'My lord.' He hesitated, the barrier of detachment breached. 'I am sorry. There was no more I could do........ Maeglor's spirit is at rest.'

Taliesin met the physician's gaze, numbness giving way to the full weight of grief. Maeglor had been but eighteen months old, an infant raised side by side with his own son, like a brother to Afaon, and one day would have been master of Braich y Dinas.

He lowered his eyes, then turned and entered the chamber, closing the door silently behind him. By the yellow lamplight he saw Kywere kneeling beside Maeglor's cradle, supported by her companion. Segnuis sat with Dyfnarth, though Taliesin barely acknowledged the abbot's presence as he went to his foster-brother.

'May God comfort you,' he said softly. 'I share the pain of your loss.'

Dyfnarth did not reply, his eyes dull and remote. Instead, Segnius spoke.

'The child will be welcomed in Heaven. Though we mourn their passing, the dead are blessed, as we who yet live are not.'

Even at such a time, Taliesin heard an edge to the abbot's voice, though he knew he spoke true. He remembered the golden halls of the Otherworld, the intoxicating music, the freedom that he had given up to learn the ultimate lesson of his human frailty.

Slowly, he walked to the cradle where Maeglor lay motionless, his face no longer contorted with suffering. Taliesin felt an aching sorrow, unable to reason why one so young had been taken. Rhodri had at least lived long enough to win glory and a name that would be remembered.

But the gods took, without pity, in defiance of human understanding.

* * *

Throughout the dark days of autumn Taliesin drove himself hard. He lived at Talhaearn's settlement, as if he was an apprentice once more, and under the master's guidance worked to regain the power of breath and voice. When he was sick with exhaustion, or woke in the night crying out, living again the agony of his imprisonment, Talhaearn's counsel brought him the strength to continue. With the Pen Beirdd he journeyed into his own fear, to face what he had been unable to face alone. And at Calan Gaeaf, they performed the rites to honour the ancestors, and in memory of kin and comrades who had crossed beyond the threshold.

On a crisp afternoon he saddled Gleis, the cream-coloured stallion that had been Urien's gift to celebrate his recovery, and rode for Caer Liwelydd, conscious of how much stronger he felt than when he had left. After long months of fighting, he was back to health and ready to undertake the journey north to Dun Anarawd. The thought filled him with hope, a sudden brightness like the winter sun shimmering on the frosty road ahead.

In the hall, the welcome was as bright. A goblet of the finest wine was placed in his hand and he was offered a seat at the king's side.

'You are missed.' Urien's heavy face was flushed, his moustache moist with wine. 'Are you to stay? Is that the reason you're back, or to hear the beauty of my voice?'

'I will return soon, my lord, and then for good.' Taliesin knew that the king's cheery humour would be short-lived when he said what he had come to say. 'But first I must see my son.'

Urien grunted, lowering his brow. 'Travel is bloody treacherous so late in the year. I'll not have you risk your safety.'

Taliesin looked at his patron. He had hoped for

understanding, that after the gravity of his sickness Urien might acknowledge that he was not only Chief Bard but a mortal man, a father separated from his son, who like all men did not know what the next day would bring. But when finally he was able to live again, Urien sought to restrict him. Would the king rather have him an invalid, confined to his bed where he could come to no harm? Or preserved like some holy relic? He bit back the anger, ensuring no trace of it crept into his voice.

'The journey is not long, and I'll be back before Christmas..........to resume my duties.'

'That news at least is wealth to my ears.' But Urien's expression had not lightened, and there was silence between them. Eventually, the king sighed and turned to Taliesin. 'Go then, I see you are resolved. Take your choice of warriors as escort.'

'I'll not put myself in danger. My life is as precious to me as it is to you.'

Gruff laughter replaced the tension. 'Feast with us tonight. Give the company a song........for the glory of Rheged.'

Taliesin inclined his head. 'It will be my pleasure.'

Relieved, he drained the goblet and got to his feet. Though the battle was only half won. Before he could see Afaon, he must gain admittance to Gwilym's fortress. If Nefyn's son refused him entry and drove him away with threats, he would have made the journey in vain. His mind preoccupied, he did not notice Dyfnarth leave his seat in a dark recess of the hall and follow him outside.

'So you travel north?' he called out.

'Tomorrow, if the weather holds fine.' Taliesin slowed his pace to allow his foster-brother to fall into step. 'It was my intention to speak with you and Kywere this forenoon.'

'You fit us into your plans, I am honoured.'

Unsettled by Dyfnarth's tone, Taliesin gave no reply.

'If you're fit to travel, father expects you. Do you forget

your debt to the man who raised you like a blood son?'

Taliesin continued walking. The barb in Dyfnarth's words brought pain even now, though he had no desire to return it. And he struggled to understand the reason for this sudden hostility when all had been well between them for so long.

'I'll not neglect my duty, either to my foster-family or my blood kin,' he replied evenly. 'Dun Anarawd is half a day's ride away, Gwynedd many day's journey. In the spring I will go and see father.'

Dyfnarth sneered. 'Only an ageing man awaits you in Gwynedd. Nothing to the welcome of a woman's bed in Dun Anarawd.'

Again, Taliesin kept silent, refusing to be provoked and drawn into an argument.

But Dyfnarth persisted. 'Or do I flatter you? After cowardice in battle, nothing brings greater shame than a man's wife deserting him.'

Finally, Taliesin met his eye, still speaking evenly. 'Nothing but the tongue of a hag in the mouth of a warrior.'

Dyfnarth stared at him, then cursed, rage and grief etched across his features. Then he turned on his heel and strode towards the stables, his hand clutching the hilt of his sword as if he longed for a physical enemy he could fight in open combat.

The winter was long and bitter, setting in shortly after Taliesin returned from seeing Afaon, and from that time he remained in Caer Liwelydd, confined by alternating snow and flood. But once the tracks were again passable he could no longer avoid his own hall, and the need to ensure that everything was in order at the settlement forced him to overcome his reluctance to return to the home where, for a few short years, he had known happiness.

Though patches of snow still lay on the ground and the

pools were brittle with ice, Taliesin sensed new life awakening in pasture and copse. Yet the journey seemed longer than it used to, the old sense of freedom gone.

As he headed from the metalled road down the unmade track to Llyn Glas, a liquid freshness filled the air, and the trunks of the birches stood in silhouette against the pale sky. He dismounted outside the palisade and looked back across the lake, thinking of the times he and Nefyn had walked along its shores, of when he had sat with Afaon on his knee, watching the changing patterns of the water. Branwen had been but a child when the hall was built, Bedwen a restless youth.

Eventually, he turned and led Gleis towards the gates, calling for an attendant to unbar them. The sound of women singing came from the roundhouse where Finllian worked with her priestesses, but he saw no one as he crossed the courtyard. The hall, too, was empty.

Embers smouldered in the central hearth and an oil lamp stood on the table, illuminating the furniture and tapestries. Seeing them again, he felt he had entered a feverish dream where all that was familiar had grown tarnished. The place that had once been filled with voices and laughter now seemed remote. He stoked the fire until it blazed into life, then waited by the hearth, his thoughts drifting.

The creak of the door made him turn.

'Taliesin, it is good to see you.' Finllian hurried across to him, taking his hands. 'And looking like yourself again, no longer so painfully thin.'

'I've had a winter of feasting in the king's hall to remedy that.' He smiled affectionately, kissing her cheek.

Finllian began walking to the table, where a flagon of wine and silver goblets had been placed. But before she reached it she stopped.

'Why do you stand, and still in your cloak and boots as if you are ready to flee? Are you not staying?'

'I will stay one night, no more.' Taliesin threw his cloak aside and sat down. 'The king requires my presence in Caer Liwelydd.'

Bringing two goblets, Finllian came to the hearth and seated herself beside him. Her expression was searching.

'I am deeply saddened that you and Nefyn are not reconciled,' she said softly. 'I believed that you were content........By the Lady, perhaps the fault is mine, for my early treatment of you.'

Taliesin shook his head. It was many years since he had blamed Finllian for his own failures.

He felt the scrutiny of her gaze.

'Will you not ask her to return?' she said. 'Nefyn is a dear friend of mine, and it distresses me to know she suffers.......as it does to see you suffer.'

'That is not what either of us wants.' Taliesin took a draught of wine. 'And it is a private matter, between us alone.'

Finllian sighed. 'Very well........My concern is only for your happiness.' She held her hands out to the warmth of the fire, considering how to frame her words. 'While you are here, there is something I wish to discuss........The harshness of this past winter has made me think of my future. I am getting no younger, and the priestesses I've trained are grown women, more than able to find their own way in the world.'

She looked up, seeing the apprehension in Taliesin's eyes. 'Last summer Branwen asked if I wished to join her household. Then, I was unsure. I have become fond of Llyn Glas.' She gave a faint smile. 'But now she is with child again, I believe it is the right time, so I can be of support to her.'

After a barely noticeable pause, Taliesin replied. 'This place is no longer what it once was, for either of us........ I shall have to consider what to do with the settlement. I have no plans to live here again.' He saw her look of disappointment - or accusation? Concealing his feelings of guilt and regret, he tried to keep his voice even. 'I pray you understand?'

Finllian laid her goblet aside. Then her expression eased. 'Who knows better than I that the past cannot be undone.'

Urien's sword flashed in the firelight as he checked the edge for sharpness. Then, replacing it in the sheath which lay on the table between him and Taliesin, he met his bard's eyes, steely as the blade.

'Is it *my* life of which we speak?'

'I want no quarrel with you, Taliesin.' Urien's voice was firm. 'But you will take no more risks. Remember your oath.'

'To serve, not to sit at the fireside like a spinster.' Bitterness gnawed at Taliesin's guts. 'Life is already over once a man fears to risk it.'

'You cannot serve if you lie in your grave. And you came too close, too damn close.'

'And when the warband rides into battle? Will I be buried alive in the safety of Caer Liwelydd? Your trophy in its cedar chest?'

'That is another matter.' Urien cleared his throat. 'As Chief Bard your duties lie here until my return from the raid in Manaw.'

Taliesin stiffened, the muscles in his jaw taught, then he rose and went from the hall.

He asked himself if it would truly be another matter when Rheged's warriors advanced against the barbarians. Or would he be expected to remain behind with the old and infirm while still a man in his prime? Denied the right to meet the enemy on the field of battle, to use his power against those who believed they had destroyed him and who sought to destroy his people? Though they had beaten him until his ribs cracked and he choked on his own blood, they had not broken his spirit. He would not give in to Urien and let the king's fear become a second imprisonment.

A single drum-beat sounded, followed by silence. No one moved nor spoke, their wine left untouched. Anticipation built, tense as the pressure before a storm, until the great oak doors swung open.

Then music was heard in the hall. White-robed and raven-haired, a priestess stepped across the threshold, walking to the chimes from the silver branch in her hand. And, barefoot, she trod softly between the rows of the assembled company: the royal clan of Coel, their comrades in arms, the guests from distant kingdoms.

She had not yet reached the centre of the hall, when again the drum sounded, and again the company turned towards the entrance, where Taliesin stood, torches burning to either side of him, his figure bright against the darkness beyond. The tale of his captivity had travelled the four quarters of Ynys Prydein on the lips of bards and merchants, and the company saw a man who seemed not fully of the mortal world – one who had known death, yet still lived. Clad in a robe of many colours, his hair shining silver, he bore a feathered cloak across his outstretched arms.

He measured his steps by the priestess', keeping a distance between them as they drew nearer to the master bards who formed a circle around Bedwen. When the priestess stopped, Taliesin too was still, experiencing only profound peace - all sorrow and conflict laid aside. It was a moment he had not thought to see.

> 'A branch of the apple tree from the Glass Isle
> I bring, like those we know;
> Twigs of white silver are upon it
> Crystal grows with blossoms.' [7]

In the priestess' clear voice Taliesin heard the words that had once been spoken to him, conscious that all who wielded the silver branch were one, from ancient times to the day when the last of the bards would take the sacred oath.

The priestess turned, her slight form passing him as she moved towards the door, and he and Bedwen faced each other within the circle of bards. The chant escalated, resonating through the hall. And as Bedwen lowered himself onto one knee, Taliesin knew beyond doubt that he had earned the silver branch which rested in his hands.

He looked at the bowed head in front of him, feeling pride and the warmth of affection, then draped the feathered cloak across his apprentice's shoulders.

'Bedwen,
enter now the invisible door,
flame in the fire of Bright Knowledge,
bard amongst bards.'

Slowly, Bedwen got to his feet, his eyes meeting Taliesin's. His expression was intense, as it always would be, though the wild-fire was gone, replaced by controlled power. It was hard for Taliesin to imagine a time when Bedwen was no longer his apprentice, walking the perilous journey together. He had been a thorn in his side for so many years that he would miss the pain. Had Bedwen failed, that failure would have been Taliesin's own, but through the darkness and confusion he had always known there was gold to be mined. Now it was found, and he must let go.

Withdrawing his presence, he stepped back to become one of the circle, once more aware of the hall and its assembled company. Through dazed eyes he saw the torches blaze, glinting off brooch and torc, the brilliant hues of gown and tunic, meat on bronze platter, wine in silver cup. And at the centre Bedwen stood alone, his voice raised in song.

chapter seven

The wind blew in chill from the sea as Taliesin and Owain rode, salt air stinging their eyes. Neither slackened their pace until the sweep of Merin Rheged filled the horizon. Then, reining their horses in, they looked west to where the tail of the Wall touched the coast.

'I miss this land of my ancestors.' Owain raised his voice above the rush of the wind. 'It seems a lifetime since we raced like this.'

'A year almost.'

Taliesin replied flatly, though he was glad to be in Owain's company, and uplifted by the exhilaration of the ride, of leaping stream and ditch, Gleis' hooves thudding on the earth.

There was a pause as Owain remembered the last time they rode, after the great victory at Argoed Llwyfain......and his visit to Caer Liwelydd a month later, when Taliesin was grievously wounded. He spoke again, the enthusiasm gone. 'I'm sorry.........that remark was ill considered.'

They continued to gaze out across the estuary, until at last Taliesin broke the silence. 'I no longer have your dagger,' he said. 'Everything of value was taken from me during my captivity, like the stripping of a corpse. No doubt it rests at the belt of some barbarian when it is not being used to slit British throats.......It will never now be Afaon's.'

From the corner of his eye he saw Owain move, but did not turn. More, so much more, would never be Afaon's: his own companionship, his care and teaching. He had given up his wife and son, but was still without Gwenddydd - a fool, and treated like a fool by Urien, commanded as the king commanded his hounds.

'Taliesin.'

445

He wrenched his thoughts back to the present, and looked at the dagger which Owain held out to him, its hilt and scabbard richly inlaid with jewels and of exquisite workmanship.

'A traveller brought it from the east. They say it was made in the days when the Empire was great, as Ynys Prydein will be again. May we live to see that time, a time we have fought for, each in our own way..........Take it, or I shall regard your refusal as an insult.'

Taliesin raised a brow. 'I have won no contest.'

'Then accept it as a reward for songs not yet sung in my hall. The hospitality of Galloway awaits you.'

The golden hilt flashed as rays of light lanced through a break in the cloud. A bright hope. The reward for future songs? Finally, Taliesin reached out and took the dagger, re-sealing the bond of comradeship.

'You are generous, thank you.'

They passed a wine-skin between them, feeling the growing warmth of the sun in the stillness between gusts.

'Tomorrow I and my men hunt boar,' Owain said. 'He is angriest at this season and the chase will be good sport. Will you join us?'

'If I do, there is one who'll be angrier still.'

Owain frowned, then realization dawned and he looked enquiringly at Taliesin. 'Since I arrived at Caer Liwelydd I've noticed tension between you and father. There has never been bad feeling between you before.'

Taliesin turned the dagger over in his hands, admiring the engraved scrolls, the twisting vine leaves and grapes of ruby, the beasts with eyes of sapphire.

'Speak your mind.' He heard sympathy in Owain's voice. 'Father refuses to. He says it is none of my concern. Have you argued?'

'I will not argue with my lord and king, but.........This must go no further.'

'On my oath.'

Taliesin chose his words with care. 'Once Urien was glad for me to ride with his warband, now he'll not have me accompany him even when he raids cattle in Manaw, and he becomes ever more fearful over my safety.' The strain of the past weeks began to tell in his voice. 'He has Talhaearn to work the spirit rites in seclusion from the world. I can best serve this kingdom by wielding my power on the field of battle.......as I always have.'

'Father's age makes him anxious, though it is because he values you as a comrade, and because you are valuable, beyond price, to Rheged.'

Taliesin gave a dry laugh. 'Composing verse from second-hand reports......Inspiring valour by standing before the warband in the feast hall when I am no longer with them as they face the enemy.' He rested a hand on Gleis' neck as the horse began to stamp uneasily. 'Again, I speak in confidence.' For a moment he hesitated. 'Since my separation from Nefyn and the completion of Bedwen's training I've no obligations here, except to Urien, who will not allow me to fulfil them. And I have grown restless. For many reasons, I feel I cannot continue as Chief Bard, that it is time for another man to take the Chair.'

At first Owain said nothing, his dark eyes reflective, then he spoke with boldness. 'The lords of the Britons will fight over you......I expect you to give me first refusal.'

When Taliesin remained guarded, he continued,

'Do you recall the day we rode together the first year you were in Rheged, and drew to a halt where we sit now, overlooking the estuary?'

'It was a long time ago.' Taliesin shrugged. 'Even a bard does not recall everything.'

'I declared that when I was lord over my own kingdom I

447

would have you for my Chief Bard, in my folly believing that when that day came we would have driven the foreigners from our land.'

'And I replied that perhaps it was my destiny.'

'So you do recall.' Owain unstopped the wine skin and took a draught. 'To the future, whatever it may bring.'

He passed the skin to Taliesin, who drank deeply. As he returned the flask, Owain held his gaze. 'Think on it. No bard of mine would be denied the right to ride into battle. I would be honoured to have you at my side.'

'And what of your father? If I go to your hall it will cause a rift between you.'

'That is a risk I'm prepared to take........In the meantime, come as my guest to Galloway. Accompany me when I return.' Owain grinned. 'I will keep you safe.'

Seeing the look Taliesin cast him, he threw back his head and laughed, spilling wine on his cloak. Taliesin found himself laughing with his comrade, carelessly as they had when they were youths. Though the situation was no matter for mirth, he felt a relief that was like relief from pain - that his plans, his burdens, were shared with a man who knew better than any the stifling power of Urien's stubbornness.

The council of elders were gathered about their king as he sat in the great hall of Caer Liwelydd. Though, for once, Taliesin did not take his place amongst them.

Urien looked at him from beneath heavy brows, then motioned him to the seat which stood vacant at his side. Taliesin declined and remained standing, wondering how long that seat would remain empty, and who would be the next to occupy it.

When he addressed the council, his voice resounded in his ears as if it was another who spoke. 'I requested this assembly to inform you of a decision I have reached, after long and careful deliberation.' He looked at the men before him, then turned to Urien. 'My lord, it is my wish to relinquish the Bardic Chair of Rheged.'

Amongst the elders there were murmurs of shocked surprise. Urien had the look of a man who had received a fatal wound, who felt his life-blood seeping away, but did not believe in his own mortality.

'You offer us no reason.' His voice was hollow.

He sat motionless as Taliesin faced him, speaking again.

'I intend to travel, to be of no kingdom and of all, given to God and the people. I serve not only Rheged, but all Ynys Prydein.'

During the silence that followed, he questioned if Urien knew that it was his own refusal to compromise which had brought matters to this end, though at the root of his decision lay causes too complex to state before the elders, nor would he have been willing to discuss them with the king in private council.

'You are your own master. I have no hold on you.' Urien replied as if no loyalty, no comradeship, had ever existed between them. It was Tewdwr who spoke the words that should have been his.

'You have served Rheged well, Lord Taliesin, and Rheged has honoured you. Is it the time to take such a step now, so shortly after a grievous sickness? You have travelled before, and returned to your office.' The veteran warrior looked towards his king for acknowledgement, but received none.

Instead, Urien's third son Riwallon leant forward. 'What other man can do justice to that office as you have?'

Still, Urien sat stiffly, his florid face unusually pale, as Tewdwr spoke again.

'Will you not reconsider? The enemy grows ever more bold, and we need men of power.'

One by one the elders addressed Taliesin, Riwallon speaking last.

'Your resignation will bring much sorrow to the kingdom.'

Once more, Taliesin glanced round the circle, seeing the men incline their heads in agreement, and the look of victory in Segnius' eye.

'My love for Rheged and its people is unchanged,' he said quietly, 'and will remain so, however far or long I may travel.' For a moment, he asked himself if he was simply fleeing. At the age of thirty-six could he truly start anew, find a better way in which he might serve? Even now a shadow waited at his shoulder. When he was no longer trapped here by inactivity and frustration, would he still be trapped by the memories he could never banish?

'The decision has been hard, but I believe it is right.' Finally, he turned back to Urien. 'My lord.'

'As you say, you have decided.' Urien's stony expression had not softened. 'I'll recall the council when I have consulted Talhaearn.'

At noon the following day Taliesin rode out from Caer Liwelydd, driven by a longing for solitude. And to bid farewell to the land he loved - its flesh and bones and spirit - the land which had shared its gifts with him since his initiation. When he found himself heading blindly towards Llyn Glas he veered south, and continued until he came to Llwyfenydd, where heather-covered slopes rose towards hazy peaks.

He returned with the dusk, the hour he had asked Dyfnarth to come to his quarters, knowing he must tell him his plans before he learnt of them from another. Recently, he had been too ready to find insult in all Taliesin did.

From the moment the attendant admitted him, Dyfnarth appeared tense and hostile. But he accepted a seat and the cup

450

of mead that was offered.

Taliesin took a long draught to ease his own tension.

'Is Kywere well?' he asked. 'I've not seen her in the hall of late.'

'Well enough.' Dyfnarth stared at him. 'Did you invite me here to exchange pleasantries?'

Faced with his brother's hard, uncompromising gaze, Taliesin fought to keep his tone civil. 'I wanted to speak to you as foster-kin.'

'You finally condescend to see father?'

'I will travel to Gwynedd, yes, and elsewhere in Ynys Prydein. That is why I wish to talk........When I leave I shall not return to Rheged, except as guest. I have spoken with Urien and the council of elders, informing them of my decision to resign from the office of Chief Bard. Apart from this, you are the first to know.'

Dyfnarth slammed his cup down on the table. 'I do not drink with traitors. Who has offered you greater rewards? Land, is it? Gold?'

Outwardly calm, Taliesin recoiled from the pain of Dyfnarth's accusation. 'I think you know it is neither, but I do not know why you seek a quarrel with me.'

'Because we were raised together. Because I see who and what you are, though Urien is blind to it.'

Dyfnarth's contempt seeped through Taliesin like venom. 'Yet it was you who brought me out from captivity.'

'And this is how you repay your king, the man who ordered your rescue. Now you spit in his face.'

'It is pointless to pursue this.' Taliesin spoke under his breath. 'Your reason is clouded, though you leave your mead untouched.'

'The insults of traitors are blunt spears.' But Dyfnarth's cheeks were livid, his jaws clenched. He got to his feet. 'May the fool who has offered you glory and riches have joy of you.'

451

Taliesin watched him go, filled with regret, unable to comprehend why Dyfnarth had turned against him. Though he had hoped for reconciliation before he left Rheged, there was no more he could do. Whatever the cause of his foster-brother's bitterness, his relinquishing the Bardic Chair only supplied him with a fresh weapon for attack. Nor could he find reconciliation with Urien.

He drained his cup and poured another. The following day he would summon Bedwen and tell him that the hall at Llyn Glas would be given over to his care, to found the bardic college where he could fulfil his ambition to teach. Then, without delay, Taliesin would make arrangements to journey south to Gwynedd and Braich y Dinas. And after? To Ystrad Glud? In Rhydderch's hall, in the fortress on its crag above the Clud, briefly he could be with Gwenddydd, though whether it would bring comfort, or more pain, he could not say.

Part six

Twilight and Darkness

Am I not a candidate for fame, to be heard in song?
In the four-cornered Caer, the Island of the Strong Door,
Where twilight and darkness meet together,
Bright wine is the drink of the assembly. [16]

chapter one

Taliesin and his attendant headed into Galloway by the lowland pass, beneath mountains where snow still lingered. Lone farmsteads built of stone nestled amongst the bracken, and cattle in their winter pastures cropped the thin grass, their shadows lengthening as the sun sank towards the horizon before the day was half done.

The travellers were growing weary when the attendant nodded towards a cluster of buildings set back from the road, sheltered by a barrier of stunted trees. The sound of hoof beats brought the woman of the house to the door - dark and thick-set, with a fretful child clinging to her skirts. She eyed the strangers warily, her gaze coming to rest on Taliesin.

He reined in and dismounted. 'Peace be upon you. We've travelled far and are making for the stronghold of Din Carreg. Are we close to our destination?'

'Peace be upon you......Just keep on the road as it goes. There is......'

She fell silent as a man called out from the byre that adjoined the dwelling.

'Good day. My wife does poor justice to our hospitality by leaving you to stand on the threshold. Will you not rest here a while? I will tend the horses.'

Taking the seat offered on a bench by the hearth, Taliesin unfastened the plain brooch that secured his cloak and stretched his hands out to the warmth. The guests were served broth from a cauldron that boiled over the fire, and left to eat undisturbed as custom dictated, though the children stared, curious and solemn. Taliesin looked back at a boy who sat on the far side of the hearth, recalling the joy of seeing Branwen's three children when he returned through Rheged on his way

457

north. But he had not seen Afaon for over two years, and knew that his son would no longer recognize him.

Finally, wooden bowls were laid aside and, as the woman served ale from an earthenware flagon, their host addressed Taliesin.

'You said you've travelled far. Do you journey from south of the Wall?'

'We spent the winter in Elmet.'

'Ah.' The man paused for a moment, a dozen questions on his lips, but instead he replied heartily, 'King Owain's stronghold is but a short way. You'll be there soon with fine horses like yours.'

Taliesin leant close to the fire and took a draught of ale, his thoughts drifting. Since he resigned the Bardic Chair of Rheged he had moved from kingdom to kingdom, hall to hall, seeking something he could not find. Would it be any different in Galloway, in Owain's stronghold? Would he stay days, or months? He came without plans, without ambition, as he had gone to Elmet from Alclud, from the rare moments spent alone with Gwenddydd. And before Alclud: Powys, Dyfed and Gwynedd, travelling between his foster-home and King Rhun's fortresses of Deganwy and Aberffraw.

Distracted by a sense of being watched, he turned and saw that the boy had crept round to his side of the hearth.

The child stood with his head tilted, then took the finger he had been sucking out of his mouth and spoke. 'I know lots of songs,' he whispered. 'Do you?'

'Oh........I know a few, but I'm sure your songs are better.'

The boy giggled, drawing his mother's attention.

'Come here. Don't trouble our guest.........I'm sorry, he's over bold.'

Taliesin looked up. 'There's no harm in boldness, he's a boy to be proud of. I have a son of the same age.'

The guests sat for a while longer, growing sleepy in the

smoky heat of the house, talking of horses and cattle, and sharing news from Elmet and Rheged. But Taliesin, clad in rough travelling clothes, disclosed nothing about himself. When he had finished his second cup of ale he turned to his host.

'We must be on our way. Time passes quickly by a warm fire and we need to reach Din Carreg before nightfall.' Remembering the boy's words, he continued. 'Allow me to repay your hospitality with the gift of a song.'

The man gazed at him inquiringly, as he had since Taliesin first stepped across the threshold, then nodded. 'That I'll gladly accept, if you have such a gift to offer.'

Taliesin surveyed his audience: eight children from infant to youth, the master and mistress of the house, and a young cattle-hand, fire-light flickering across their attentive faces. The last time he had performed was in the hall of Gwallawg, Lord of Elmet, the next would be before Owain's court at Din Carreg. He questioned which song to give them, then straightened, drawing in his breath. They would have an old song from many years ago, one he had composed to entertain Owain and his companions on the hunt in the days when he was still a prince of Rheged.

Not harp music, but the crackling fire and bubbling cauldron were his accompaniment. Even the children grew still, sitting glassy-eyed as he sang. But when he finished they exchanged glances, speaking in whispers.

His host raised a cup towards Taliesin. 'Such a voice has never been heard in this house before. You did not say you were a bard.' He paused. 'Nor have you told us your name.'

'My name is Taliesin.'

The woman turned sharply, and for a moment their jovial host was silent. When he found his tongue he spoke with a new deference.

'My lord, you travel to Din Carreg to take up a post as royal bard?'

'I go as King Owain's guest, nothing more.' Taliesin refastened his cloak and got to his feet, reluctant to leave the humble company, though honour, and the finest of meats and wine, awaited him. He looked from the man to his wife. 'Thank you for your hospitality. Good health and prosperity attend you.'

'We will always remember this day, my lord. My children will speak of it when they are grown.'

Taliesin preceded the man to the door, catching his son's eye and winning a smile in return. The name of their visitor meant nothing to him, the boy knew only that he had made a friend.

Out on the cold road, Taliesin wrapped his plaid cloak more tightly around his shoulders, though he felt lighter in spirit, touched by the peace he had found at the farmstead and glad that their journey was almost done.

He and his attendant were heading north again, into the biting wind, when he noticed that the road had widened, the settlements become less scattered. And as darkness gathered, a fortified hill came into view, fiery torches on the ramparts illuminating the sky. The road curved eastward, skirting the base of the hill, and the travellers slowed their pace to ford the river that separated them from the track to the fortress.

They reached the far bank wet and mud-spattered, and following the guiding beacons, began a steep ascent. Smoke filled their nostrils, driven on the wind, then drifted away as the wind veered, leaving mountain air that was clear and brittle. Outside the palisade Taliesin drew to a halt, looking out across the darkening landscape before he guided Gleis towards a stone-built gatehouse. Though he could see no one, a voice called out a challenge.

'Who comes?'

'It is Taliesin, bard of Ynys Prydein.'

460

Not of Rheged, nor Powys, but his own master, Ceridwen's vessel, bard of all kingdoms and none.

There were shouts, commands.......finally, the creak of wooden bars being lifted, and the gates opened to reveal a courtyard radiant as the illuminated ramparts. At the centre stood Owain, clad in a scarlet cloak, his warband gathered about him.

He strode forward as Taliesin dismounted, and embraced him like a brother. Then, side by side, they led the way into the hall where the women sat at tables decked for a feast. Taliesin's tiredness slipped away, forgotten in the warmth of the welcome. He was given the seat of honour at Owain's right hand and a goblet of wine was placed before him. Penarwen sat to her husband's left, with the eldest of their six children, now grown to manhood. Though she and Nefyn had been close companions, her greeting was warm as Owain's, untarnished by the bitterness of Taliesin's and Nefyn's parting.

As the feasting began he sensed an overflowing energy and optimism, those things which had grown faint at Urien's stronghold, where a gloom, an ageing despondency had set in. Here, all was bold and bright. Here, the children of the Great Queen had not forgotten that they embodied the glory of their ancestors.

The fortress of Din Carreg lay between two rivers, just north of the confluence and protected on three sides as if by a forked staff. With daylight, Taliesin was moved by the stark beauty of the surrounding land. Shadowed by mountains, which rose to the north-west, the stronghold overlooked a deep valley through which the main river flowed south to Merin Rheged.

While Owain was called to settle a dispute, Taliesin left the fortress alone, riding downstream. The air cleared his head after the previous night's drinking, and he returned calm and

461

refreshed.

He was walking from the stables when Owain rode into the courtyard and dismounted beside him.

'My apologies for being so poor a host, but the crises of the kingdom make no allowance for comradeship. I would that I'd been able to accompany you.'

Taliesin shrugged as they headed towards the hall. 'I know the demands of kingship all too well. You have no need to apologize to me, who lived at a king's side for ten years.'

'I take it you know that father has been ill over the winter?' Owain lowered his voice. 'He is recovering, but there's uncertainty over whether he'll be fit enough to lead the warband in the coming season. Riwallon may have to command in his stead.'

His comrade's words rekindled memories Taliesin had chosen to forget. He, too, spoke in a low voice,

'I did not visit Caer Liwelydd on my journey. I doubt if I'd have been welcome. I received news of the kingdom from my son-in-law and from Bedwen, news that grieved me. With land lost to Fflamddwyn, Rheged has again lost confidence.'

They entered the hall, where bright tapestries and polished weapons decorated wall and pillar. Amongst them was Owain's shield: gold and scarlet, the three ravens of Galloway emblazoned in the centre. For a moment Taliesin's gaze rested on it, then he took a seat opposite his comrade.

'Father cannot accept that he is no longer a young man and lacks the strength to fight as he used to,' Owain said. 'And he still treats Riwallon like a boy with no mind of his own.'

'Riwallon has my sympathy.' Taliesin gave a wry smile.

Owain looked at him closely. 'Ysfael was offered the Bardic Chair, but he refused to take it and a master from Elmet was appointed. Within a year the man resigned and left Rheged, struck down by an unexplained sickness. Since then no other has come forward, nor has father attempted to find a replacement. Your Chair stands empty, and it is said that only one man is worthy of the office.'

Taliesin turned away, avoiding Owain's gaze. Then he asked himself why he should be burdened by guilt? Why take the blame for Rheged's suffering? He had never sworn to be bound to one kingdom for life.

'Then it must remain empty,' he replied under his breath.

Owain continued to face him. 'And will you seek a Chair elsewhere?'

He received no answer.

'You are here as my guest, and welcome to stay as such for however long you wish. But is that your reason for coming to Galloway? You have not spoken of your plans.'

'I have none.'

Owain frowned. 'You were once so certain in all you did. You saw a path and followed it, never hesitating 'til you reached your destination.'

'Now I simply follow the path. Nothing is set in stone, all things change, except those we most want to.........' Taliesin stopped, remembering himself. 'You are asking if I will remain here as one of the royal bards?'

'As Chief Bard. It would be an insult to offer you less. My warriors, my people, are strong. Our glory is on the ascendant, and with your presence on this soil it can only increase.'

They were words Taliesin had heard before, in each kingdom he visited, until he thought he had grown immune to them, but on Owain's lips they carried a new weight. 'I would we had not spoken of this so soon, and you have a Chief Bard. I've already incurred the wrath of too many without contesting with Cian.'

'Should you accept my offer, there would be no obstacles in your way.'

Taliesin felt uneasy, disliking the tone of Owain's voice but unable to believe that he could act dishonourably. Or did he think the gods themselves would resolve the matter without human intervention? Even if it was so, Owain was a fool if he imagined that their will inevitably reflected his own. It would be hard to avoid conflict, and he had no wish to waste his energy debating with Owain, or within himself.

'I've not yet been here a week,' he answered quietly. 'I need time before reaching a decision.'

'Of course, there's no need for haste..........But enough of talking. Will you have a game of gwyddbwll? It's too long since I've challenged a worthy opponent.'

Taliesin inclined his head, and Owain called for an attendant to bring the board of carved oak, and pieces inlaid with gold and silver. The man filled their meadhorns, then set the game in front of them: the king at the centre, guarded by the four lords of the caers; at either end, the warriors in battle-line opposing each other.

Immediately, an eager crowd pressed around them, watching as the game progressed. Penarwen stood at Owain's shoulder, and when his concentration relaxed for a moment Taliesin became aware that her widowed sister Angharad stood at his own shoulder, still and silent.

Keeping his eyes on the game, he allowed them to slip out of focus until the chequered board became the sacred land. In the centre lay Rheged, where Urien sat in council with the four lords of the caers: Rhydderch of Ystrad Glud, Gwallawg of Elmet, Morcant of Manaw Gododdin, and Owain, Lord of Galloway. He felt that he spiralled inward, though when he threw off those who tried to oppose him, he was unsure if they had been forcing him on or holding him back.

He blinked the image away and made his move. Owain now stared at the pieces, frowning. There was a long pause, then he too made a move, though he knew he was defeated.

His face a mask, Taliesin reached across the board, the spirals tattooed on his flesh poised above the squares like the path of his vision.   The king was captured, the game ended.

He felt the tension amongst the onlookers ease, and heard Angharad's laughter as Owain raised his meadhorn, generous in defeat.

'Let us drink to the victor.'

Angharad took a sip of mead, then glanced towards her sister with a look of triumph and a challenge in her voice.

'Will you play again? We wish to see more of your skill.'

'Taliesin?' The light in Owain's eye told that he saw a deeper significance to the contest. He had had to concede defeat on two counts, and, despite his good-humour, he was not a man to surrender easily.

'The day is young, and there are many battles to be fought.'

'Well said.' Owain waved a hand to the attendant, who once again set up the board.

Over the following days Taliesin rode and walked the land, trusting that in time the earth of Galloway would tell him if this was a kingdom where he could live as Chief Bard. And in the hall with its blazing torches, he sat to Owain's right, the guest of honour.

Now his place at the feast table stood empty as he faced the company, giving voice to the boldness and energy he found amongst Owain's people.

'Fierce in the fight,
gentle, generous at home,
the Lord of Din Carreg.
Giver of golden mead
and bright laughter in the hall,
the hall of Din Carreg.

Ravens,
black winged in fury,
terror to the Angles,
the ravens of Din Carreg.......'

He raised his eyes to the shield hanging on the wall behind Owain's seat, and saw the ravens fly from its leather covering, east to Bernicia, driving the enemy from the sacred soil.

When the Awen flowed through him it no longer mattered whether he performed in Urien's hall or Gwallawg's, Owain's or Cynan's. He was bard of Ynys Prydein, and whatever choice he made that would remain unchanged.

'Saeson and Angle scream
on the sword of my tongue:
fire-scoured,
earth-crushed,
drowned in the deep.
Ravens pick their bones,
the poison-seed uprooted.'

The hall rang with shouts and battle cries as he re-took his place between Owain and Angharad. But it was the golden-haired sister of one of Owain's warriors who leant across his shoulder to fill his meadhorn, the skin of her bare arm brushing against his.

Angharad had begun to drink, but stopped and fixed her with a dark gaze until she retreated.

'Your bardcraft works magic here, my lord.' She watched the woman's departing figure as if she had crushed an insect, then met Taliesin's eyes. Her own were hazel, with flecks of flame, like her hair. 'Your words are a weapon more dangerous than my brother-in-law's blade.'

Taliesin looked back at her, though he said nothing, struck

by her fierce beauty.

'Here in Galloway we are far from the barbarians,' she continued. 'I've never seen them nor listened to their speech, though I've heard men say that their language is as ugly as their ways. Perhaps it's because they do not understand the true nature of poetry that they have no bond with their homeland and are driven to steal ours. Life is like a dreamless sleep without the poetic spirit.'

Taliesin inclined his head. 'That is one of the great truths. But many Britons have forgotten it.'

'Surely not in the halls where you've performed. Was it to ensure that the Tradition lives that you travelled so long?'

Taliesin smiled. 'I can tell you the genealogy of kings and the teachings of natural philosophy........but not the answer to that question.'

Angharad returned the smile, and was about to speak again when a hush fell and Cian made his way to the centre of the hall. As he passed them, he cast Taliesin a glance that held the cold gleam of a newly-whetted sword. Aware that Cian distrusted him, Taliesin paid no heed. It was only when he noticed the look in Angharad's eyes that he felt a moment's disquiet.

CHAPTER TWO

Sunlight spilt across the manuscript that lay open on Taliesin's knee - one of the valuable texts that Owain had collected and kept locked in an oak chest. It was not the first time he had read it, nor the second, as he continued to linger at Din Carreg while the season turned to spring, then to summer.

Distracted by the sound of voices, he looked up and saw his comrade enter the hall with a man whose face he recognized from Urien's household.

He rolled the manuscript, and laid it aside as the man spoke.

'I bring news from Caer Liwelydd.' The messenger turned to Owain. 'Rheged's warriors, under the command of Prince Riwallon, engaged the Deirans south of Catreath, suffering heavy losses. As the warband fought to hold our position, Riwallon sustained a head wound.......The king has sent me to summon you, my lord. Your brother is gravely ill.'

Owain looked back in silence, and a chill filled the hall even as the sun shone in the courtyard and flies buzzed beneath the roof timbers. All who overheard had been eager for news, praying it would be word of victory. But still the tide ran against the Britons.

When the messenger went to rest, Taliesin stayed with Owain, though neither had the heart to talk. There were no answers, only questions. And a doubt that permeated everything. For ten years Taliesin had given himself to Urien's kingdom - a land he loved, the land where his children dwelt - yet now he knew of its struggle only through second-hand reports.

Before long he left Owain with Penarwen, and needing to be alone walked from the fortress. He had begun to descend the steep track to the river when he noticed movement beside a stand of trees. Even at a distance, the figures who vanished into the shadow were unmistakable: Cian, black-haired and draped in a green cloak, and the tall spindly form of his apprentice. The Chief Bard and three of the warriors who sat on the council of elders had been absent when Owain summoned them, but in Taliesin's fear for Riwallon, Cian's manoeuvres seemed of little importance.

Oblivious to distance, he walked north until he came to a rocky gully, remote from road or dwelling. He seated himself on a boulder and raised his eyes to where the mountains broke the skyline. Again and again there were reports of defeat. The barbarian incursion had begun in the south-east of Ynys Prydein before his birth, but was stemmed for so long that the Britons grew complacent. While they fought amongst themselves, and bragged of gold and valour, the disease started to spread once more. Elmet suffered, then Powys, but Rheged had always held firm. Now Urien, too, was losing his grip.

A faint breeze stirred the dust at his feet. Above, clouds were massing over the mountains, extinguishing the last of the sunlight. In the tension of the approaching storm Taliesin felt Ceridwen's presence. In the darkened sky he saw the face of his initiator, the goddess he had sworn to serve.

Suddenly, despair gave way to anger, and he spoke aloud, his voice rebounding from the rocks, raging back at him.

'Lady, why do you allow the sacred land to be taken? Why do you allow your people and the Tradition to die? Twice you released me from Annwn, because you told me my work in this world was unfinished. For years I have struggled, sacrificing the happiness I could have had with Gwenddydd to fulfil my oath. I was ready to give anything, suffer anything, if my land and people could be free. Why did you let me live? Nothing I have done has made any difference.'

The fire left him, and he looked down as the echo of his

words returned in mockery. Then, from the mountains and the rocks and the earth, she replied,

'I withdraw from those who cease to seek me, who discredit my wisdom and believe they are wiser than I. And you, Taliesin, filled with self-pity you ask me questions like an apprentice; and blame me for your own failure. Ask yourself, are you worthy of the task you believe to be your divine purpose? Are you strong enough?'

In the past Taliesin would have declared that he was strong and would fight to the end. But all he could think of was the haggard face of the messenger from Rheged, and Owain's grief when he learnt that his brother had been wounded. He remembered the burnt-out villages, the piles of corpses lying unburied because there was no one left alive to bury them, stinking in the summer's heat; remembered his days in captivity, broken and helpless like a beast caught in the hunt - a helplessness that remained with him though his body had long since healed.

He knew how much Owain wanted him to stay in Galloway, to accept the Bardic Chair, yet he could not make that decision. There was something that always held him back. And he realized now that his despair stemmed not only from the suffering of his people, but from an awareness that everything he held sacred might be lost from Ynys Prydein for all time, that the Bright Knowledge, the Tradition, would fade if there was no bardic memory left to preserve it.

Though the afternoon was golden, on the cusp of autumn, and an aura of peace hung over the mountains, Taliesin felt drained, suddenly old.

As he left the hall, the setting sun dazzled him, and it was only when he reached the shadow of the palisade that he saw Angharad heading from the women's bower. Her step was brisk, and she smiled brightly.

'Good day, my lord.'

But when she stood at his side and looked at him, the smile faded. 'Forgive my boldness,' she said, 'but I hope you're not ailing?'

Taliesin sighed. 'Simply preoccupied.'

'Perhaps talking will lighten your burden.......Let us make the most of the lingering summer.'

She began moving towards the gates, and neither spoke until they were beyond the fortress.

Angharad frowned into the glow on the western horizon. 'An elderly brother at Candida Casa once told me that in his childhood he knew families whose kin had been taken by Hibernian raiders from across the water, and the bards recount how the holy Patrick himself was taken. Because he taught the Hibernians to accept the true faith, we are no longer threatened from the west.........He must have had great courage to initiate the conversion of a barbarian enemy.'

Taliesin inclined his head, his expression distant as Angharad continued.

'I cannot see that the Angle and Saeson will ever be converted; sooner slay them than wait for our monks to baptise them.' Her tone altered. 'I hear that Urien has suffered yet another defeat. No doubt grief over Riwallon's condition weakens Rheged's morale........And that they have no Chief Bard.'

Taliesin watched the last sliver of sunlight dip behind the mountains. There was always a sense of loss at that time of ending, though dawn followed darkness, winter was but one season, and death brought eventual rebirth. But if Ynys Prydein was conquered, each kingdom in succession falling to the foreigners........

'Lord Taliesin? I fear that you are ailing.'

He hesitated, knowing he could not tell Angharad the

471

truth, of the hopelessness that dragged at him like a drowning man's clothes. Only after a moment did he reply. 'I was thinking of the cycles of life.......Sorry, you spoke of Urien......'

Angharad, too, paused, disconcerted. 'Do you plan to return to his hall? Or will you remain here with us? Both Owain and Penarwen wish it.'

'Perhaps Penarwen has sent you to walk with me?' Taliesin looked at her quizzically. 'Because she believes that you alone can obtain an answer.'

'I ask because I hope you will accept Owain's offer and that I shall have more of your company.' Though they were alone, Angharad lowered her voice and glanced back towards the gates. 'I am also concerned for you.......Cian is a dangerous enemy, and I've watched him of late, noticed how he and his comrades are often from the hall. Perhaps his fear of your power, of what happened to the bard who took the Chair of Rheged after you, will restrain him, and perhaps you think I'm a prey to foolish anxiety, but I could not leave this unsaid.'

Taliesin looked down into the river valley, already in shadow as the land lay poised between night and day, then met Angharad's gaze.

His tone was gentle. 'Do not be concerned; whatever Cian may attempt, I am prepared.'

'He will not rest 'til he has driven you from Din Carreg. You must know that.'

'Then he will grow weary. No man dictates whether I leave or stay, I obey only the will of the........of God.'

Angharad stood close, looking up with a tenderness that cut through him. And when she turned away without speaking, he felt relief, because he could not have answered the question he had seen in her eyes.

Red and purple berries, and mushrooms gathered in the

woodlands, were served from silver platters set out on the tables of the feast hall. Outside it was frosty, but the blazing hearth-fire kept the cold and the night at bay.

Dazed by mead, the company followed Taliesin's voice beyond the boundary of time and place. Each verse drew them deeper, until the final note shuddered through the quiet hall. For a moment the enchantment held, then broke in a wave of shouts and cheering as the assembly rose to their feet.

Taliesin turned to retake his seat, but stopped when he saw Cian step forward. The Chief Bard's jaw was set, his eye hard and sharp as a spear-point. By contrast, his speech was flawlessly courteous.

'Master Taliesin, I commend you on your song.'

'And I you, on the inspiration of your earlier tale.'

As the two men faced each other the cheering subsided, and one by one the company fell silent. Cian waited until all sound had ceased.

'When the bull's horns are blunted, the bold flight of ravens draws the silver fronted salmon from Llew's stronghold to contend for the Chair that is well defended.'

Taliesin responded effortlessly. 'My Chair is in Caer Siddi, where age and sickness are unknown. Three rings of flame around it. Three mighty fountains flow before it, their mead the stream of song. There is but one defence of the pre-eminent Chair.'

A flicker of doubt broke through Cian's composure, but was quickly masked. 'The hazels are my gift. Beyond the seven caers, my achievement - to taste of the cauldron, pearl white berries at its rim.'

'Soft the breath of the nine maidens, crimson the fruit, bright the dew, and ocean's foam. Does the hound take three drops that kindle fire in the head, or drink the deep draught of poison after the three drops are won?'

'Three drops of art, three doors of truth, three pillars of

light.' Cian drew himself up to his full height, his voice resonating in the stillness. 'The hound is the stout guardian at the portal before the rock.........'

He surveyed the company in the hall, who only half understood as they sat motionless, tension mounting.

'.........Annwn is dark. Stones are sharp. The salmon swims to spawn venom when the three sacred drops are spilt.'

Unconcealed ferocity drove Cian's words, but Taliesin countered them in the melodious voice of bardic recital. 'The salmon swims to spawn a stream of Bright Knowledge, from the Well of Wisdom and the Silver Wheel, from the ramparts of Caer Gwydion and Llys Don, from the horns of the Starry Ox and the shining White Throne. From root to crown.' Still, he addressed Cian in the same melodic tone. 'Gwair is freed, the eagle soars, the salmon dives. When the hound guards the Chair of the rock a heavy chain binds, with bitterness on the tongue.'

He saw the dangerous expression on the Chief Bard's face, and waited for a response. But Cian said nothing. He remained where he stood, staring in silent confrontation.

No one moved until Owain spoke.

'Let the mead jar be passed round.' There was an exaggerated boldness in his voice. 'No cup shall be empty in the hall of Din Carreg.'

(See note on page 544)

It was the day of All Hallows, the feast when prayers were offered for the dead. For weeks there had been rain, and the waters of the swollen river rushed below the bank where Taliesin walked, thinking of Riwallon. Since he was wounded, struck by an axe blow to the skull, he had declined slowly, dependent as an infant and unable to recognize his loved ones, until the end came as a mercy. Taliesin grieved deeply for him, a man who had remained a loyal comrade. He had not turned against him before he left Rheged, accusing him of betrayal, nor shared Urien's cold unspoken anger. But the past was done, the future an empty vessel. There was only the present.

Taliesin stopped, and spread his cloak on the ground where a thicket offered some shelter, then lay on his back and gazed up through a tangle of branches, listening to the last dry leaves rattling in the wind. He had never felt more glad of solitude, to be where there was no human conflict, away from Cian's jealousy and from the weight of the praise that was heaped upon him - praise he found increasingly hard to accept. The Angles were advancing in the north, the Saeson in the south. What was there to praise in his gifts, or his achievements? He had failed as mediator with the gods, failed to inspire the warriors to win victory. He had become nothing but an empty performer.

The branches above him swayed. He felt as if he was falling, sinking through the earth, all that was visible dissolving into mist. But when the mist cleared he found that he was behind his own hall, on the shores of Llyn Glas. The birch trees were recovering, new saplings sprouting on ground that had been charred by the fire. He could hear their leaves rustle as he sat on a log bench, looking down at the upturned face of the youth who knelt at his feet. As the face became more distinct, he realized that he was looking at himself.

'Master, will you not speak to me? Tell me the truth.'

Taliesin met eager eyes, wondering how different things would have been had he known then what he knew now. He spoke slowly, 'If you sow, you labour; yet, though you labour, still you do not reap.'

His youthful self looked puzzled, his expression resolute. 'I shall reap the harvest of the river: the salmon of wisdom. And the barley, the grain in the sacred cup that makes the vision flow. I shall work until I reap, until I am bard to the greatest of lords, until Angle and Saeson are drowned in the eastern sea. And my name will be known to generations beyond imagining.'

Taliesin smiled, thinking that perhaps it was the youth who was teaching him. 'Yes. Though a late summer brings a late harvest, it is not necessarily a meagre one. There are many lives to reap what we sow in this, and have sown in the past.'

He gazed over the youth's shoulder, at the cattle on the far shore of the lake, and when he turned back to his apprentice he saw that he had been mistaken. It was not his youthful self that he was speaking to, but a dark-haired, oval-faced boy with solemn brown eyes.

'The truth is that we sow the answers and reap the questions.'

'Master?'

'Wherefore should a stone be hard;
Why should a thorn be sharp-pointed;.......
Who is salt like brine;
Who sweet like honey;
Who rides on the gale....' [20]

The boy frowned, but in his eyes there was a dawning realization.

'My lord, here........'

An urgent voice cut the frosty air, and Owain ran towards it.

'My God!' He crouched down and held a blazing torch over Taliesin's motionless figure. As he lay on the ground, there was a strange look of peace on his features, like the peace of death.

The spearman who had found him crouched at Owain's side.

'He breathes. Shall I try and rouse him?'

Owain pushed the man's arm away as he reached out. 'Don't touch him. Lest it cause shock.'

But he removed his own scarlet cloak and carefully placed it over Taliesin, then leant closer, the torchlight flickering on Taliesin's closed lids.

As the men who had accompanied their king gathered round, Owain fought not to give in to the suspicion that had crossed his mind many times while they scoured the river banks in the darkness, not knowing what they might find. Yet still it plagued him, together with the knowledge that his own behaviour had enflamed Cian's anger. He had treated him with disrespect. His affection for Taliesin and the ambition to have him as Chief Bard, and so make Galloway the envy of larger and more powerful kingdoms, had made him act like a fool.

After a wait that seemed as long as the search that had preceded it, Taliesin opened his eyes, recoiling from the light.

Owain's tension eased. 'Taliesin, do you hear me? Are you able to speak?'

He frowned, then replied in a whisper. 'It is night.'

'You've been away from Din Carreg since noon. We began searching when you did not return to the hall to dine. A man can perish out here within hours once the sun sets......... Are you sick........injured?'

Owain extended a hand to help him sit up and was startled by the warmth of Taliesin's skin, as if he had been lying by a hearth-fire. Again, alarm flared.

'You have a fever. You must see my physician without delay.'

But Taliesin got easily to his feet, and returned Owain's cloak with a nod of thanks. Then he stooped to retrieve his own, slinging it over his shoulders though it was soaked with damp from the riverbank. Owain's companions looked on, confounded, half-believing that he had risen from the dead.

477

Nor, they thought, would it be the first time.

He turned to Owain, who watched him with concern.

'I've come to no harm. Allay your fear.'

They began to walk ahead of the others.

'I refuse to dismiss this so lightly. By morning I would have found a corpse. You must tell me what happened.' Owain spoke under his breath. 'Was Cian responsible for your collapse?'

'I was in trance........of my own accord. Cian is in no way to blame.'

Owain shook his head. 'Tonight you alarmed me as you did when we were youths, when you swam under water for a time that would have drowned any other man. I see now that it's something I must accept, though I'm damned if I'll ever understand.'

chapter three

Harp music filled the hall, though there was only one man in Taliesin's audience - a young warrior who had been wounded that summer and was unable to join his comrades on the hunt.

Taliesin had just begun a new refrain, when a draft fanned the hearth-fire and Cian crossed the threshold, accompanied by the tall spare figure of his apprentice. Taliesin kept his eyes lowered, his fingers continuing to ripple across the harp strings. But he could not ignore the footsteps which came to a halt a few paces away, and eventually he looked up, still playing.

Cian's voice jarred against the music. 'You show discourtesy towards your host's Chief Bard.'

'My apologies.'

The deference of the soft spoken reply made Cian bristle. 'Six months have passed since you arrived at Din Carreg, exploiting the king's hospitality........unless you see yourself as other than guest.'

'I can be generous with my knowledge.' Taliesin maintained his tone of deference, letting the harp fall silent. 'Do you recommend that I repay the king's hospitality by seeking an apprentice - to increase the learning in this hall?'

The younger bard gave a snort, and edged nearer to his master as if to defend him from physical attack.

Cian's lips were pinched. 'Generous, as the hunter is. Teaching the stag the thrill of the chase before driving a spear into its heart.'

'Knowledge does not come without pain.'

There was a brief pause. 'The Chair of Rheged stands empty, poisoned by its last occupant, bringing ruin on Urien's kingdom. My advice is that you consider your position, your health, your future.'

'No doubt they will flourish, along with your own.' Taliesin turned away, plucking a single note, then taking up the music where he had left off.

He did not see the bard's expression, or the contemptuous glance his apprentice cast him before following Cian across the hall. All he saw was the fear on the face of the young warrior - a fear that he sensed was not only for, but of, himself.

As he left the stables Taliesin was in a dark mood, though it lightened a little when he saw Angharad walking towards him, muffled in a russet cloak the colour of her hair.

They fell into step and entered the hall together in quiet companionship, finding a seat away from the dice players and youths who clustered round the hearth.

'It's impossible to find peace when we're all heaped upon each other like fish in a net.' Angharad unpinned the brooch that fastened her cloak, then looked at Taliesin. 'No doubt you agree, if you've been riding in this weather.'

Taliesin spoke under his breath. 'I've not been riding. Gleis is sick. The groom summoned me not an hour ago, concerned by the sudden severity of the symptoms and afraid I'd put the blame on him.......In Rheged I have a stable of pure-bred horses, yet none could replace Gleis, the companion of my travels.'

'I know.' Angharad smiled in sympathy. 'I would be upset if........' She stopped abruptly. 'Do you think the sickness may be due to........not of natural cause?'

She received no reply, only a look of dismissal.

'Taliesin, have a care. This time it is Gleis, but.......'

'I should not have mentioned it.'

'Do not treat me like a child.' Angharad sighed. 'I've witnessed enough of life......and death. And I see the hostility in this hall, though Owain turns his back and does nothing to

480

resolve it.'

'Then perhaps I should........I cannot remain here for ever.'

'Your leaving would appear as if you were giving in to.......him.' Angharad paused, and when she spoke again there was frustration in her voice. 'You know that is not the reason why I wish you to stay.'

The shouts and laughter from the youths at the hearthside continued as Taliesin and Angharad lapsed into silence. He tried to find an answer, to understand what he truly felt. But though he admired her, desired her, he could not respond as she wanted him to.

'Your thoughts are always concealed,' she said eventually. 'Your feelings too........Is it because of Nefyn that you keep your distance from me?' The name was spoken like a challenge, a cipher broken. 'Is it because you love her still?'

Taliesin was startled by her directness, and threw her a questioning glance.

'Penarwen told me that you have a wife and son.'

'Nefyn and I have been estranged for many years, with no likelihood of reconciliation,' he replied quietly.

Angharad looked at him. 'Then there is another.'

At first Taliesin thought of denying it, but she was too shrewd, and the truth would be easiest and kindest. His voice remained low.

'Yes, there is another.'

He expected anger, for her to accuse him of having encouraged her affection. Instead, she rested her hand over his, and waited until he faced her.

'Did you really think I would be vain enough to be insulted?' she said. 'Bitter at losing what I never had? That would be a pitiful waste of energy.' Her grip on his hand tightened. 'I've known many who dreamt of love tomorrow, but who were taken by fever or slain in battle before tomorrow came........I only pray you are not throwing your life away on

481

dreams.'

Rain lashed across the courtyard, driven in sheets against the stable where Taliesin stood, twisting a bundle of straws between his fingers in agitation. Gleis had not taken any food for two days, and could no longer stand but lay with sides heaving and eyes wild, a froth around his mouth. The grooms swore they had never seen such a sickness, and neither their remedies nor Taliesin's own had brought a cure.

He took a final look at Gleis, then unlatched the door. As he opened it he saw Cian hastening past, alone, without his stick-thin shadow. The bard looked over his shoulder, then stopped.

His expression was detached, though his words flowed like syrup. 'I hear your horse is ailing. It would be most unfortunate to lose a good beast, and one so young.'

In his mind Taliesin saw Gleis' agony, remembering how he had raced him along the riverbank only a week before, when he had been strong and in fine health.

'I have confidence that he'll recover,' he said, 'as the sickness returns to its source.'

There was no change in the mask that was Cian's face. Taliesin was about to let the straws he held fall to the ground, and leave the stable, when he hesitated. Despite the Chief Bard's learning, he had noticed how Cian was a prey to the darkest and most primitive fears.

Suddenly, Taliesin raised his hand, flinging the straws towards him. Only then did the mask crack. And Taliesin glimpsed a look of horror, before Cian drew his cloak tightly about his shoulders and walked away through the downpour.

As the rains continued, few ventured from Din Carreg, where

mead and song brightened the short days. But Cian was absent from the company, struck down by stomach cramps that made him vomit whatever he tried to eat. There were whispers in the stables as the grooms watched the improvement in Gleis' condition, and murmurs amongst the warriors of a 'druid's wisp', while those who had looked askance at Taliesin before, now avoided him. Owain never broached the subject. Only Angharad dared, though she learnt nothing.

A week before Christmas Taliesin sat with his comrade in a hall decked with evergreens, torchlight flickering across the boughs.

'Tomorrow we expect a clutch of brethren from the foundation, as always at this season. To make certain we remember the holy nature of the festival.' There was a glint in Owain's eye. 'Though we give them more mead and pork in a week than the abbot allows in a year.'

'I'm sure their only concern is for your souls.' Taliesin smiled. 'Even in Gwynedd people speak of the library at Candida Casa, the greatest in all Ynys Prydein it is said. I look forward to discussing its treasures with your guests.'

'Unrepentant Pagan though you are, according to old Segnius.'

Again, a faint smile touched Taliesin's lips. 'I make no distinctions. Wisdom is wisdom by whatever name.'

Owain nodded. 'No doubt......The man who is favoured to be the next abbot may be amongst the visitors. Last year he proved excellent company - no tight-faced hypocrite, but a man of character, who has a reputation for performing miraculous cures. He'll be glad to discuss the library, and have you as guest if you wish to see it for yourself.'

Overnight the skies cleared, and around mid-afternoon, as the sun sank behind the western mountains, four men in grey cloaks forded the river and rode up the track to Din Carreg. Taliesin was not amongst the party that greeted them in the chill courtyard before they were escorted to their quarters to rest. Only that evening, when the company gathered for the welcome feast, did he see them for the first time. They were all young, apart from one, and as the little group made their way into the hall Owain glanced towards him, addressing Taliesin.

'This is the man I spoke of.'

But Taliesin's attention had already been drawn to the senior brother, whose appearance brought a strange disquiet, like a half-remembered dream. The monk was small in stature and gaunt from years of fasting, his greying brown hair tonsured from ear to ear like his fellow brothers'. Nothing to set him apart. Then, as he passed Taliesin, he turned.

The movement of his head, his smile, were unmistakable, his greeting filled with warmth.

'May God be praised!'

Taliesin returned the smile, and with his spirit-vision saw the radiance that surrounded his old comrade. 'Rhys, this is a great joy.'

Owain looked from one to the other, then laughed. 'Clearly, you need no introduction.'

'We knew each other as boys, my lord.' Rhys replied. 'A long distance away and a long time ago.'

'Then I am glad you are reunited in my hall, in this season of goodwill.'

The next morning, after Rhys had finished leading the prayers in Owain's chapel, he and Taliesin broke their fast together. When they talked it was as if the years had been wiped away, as if it was only yesterday that they sat side by side on a pallet bed in the apprentices' hall at Deganwy. The sensitivity of the boy Taliesin had known still lay behind the quiet strength of the man who now faced him, speaking in a gentle voice.

'I've followed your progress, listening whenever pilgrims brought news from Rheged, and before that from Powys. When I learnt you were in Galloway, I looked forward to making the journey to Din Carreg.'

Hearing Rhys' words, Taliesin asked himself if it was for this that he had lingered so long at Owain's stronghold, guided by the will of the gods. 'I knew nothing of your whereabouts,' he said, 'but I thought of you often, and wondered if you'd taken holy orders as you wished.'

'The decision to give up bardic training was one of the hardest I've had to make.' Rhys met his eyes. 'Your friendship gave me courage, helping me not to surrender to weakness, and so find my true path. I've never forgotten that.'

Taliesin replied softly. 'If I had some small part to play, it gladdens me........Owain says you are favoured as successor to the abbacy of Candida Casa.'

'He speaks true, though high office was never my ambition.' Rhys paused. 'At one time I would have refused, but I now realize the unique opportunity it offers to do the Lord's work, and will accept the honour should it be offered. It is the wish of Brother Cadoc, the present abbot, who is past his seventieth year and growing frail.........But I dislike speaking of myself. It surprised me to learn that you'd resigned the Chair of Rheged. Do you plan to remain as King Owain's Chief Bard if Cian's health fails to improve?'

Taliesin took a draught of mead, hoping that Rhys would not come to hear the rumours about the cause of Cian's sickness. And once again he was being questioned. The question no one would let rest.

His tone was reflective. 'I always believed that I knew my vocation, but after I was held prisoner every certainty has been undermined.' He no longer attempted to conceal the despair. 'I left Rheged because there was nothing more I could achieve as Chief Bard to Urien. I thought I would find resolution through travel, that I would be shown how I could best serve our people. Yet that has not happened.'

Rhys inclined his head. 'I am no stranger to such dilemmas, as you're aware. Where we differ, perhaps, is in priorities. I serve God above all else. Though I love this land, there is a greater kingdom than Galloway or Rheged, or all Ynys Prydein, where even the weak and defeated are free.'

For a moment Taliesin was silent, remembering. To Rhys the realm that lay beyond the threshold was the Kingdom of God, where the soul remained eternally after death. Those of the Old Faith saw it as a place of rest before rebirth in another form. In many ways their beliefs were as one, yet.........

He raised his eyes. 'The land that supports us is sacred, and earthly life precious, though transient. While we have breath in our bodies, should we not strive? For future generations, to uphold the Tradition, to bring some of..........Heaven, through to this mortal world.'

'You do not sound like a man who has lost his conviction.' Rhys looked at him searchingly. 'Yet fear and doubt stand between us and the wisdom of God......' he smiled, '.......the gods, and spirits of the land. When we fight an inner battle, we allow the mind to place obstacles in the way of what the spirit knows.'

As Taliesin listened, it seemed that Cadfarch and Tegai and Talhaearn spoke with the voice of the future Abbot of Candida Casa. But the power was not in what Rhys said but in himself, in the strength and the selflessness, and the courage of one who had conquered his own darkness. In his company, Taliesin felt a hope that he had not thought to feel again.

And after the monks' departure, as the days dragged by amidst hail and snow, he found a new sense of purpose. The question was finally answered - he would remain at Din Carreg. Not to usurp Cian's Chair, but as a bard amongst others, unless a time came when the Chief Bard stepped down of his own free will.

Winter still held the land in its grip, though the warriors had resumed training. Their shouts rang in Taliesin's ears as he forced himself to concentrate on the composition he had begun. But it was not outer distraction that made him put his harp aside and reach for his cloak. Plagued by an uneasiness he could not explain, he left the guest quarters, making his way across the courtyard where the men practised.

He descended the track from the fortress on foot, walking steadily, his breath turning to vapour in the icy air. Even in the peace of the valley, restlessness drove him on, and he increased his pace, heading upstream. Finally realizing he could find no escape, he sat on the riverbank, stilling his mind as he watched the fast-flowing water.

As his consciousness began to shift he lay back, the river's race becoming the sound of the sea echoing in a rocky chasm beyond an archway of yews. Under the arch he saw Talhaearn, his gaunt figure straight, his eyes shining with a silvery brightness. With him were Bedwen and Ysfael, Talhaearn's master, Menw, and men who had been his apprentices since before Taliesin's birth, many old themselves, or long since departed from the mortal world.

Taliesin remained where he stood, angry at himself, and unwilling to acknowledge what he now knew. He waited until Talhaearn addressed him, the familiar voice rich and melodious.

'My work in Abred is complete in this life, yours scarcely begun. You are my heir, Taliesin. That is why I defied the natural laws to guide you back when you began the final journey too soon.'

As he struggled to accept the truth, Taliesin's speech faltered. 'I would have come to be with you in body, had I known you were ailing........But I was closed, blinded by my own worldly cares.'

The reply was gentle. 'I am not ailing, just old, and my heart grows weak. Your presence here in spirit is enough....... It is unnecessary for *me* to remind you what you must do for your people: Pen Beirdd of Ynys Prydein.'

The meaning of the words scarcely registered. At that moment Taliesin thought of himself only as Talhaearn's apprentice.

'Master, I wish to journey with you now,' he said, 'to be your companion on this last voyage as you would have been for me.'

Talhaearn smiled faintly, giving his assent, and Taliesin took a step forward to stand beside him under the arch. Memories flooded over him, of the greatest freedom and beauty. Of all he had sacrificed to follow Talhaearn back to the world of men. Though this time he would return alone.

Owain lowered his black brows, reminding Taliesin of Urien.

'You asked to speak in private.'

Taliesin replied evenly. 'I wish to tell you of my plans.'

The frown deepened, though Owain remained silent.

'A year ago you did me the honour of offering me the Bardic Chair of Galloway, and I have delayed giving you an answer for too long......You've shown more patience than I deserve.'

Owain sighed. 'To have you as guest has required no patience. But it does not take a prophet to know what your answer is to be now - you will to return to Rheged.'

'I must. The death of the Master Talhaearn has brought me to a decision. And Rheged under Urien is the centre that will unite the north against the foreigners........Soon, this year or next, the Britons will be given an opportunity we've not had for over a generation.'

'You have seen this? In vision?' Owain shook his head. 'Your gifts are rare indeed, invaluable to any lord, any kingdom. Though it was because of our comradeship, as much as for your gifts, that I prayed you'd accept my offer. For that I was willing to risk father's wrath, and Cian's. But in some part of my mind I always knew you would leave, that a power greater than mortal ambition ensured that the Bardic Chair of Rheged remained vacant, awaiting your return.'

Taliesin glanced at the raven banner of Galloway, the banner he had once thought he would follow into battle, riding at his comrade's side. 'Cian, at least, will be glad to see me go,' he said.

'But only he.' Again there was silence, then Owain reached for his mead-horn. Slowly, he raised it, mustering some of the old enthusiasm. 'I drink to the Chief Bard of Rheged......the Pen Beirdd of Ynys Prydein. May your inspiration guide us to victory.'

chapter four

'I shall not cast aside
the bravest leader,
I'll go to Urien,
to him I'll sing.' [21]

Taliesin faced his patron across the smoky hall. The furrows on the king's brow had deepened, his iron grey hair turned to white, but the old strength, the power that made him a leader amongst leaders, had returned. Urien's gaze was steady, though there was no welcome in it, and Taliesin knew he had only been received back for the good of the kingdom.

Around their chieftain he saw familiar faces, bronzed by the torchlight; others of the warband were missing, slain in the three years he had been away. And he felt the emptiness of the hall without Nefyn. In Rheged, surrounded by the places which had been a part of his life for so long, he could not evade the past, nor attempt to outrun the tide of change.

He struck the final chord and got to his feet, shouts and cheering loud in his ears, and as the warmth of the people touched him, he questioned what the future held for all who listened to his words that night.

Bedwen came out to meet Taliesin as he dismounted within the palisade at Llyn Glas, and together they crossed the courtyard, the uncertain harp playing of a student at practice clear in the stillness.

'There's a matter I need to discuss with you,' Bedwen began slowly. 'It has been troubling me for some time, so I'm glad of the opportunity to speak face to face at last.' He cleared his throat. 'One of my pupils, Hywel, claims that he received the bardic name of Taliesin during his initiation six months ago........that it was bestowed upon him by the Lady Ceridwen herself.'

'I see.' Bedwen noticed a flicker of amusement in Taliesin's eye. 'Why should that trouble you?'

There was an awkward pause. 'Because it seems like presumption. Perhaps because I thought it would displease you, or others........a dozen reasons. He also claims that he has been communicating with you in spirit, journeying to a wild mountainous kingdom where he receives verse from you.' His tone lightened when Taliesin showed no sign of anger, only growing interest. 'I have to admit that he composes some remarkable work for a lad of his age and experience, yet I find it difficult to accept the truth of his words.'

'You're troubled when a pupil excels in the very thing you've been teaching him?'

Bedwen smiled, and shook his head. 'I think I'm entangling myself in my own web.'

'I should like to speak with this boy.'

The smile became a grin. 'Not for the first time, as he'd have me believe.'

Bedwen held the door open for Taliesin as they entered the hall. 'I'll send for Hywel now if you wish,' he said. 'You can help me separate fact from fantasy.'

A group of youths got hurriedly to their feet at the sight of the Pen Beirdd, but Taliesin paid them no attention and took a seat on a bench beside the hearth, remembering when this had been his home. It was no longer richly furnished, with no inlaid chests or costly rugs for the boys to spoil. All was plain and practical, like the apprentices' quarters at Deganwy.

He had little time for reminiscence before Bedwen returned, followed by a solemn-eyed youth, his face familiar as Bedwen's own. The boy, too, looked at Taliesin with recognition.

There was a note of severity in Bedwen's voice. 'The master wishes to speak with you concerning your visions.'

'Sit down, Hywel.' Taliesin indicated the bench beside him, his tone gentle. 'It is good to meet again.'

'I am honoured to meet you, Master, in this world.'

Even the fine tuneful voice was familiar. Taliesin thought back to when the boy had first appeared in his spirit landscape, unbidden, emerging from his own youthful self, and of how he claimed to have earned the name Taliesin. He had never felt the need to ask his birth name, nor to question him as he must now. They had only ever spoken in the instructive dialogue of master and pupil.

'Did you come seeking me?' he asked.

Suddenly Hywel sounded wary. 'Was I wrong to?'

Taliesin frowned, deep in thought. 'It is rather irregular. Was Bedwen's instruction not enough for you?'

'No.......no that was not my reason. I respect him more than any man, except.......' The young bard looked up at Taliesin. 'I.......I wanted to see if I could find you, to test myself to my limits. I felt I had to do it, though I cannot explain why, and though I realized that the Lady Ceridwen would teach me a severe lesson.......destroy me even.......if I was in error.'

'Yet she rewards courage.'

Taliesin met Hywel's eyes, large and dark like a doe's. There was an air about him, something his spirit resonated with. His own natural successor? The words Talhaearn had used about himself. Words that rang through his head like the chiming of a silver branch as he wondered why he had never resented this stranger's intrusions into his trance and put up a barrier to keep him out. Instead, he had welcomed him, been keen to teach him. And he realized that during the months at Din Carreg, instructing Hywel had filled a void left by the completion of Bedwen's apprenticeship.

'I should like to hear you perform,' he said. 'My time is at a premium, but I'll come back here in a week, at the full of the moon.' He got to his feet. 'Prepare a song and a tale by then, and I shall test you on your mastery over the elements.'

The youth rose too, and despite his apparent self-assurance there was a slight tremor in his voice when he replied,

'I'll be prepared, Master.'

'At last Elmet is ready to grasp Rheged's hand in friendship. Gwallawg has taken a lesson from Cynan's folly and will do anything to hold Cryda back.'

Urien's voice growled across the table. The elderly Tewdwr was still at his side, his flesh like dried leather but his one eye bright as a young man's.

'We've had no quarrel with Gwallawg for half a generation. I say we send reply to his embassy and invite him to the council of Britons.'

'He knows me well. If you're in agreement, I'll lead the deputation.'

The king looked at Taliesin, his expression set. 'It does not need a man of your rank to deliver messages.'

Taliesin did not argue. He had returned with no illusions, and was prepared to compromise, more patient and stoical than he had been three years ago.

Without pause for discussion, Urien continued, 'And we must consider Morcant of Eidyn.......'

Several of the men exchanged glances and swore under their breath.

'We'll raid the coward's cattle, not have him rut with our maidens.'

There was a rumble of laughter. The king's stare silenced it.

'This is no time for cursing, for Briton against Briton.'

'If we ally with Morcant, he'll let our men die to protect his borders, then overrun ours.' Dyfnarth's words were greeted by nods from around the table. 'It won't be the first time, nor the last.'

'And what of Rhydderch?' Tewdwr turned to Urien. 'Though he's willing to renew the alliance with Rheged, there's hostility between Ystad Glud and Manaw over the matter of his refusal to let Morcant marry his neice. Will he tolerate Morcant on the council? Or Morcant may harbour resentment and refuse to sit at Rhydderch's side.'

Once more the elders nodded. 'We'll have battles at the council table if we draw enemies into this hall and expect them to share a cup of peace and become sword friends.'

'We will have neither peace nor territory if we cannot put aside our differences.' Taliesin spoke firmly. 'The foreigners manage to ally with the Picts, driven by nothing more than greed; we fight for our sacred land, for our ancestors, our descendants.'

Dyfnarth's eyes flashed, but his question was asked calmly. 'And who would you choose for an ally? Rhydderch or Morcant?'

'Let us hope it will not come to a choice, that we will pit our united strength against the Angles, not divide against each other.' Taliesin looked at his foster-brother's weathered and scarred face, the hard set of his jaw, thinking how the same was true within Caer Liwelydd, and amongst clan and kin. Though Dyfnarth had shown no open hostility since his return - perhaps joy at the birth of a daughter had helped heal past grievances - an underlying tension remained.

He continued, finding it difficult to speak of Rhydderch, not to allow personal feeling to affect his judgement. 'If either is excluded it will be taken as a graver insult than the offer to sit in council together. With his kingdom under imminent threat - the Picts attacking from the north and Fflamddwyn pressing in from the south - Morcant is in no position to harbour resentment, and Rhydderch is less quick to anger than he once was. He devotes himself to the church and, since their reconciliation, Cunotigern has returned from Gwynedd to his foundation of Glas-chu. With such a man as adviser, Rhydderch should prove a steadfast ally.'

The response was swift, voices raised for and against, until once again Urien silenced them.

'A representative will be sent to Ystrad Glud without delay. Let Rhydderch answer for himself whether he will swear the oath with Morcant.'

By May Eve there had been a week of feasting to celebrate the greatest alliance since the time of Arthur Pendragon. Urien of Rheged, Owain of Galloway - heir to his father's kingdom - Rhydderch of Ystrad Glud, Gwallawg of Elmet, and Morcant of Manaw Gododdin, united against a common enemy.

The sun shone from a clear sky, and the afternoon's contests were about to begin below the walls of Caer Liwelydd. As the royal company made their way through the crowds, Gwenddydd turned to Rhydderch who rode beside her, his lined face framed by white hair, his beard as white.

'I grow tired of races and of seeing warriors fight, even in sport. Lord Taliesin has offered to escort me to the places of beauty on the land. I'd find it a welcome change, unless you wish me to stay at your side.'

Rhydderch shook his head. 'No, please go, we seldom leave Alclud and I want you to be happy whilst we are here.'

Gwenddydd smiled. 'May you have a pleasant afternoon.'

The noise from the first race faded as they rode out across spring pastures, Taliesin and Gwenddydd ahead of her two companions, making light conversation. They dismounted at the top of a rise where the view was clear as far as the waters of the estuary. But Taliesin's eyes rested instead on Gwenddydd's profile - the straight line of her nose, her high forehead - and on the rich blue-black of her hair, now streaked with silver.

Unaware of his gaze, she drew in a deep breath. 'I smell the salt on the breeze, and the sweetness of the meadows.' She raised a hand, shielding her eyes against the sun. 'Shall we continue to the mouth of the Idon?'

'Whatever you wish. But it is not far out of our way to a cairn laid in memory of Urien's brother, who was slain thirty years ago fighting the Angles. All who pass it add a stone, so each year it grows higher.'

'It seems appropriate to pay our respects at a time such as this, when Urien is Gwledig, the man who has brought the northern kingdoms together and who will lead them as one.'

Gwenddydd tightened her hold on the reins, glancing over her shoulder at her companions. She was about to remount, when she looked at the youngest with concern.

'Morwen, are you unwell?'

The woman frowned. 'I have a severe pain in my head. I fear it is the heat that disagrees with me.'

Taliesin unstopped his drinking flask, though Morwen took only a small sip before returning it. There were beads of sweat on her brow, and she gripped her companion's arm. 'I am sorry,' she said shakily. 'But I think I must return to Caer Liwelydd, where I can lie down in darkness.'

Gwenddydd hesitated, torn between responsibility and her reluctance to turn back.

It was the other woman who broke the silence. 'I'll accompany her, my lady. There is no reason for you to alter your plans.'

After a brief pause, Gwenddydd replied, 'Very well.' And addressing Morwen, said gently, 'I hope to find you fully restored to health by evening.'

She and Taliesin watched the women manoeuvre their horses and head in the direction of the town. At first neither spoke, as the solitude of the place washed over them. Eventually, Taliesin turned to her.

'Do you still wish to go to the cairn? The estuary?' His tone was neutral, but the look in his eyes over-rode the question.

As she returned his gaze, Gwenddydd felt as if she was drugged, unable to think rationally. For a moment she forgot what he had asked, then managed to find her voice.

'Do you?' She glanced at the two figures receding into the distance. Soon they would be out of sight. 'Perhaps Morwen was right,' she said vaguely. 'It is over hot for riding.'

'The hall at Llyn Glas will be cooler, and quiet. No one's there except the attendants. Bedwen and his pupils are watching the contests.'

They were standing side by side, and Taliesin reached out and took Gwenddydd's hand, pressing it to his lips. Her husband, kingdoms, alliances blocked from his mind. He had made too many sacrifices, suffered too many years alone.

As Taliesin and Gwenddydd entered the gates of the bardic college, a man stepped across their path issuing a challenge, another appearing from the stables in response to his comrade's call. A moment later both stood at ease, and Taliesin recognized the second man as Ieuan, little changed from the days when he had been Talhaearn's attendant.

For appearances sake, Taliesin asked him to serve in the hall, where he offered Gwenddydd a seat on the rough bench that had replaced the couch at the hearthside. Slowly, wine was poured into his goblet, but Taliesin had ceased to feel irritated by the formality, the farcical game they must play. It had become part of the beauty of the moment, the growing

497

anticipation, with Gwenddydd so close yet untouchable. He found pleasure in the last minutes of separation, the pretence, even the risk.

When Ieuan went to leave, he rose and accompanied him to the door. 'My guest is tired and wishes to rest,' he said. 'Ensure she is not disturbed.'

He waited, gazing across the empty sunlit courtyard, watching the man's departing figure until he entered the stables. Then Taliesin shut the door, and lifted the heavy wooden bar to secure it.

'I see you intend to hold me prisoner.' Gwenddydd looked round, giving a faint smile. 'After bespelling my companion.'

'Ah, you have found me out.'

She smiled openly now, setting her goblet down and getting to her feet.

'Nothing could give me greater joy than to be together on your birthday,' she said softly. 'At the celebrations tonight, the lords will bring you gold and jewels, yet I have brought no gift.'

Gwenddydd's pupils were dark, her face close to his, and Taliesin put an arm around her waist, drawing her nearer.

She went with him unquestioningly, holding him as they walked towards the partition that divided the main hall from the chamber beyond. Though the chamber was Bedwen's now, it was still furnished with costly objects - the tapestries and metalwork, the carved chairs and chests that were an accumulation of Bedwen's growing riches and Taliesin's own, the things left behind when he began his years of travel.

In silence, he laid his night-blue cloak across the bed, then lit a single oil lamp beside it before returning to Gwenddydd. She stood watching him, the light giving a creamy warmth to her cheeks, reflected flames glancing off the gold at her throat and the royal circlet set with gems.

He stroked her hair back from her brow, then lifted the circlet and the pins that held the braid coiled about her head.

As her hair fell free, reaching to her hips, he took her hands.

His voice was little more than a whisper. 'Only the greatest fool would have allowed himself to lose you.'

'Do you truly believe you ever lost me?' Gwenddydd looked up at him. 'My innermost self has never been Rhydderch's........never. I thought of you each day during the time you were travelling, praying you were not placing yourself in danger.' She paused. 'We are no longer young. We have been close for so many years, yet I think we have also been afraid. Of doing wrong as the world would see it? Or were we afraid of each other, of breaking the dream?'

'What does it matter?' Taliesin kissed her. 'Fear is only in the mind.'

He kissed her again, longer and harder. No, they were not young, but she was still the girl he had known in Deganwy, grown more beautiful with age, who could never be anything but beautiful: maiden, mother or crone.

He unfastened the enamelled brooches that secured her gown, and she slipped it from her shoulders as Taliesin removed his tunic and breeches. She had held him often, but always through the barrier of garments, and the greater barrier of doubt. Though she saw him naked for the first time, she already knew his body, lean and well-muscled, without a warrior's sturdiness. The scars across his ribs and stomach showed clearly against the whiteness of his skin, a reminder of how death had almost taken him from her. Awareness of his mortality, of their mortality, intensified her love for him. She reached out, and felt his arms around her, his flesh warm against her breasts, the taste of his mouth on hers.

Still with their arms about each other they crossed the room to the bed, and lay together on Taliesin's cloak, the lamp bathing their bodies in pale light. At last there was no guilt, no fear, only a deep knowing. The storm pulse burned through Taliesin, Gwenddydd's touch awakening the power of life.

Lover, queen, goddess, part of his own soul.

She drew in a shuddering breath as the fire of Beli kindled within her. The greatest sacrament, not the dull duty of pleasing her ageing husband. She knew this could never destroy the dreams of half a life-span, but only make them real in the world, grounded in earthly love and in memory. She and Taliesin were one as they had always been. A wave carried them, lifting them to a place of ecstasy, of fire and water, then the softness of a dark ocean.

Gwenddydd looked at Taliesin resting beside her, at a strong-boned face surrounded by ruffled hair, his arm, with the blue spiral tattoos of an initiate, relaxed across her belly.

She could think of neither past nor future. Nothing existed but the brief hours spent lying with the man she had loved since their youth - knowing the fiercest intensity and the greatest tenderness, beyond anything she had let herself imagine in the loneliness of Ystrad Glud. Beside her was the man honoured above any in Ynys Prydein, above kings, worshipped like a god, but feared, misunderstood.

He opened his eyes, meeting hers, and kissed her, then held her to him. They pulled the edges of the cloak around themselves, drowsy in each other's warmth, and finally fell asleep.

The mid-morning sun shone above the Wall as Taliesin rode through the southern gate of Caer Liwelydd, immune to tiredness.

Throughout the previous night he had celebrated with the noble company, and while chieftains and warriors from five kingdoms drank his health, he had sung as always, rewarded by praise and gifts. In the early hours, when the feast was at an end, he returned to Llyn Glas, alone, to be ready for the dawn, to lead Bedwen and his apprentices in the rites of Calan Mai.

Gleis' hooves clattered over broken cobbles as Taliesin passed dwellings and workshops, the streets crowded with people. He dismounted in front of the royal stables and threw the horse's reins to a groom, noticing that Rhydderch and his advisers were approaching the hall.

They reached the entrance together, and Gwenddydd's husband nodded towards him with a look of respect.

'The first day of summer, Lord Taliesin,' he said cordially. 'An apt day for swearing trust and friendship between kingdoms.'

At the council table Taliesin took his seat at Urien's side, facing the assembled men: Owain, bold and strong, leaning forward as he spoke with the ageing Gwallawg; Rhydderch, clothed in dark garments, a cross at his breast - one of the most powerful and wealthy kings of Ynys Prydein clad plainly as a holy brother; and Morcant of Eidyn, with his crimson tunic and emerald cloak, jewelled rings on each finger flashing in the torchlight. His hair was the colour of a fox's pelt, his eyes and movements keen.

Taliesin wondered if those who still distrusted him were right to do so. But he and Rhydderch had put aside past differences for the sake of the alliance, and though Morcant had once been all too ready to deceive neighbour or ally, in recent years he seemed also to have put aside selfish ambition.

Distracted by a sense of being watched, Taliesin turned, and caught Dyfnarth's eye before his foster-brother looked away. He could find no reason for the hostility he had seen in that look. But there was no time to question. No time for his own concerns during the hours that followed, as the alliance was sealed with mead and oaths.

Not until daylight faded did Taliesin leave the hall to prepare for the recitals he would perform at the farewell feast.

He had barely taken ten paces across the courtyard when Dyfnarth came up alongside him, silent and inescapable as a shadow.

At the door to his quarters, Taliesin stopped. 'I assume you want to speak with me?'

Dyfnarth gave a curt nod and strode into the chamber. Taliesin felt as if they were re-living the day three years ago when he announced that he intended to leave Rheged. He dismissed his attendant, knowing words would be exchanged that he did not want the man to overhear or repeat, then sat down, indicating for his brother to join him.

'This should be a time of unity,' he said quietly, 'not of divisive barriers, least of all between foster-kin.'

'Once a damned traitor, always so. It were better for Rheged had you travelled for the rest of your days.'

Taliesin looked at Dyfnarth, feeling vulnerable in his recent happiness. 'Your dislike of me is plain enough,' he replied, 'but what you accuse me of is not.'

'You betray the laws of hospitality, the trust of kings, God's own law. You, Urien's Chief Bard, copulate with Rhydderch's wife while they swear loyalty to the death.'

Taliesin forced himself to remain calm.

His voice was lowered, not raised. 'You make a dangerous accusation.'

'I have proof. Witnesses.' A crooked smile spread across Dyfnarth's face. 'You cannot deny that you paid off Queen Gwenddydd's companions to leave her alone with you, that you took her to your hall, barring the door, and lay with her.' The smile widened, stretching the scar on Dyfnarth's cheek, showing missing teeth. 'I hope she was worth it.'

'What do you hope to gain by confronting me with these lies?' Taliesin kept his voice low. 'Do the bonds of foster-kinship mean nothing? The memory of the mother whose love we shared? Our father, who lives still?'

'And your oath to lord and land? Your lust endangers kingdoms, the entire territory of Ynys Prydein. What if Rhydderch should hear of this?'

'He will not hear of it, unless you are fool enough to go to him.' The tone of Taliesin's voice had darkened. 'What I might suffer as a result is nothing compared to the suffering it would cause our people. You speak of treachery. Would you let your hatred of me divide the Britons, destroying our last hope of driving the enemy from our shores? Think before you do anything you may live to regret.'

'As I'm sure you did.' Dyfnarth laughed harshly. 'As you felt the warmth of her thighs.......'

Taliesin got suddenly to his feet, Dyfnarth instinctively doing the same, bracing himself to deflect a blow.

'How dare you.' Finally, the rage was unleashed. 'Get out!'

Dyfnarth's hand dropped weakly to his side. As long as he lived he would never forget the inhuman glare in Taliesin's eyes, the white fire. He could feel it starting to burn through him as he hastened towards the door, terror-struck, knowing what Taliesin's anger had done to Glinneu when he was only a boy, untrained in whatever unspeakable arts he now practised.

Chapter Five

Summer rain lashed against the roof, accompanying Hywel's words.

'The three inventors of song and record of the Britons: Gwyddon Ganhebon, who was the first in the world that composed vocal song; Hu the Mighty, who first applied vocal song to strengthen memory and record; and Tydain........' [22]

As the boy spoke, Taliesin would suddenly see Cadfarch looking back at him through the nut-brown eyes, or evoked by a chance mannerism. He had no regrets over taking Hywel on as apprentice, and teaching brought a welcome distraction from the concerns that weighed on his mind. It was two weeks since Rhydderch left, an ally still, so Dyfnarth had seen sense and kept his knowledge to himself, though Taliesin wondered if even now his brother's tongue might be loosened in a fit of drunken temper.

'.......from what was done by these three men, originated bards and bardism, and the privilege and........' [22]

Hywel stopped at the sound of a single knock on the door and, looking over his shoulder, Taliesin called out in reply.

The attendant who entered was accompanied by a stranger, his hair and cloak soaked by the downpour. At first Taliesin felt annoyance. The weather had prevented him from taking Hywel out onto the land to conduct his lessons, yet it never spared them from interruption.

'My lord. Gareth, spearman to Gwilym ap Ederyn of Dun Anarawd.'

The man crossed the chamber and Taliesin rose to greet him. Hearing his name, annoyance became foreboding, but he kept his voice even as he turned to Hywel.

'There'll be no more lessons today, you may go.'

504

The youth stood, and picked up his leather pouch of Ogham staves. For an instant he paused, curiosity in his eyes, though he knew it was not his place to question.

'I'll prepare the triads for tomorrow,' he said, glancing uneasily at Gareth. 'Good day, Master.'

Once Hywel had left, Taliesin's attendant poured the spearman a cup of mead, then spread his cloak on a bench to dry. For three years Taliesin had not seen his son, and his thoughts were of Afaon as he faced the man opposite him.

Both remained standing.

'My Lord.' Gareth spoke slowly. 'A week past, Lady Nefyn was taken ill, suffering from a fever of the brain. A skilled physician was summoned, but the sickness was grievous........'

In silence, Taliesin waited.

'It brings me sorrow to tell you what I must,' Gareth spoke again, 'that early this day she passed from the world. God rest her soul.'

Taliesin sat now, staring at the cold hearth, and as the rain continued to hammer against the roof, struggled to accept what he heard. Nefyn had always been strong, even when she bore a child late in life. And despite their separation, her bitterness towards him, he had never ceased caring for her, carrying the memory of her beauty and vitality, and a burden of guilt at the suffering he had caused.

Finally, he raised his eyes.

'My son. Is the sickness contagious?'

'Your son remains in good health, my lord.'

Taliesin sighed. In a week Urien's warriors would head east at the start of the united campaign against the Angles. He was to ride with them, a time he had long anticipated. But he had to see Afaon. He had to be certain that he was well cared for and speak with Gwilym about his future upbringing.

He addressed the spearman. 'If you can delay your

departure until tomorrow, I will accompany you to Dun Anarawd.'

After Urien's warriors joined forces with the men of Din Eidyn they encountered an Anglian raiding party on the border of Manaw. With advancing years and his recent illness, the king led only as strategist and adviser, and it was Dyfnarth who commanded in battle - Rheged's captain now Riwallon was dead.

The fight was short but bloody, the track stained red and the pasture scattered with corpses by the time the enemy retreated. In its aftermath, Urien walked amongst the wounded, praising courage, promising victory.

As men mourned their comrades, he returned to Taliesin's side, surveying the field.

'Once the casualties are tended we move. This place is a death trap if the barbarians drag up more scum from the forest.'

'Yes, we come to hunt, not be hunted.' Morcant's hazel eyes gleamed like a wild cat's. 'And it is but a short distance to our rendezvous where the legionary road crosses the river.'

Taliesin turned away, oppressed by the cries of the wounded and dying.

He had ridden hard from Dun Anarawd, only returning to Caer Liwelydd as Rheged's forces were on the point of departure. Throughout the journey back, he had seen Afaon in his mind's eye, not the infant he remembered but a sturdy boy of five summers, so like Nefyn with his oval face and black curls. He was just beginning to lose his wariness of his father, who was nothing but a stranger to him, when Taliesin had had to leave once more.

Exhausted from lack of sleep, he questioned if he had made the right choice in accepting Gwilym's offer to raise Afaon with his own children. Believing it kindest not to tear

506

him away from all that was familiar, Taliesin had thought he acted in his son's best interests. But Caer Liwelydd was at the heart of the kingdom, a place filled with opportunity, Dun Anarawd a backwater in the wilds north of the Wall. And in letting him remain, did he risk that Afaon might suffer feelings of rejection, the pain of the outsider that he himself had known?

Under a blue sky, with cloud building on the horizon, the warriors of Rheged and Manaw Gododdin made their way along an ancient hilltop track. Before the sun reached its zenith there was a second skirmish, Morcant's men riding in pursuit of a band of Angles who were spotted in the valley below, slaying half their number. Encouraged by their success, they continued onto the metalled road which cut through the land like a knife slash, the day growing hot and dark as they neared their destination.

Warbands were already assembled at the ford, cavalrymen holding horses which stamped and snorted, tails flicking at the flies that bit savagely in the heat. A swelling sea of man and beast gathered, while small parties rode further afield, raiding into Bernicia, burning the ripening corn and levelling villages, sparing only women and children. They would sting Theodoric Flame-bearer, like the flies stung the horses, until he kicked out, ignorant of what lay in wait for him when he did.

As Urien's men dismounted, Owain clasped Taliesin in greeting, then addressed him, his voice low.

'Penarwen and I were deeply saddened to hear of Nefyn's death,' he said. 'She was a dear friend to us both.'

Though noise and commotion surrounded them, Taliesin spoke confidentially. 'I would that she and I had not parted with such coldness when last we met.' He felt grief burn behind his eyes. 'And I regret that I did not see Afaon more. But during the years I spent travelling I was only half aware of the world.......Not until recently has my mind become clear again.'

Owain's gaze was steady. 'You did right to return to

507

Rheged, though it was my loss......Today we stand on the threshold of a new era.'

Watched by a circle of elite warriors, Urien strode into the waters of the ford. He looked at the men around him, then drew his sword and offered the hilt to Taliesin, the kings of the five northern British territories placing their hands upon the blade.

'My lords, your oath before God and those who bear witness.'

Taliesin's voice resounded in the silence. It was followed by Urien's.

'In the name of Almighty God, I swear to uphold the alliance; in word and deed, to be guided by truth and justice. May the Lord be with us and grant us victory.'

As each king took the oath, dark clouds were mirrored in the water that swirled about their feet as if they stood in a maelstrom. Taliesin held the sword steady - the blade that bound old enemies together in friendship: Rhydderch's ageing hand beside Morcant's, broad and smooth, the bitterness between Urien and Rhydderch over Arderydd buried in the past, Gwallawg's face resolute yet calm. Only Morcant's eye flickered, the corner of his mouth tightening.

'...........May the Lord be with us and grant us victory.'

Owain was last to make the pledge. Echoing his words, the warriors broke into a chant that was taken up by the assembled host, a wave of voice that rolled across the land. In the moments that followed, toasts were drunk and strategies finalized before the forces separated, Morcant, with his foster-brother Cynddylan at his side, preparing to lead the warriors of Manaw from the ford.

The two men, so alike they could have been blood-kin, spoke in undertones as they walked to where their horses were tethered.

'It sticks in my gullet watching two old men lord it over us. Urien imagines himself as High King, while Rhydderch, that sanctimonious bastard, thinks he is holier than Christ himself. He reckoned his mousey niece too good for me to take as wife.'

Cynddylan nodded. 'He allows another to lead because his own arm is too weak to wield a sword. Men need a king who can fight, inspire by example. He can do no more than set an example to a choir of monks.'

'The warriors only accept these ancients because they remember what they once were.' Morcant glanced towards his foster-brother with an ironic smile. 'After so many years waging war, our noble ally has earned his rest.'

There was a pause.

'I did not think the Pen Beirdd would be here,' Cynddylan said, unhitching his horse's reins.

'You believe what is told of him! Stuff for snivelling children.'

Cynddylan bristled. 'He has strange eyes, eyes that see what others do not.......I say be on your guard, take nothing for granted.'

'If that is what you say, dear brother, that is what I must do.' Morcant grinned, then yelled to the warriors behind them. 'Continue into the scrubland and lay low. We camp there 'til I give the signal.'

Evening drew on, the men of Rheged and Galloway watching at the ford while scouts combed the surrounding land. Out of sight, their allies waited, ready for action, but by nightfall there had been no movement from across the Bernician border. Fires were lit only in the main camp, and as the waiting continued throughout the dark hours Taliesin related tales of past glory: Urien's victories, and the deeds of his father and grandfather, and of the warlord Arthur Pendragon - first to unite the Britons as one. An increasing company gathered round, courage roused, and the fires had burnt low before they took their rest. Wrapped in his cloak, his pack of provisions beneath his head, Taliesin lay down with them, eventually slipping into a fitful sleep.

He woke suddenly, startled by the blast of a horn, and though it seemed that no time had passed he opened his eyes to the grey light of dawn. Dew lay on the ground and there was a chill in the air, air that carried the scent of the sea.

Owain sat up beside him, easing his leg to relieve the ache of an old wound, but he spoke with youthful confidence.

'Our descendants will remember this day, a day the Angles will wish they had not lived to see.'

In the camp, men snatched a drink of mead or a bite of oatcake as they made ready, fitting harness and taking up weapons amidst the clang of metal and stamp of hooves. Still, there was no sign of the enemy. The message had come from far to the south. And, at a distance, the forces of Ystrad Glud and Elmet and Manaw prepared for battle.

A second horn signalled for the Britons at the ford to take up their stations.

Sitting astride Gleis, Taliesin looked towards the southern horizon. Tension mounted amongst the men who watched with him as the enemy came within sight, on foot but advancing swiftly. A dark shadow, a flood-tide of destruction. They surged onward while the Britons stood firm, biding their time; drawing nearer until Taliesin was able to make out Fflamddwn's squat figure at the head of his forces. The enemy numbers were vast, mustered by the Bernician lord since British raids on his territory began, his ranks reinforced by Deiran fighters and bands of Picts.

Then the shout came. 'For the glory of Rheged, for the glory of Ynys Prydein.'

Dyfnarth urged his horse into a gallop, leading Rheged's warriors while Owain's men held the ford. Drums beat to the thunder of hooves. Pipes shrilled. And where the land rose above the river, the sides locked in combat.

The enemy, confident in number, believed they met a lesser force. Relentless, they advanced. Then, appearing from out of the mist like spirit warriors, Morcant's warband rode at them, roaring the battle cry. Thrown spears - raptors taking their prey.

The rush of cavalry brought confusion to the Angles, but they fought fiercely, unyielding.

Finally, Owain gave the order to charge.

As he restrained Gleis from running with the other horses, Taliesin followed his comrade's progress. In the path of Owain's onslaught dozens fell. Shrieks and the clash of iron tore the air. The fight intensified, both sides matched in ferocity.

Sunless, noon passed, and the Angles began to gain the advantage. Bloodied corpses trampled beneath their feet, they pressed forward and, seeing the men of Ynys Prydein weak and outnumbered, summoned the last of their reserves.

But at the moment when Fflamddwyn believed victory was his, a mighty host blotted out the horizon - cavalry to the fore, at the rear, warriors on foot, spears raised in a forest of death. Rhydderch's standard of the holy cross on a blue ground was carried beside Neithon, his cousin and heir, who commanded in his stead; the eagle banner of Elmet flew over Gwallawg's men. The full strength of the alliance launched against the enemy.

Taliesin beheld a force greater than any he had seen, and felt the hope that had faded over the years rekindle. In humility, he called upon the power of Beli, praying that the Britons might yet free the sacred land. If they won victory in the north, it would reinforce Selyf's morale in the campaign to save Powys, upholding the honour of his late father......give courage to the men of Dumnonia.

Above the seething mass of man and horse, he watched the red dragon blaze, entangled with the white, a ghost from the ice of winter, the colour of corpse flesh. Spitting vapour, the white dragon writhed in helpless fury, and leaving a track of dead and wounded the enemy retreated. Oaths sworn by warriors in the mead hall for as long as Taliesin could remember, that they would drown the Angles in the waters over which they had come, seemed destined to be fulfilled.

Though the Bernicians had a fortress on the coast, Morcant's men cut off their chance to reach its refuge. The Lord of Eidyn, fiery hair and emerald cloak bold in the grey morning, fought fiercely, his action ensuring that the Angles remained in the open, only a small band escaping into the wilds to the south.

Gulls screeched overhead, waves pounded at the enemy's back as the tide rose. While the battle raged on the shore, sea reclaimed sand. And after a last desperate clash, before the chance was lost, the Bernicians fled, not to a watery grave but towards sanctuary on the tidal island of Metcaud.

Owain rode at Neithon's side, their comrades behind them, plunging through the rising water in pursuit, wanting to finish it then and there. Yet, faster and faster the sea rushed in, water dragging at the horses' legs, undermining their foothold until, cursing, the men were forced to turn back.

Dawn silvered the horizon, the mists which drifted over the Northern Sea making Metcaud appear deceptively ethereal.

All night the Britons had camped above the beach, watch-fires glowing in the moist air. Taliesin and Dyfnarth were amongst the men closest to Urien, seated with him whilst food was shared, at each other's side when the allies met in council, but they had not spoken, nor acknowledged each other, since they argued. Taliesin had felt easier with Rhydderch back in

Alclud, many days journey away. Now it was again possible for Dyfnarth to go to him and voice his suspicions, though it seemed unlikely that he would do so until the Angles were defeated.

Needing peace to think, Taliesin stood on the shore, watching the incoming waves. Far across the grey waters to the east were the homelands the barbarians had left, some a generation or more ago. He questioned why they were not content to remain there, honouring the sacred places of their ancestors, thriving on the soil that had always nourished them. Had their lands become so desolate and infertile that the need to find new territory was worth decades of slaughter?

The question still in his mind, he turned and headed towards the tent where the kings were assembled. A circle of swords lay on the ground at their feet, blades pointing in to the centre like the spokes of a wheel.

When Taliesin was seated, Urien addressed the council. 'My lords, there's little time for discussion if we're to storm the island this forenoon. Soon the tide begins to ebb......Or do we lay siege until the enemy weakens? Or attempts to break out?'

Almost before Urien had finished speaking, Morcant replied boldly. 'By delaying we consolidate our advantage. The enemy have no food. Let us starve them into defeat........'

As he continued, he held the men's attention, and Taliesin alone noticed Cynddylan watching Rhydderch with a look of veiled contempt.

Gwallawg shook his head thoughtfully. 'Our warriors will grow weary with constant vigilance. I believe we should act now.'

Silence followed. Tinder ready to ignite, pride and old grievances smouldered close beneath the surface. Yet Rhydderch's voice was reasoned when he broke that silence.

'There is sense in both options. Though I suggest a compromise. We lay siege for two, at most three days, then mount an attack, using the pick of cavalry from our combined ranks.'

Urien's gaze moved round the circle, pausing as each man responded, uncertainty resolving into agreement. Lastly, he faced Morcant, staring at him from beneath lowered brows. 'What say you?'

Morcant's gaze now moved round the circle. 'Experience alone will tell,' he replied. 'I bow to your wisdom.'

The storm had dispersed, and Taliesin felt the tension ease. He glanced again at Cynddylan, trying to reassure himself that he had become over-suspicious as tiredness and strain took its toll.

Urien's voice was firm. 'We must deal quickly with the foreign filth that headed south, in case they return to bite our heel. I will lead a foray to track them down.'

No longer content to remain inactive, the Lord of Rheged rode out along the coast with a band of warriors. The rest waited throughout the day, monitoring the tide and watching for any movement on the island. As light began to fade, Morcant sat playing dice with his comrades. Owain, too, sat with his comrades, while Rhydderch retired to his tent, alone. There was no sign of Cynddylan.

Though Taliesin attempted to relax, to distract himself by listening to the battle tales the men recounted, he was plagued by uneasiness. Remembering the look Morcant's foster-brother had given Rhydderch, and Morcant's words at the war council, he got to his feet, leaving the camp-fire.

He stopped outside Rhydderch's tent and spoke his name, fighting his own darkness, the inner conflict he could not acknowledge. When his greeting brought no response, the conflict intensified. If Gwenddydd's husband was slain.......

Then he heard a familiar soft-spoken voice.

'Lord Taliesin. Come in.'

Pushing the tent flap aside, he saw Rhydderch rise from his knees.

'My apologies, I have disturbed you at prayer.'

'No, please stay.......Has King Urien returned?

'Not as yet.'

Taliesin met Rhydderch's eye, realizing how long the assault party had been absent, knowing that as time passed it increased the possibility they had been caught in an ambush or underestimated the number of fugitive Angles. And they were without reinforcements.

Rhydderch read his expression. 'I, too, am concerned, but we must have faith.'

Together they walked to the water's edge, speaking not of the siege nor the forthcoming battle, but of Cunotigern's foundation at Glas-chu, and of Taliesin's reunion with Rhys and his visit to Candida Casa. The conversation was gradually becoming less forced, when an uproar in the camp made them turn.

Two of Urien's comrades had Cynddylan in a rough grasp, his face and cloak soaked with blood as he struggled like a man crazed, yelling curses with each attempt to free himself. Taliesin hurried back up the beach, seeking Urien amongst the warriors of his band who surrounded the captive. But even as he searched, he was overcome by a certainty chill as the northern sea.

chapter six

They laid Urien's body in the tent where the previous day he had led the war council - his shoulders draped in the purple cloak of kingship, his calloused hands crossed at his breast, over the hilt of the sword the alliance had been sworn upon.

Standing beside Owain, Taliesin recalled his years as Chief Bard to the Lord of Rheged, aware that all they had striven for had been destroyed at the moment when ultimate victory lay within the Britons' grasp.

The wound in Urien's neck, caked with blackened blood, showed where Cynddylan's spear had struck its mark. But the traitor had been too slow to get away, and, believing they went in pursuit of an Anglian spearman, Urien's men had captured him as he attempted to flee through the undergrowth.

His head lowered, Owain stepped back from his father's body and left the tent. He glanced to where the men of Manaw had been camped, then faced the chieftains gathered with their warriors above the beach, the pain of loss over-ridden by rage.

'I'll take my warband and go after them. My father's death must be avenged before his spirit can rest.'

His declaration met with silence. Neithon shifted awkwardly, Rhydderch grave and motionless at his side. Gwallawg frowned, biting back the words on his tongue. The tide had begun to turn, the gulls massing in the shallows with raucous cries.

Only Taliesin dared speak his mind. 'Would you risk allowing Fflamddwyn to escape and rebuild his army? There is time enough to make Morcant pay for his treachery once we have finished our work here.'

Owain's gaze was dark, and without replying he looked towards Metcaud, at the narrowing barrier of water which separated Angle from Briton. For a long while he remained in thought before addressing his allies.

'My lords,' he tried to hold his voice steady, 'allow me to command the assault on the island.....now, before another chance is lost.'

Rhydderch replied softly. 'May God go with you.'

Gwallawg inclined his head, echoing Rhydderch's words.

Intending to remain behind, Taliesin gave Owain his blessing and walked towards the tent where Urien lay. While the warriors fought the decisive battle he would sit in vigil - pay him due honour, and ease his spirit that had been driven from his body unprepared.

But Owain went after him.

'Ride with us, Taliesin,' he said. 'The men need your presence.'

Taliesin hesitated, feeling bound by a debt of duty to Urien, resolved not to fail him in death as he had in life. He was about to refuse Owain's request when he saw the desperation in his eyes, and questioned if his own decision might hold the balance between victory and defeat. Again he hesitated, his resolve weakening.

With a brief word, he turned and accompanied his comrade to where Gleis was tethered.

The warriors made ready, watching the waters recede, impatient for action after hours of uncertainty and enforced idleness. The last moments dragged by as the land emerged from beneath the waves, yet Owain restrained his own impatience.

He glanced at the men behind him, and back towards Metcaud, the expanse of sea that had made it an isle now no more than a ribbon. Then, raising his sword, he gave Urien's battle cry.

'For the glory of Rheged.'

Digging their heels into their horses' flanks, the Britons raced across the exposed sands into shallow water, striking up a riot of spray. The wind stung Taliesin's eyes and filled his mouth with the taste of salt, catching at the folds of his cloak as it lashed behind him.

They were halfway to the island when the sun burst through the cloud, creating a shimmering track to Metcaud. Once they came within range, a hail of spears flew from its shore, flashing in the light. Two men were hit, their mounts charging on riderless as the attackers burst on the enemy defence. Horses screamed, panicking in the crush, fallen warriors trampled beneath flailing hooves.

Seeing the Britons fail to gain the advantage, Neithon raised the war cry of Ystrad Glud and led his men in the second onslaught. On the shores of Metcaud they used their thrusting spears on the Angles that came to meet them, leaving them gasping like beached fish where they lay at the water's edge.

Taliesin held Gleis still, aware that he was an easy target for any Anglian spearman who was given respite to take aim, but his concern was not for his own safety. Seeing him with them brought courage to the warriors who fought on sands churned and blood-stained, and he remained close to the action, though he took no part in it. Looking to where the battle was at its fiercest, he glimpsed a scarlet shield in the thick of the fight. Gradually, the press of men thinned until his comrade was clearly visible, facing Fflamddwyn in single combat.

As Owain struck with brutal force, the Angle raised his shield to deflect Owain's blade, sending him off balance. He righted himself and again attacked - tireless, filled with battle fury. Fflamddwyn stood firm, his body like a rock, his hand and mind as steady, waiting for Owain to make a fatal error. It was plain to Taliesin that his comrade fought in blind rage. Each thrust he made was Morcant's death blow, though he

518

knew that unless Owain curbed his recklessness he would not live to deal that blow to the traitor.

Taliesin had lost one lord and comrade that day, he would not suffer the loss of another. Detaching himself, he prepared to raise the white fire. But as he began to circulate the sacred breaths, the din of combat and cries of death rang out over the island in a voice of eerie beauty.

'Do nothing. Owain must make his own destiny. It is not for you to alter its course.'

Shaken and distraught, Taliesin earthed the energy he had summoned, not understanding why his goddess stayed his hand.

Once more he watched Owain strike out, putting his full weight behind the thrust. Fflamddwyn struck back, his blade glancing off the edge of Owain's shield, chipping away the wood and biting into his arm. Owain cursed and dropped the shield, as Taliesin felt the grip of fear. But pain and danger fuelled Owain's fury. He leapt to the left, confusing Fflamddwyn, then crouched and drove his blade up under the Angle's shield, beneath the mail and leather, into his belly. Belching a stream of blood, Fflamddwyn keeled forward into a pool of his own gore, while Owain stood as if paralyzed, his gaze fixed and staring, then collapsed unconscious beside the body.

Owain, Lord of Rheged and Galloway, sat in the great high-backed chair in the hall at Caer Liwelydd as Taliesin recited in praise of his courage.

That morning the oath of kingship had been sworn before God in the chapel, the ceremony conducted by Segnius' successor. Then, known only to Taliesin and initiates of the Old Faith, out on the land Owain gave himself to the Great Queen in love and loyalty. Now was the time for celebration - a week of feasting, contest and song.

As Owain's ally, Rhydderch was given the place of honour at the royal table, Gwenddydd seated beside him, serene in a gown of dawn blue, black braids streaked with silver coiled about her head. Taliesin kept his eyes from her, seeing her only when he looked towards his comrade. The pain of continued separation was like a sickness, disabling and inescapable, except through oblivion.

Losing himself in the words of his eulogy, his voice rose, rich and clear,

> 'No equal will be found
> to a lord
> of dazzling joy,
> enemy-reaper, grasper,
> with the nature of his father
> and his grandfather.' [23]

To a silent hall, he recounted Owain's victory over Morcant of Eidyn and the traitor's death, drawing the company with him through war and triumph. Yet, as the final applause rang out, Taliesin thought how all triumph was hollow, and that in each victory there was defeat.

The following day Gwenddydd went openly to Taliesin's rooms. Finllian was in Caer Liwelydd for the festivities, and in the eyes of the royal household it was she whom Gwenddydd came to see. But after a brief greeting Finllian retired to an inner chamber, leaving them alone.

When she had gone, they faced each other in wordless communication, too deep to voice. Then Taliesin drew Gwenddydd to him, finding strength in her closeness, a brief respite from grief.

Afterwards they sat together, drinking wine and speaking softly.

'Is it truly less than two months since we last met? That time seems so long......and it has brought nothing but sorrow.' Gwenddydd sounded weary. 'I cannot believe that Urien is slain. I thought we'd finally found peace between the northern kingdoms. But again Rheged and Ystrad Glud are at war with Manaw.'

Taliesin's expression was grim. 'I'm sure Fflamddwyn's heir Hussa will take full advantage. The Angles of Bernicia are defeated, but not crushed. And now the alliance is broken we cannot follow up our victory with the second campaign planned by the war council, Morcant and Urien drinking mead together.......' He sighed. 'I am sickened by it all, this futility.........My place is no longer on the field of battle, nor composing verse in praise of slaughter.'

Gwenddydd frowned. 'But you and Owain are comrades. Surely you are glad to be his Chief Bard, he to have you at his side?'

'The battle is not only fought with sword and spear.' Taliesin lowered his voice, anger giving way to a remoteness that made Gwenddydd uneasy. 'Though the future may bring defeat, our people be slain or driven from the sacred land, if the ancestral wisdom is preserved our spirit will be victorious.'

For a moment Gwenddydd said nothing, then replied gently. 'I don't like to hear you speak this way. You are exhausted, grieving for Urien.'

'That does not alter the truth.' Taliesin paused. 'I've not yet spoken of this to anyone, but now Urien is dead I shall not stay on as Chief Bard. I shall go to Llydaw and live quietly, carrying on my teaching work away from all who know me. Bedwen is master of the bardic college, others can sing the king's praises.'

When he looked at Gwenddydd, her expression reminded

him of when they separated in the orchard at Deganwy twenty-four years earlier. 'This means I may never see you again,' she said. 'Is that what you want?'

'Do you want us to go on as we are now? Unable to be together, nor remain apart. With Rhydderch as Owain's ally this farce will continue without end.' Taliesin's voice faltered. 'I cannot endure it for the rest of my days.'

'So it's because of me that you are leaving?'

Taliesin turned away. 'There is no more I can do in Rheged,' he said under his breath. 'And my duty as an initiate has been neglected. Living a simple life, free from the demands of public office, I will be closer to the gods, better able to journey in spirit and summon power to help Ynys Prydein.'

'You do not have to leave to do that........Think again. And think how I feel, believing that I've deprived Owain and the people of your presence. You know there is no one who can replace you, how much they love you.'

'I will continue to work for our people......only in another way.'

The finality of his words resounded in Taliesin's ears. Yet there was one finality he could never accept, one question he must ask. For too long he had attempted to push it into the shadow, though it allowed him no peace. He recalled standing outside Rhydderch's tent above the strand overlooking Metcaud, the turmoil in that moment of uncertainty.

As Gwenddydd reached for his hand, he looked up. 'Perhaps I am wrong to speak of this.......selfish, but I beg that you answer me.' He met her eyes. 'Should we both outlive Rhydderch, however far in the future that time may be, would you come to Llydaw so we could be together? To be my wife?'

He felt her grow tense, then saw that her eyes glistened with tears. 'How could you doubt it?' she said softly. 'But it is only a dream. Who can say what will happen to any of us.'

She leant against him, and he held her, aware that it was

probably for the last time. He thought for a moment that he could not do as he had said, that he would take the coward's choice and stay to escape the pain of parting. But he knew the years would bring yet greater pain if he remained.

The loneliness Taliesin felt at Gwenddydd's departure from Caer Liwelydd hastened his preparations for his own departure, and he knew that speaking to Owain would set the final seal on it.

In a private chamber, the two men took their seats.

'Why do I sense that I shall not like what you are about to tell me?' There was an edge to Owain's voice.

Taliesin faced his comrade. 'Once we believed that fate had decreed I would be your Chief Bard, though it seems that fate, the will of the gods, whatever we may call it, has proved us wrong.'

He thought back to when he first met Owain, the times they had shared confidences, ridden at each other's side into battle........ 'This is not easy for me to say,' he continued, 'but I make plans to travel, and before the summer is out I set sail for Llydaw.........I do not intend to return.'

He saw Owain's lips tighten, the spark of anger in his eyes.

'You would be Chief Bard to my father and not to me.'

Taliesin replied quietly. 'The reasons are personal, and I mean no insult to you……An inner voice summons me to withdraw from the company of men, to carry out my spiritual work where I am unknown. And where I need play no part in the continual feuding amongst our people.'

Owain looked at him closely, and after a moment said,

'Do you tell me the full truth?'

Taken off-guard, Taliesin hesitated, ready to defend his motives and swear comradeship. But Owain spoke again.

'Is it not also that you wish to place a distance between

yourself and Queen Gwenddydd?'

Though there was no note of accusation, the words hit hard. It was one confidence Taliesin would not willingly have shared. Yet his comrade knew him too well......or had Dyfnarth betrayed him? When he had finally ceased to think of his threats.

Owain replied to the unvoiced question. 'Your brother thought father should be told of your.......relationship, and he confided in me.'

Taliesin said nothing.

'It was on the campaign against Fflamddwyn that Dyfnarth spoke out, thankfully not to Rhydderch.'

Taliesin lowered his eyes, feeling a bleakness worse than physical pain.

'Then you will see that it is best I am away in Llydaw, where I cannot add to the troubles of this land.'

Owain looked at him still.

'You've done immeasurable good for Ynys Prydein,' his voice was firm, 'and would continue to do so in future, should you change your mind and remain.'

But the words brought no comfort, and Taliesin wanted only for the discussion to be at an end, to be freed from the endless questions, the expectations he could no longer fulfil. 'I cannot be persuaded to reconsider,' he replied flatly. 'Too much has already passed.'

In the silence of the chamber, insects hummed beneath the smoke-blackened rafters, and from the courtyard came the sound of men's voices.

At length Owain got to his feet.

'Then I must call the council of elders........and begin the search for a Chief Bard. This has been a dark summer, and it is not yet done.'

* * *

With a sense of detachment, Taliesin continued to prepare for his journey, though he delayed breaking the news to Bedwen. Not until two days later did he ride out to Llyn Glas to let him know of his plans. He was thankful to see no sign of Ieuan, and as a new attendant brought them mead they spoke more freely than they had before, their cups refilled over and again.

Night had long since fallen when Taliesin rose to leave, unsteady on his feet. As he grasped the bench for support, Bedwen turned to him.

'You need not go back tonight,' he said. 'Have my bed, and I will sleep by the hearth.' A note of amusement crept into his voice. 'I should not like to think of you lying unconscious in a ditch.'

Taliesin gave a vague smile. He was reluctant to accept the offer of hospitality, but the road to Caer Liwelydd was long and dark, and no welcome awaited him at the end of it.

'Thank you. The hearthside will be adequate, and more comfortable than a ditch.' Retaking his seat, he reached for the mead jar. 'Though a ditch is sweeter smelling than the town in mid-summer.'

Bedwen laughed. 'I'll join you for a last cup. We may not have another opportunity to talk like this.'

But as he lay fully awake hour after hour, listening to Bedwen's regular breathing, Taliesin knew he should have left, however late. The chamber held too many memories. In his mind he saw Nefyn seated by the fire, a silver mirror in her hand; and Afaon, chuckling as he played with a hound pup. Finally, it was Gwenddydd who stood before him, black hair falling across her naked breasts.........

Impatiently, he pushed the rug that covered him aside, and searched for his clothes without kindling a light. And while Bedwen slept on, oblivious, he left the hall.

Once Taliesin was outside the palisade he paused, breathing air filled with the scents of the night: wild flowers and grasses, and the salt tang of the sea. Then he began to walk, without destination, walking his farewell to the land that had been his home, as the spirits of place, of human companions, merged with the presence of his goddess. He continued walking across pasture tinted blue by the ghost-light of the moon, receptive to her as he had not been since the siege of Metcaud.

An owl, spectre white, swooped across his path. A cow in calf lowed from the shadows. He felt Ceridwen draw closer still, in the claws of the Crone and the milk of the Mother, in the cauldron where the sweet mead of inspiration and bitter poison were brewed as one.

'Taliesin.'

Her call made him stop, unable to take the next step. A sense of despair, of over-riding failure, drove out all other thought, striking him like the blows of his Anglian torturers, forcing him to re-live the full agony. Pressing his palms to his brow, he shrank from what he could not escape. Then slowly the pain began to subside.

He raised his head, numb at first, until in time he was able to think clearly, to remember.

Calm now, he listened.

'Once, you asked, 'Why have you turned your back on me?' Now I ask the same of you. If you cannot face Gwenddydd, you cannot face me. If you cannot face loss and grief, you cannot face me. You betray me when you put sentiment above your sacred oath.'

Looking into the eyes of Ceridwen was to see all ages: when the first creature crawled from the chaos of Annwn, when humankind found its place on the lands of the earth, and a future harsher than the cruellest battle slaughter he had witnessed, colder and bleaker than the worst he had known man to inflict on man. And it was to see into the depths of himself, to be faced with all that he had tried to evade and distort.

'If you honour me you will not flee Rheged like a coward.' Ceridwen's voice was uncompromising. 'You will lend your powers to the king, giving him strength in the years to come. Those years will not be without their testing, and though your life will be long, it will be hard.'

The sigh of the wind filled the night, then once more Ceridwen spoke.

'The cauldron is slipping from the grasp of my people. Only a few have drunk of its Bright Knowledge, and in time there will be yet fewer, but it will not be broken or destroyed. After you have joined me beyond the threshold, your works will be passed from master to apprentice through the generations, and again passed from generation to generation through the inscribed word. They will inspire seekers who live in a distant age, when the body of the Great Queen is raped and plundered. That is when my cauldron will return to the people. When many will again know my life-giving wisdom.'

Taliesin stood motionless, experiencing profound peace, the inner battle finally over. If it was his goddess' will, he would remain in Rheged as Chief Bard - as Pen Beirdd of Ynys Prydein.

He looked out over the sleeping land, his voice carrying far in the stillness.

'My Lady Ceridwen, all that I am is yours.'

Author's Note

Taliesin is an enigmatic figure, probably best known as the mythical hero of the 'Hanes Taliesin' ('Story of Taliesin'), in which he begins life as a boy named Gwion Bach, and after a series of transformations becomes a prodigy capable of powerful bardic composition and magic.

There are, in effect, two Taliesins - the one mentioned above, and a real person who lived in the sixth century AD. The factual Taliesin was bard to several kings of his time, most significantly Urien of Rheged (centred on the modern county of Cumbria), for whom he composed eight eulogies still extant.

In the novel I have used what facts are known about the sixth century bard and added various mythological elements, so amalgamating the two Taliesins into one character. Taliesin's eulogies, of which there are twelve in all, are recognized by experts as being by the historical person. As a source of information for these I have used Meirion Pennar's translation of the poems from the late thirteenth century 'Book of Taliesin' (see References).

In addition to the eulogies, 'The Book of Taliesin' contains a number of poems involving mystical lore, almost certainly not composed by the historical bard, but the product of an oral tradition with roots stretching back hundreds of years and only recorded in written form during the Medieval period. They may even contain clues about ancient druidic practice from before the Roman conquest. The name of the great bard has been attached to such poems in order to emphasize their importance amongst later followers of the tradition who were working to ensure its continuity.

Part One, Chapter One and Part Two, Chapter One of the novel are based on the 'Hanes Taliesin', and I have quoted from the poetry found within Lady Charlotte Guest's translation of the story, which appears in her 'Mabinogion Legends'. The 'Hanes' was first written down in the sixteenth century by a bard named Llewellyn Sion, and there are four different versions recorded in various manuscripts. There is also an incomplete version, transcribed by Elis Gryffudd around the same time as Llewellyn Sion's, and translated by Professor P K Ford.

Several esoteric poems ascribed to Taliesin, but not contained in the 'Hanes', are also quoted in my novel, or have acted as inspiration for some of his spiritual experiences. These are translated by D W Nash in 'Taliesin, or the Bards and Druids of Britain' (see References), using source material from the 'Myvyrian Archaeology of Wales' - a collection of early Welsh literature published in the nineteenth century, which includes the poetry from the 'Book of Taliesin'.

Myrddin has a similar dual existence to Taliesin. As the wizard Merlin, he plays a major role in Medieval Arthurian romance but, though there is debate amongst literary scholars as to whether such a historical person did exist, he is thought to have been a sixth century bard. It is the Myrddin whose life and personality are revealed in the poems attributed to him, and in Geoffrey of Monmouth's 'Vita Merlini', on whom I have based my character.

The plotline involving Gwenddydd, Rhydderch and Myrddin is inspired by a poem entitled 'Afallennau' ('Apple Trees'), which is found in 'The Black Book of Carmarthen', a thirteenth century compilation of Welsh bardic poetry (see the Llanerch edition translated by Meirion Pennar). Like Urien and Rhydderch, the other kings of northern Britain who feature as characters in the novel were actual people, and the events associated with the alliance are based on paragraph sixty-three of Nennius' 'British History' (Phillimore & Co Ltd, London 1980).

For information on Angle and Saxon kings, and some of the battles fought against the Britons, I have referred to 'The Anglo-Saxon Chronicle' (J M Dent, London 1996).

Though 'Radiant Brow' is predominantly imagination, and written on a laptop rather than performed aloud, by laying its foundation in Welsh myth and the hazy fragments of Dark Age history, I have tried to remain true to the spirit of the bardic tradition - which has never been static - keeping the characters and their tales alive.

H. Catherine Watling
Glastonbury
2014

CHARACTERS

Gwynedd

Braich y Dinas
Alarch - Taliesin's younger foster-sister
Cadfarch - Gwyddno's Chief Bard. Taliesin's first bardic
master
Collen - Drych's son
Docmael - Taliesin's tutor
Dyfnarth - Taliesin's elder foster-brother
Drych - Elffin's manservant
Eilonwy - Taliesin's foster-mother
Elffin - Taliesin's foster-father
Finllian
Glinneu - Taliesin's elder foster-brother
Gwyddno - Elffin's father. Brother to Maelgwn, King of
Gwynedd
Henwyn - Taliesin's boyhood friend
Taliesin
Tanwen - Taliesin's elder foster-sister

Deganwy
Griffudd - Monk from the monastery of Llandrillo
Gwenddydd - Perwyr's companion
Heinin - Maelgwn's Chief Bard
Maelgwn - King of Gwynedd
Olwen - Rhun's wife
Perwyr - Maelgwn's wife
Rhian - Perwyr's companion
Rhun - Maelgwn's son
Tegai - Master of Deganwy Bardic College. Taliesin's second

bardic master. Rhun's Chief Bard

Apprentices at the Bardic College of Deganwy:
Ewyn
Iddig
Meriadoc
Rhys

Rheged

Afaon
Bedwen - Taliesin's first apprentice
Branwen
Credan - Physician trained by Iorwerth
Elffin - Urien's second son
Gruffydd - Mair's father
Hywel - Taliesin's second apprentice
Ieuan - Talhaearn's servant
Iorwerth - Urien's chief physician
Mair - A bondman's daughter
Megan - Mair's sister
Morfydd - Urien's daughter
Myrddin - Gwenddydd's twin brother
Nefyn
Owain - Urien's eldest son
Penarwen - Owain's wife
Riwallon - Urien's third son
Segnius - Urien's Bishop
Talhaearn - Chief Bard of Rheged. Taliesin's bardic master
Tewdwr - Veteran warrior and elder
Urien - King of Rheged
Ysfael - Taliesin's fellow apprentice under Talhaearn

Ystrad Clud

Neithon - Rhydderch's cousin
Rhodri - Rhydderch's son
Rhydderch - King of Ystrad Glud

Gallowag

Angharad - Penarwen's sister
Cian - Owain's Chief Bard
Owain - Urien's son. King of Galloway
Penarwen - Owain's wife.

hISTORICAL pERSONS
referred to in the novel

BRITISh kInZs
Cynan Garwyn - King of Powys
Gwallawg - King of Elmet (Leeds area)
Selyf - Cynan's son. King of Powys

AnZLes
Aelle - King of Deira
Aethelric - Ida's son. King of Bernicia
Cryda - King of Mercia
Ida - King of Bernicia
Theodoric ('Fflamddwyn') - Ida's son. King of Bernicia

Saxons
Ceawlin - Cynric's son. King of Wessex
Cerdic - With Cynric, he began the conquest of the area that
was to become the kingdom of Wessex
Cynric - Cerdic's son, possibly grandson. King of Wessex

plAces

Afon Hafren - River Severn

Alclud - Dumbarton

Arderydd - Longtown, Cumbria

Argoed Llwyfain - Bewcastle Fells, north-east of Carlisle. Site of battle

Braich y Dinas - A fortress in Gwynedd

Caerfyrddin - Carmarthen

Caer Liwelydd - Carlisle

Caerwenddolew - A fortress near Longtown

Candida Casa - Monastery of Whithorn, Galloway

Catraeth - Catterick

Celyddon, Forest of - Between Arderydd and Alclud

Deira and Bernicia - Anglian kingdoms that were amalgamated to form Northumbria

Din Eidyn - Edinburgh

Dumnonia - Devon, Cornwall, Somerset

Dyfed

Ellan Vannin - Isle of Man

Elmet - Leeds area

Eryri - Snowdonia

Gwen Ystrad - Wensleydale. Site of battle

Gwynedd

Hibernian Sea - Irish Sea

Idon - River Eden

Llydaw - Brittany

Manaw Gododdin - Kingdom centred on Edinburgh

Merin Iudeu - Firth of Forth

Merin Rheged - Solway Firth

Metcaud - Lindisfarne

Mor Hafren - Bristol Channel

Penrhyd - Penrith

Rheged - Kingdom centred on Cumbria
Ynys Mon - Anglesey
Ystrad Glud - Strathclyde

Glossary

Abred   The earthly, mortal realm, according to Welsh
             bardic tradition.   The stage of struggle and
             evolution.

Annwn   The Underworld.

Arawn   God of the Underworld. Hunter who
             possesses a pack of supernatural white
             hounds with red ears.

Arianrhod   Celestial goddess associated with the moon
             and the Corona Borealis - Caer Arianrhod/
             Caer Siddi. Mythologically, this is the Glass
             or Spiral Castle where shaman-bards receive
             initiation and the spirits of kings and heroes
             reside between death and rebirth.

Awen   Flowing spirit of inspiration.

Beli Mawr   (= Beli the Great) Divine ancestor of several
             ancient British gods. Husband of Don. The
             poem 'The Protection of the Honey Isle' in
             'The Book of Taliesin' makes a connection
             between a dragon and Beli: defender of The
             Honey Isle (Britain) (ref. translation in John
             Matthews' 'Taliesin - Shamanism and the
             Bardic Mysteries in Britain and Ireland',
             Aquarian Press 1991).
             Belenus was worshipped in Celtic Gaul as a
             solar deity and god of light. He also had

Underworld associations.

Blodeuwedd   Supernatural bride created for Llew out of the flowers of oak, broom and meadowsweet. She betrays him with Goronwy and is turned into an owl as punishment.

Bran   (= Raven in Welsh) Underworld god of prophecy. Possessor of a cauldron which can restore the dead to life.

Bright Knowledge   Bardic wisdom. Used in the cause of good/ light.

Caer   Castle/fortress, in the earthly realm or in the Otherworld.

Calan Gaeaf   31st October. Irish - Samhain. Fire festival to mark the start of winter. Feast of the dead, of the ancestors.

Calan Mai   1st May. Irish - Beltane (= Bel's Fire) See 'Beli Mawr' above.
Fire festival to mark the start of summer.

Ceridwen   Her name occurs in the 'Hanes Taliesin' and Medieval bardic poetry as the owner of a cauldron of initiation/inspiration/wisdom. The tale also reveals her dual aspect as a goddess of birth/fertility and harvester/ destroyer.

Don   Ancestral British goddess. Mother of several deities.

Goronwy	Blodeuwedd's lover.
Gwydion	Deity of bardcraft, magic and shapeshifting.
Llyminawg	Companion of Arthur. May be an early version of Lancelot.
Llew/Lleu	God of light.
Mabinogion	Collection of ancient Welsh myths.
Mabon	(mab = son in Welsh) Found as an archetype in Celtic myth - a divine child who possesses unique gifts.
Manawyddan	Son of the sea god Llyr. Manawyddan equates with the Irish Manannan, god of the sea, though in 'The Mabinogion' he does not appear as a nautical deity.
Math	Magician deity
Ogham	Celtic alphabet, probably originating in the 2nd century AD, in which each letter/symbol corresponds to a sacred tree. Other letter correspondences were also used by bardic initiates.
Preiddeu Annwn	Poem attributed to Taliesin in which Arthur and his companions journey to the Underworld on a quest for the cauldron of the Lord of Annwn.
Rhiannon	Horse goddess, associated with the

Underworld and fertility. Her name derives from Rigantona (Great/Divine Queen). According to Celtic belief the horse goddess represents the sacred land.

Salmon   Associated with wisdom in Celtic tradition.

Secret   Cipher using Ogham correspondences.
Language   Communication could be silent, by indicating
of the Bards   a part of the finger corresponding to the
                  relevant letter.

Taranis   (Taran = peal of thunder in Welsh) Gaulish
                  god of thunder. During the Roman
                  occupation, an altar was dedicated to him in
                  Chester.

Guide to Welsh Pronunciation

Consonants:

ch - pronounced as in 'loch'

dd - 'th' as in breathe

f - as the letter 'v' in English

ff - as the letter 'f' in English

ll - similar to 'ch', ending with a faint 'l' sound - made by placing the back of the tongue against the palate.

rh - as in 'perhaps', with a trilled 'r' sound

si - 'sh' as in show

th - 'th' as in thank

Vowels:

y - 'i' as in sit, or 'ee' as in need, when y occurs in the last syllable of a word. Pronounced 'uh' as in run when it occurs in any syllable other than the last. In words of one syllable, eg. y (the) pronounce 'er'.

u - in South Wales, pronounced 'i' as in 'him', or 'ee' as in need, depending on the consonants that follow. In North Wales, like the French pronunciation of the word 'du'.

ae/ai - pronounced 'eye'.

au - similar to ae/ai in South Wales. See 'u' for North Welsh
     pronunciation of that letter.

aw - pronounce a short 'ah' closely followed by a short 'oo' sound.

ei/eu - pronounced 'eye'.

ew - a short 'eh' followed by a quick 'oo'.

oe/oi - as in oil.

w - 'oo'

wy - a short 'oo', followed a short 'ee' sound

Cian: 'Because Urien (the bull - he is described as one of the 'three Bulls of Battle of the Isle of Britain' in Triad 72. See ref. 22) is losing power, Galloway (with its raven banner) attracts you (the salmon is Taliesin's totem animal) to leave Caer Liwelydd (Llew's Stronghold). You come here to take my Bardic Chair, which I will fight for.'

Taliesin: 'I am not interested in your position because my Bardic Chair is not of this world, but in the Otherworld (Caer Siddi). (Based on a line from 'Kerdd am veib Llyr ab Brochwel Powys' - 'Song concerning the sons of Llyr ab Brochwel Powys', trans. D W Nash. See ref. 4. In the poem fire and water are mentioned in connection with the Otherworldly Bardic Chair.) Only a true initiate of the Bardic Mysteries can hold my Otherworldly Chair.' (By implication: 'I do not find you a threat because you are not worthy.')

Cian: 'I have studied the poetic arts (in Irish myth magical hazelnuts are associated with poetic gifts. The nuts that fall into the sacred pool of Segais are eaten by the Salmon of Wisdom, and whoever eats the Salmon of Wisdom, ie. Finn MacCumhal in the tale, receives inspiration. Ref. 'Celtic Myths and Legends,' T W Rolleston, Bracken Books, London, 1986). I have made shamanic journeys to the seven castles of the Otherworld (these occur in 'Preiddeu Annwn', see ref. 16), and have found sacred inspiration and wisdom (from Ceridwen's cauldron, as in 'Hanes Taliesin' in 'The Mabinogion', see ref. 1; and the cauldron of wisdom surrounded by pearls in 'Preiddeu Annwn').'

Taliesin: (The breath of the nine maidens fills the cauldron with inspiration in 'Preiddeu Annwn'; the rowan berries, dew and sea water are ingredients of the bardic initiation drink from 'Kadeir Taliesin' - 'The Chair of Taliesin', trans. D W Nash, see ref. 4.) 'Have you (the hound is Cian's totem) really found wisdom? (It is the first three drops from Ceridwen's cauldron that bestow wisdom, the remainder of the contents is poisonous.)   Or have you over-reached yourself through ambition and lost your true gifts?'

Cian: 'I do retain true wisdom.'   (The three doors of truth can refer to any of the sacred Druidic triplicities, or to the Triads. Three pillars of light /I \ is the symbol which represents the Awen.)

...........'It is you who causes strife because you did not succeed in your initiation.' (ie. the drops of wisdom were spilt, not consumed.)

Taliesin: 'I carry the Bardic Tradition (the stream of Bright Knowledge) from the well, pool or cauldron of the Underworld/subconscious and from the Upperworld/spirit/ celestial realms. (The Silver Wheel = Corona Borealis, Caer Gwydion = Milky Way, Llys Don = Cassiopeia, The Starry Ox = Taurus, Taliesin's own birth sign, The White Throne = the star Spica in Virgo.) From the root to the crown of the World Tree.'

'Through my influence there will be positive transformation - Gwair is freed from his prison in the Underworld: ie. comes through the ordeal of initiation (Gwair is mentioned as a prisoner in 'Preiddeu Annwn', see ref. 16), the eagle soars: ie. the spirit gains illumination, the salmon dives: ie. wisdom is found in the deep pools of the subconscious/Underworld.) But because you are so preoccupied with your earthly position you are unable to find your Awen and inspire others.'

References

I have used the following as sources for the poetry in 'Radiant Brow'. Where there is no reference beside a poem, it is my own.

1. From 'Taliesin' in 'Mabinogion Legends', translated by Lady Charlotte Guest, Llanerch Publishers, Felinfach, 1992.

2. See ref.1.

3. See ref.1.

4. From 'Angar Cyfyndawd' ('The Hostile Confederacy') in 'Taliesin, or the Bards and Druids of Britain', translated by D W Nash, J Russell Smith, 1858. Reprinted by Kessinger Publishing, www.kessinger.net.

5. From 'Kadeir Teyrnon' ('The Chair of the Sovereign'), trans. D W Nash. See ref.4.

6. From 'Cad Goddeu' ('Battle of the Trees'), trans. D W Nash. See ref.4.

7. Adapted from a verse in 'The Voyage of Bran MacFabel to the Land of Faery', translated by K. Meyer, D. Nutt, 1895.

8. From 'Angar Cyfyndawd' ('The Hostile Confederacy'), trans. D W Nash. See ref.4.

9. From 'Gwaith Gwenystrad' ('The Battle of Wensleydale') from 'Taliesin Poems' translated by Meirion Pennar,

Llanerch, Felinfach, Wales, 1988.

10. From 'Gwaith Gwenystrad' ('The Battle of Wensleydale').
    See ref.9.

11. Adapted from 'Angar Cyfyndawd' ('The Hostile
    Confederacy'), trans. D W Nash. See ref.4.

12. From 'Cad Goddeu' ('Battle of the Trees'), trans. D W
    Nash. See ref.4.

13. From 'Urien Yng Ngorffowys' ('Urien at Home'), trans.
    Meirion Pennar. See ref.9.

14. From 'Urien Yng Ngorffowys' ('Urien at Home'), trans.
    Meirion Pennar. See ref.9.

15. Adapted from 'The History of the Kings of Britain' by
    Geoffrey of Monmouth, translated by Lewis Thorpe,
    Penguin Classics, London, 1966.

16. Adapted from 'Preiddeu Annwn' ('The Spoils of Annwn'),
    trans. D W Nash. See ref.4.

17. From 'Arddwyre Reged' ('Rheged Arise') trans. Meirion
    Pennar. See ref.9.

18. From 'Gwaith Argoed Llwyfain' ('The Battle of Argoed
    Llwyfain'), trans. Meirion Pennar. See ref.9.

19. From 'Kadeir Teyrnon' ('The Chair of the Sovereign'), trans.
    D W Nash. See ref.4.

20. From 'Taliesin' in 'Mabinogion Legends'. See ref.1.